The Bucket List to Mend a Broken Heart

Anna Bell currently writes the weekly column 'The Secret Dreamworld of An Aspiring Author' on the website Novelicious (www.novelicious.com).

Anna is a full-time writer and loves nothing more than going for walks with her husband, two young children and Labrador.

You can find out more about Anna at her website: www. annabellwrites.com

Also by Anna Bell

Don't Tell the Groom
Don't Tell the Boss
Don't Tell the Brides-to-Be

The Bucket List to Mend a Broken Heart

ANNA BELL

ZAFFRE

First published in Great Britain in 2016 by
ZAFFRE PUBLISHING
80-81 Wimpole St, London W1G 9RE
www.zaffrebooks.co.uk

A CIP catalogue record for this book is available from the British Library.

ISBN: 978–1–785–76037–2

also available as an ebook

1 3 5 7 9 10 8 6 4 2

Typeset by IDSUK (Data Connection) Ltd

Printed and bound by Clays Ltd, St Ives Plc

Zaffre Publishing is an imprint of Bonnier Publishing Fiction,
a Bonnier Publishing company
www.bonnierpublishingfiction.co.uk
www.bonnierpublishing.co.uk

For Evan and Jessica: Here's to starting our very own bucket list of family adventures

Prologue

I'm late, I'm late, for a very important date, I sing to myself as I hurry down the road – half-walking, half-running. It's as if everything's conspiring against me to get to Joseph's house: the pesky dog walker with his out-of-control terriers and their ridiculously long leads that seemed to be attempting to trip me up; the traffic getting out of Portsmouth, that saw me getting stuck at every single red light; the lack of car parking spaces anywhere near his house.

I'm desperately trying not to be any later as Joseph hates tardiness. It's high on his list of pet peeves. I know he'll tell me that I should have left earlier, but I thought I'd have plenty of time.

Even the little kitten heels I'm wearing aren't helping. They're those annoying shoes that fool you into thinking they're practically flat until you have to get somewhere fast and you realise that you're tottering about. I should have worn some killer skyscraper heels – at least they would have given me that sexy long-leg look.

I finally arrive at Joseph's town house, and ring the bell. I see his outline walking towards the opaque glass of the door, and, despite the fact that we've been together for almost a year, I get butterflies in my stomach. Proof that it must be love.

'Ah, hello. At last,' he says as he opens the door.

'I'm so sorry,' I say, reaching up and kissing him, hoping to make up for my lateness. 'I was at the hairdresser and then I nipped into Waitrose to pick up dessert, then traffic was terrible and I couldn't get parked.'

I push past him, slipping off my kitten heels, so as not to mark his wooden floors, and pad into the kitchen, depositing the shopping bag I was carrying onto his long oak table. I look round the room – something doesn't seem right. It takes me a second to register that it's cold and quiet, which is surprising considering that he's supposed to be making us dinner.

'I thought I'd wait for you before I started cooking,' he says as he walks in behind me, reading my mind. He goes over to the sink and washes his hands meticulously like a surgeon and my stomach lets out a sigh of relief that food preparation is imminent. I'm starving. 'I just got us some pasta and sauce.'

My heart sinks a little. It's not as if I'd expected him to have morphed into James Martin overnight, but when he'd suggested a night in with him cooking, I imagined him slaving lovingly over the stove. We always go out for dinner on a Saturday night to some fancy restaurant that seems to feed us the same amount a shrew would eat, and I've been looking forward to pigging out on home-cooked food all day. Pasta and sauce was not what I had in my mind. I know it'll be fresh pasta and sauce from M&S, as Joseph's a bit of a supermarket snob, but still.

Thank heavens I bought an emergency cheesecake, or else it really would have been a disaster.

I try and shrug off the disappointment and go and wrap my arms around his waist. Nothing cheers me up like a kiss and cuddle. He follows suit, hugging me back and I breathe in his aftershave.

'So what do you think of my haircut?' I ask, leaning backwards and giving my long hair a little flick.

'Did you have much cut off?' He's squinting as if he's trying to see what I've had done. Maybe he can't see it properly because I'm so close to him. Or more likely he's a typical man who probably wouldn't notice if I'd had the whole lot chopped off.

'About half an inch,' I reply, shaking it about.

In his defence I do have very long hair, and half an inch is probably like throwing a pebble into an ocean, but it looks all glossy and bouncy in that way that only a hairdresser can make happen.

'Looks nice,' he says, pulling away from me.

I take that as my cue to unpack the bag of shopping. I pull out the emergency cheesecake and place it in the fridge. Sure enough, there on the top shelf is the M&S-branded tagliatelle and a pot of sauce. I can read my boyfriend like a book.

'Do you want something to drink?' he says, turning to look at his wine rack.

He's a little quiet and I'm wondering if he's pissed off that I was late, but the dark circles around his eyes bear all the hallmarks of stress. He's probably spent the afternoon working. He's been burning the candle at both ends lately with all the pressure he's been under.

Hopefully a nice night in will help to relax him.

I could give him one of my special back massages or, better yet, we could have a bath with candles and bubbles, like in the movies, in his gorgeous freestanding Victorian bath with feet.

'Earth to Abi. Drink?' he asks again, snapping me out of my fantasy in which he's wearing nothing but a beard of bubbles.

'Yes, that would be nice. I bought a bottle of Chianti,' I say, reading the label as I pull it out of the bag and put it on the table.

'It's pronounced *key*-anti,' he says, enunciating.

I blush a little. Of course it is. I'd gone down the chi route – you know, like the tea.

He playfully gives my bum a slap with the tea towel he's holding, as if acknowledging my schoolgirl error, before taking the bottle out of my hands.

Before I met Joseph I thought wines were red, white and rosé. He's been slowly trying to educate me. I'd only bought this *Chi*anti as it was half price and it'd won some wine award.

'Looks like a good bottle,' he says as he peruses it before unscrewing the cork with the fancy corkscrew that I can never work.

Pleased that he's at least opening it, meaning that it's passed the label test, I sit down at the table.

'So I was thinking,' I say, trying to cheer him up, 'about our anniversary next month. I thought we could perhaps go away for the weekend. You know, to a country hotel or spa, or to a nice city like Bath or York.'

I try and drop it into conversation as if it's no big deal, and not like it's been the only thing I've been thinking about since I had the idea last week.

'What date is it?'

'What date?' I say far too squeakily and quickly.

I'm shocked he doesn't know, but men are rubbish with remembering stuff like that, aren't they?

'Twentieth March.'

'Oh, um … it's my mum's birthday that weekend, and my sister's coming down for it. I think we're going somewhere for Sunday lunch.'

'Right,' I say, trying not to be too disappointed.

It's our first anniversary and I'm more than a little excited. It's the longest relationship that I've ever had, so I wanted to milk the occasion a little. I've already seen the perfect gift for him and made a Moonpig card with our photo on it.

'Yeah. Sorry,' he says, shrugging.

It takes me a minute to realise that he's neither suggested that I accompany him to the birthday lunch with his family, whom I've never met, nor that we go away on a different weekend.

Undeterred and ignoring the warning signs, I plough on.

'How about just a day spa?'

I can just see us in matching fluffy robes. I look up to see that he's concentrating on opening the bottle of wine like his life depends on it. 'Or we could just do the normal, go out for dinner … or even just drinks,' I say, unable to give up on the idea, my voice becoming ever more feeble.

The cork pops out with a lip-smacking noise as if highlighting the silence that has descended on the room. I watch him pour the wine into a decanter stony faced.

'Or we don't have to do anything. It's just an anniversary. No biggie,' I say, wishing that I'd never said anything.

'Abi,' he says, turning towards me and leaning back against the sideboard in a way that makes my stomach flip for all the wrong reasons. 'We need to talk.'

Chapter One

Three weeks, six days and unknown hours since the love of my life stamped violently on my heart.

I glance up at the oversized clock on the office wall and it seems to be saying it's four o'clock. I have to immediately double check it against my computer to make sure I haven't misread it. *Four o'clock?* How did that happen? I've managed to make it through seven hours of work with no tears. OK, almost no tears, but the sobbing I did in the toilet technically doesn't count as I was on my lunch break.

I know it sounds a bit pathetic that I'm excited to get through a day at work – as most normal people do day in, day out – but it's the first time that I've made it into the office since Joseph dumped me a month ago.

I'm lucky that I work as a graphic designer at a vibrant marketing agency, where my boss strongly believes that a bit of home-working fuels creativity. I can't say that it's fuelled much of mine over the last few weeks, but it has allowed me to indulge in the mother of all moping sessions. I couldn't have imagined anything worse than peeling myself out of my frumpy pyjamas, or doing such basic tasks as showering and hair-washing on a daily basis. How the non-home-working heartbroken people go out to work every day is beyond me.

But, amazingly, here I am, in freshly laundered clothes and clean hair, having lasted a whole seven hours more than I thought I would.

I hate to admit it, but my best friend Sian was right, it has done me good. Not that I'll tell her of course. I'd never hear the end of it.

I'd love to say that I came into work today of my own accord; that I'd woken up feeling a step closer to getting over Joseph, the love-of-my-life who dumped me out of the blue, but in truth my boss told me in no uncertain terms that I had to come in as not only is my work – to quote him – 'slipping', but it's agency photo day. It's the day of the year that I dread under normal circumstances, let alone when my eyes are puffy and red as a result of weeks of crying my heart out.

'You're next, Abi,' calls Rick, my boss, as he walks past my work station.

'Great,' I mutter, feigning enthusiasm. I've been hearing yells and screams emanating from the lobby all day, which hasn't done anything to ease my apprehension.

Rick hates corporate-looking photos, and he always wants our web mugshots not only to be up-to-date, but also to look like working at our agency is the most fun ever.

This year he's excelled himself. I thought it was an early April Fool's joke, but it turns out he's deadly serious. He's installed a trampoline in the lobby – the kind that seems to blight the gardens of anyone that's got kids. He's rigged up our studio's green screen behind it and the idea is that we'll all be jumping ecstatically in front of a brilliant blue sky on a summer's day that will be superimposed later.

I'm absolutely petrified of heights and the thought of bouncing up and down on a trampoline gives me the heebie-jeebies.

'If you want to come on down, you can watch Giles and then when Seb's finished with him, you can hop straight on.'

I nod and stand up to follow him out of our office and into the lobby that we share with six other companies. Just in case it wasn't embarrassing enough that I have to make a giant tit out of myself in front of my own work colleagues when I'm quaking with fear, there's also a whole host of other people milling about to witness it.

'I must say, I'm glad you came back in, Abi. I'm sorry we had to go down the formal route of writing you a letter,' says Rick. He waves his hand around in a way that suggests that it was no big deal that I got sent a letter telling me that I basically had to pull my socks up and show my face in the office or else I'd be facing disciplinary action – it had scared the crap out of me. 'You know HR these days; everything has to be done formally.'

'It's fine, really. It's about time I came into the office anyway.'

That really had been the worst post day ever as not only did I get the letter from HR, but I also got one from my letting agent to say that my rent's going up from next month. That had given me an extra incentive to get back into work because now more than ever I can't afford to lose my job.

We walk down the white circular staircase that runs around the outside of the lobby and my pulse starts to race when I see the trampoline with my colleague Giles bouncing happily on it.

'It'll be great to have these new photos up on the website,' says Rick, 'just in case the lot at Spinnaker start looking into the company.'

I nod, hoping that my photos aren't going to look so horrendous that I scare them off. Our company is pitching to do the marketing materials for the local tourist attraction the Spinnaker Tower, hopefully as a stepping stone to doing all the work for their parent company that owns other famous sites around the country.

'That's fantastic. Now jump again,' calls Seb, our usual freelance photographer.

I arrive in the lobby and watch Giles with trepidation. With his six-foot-five, lanky frame, he looks as if he's going to reach the ceiling at any minute.

Simply watching him is making me feel dizzy. I cling onto the end of the banister to steady myself. How on earth am I going to get on that thing?

'Perfect. Thanks, Giles,' says Seb.

He walks over to his laptop to review his work. 'They're perfect. Looks like you're up, Abi, but do you mind if I grab a quick coffee first?'

'No, no, take all the time you need,' I say, feeling like I've got a last minute stay of execution.

'That was awesome,' says Giles as he slides his trainers on, before bending down to tie his laces.

'You looked like you were having fun.'

'Well, that was the brief from Rick.'

We look up at our esteemed leader who's hopped onto the trampoline for a bounce. He's masterfully dropping on his bum in a seat drop and flip-flopping onto his front and his back. It's doing nothing to calm my nerves.

'So how are you, anyway?' asks Giles with his head tilted in a pity pose.

'I'm OK,' I say, lying.

'It's good to see you back at work and getting on with things.'

'Thanks.'

'Yeah, it was doing you no favours hanging around your flat. Best to get out and about.'

I nod at him, despite the fact I disagree. If Rick hadn't put a fly in the ointment with his letter, I could have stayed holed up indefinitely. Thanks to the revolution that is Internet shopping, and having every type of takeaway under the sun on my doorstep, there's really been no need for me to venture out. Before today, I'd only had to leave the confines of my flat a grand total of twice since Joseph dumped me, once on an emergency booze run, and the other when I'd forgotten to order loo roll.

'In fact, what are you up to this weekend?' asks Giles.

'Um,' I say, desperately stalling whilst I try and come up with a fake answer. 'I think I'm doing something with my friend Sian.'

'Right, well, Laura and I are going to cycle to Hayling Island with some of my mates if you fancy it. It's nice and flat so it's dead easy. I know Laura would love some female company.'

I'm sure she would. Giles's long-suffering wife always seems to be getting dragged along on his and his friends' adventures, but really, cycling from Portsmouth to Hayling Island is not something I'd do even if I was feeling on top of the world.

'Ah, thanks,' I say, a small smile forming on my face. 'But I don't have a bike.'

'Well, that's not a problem, my mate's got a bike shop and I'm sure he'd lend you a second-hand one for the day.'

Bugger. Why didn't I tell him the truth? That the last bike I rode probably had stabilisers.

'I don't think Sian's really into bikes,' I say, lying, 'so I think we'll give it a miss, but thanks.'

Giles stands back up.

'OK, but if you change your mind, send me a message.'

'OK, I will do.' Knowing full well that I will not.

'So,' says Giles, leaning in closer now that he's standing upright. 'What do you make of Linz?'

Ah, Linz. Hayley, one of my fellow designers, went off on maternity leave a few weeks ago and her cover, Lindsey, started whilst I was in hibernation. I met her briefly this morning and I've been trying to avoid her ever since. She's one of those people that's all perky and positive all the time, as if she's permanently attached to a mainline of coffee. She'd do my head in on a normal day, so in my current state I don't have the mental capacity to tolerate her.

'She seems ...' I search for an appropriate adjective, 'upbeat.'

Giles's smile grows wider. 'That's one word for her. She seems like she's settled in and got her feet well and truly under the table in your absence.'

I'm about to ask Giles what he means, when Seb walks back over to us.

'Right then, Abi, let's get this show on the road,' he says.

Giles gives me a double thumbs up in support as he heads back up the stairs and I nervously pull off my Uggs.

'Jump up onto the trampoline and I'll snap a few test shots to make sure I'm happy with the light.'

He makes it sound so easy. I can feel beads of sweat start to spread over my forehead and my heart is beating ten to the dozen.

'Are you sure this is safe?' I ask as I rest my hands on the edge. 'I mean, doesn't it usually have netting round it to keep you in?'

'Yeah, but we can't use that as it would mess up the green screen and it would be in front of my lens. But you'll be fine, we've had no problems all day and there are crash mats if you get too carried away with the bouncing.'

No chance of that.

My legs are wobbling like jelly, but the fear that I'll be ridiculed by my work colleagues for not being able to bounce on a trampoline is currently greater than my fear of heights.

I climb up with as much grace as a beached whale and find myself on all fours, too scared to stand up.

'Right then, get up so I can test the light.'

I turn round and face Seb and see that Rick is standing right beside him. He gives me a broad grin and I know from experience that there's no way I can get out of this. If I told him the truth he'd take it upon himself to try and cure me of my fear of heights. He'd probably try to push me off the roof of our building for a base jump, or abseiling, or something equally ridiculous and adrenaline fuelled.

I slowly rise to my feet, telling myself that if little kids can bounce on a trampoline, then so can I.

'Perfect, that's great. Looks like we're good to go,' shouts Seb from over near his laptop. 'Any time you're ready.'

I catch sight of Rick who's staring at me intently and, worried that he'll guess my secret, I start to bounce. Amazingly I feel myself starting to lift off the floor of the trampoline. Maybe only an inch or two, but I'm actually doing it.

My leg muscles are stiff from my recent inactivity and my muffin top is wobbling over the top of my jeans.

'Try and put your arms up like you're punching the air,' says Rick, demonstrating on the ground and causing me to stumble. 'You look like you're bracing yourself for a fall.'

That's exactly what I'm doing.

I give it another couple of bounces, but the more I try to coordinate my arms and legs, the more my face contorts in a way that must make me look like I'm constipated.

'Try and think of something that makes you happy,' suggests Seb.

I immediately think of Joseph tucked up in my bed the week before he dumped me. He'd pulled naked me into a snuggly cuddle, smoothed down my long, straggly bed hair and then traced patterns with his fingers down my arms. I don't think I'd ever been as content and happy as I was then. Which is why it was so baffling when, a week later, he broke up with me, causing my heart to shatter into smithereens.

The smile drops off my face and I can feel the tears prickling behind my eyes. I can't cry at work, and I especially can't cry in front of my boss when my every move is being caught on camera.

'That's it, that's great bouncing,' says Rick.

I dread to think what I must look like. Thank heavens I put on my baggy cowl-neck jumper. I'd put it on this morning to hide the extra pounds that had found their way onto my waistline during my hibernation, but hopefully now it's hiding my chest too. Without prior warning of the trampoline I hadn't secured my boobs into an appropriate sports bra, and they're bounding about all over the place.

'OK,' shouts Seb. 'You can stop now.'

I'm so relieved that my ordeal is over and that I've survived that I don't give any thought to stopping. I simply straighten my legs as I come down from a bounce and I can feel myself tumble forward with the impact. I'm hurtling perilously close to the edge and I'm sure I'm about to fall flat on my face.

'Whoa, there,' says Rick, jumping up onto the crash mat and holding his hands out to stop me.

He manages to break my fall and stops me before I land on top of him. God, that could have been embarrassing. I could have found myself lying on top of my boss, instead of him having stopped me by grabbing hold of my boobs.

Oh, crap, my boss's hands are on my boobs.

His hands are well and truly cupping my 36DDs and they're the only thing stopping me from falling on him. I try and push myself backwards, but I'm so off-kilter that all I'm doing is pushing closer to him and giving him more of a feel.

Why isn't he moving his hands?

It's like he hasn't noticed where they are. I know he's probably relieved that I didn't end up on top of him, squashing him with the extra weight I'm carrying, but surely he can sense what he's holding? He's gripping me so tight that I feel like I'm wearing one of Madonna's conical bras.

'You all right?' he says. 'That was quite a stop.'

'Um, yeah, I'd be better if perhaps ...'

Perhaps you took your mitts of my tits, I want to scream, but I can't quite bring myself to say that to my boss.

'... If perhaps, I was, you know ... a bit more upright.'

Rick looks down at his hands and his eyes almost pop out in horror.

'Argh!' He pushes me backwards with such force that I land on my bum with a bit of a bounce.

His hands are still outstretched in a cupping motion and he seems to be as scarred as I am by what's just happened.

'Thanks for stopping me,' I mutter, mortified. I slide off the trampoline, desperate to get onto solid ground and away from Rick.

'No problem,' he stutters, before finally putting his hands down and scurrying back upstairs, too embarrassed to make eye contact.

Once my feet have adjusted to being back on terra firma, I walk over to join Seb, who's studying his laptop, having missed the whole boob-grabbing incident.

'They're not too bad,' he says.

I squint at the thumbnails and recoil in horror.

'But they're not good,' I reply.

I can't believe that's me on the screen. I barely recognise myself. I've got huge black circles under my eyes, and my dark-brown, elbow-length hair looks matted and messy as it flies out behind me. I look like I've been electrocuted. The black jumper and jeans that I wore in order to cover up the post-break-up pounds are more frumpy than flattering. All in all, I look like I've pulled an all-nighter at a Goth convention.

'It's not as good as last year's photo,' says Seb diplomatically. 'But it's not the worst I've seen today.'

I look back at the thumbnails, hoping to see at least one good one, but they all look like I'm auditioning for a part in a zombie movie.

'Don't worry, we'll do something equally as fun next year,' says Seb.

'Something to look forward to,' I say sarcastically.

He smiles at me and goes over to talk to Pat, the office manager, his next victim. Despite the fact that she turned sixty last year, she shows no sign of fear like I did. Instead she slips off her glasses and shoes, and willingly climbs on board. I watch her do her test bounces as she soars delicately in the air.

I'm so going to win the worst photo this year.

I slip my boots back on and walk slowly back to my desk. I'm not in the mood to do any more work, so instead I turn off my computer. It is Friday, and almost knocking off time.

'How did your photos go?' asks Fran, who sits in the cubicle opposite me, as I walk past her desk. I was hoping to sneak off without attracting any attention.

'They could have gone better. How were yours?'

'They were OK,' she says, standing up and picking up her coffee cup. 'All the better for not being on that bloody trampoline.'

'How did you get out of that?'

Was that even an option?

'Well,' she says, leaning into me, 'I might have told Seb a little white lie.'

'Right . . .' I say, hoping I can learn how to get out of next year's stunt.

'I told him that I was a couple of months pregnant.'

'You what?' I say, thinking I must have misheard her.

'I told Seb that I was expecting and that it wasn't advisable for me to bounce.' She shrugs her shoulders as if it's perfectly normal to make up a fake baby at work.

'And don't you think he might tell Rick?'

'I told him not to as I'm waiting for the three-month mark before I announce it, and of course I'll tell him next time that it was a false positive on the test or that I miscarried.'

I gasp, as if she's jinxing her future babies.

'All I knew, when I saw Linz bounding around like an overexcited monkey, was that I wasn't going to go down that route. Do you know she wasn't even wearing a bra and she still went on it?' She shakes her head in disgust.

'How slutty,' I say, thinking that it's slightly ironic that Fran finds the lack of bra the disturbing part of this conversation. 'Right, I've got to run.'

'OK, have a nice weekend!'

'You too,' I say, waving as I practically run out the back fire escape. I don't want to see that trampoline ever again.

The fresh air hits me and my thoughts turn to the photos I've just seen. I knew the last few weeks had been hard on me mentally, but I didn't realise they'd left such a physical mark too.

I walk home briskly, cursing Joseph and his 'I don't think we want the same things from life' speech that ended our lovely romance. Before that I was a normal, sane human being. One that could get up in the morning without being reduced to tears at the sight of a box of cornflakes that bore his fingerprints.

It's been four weeks and I don't seem to be getting over him at all. In fact, absence truly has made the heart grow fonder and I feel like I miss him more and more each day.

I hurry back home, desperate to hide away and mope. I practically run up the steps to the entrance of my block of flats. Usually I'd take a moment to look out at the view of the tree-lined common and the seafront beyond it, but not today. Instead I want to reach the sanctuary of my flat as quickly as I can.

I unlock my front door, and I'm immediately hit by the smell. It's a musty combination of stale wine and Chinese food.

I walk into the living room and it's as if I'm seeing it for the first time. It looks like a teenager's been left at home alone for the first time. My open-plan living room is littered with takeaway cartons, wine bottles and half-eaten bags of crisps. It's hard to tell where the kitchen area ends and the lounge starts.

I hover in the doorway, wrinkling my nose. How have I been living like this?

It's not just that my flat's in a mess, I think, as I catch sight of my reflection in the full-length mirror in the hallway – I am too. I turn to study myself.

The bright lights of the photo shoot might have amplified the puffy, panda eyes, but they're definitely visible. I rake my hand through the knotty hair that's hanging limply down my back. I puff my cheeks out and prod the bags under my eyes, but it doesn't change anything. All I see when I look in the mirror is the woman that Joseph dumped.

I've desperately wanted him to see the error of his ways and come back to me, but what on earth would he think of me and the flat if he did?

I suddenly know what I've got to do.

I walk over to the kitchen and grab a pair of scissors out of the knife rack. I scoop my hair up and hold it as if I'm putting it into a loose ponytail.

Positioning myself back in front of the mirror, I take a deep breath before taking the scissors up to my hair and snipping. I wince slightly as the blades squeak as they cut through, but it only lasts a second and then I'm left clutching nine inches of my hair.

It's as if I've suddenly realised that I've got to take control of this post-break-up existence. I've already got one pretty major obstacle in the way of Joseph and me getting back together – him – so I don't need anything else.

I look back down at the hair in my hand and laugh. It's probably the craziest thing I've ever done, but somehow it seems like the sanest decision I've made in weeks.

Chapter Two

Four weeks exactly since I was dumped and twenty-two hours since I hacked off my hair.

Waking up to my new hairdo this morning was a bit of a shock. I've had long hair my whole life, or at least I would have done if my sister Jill hadn't got bored of her Dolls World Styling Head and chopped my hair instead. But aside from that unwanted pixie cut when I was six, my hair has always hung like a shiny mane far down my back and sometimes skimming my bum. So when I sleepily went to scrape it back, I wasn't expecting that I'd have to hunt around for it.

I can just about make a ponytail out of my new hair, which is marginally better than the scarecrow look I have when it's down.

It might have been symbolic – cutting away the dead ends of my hair as if cutting away the dead ends of my life – but I hadn't really thought through the consequences for my appearance.

Thank goodness it's Saturday and I've got time to get it sorted.

I manage to nab my hairdresser's last available appointment, and luckily for me it's a freezing March day, so I can legitimately tuck my scrappy bob under a beanie.

'Abi!' says Carly, my hairdresser, as she walks across the floor. 'You're not due another cut already, are you?'

'No, but I, er, needed a bit of a change.'

She puts a silky black robe over me and I follow her over to a comfy black chair.

My last haircut was the weekend that Joseph broke up with me. I feel foolish thinking that I'd sat in this very chair telling Carly how amazing my boyfriend was, only for him to end things with me hours later.

She pulls off my hat and gasps.

'What the hell happened?' she shrieks. She starts pulling clumps of my hair up and letting it fall back down.

'I needed a change,' I say again, feeling a bit like a broken record.

'You did this to yourself?' she asks in disbelief.

'Uh-huh.'

'Whilst sober?'

'Yep,' I say, embarrassed.

She looks at my reflection in the mirror as if searching my eyes for an answer.

'You broke up with your boyfriend,' she guesses, gasping again.

I pull my lips into my mouth and bite down on them, trying to stop the tears from falling. I can already feel my eyes glistening.

'Well, don't worry. We're going to have you looking hotter than ever. You know, bobs are bang on-trend,' she smiles, and as I listen to her I start to feel the need to cry ebb away. 'I think with a little bit taken off the front here to shape it, and maybe putting a few layers in here, it'll look really good.

'I'm just gutted that I wasn't the one to do the initial snip. I've wanted to change your hair for years and you've never let me take more than an inch off, and the one time you want something drastic done, you ruin the fun for me.'

'Sorry,' I say, smiling.

'Well, let's get you over to the sinks and then we can get started. I'm so excited. I think you're going to look amazing. I don't usually advocate self-mutilation, but I think in this case it's going to turn out just fine.'

After what seemed like the quickest hair wash ever, thanks to the seventy-five per cent reduction in my hair, Carly gets to work. She rakes up tiny bits of hair at a time and snips away what seems to be an awful lot considering she doesn't have much to work with. My heart is racing quicker with every cut. It isn't until she starts to blow dry it, and I begin to see it taking shape, that I start to relax.

By the time my bob has been masterfully flicked around my face, in a way that I'll never be able to replicate, no matter how hard I try, I barely recognise the person in the mirror.

OK, so I can still see it's me, thanks to the saucer-like dark circles under my eyes, but I look different. I look all right. In fact, I look pretty damn good.

I wonder if Joseph would like it?

No, no, no, I think, shaking my head and invoking the wrath of Carly, who almost takes a chunk out at the front of my hair.

I apologise before trying to banish thoughts of Joseph from my mind. I'm not thinking about him today.

I'm so busy trying to rid myself of thoughts of my ex that I haven't been paying attention to the finishing touches Carly is doing.

'Ta-daa,' she says theatrically. She picks up a round mirror and holds it behind my head so that I can see the back of my hair.

'Bloody hell,' I say. She's clearly run a product through my hair that's given it a sheen and shine that makes it look as glossy as chocolate fondue.

'It really suits you. See, you should have let me do this type of cut years ago.'

I put my hand up to it, and recoil almost immediately, too frightened that I'm going to mess it up.

'I can't believe it's me,' I say in a whisper.

'You look gorgeous,' says Carly. 'Now, I hope you're going to go somewhere good tonight to show it off?'

'I'm not sure yet.'

'Well, make sure you do,' says Carly.

She pulls my chair back and I slowly rise to my feet and follow her over to the till, paying and thanking her profusely as I leave.

I shove my hat into my bag – there's no way I'm going to put that on now, even if it means my ears are going to get a little chilly.

I have a spring in my step as I walk down Southsea High Street to meet Sian, and I find myself grinning at strangers.

My mouth muscles start to ache, unused to all the smiling, but I don't care. For the first time in weeks, I feel happy. It's like I've seen a glimpse of my old self.

I spot Sian in the distance standing outside the department store where we planned to meet. As I get closer to her I start to feel nervous and begin to doubt my radical new hairdo. What if it's too drastic? Sure, Carly said she liked it, but can you really trust a hairdresser that you once saw with half her hair cut in a pink bob and the other side completely shaved off?

Sian hasn't noticed me yet; she's too busy scrolling on her phone. I walk right up and stand in front of her. She glances up momentarily, but she doesn't say anything and instead turns her attention back to her phone.

Has all that time hiding in my flat turned me invisible? I continue to stand there, waiting for her to notice me.

She looks up again, this time with a hint of annoyance on her face, before her jaw drops open.

'Oh, my God. Abi!'

'Hiya,' I say, laughing. It's not often that I shock my friend.

'I can't believe it's you. Look at your hair.'

I tuck a bit behind my ear, self-consciously.

'Do you like it?' I say, holding my breath.

'I don't like it,' she says, causing my heart to sink. 'I love it! It really suits you. Wow. I can't believe it's you.'

I catch my reflection in the shop window, and I can't believe it's me either.

'You're like a completely different Abi from the tear-stained mess I left on Thursday night,' she says, shaking her head, her mouth still hanging open. 'You look bloody amazing.'

'Thanks. It's nice not to be told I look like shit.'

She's been saying that to me so much lately that it has almost become her catchphrase.

'You know I only told you that because I love you and I wanted you to crawl out from the rock you were hiding under, and see, now you have.'

I smile with a little bit of pride.

'So shall we go for a coffee?' I say.

'Oh no, we're going shopping. Hair like that deserves new clothes.'

'I don't know …' I say, prodding my belly. I wanted to lose the extra break-up pounds before I bought any new clothes.

'Nonsense. Come on.'

Sian turns and walks straight into the department store and makes a beeline for Womenswear. She's like a woman on a mission as she flicks through the rails of clothes, holding up dresses here and there in my direction, before wrinkling her nose and returning them to the rack.

'So what happened?' she asks as she starts piling items over her arm. 'I've been trying for weeks to get you to leave the house, and not only do you agree to meet me in town, but you also turn up looking like a model.'

'Ha, a model in need of a lot of airbrushing,' I say, shuddering at the thought of yesterday's photo shoot. Sian looks back at me expectantly as if I haven't answered her question. 'I was feeling pretty crap as I'd had my photo taken at work and I looked awful. Then I walked into my flat and saw how gross it had become. And then it hit me that my flat was a reflection of me. So I felt like I needed to take matters into my own hands and I chopped my hair and spent the rest of the night cleaning.'

'Wow, so you don't need a biohazard symbol on your door any more?'

'Very funny.'

I'd love to protest that it wasn't that bad, but it really was.

'Well,' she says, 'I'm glad as I was going to don my Marigolds and head over with a bottle of Cillit Bang.'

Blimey, that would have been proof of true friendship. I wouldn't have wished last night's cleaning on my worst enemy.

I watch as she throws a dress that is breaching the Trade Descriptions Act as it's short enough to be a top over her arm.

'Try these on,' she says, thrusting the pile of garments at me.

I take them and walk towards the fitting room, managing to lose the top masquerading as a dress along the way. There's no way that even Sian's persuasive skills would have been able to get me and my tree trunk thighs to wear that.

I try the first dress on and stand back to look at myself for a moment before opening the curtain and allowing her to see.

'That looks all right,' she says. 'But try one of the others on.'

I do as I'm told, and after putting a metallic body-con dress to one side – that ain't ever going to happen – I settle on an electric-blue skater dress instead. At least it covers my bum and the skirt juts out, hiding my thighs.

'That's the one,' says Sian, before I've barely made it out of the cubicle. 'That'll be perfect for going out for a few drinks tonight.'

'Tonight? I'm still not sure I'm ready to go out,' I say as I shut the curtain and slip the dress off.

'With that dress, your new haircut and a bottle of wine, you'll feel differently. We'll go back to yours and shove some tunes on to get you in the mood.'

I slip my jeans and baggy jumper back on, and wonder if I could face going out.

I pay for the dress and we leave the shop, walking in the direction of my flat.

'Look at the difference forty-eight hours makes,' says Sian as we walk away from the High Street, and the shops give way to letting agents and restaurants.

'I know. I'm beginning to feel a bit more like the old me.'

'That's good, I've missed her.'

The closer we get to the flat, the closer we are to the seafront and the biting wind that blows along it. The sun's started to set and a chill's descended on the air. I pull my coat tighter around me and Sian links her arm through mine.

'So with all this change, does that mean that you're getting over Joseph?'

'I wouldn't say I'm over him, but there's no point moping around my flat. Consuming my bodyweight in crisps isn't going to get him back.'

'And having your hair cut is?'

I smile, and keep looking straight at the road in front of me. Sian knows me too well.

'Well, it's got to be a better look than hair so greasy I could cook chips in it.'

'So you do still want him back then?'

'Absolutely. He's the one.'

She doesn't reply and I can tell she's itching to say something.

I'm not the only one who's been acting out of character over the last few weeks. Sian's one of the most outspoken people I know, but since I got dumped, she's been unusually quiet.

For reasons I've never understood, she's never been Joseph's biggest fan, yet since we broke up she's barely uttered a word against him. Sure, she's trotted out the usual, 'if he can't see you're wonderful then he's not worth it' and 'who needs a man to be happy', but she hasn't got personal.

'I know you don't think that he was the one,' I say, 'but I really do, and I don't think that feeling's going to go away any time soon.'

Sian sighs and I can't take it any longer.

'You can tell me what you really think.'

I stop walking and unlink our arms. I close my eyes and tense my body, waiting for what she has to throw at me.

'It's just …' she hesitates. 'I never got the impression that he was that into you.'

'Not that into me? He was the one that insisted we were boyfriend and girlfriend from our second date,' I reply, momentarily stunned. Of all the men I've dated he was the most committed – he would happily throw around the L word, and introduce me as his girlfriend to people we met.

Joseph's the polar opposite of his best friend Marcus who's dated more women than I've had hot dinners. He's a Tinder cruiser, hooking up with girls who are lucky if they're even taken out to breakfast. But Joseph's like the anti-Marcus, monogamous to the max and happily so.

'Not that into me ...' I repeat, this time with a hint of a laugh and a shake of my head. 'Whatever gave you that impression?'

'Well, you were dating for almost a year and you never made any plans for the future. You never booked any holidays together, he took his sister as a plus one to his friend's wedding that time and he never introduced you to his family.'

I make a guttural noise and try to hold my tears at bay. They're all observations that have played on my mind in the weeks since Joseph dumped me, but it's something else to have someone say them out loud. That's the problem with having a best friend that you tell absolutely everything to – they can use their knowledge to hurt you at a later date.

Over the weeks I've tried to think of plausible reasons for Joseph's odd behaviour. We never made future plans, like moving in together, because Joseph liked coming and spending time in my seafront flat. And as much as it would have been a godsend financially for me to have moved into his three-bedroom town house, it would have been a right pain in the arse for me to get to and from his for work.

With regards to that wedding, it did make more sense to take his sister as she had met his uni friends on numerous occasions, whereas I had only met them in passing once. Not everyone is like me and goes so completely mushy at weddings that they want to spend the whole night whispering sweet nothings and fantasising with their other half about their own magical day.

And from what Joseph told me about his family, he did me a favour not introducing me to them. They sound like a nightmare – all intense and clingy. Joseph said that if I met them we'd be expected at their house all the time and his mother would keep inviting me to the opera or the ballet, and Joseph wanted me all to himself instead. If anything that proves that he was too into me.

'Those are exceptions to the rule,' I say, knowing that Sian will never understand. 'And besides he always took me on all those romantic dates.'

Sian's lips are still pursed.

'Come on, we were always doing romantic things. Going to the theatre, eating at fancy restaurants, exploring National Trust properties.'

'I wouldn't exactly call them romantic,' she says, rolling her eyes.

'Of course they were. There was no shortage of candlelit suppers or roses in our relationship. You, Miss Ice Maiden, don't get it as you don't have a romantic bone in your body.'

'OK, I know I'm not all into hearts and roses, but really, was that stuff actually romantic? I mean, it always seemed so clichéd and before you got together with him I never thought it would be the kind of stuff you'd like doing week in, week out.'

I try and avoid eye contact. I can't say that I am a natural theatre-goer, and before I met Joseph I thought a sommelier was someone from Somalia, but that doesn't mean to say that I didn't grow to enjoy our dates.

'And don't you think that it was a bit weird how you went from one date to being all loved-up? It happened so quickly and whenever I met him, I got the impression that he didn't seem to really know you at all.'

'Sometimes you don't need to know each other first; sometimes there's just that spark,' I say, wishing I'd never asked Sian what she thought. I start to walk again and we hurry across a road whilst there's a gap in the traffic. 'I knew the day I met him that he was the one. Back in the –'

'Back in the coffee shop, I know. You told me the story. He took your caramel latte and you took his mocha choca-lata-ya-ya – or whatever.'

I've probably bored her to death with the story of how we met a hundred times, but she still doesn't get it. She doesn't understand the connection Joseph and I had. The jolt of electricity I felt when we first touched hands as we swapped drinks. The look he gave me when he stared into my eyes, as if he was looking right down into my soul. The warmness I felt for him when he rambled along, apologising profusely for nibbling my cream, and then blushing in recognition of what he'd said.

It was then that I knew that I was destined to fall for this man. And fall for him I did. It felt like I'd gone head-over-heels and tumbled down a million flights of stairs. It's going to take me a bloody long time, and more than a haircut, to get back up that staircase.

I blink back a rogue tear. *I will not cry. I will not cry.* I've come so far over the last twenty-four hours; I don't want to go back to that pathetic excuse for myself.

We round the corner of my road, and Sian relinks her arm through mine. We're pushed along by the strong wind whistling off the sea behind us and it propels us closer to my block of flats.

'Look, Abs, I don't want to upset you. I know it's going to take time for you to get over him, and I'll be here whilst you do.'

I try and smile. I know she's doing her best, but it's hard when she doesn't appreciate what I've lost. She doesn't understand relationships full stop, they're not how she operates. I guess, thinking about it, she's the less extreme, female equivalent of Marcus.

We walk the rest of the way to my flat in silence.

I'm on autopilot as I unlock the communal door and go through the lobby area, past the post-boxes. I'm too lost in my memories of Joseph to notice that Sian has stopped.

'Abi, this is for you.'

I turn to see her manhandling a large, brown box off the floor.

The flaps are still open at the top – it's clearly been hand delivered. A funny feeling washes over me and I know instinctively what it is and who it's from, even before I recognise the handwriting.

'What is it?' asks Sian.

'It's the stuff I left at Joseph's.'

I can't believe he was standing here in my block of flats, in this very spot.

I'm gutted that I didn't see him, and especially now that I'm sporting my super-hot I-don't-care-about-you-honestly-I-don't hair, but it's more than that – that stuff was my only legitimate reason for seeing him again, and now he's taken it away from me.

The only comforting thing in this whole break-up was that part of me was still at his house, even if it was in the guise of old CDs, books and a random assortment of clothes. I always thought that when I got myself a bit more together I'd casually drop by to pick them up looking like a super fox, and of course Joseph would realise the error of his ways and beg me to come back. Only now my stuff has been boxed up and rejected from his life like I have been.

'Oh no,' says Sian. 'Don't you dare turn back into a melancholy moper.'

'Too late,' I mutter, as I feel myself getting sucked back under the wave of sadness – only this time I don't know if I'm strong enough to fight it.

Chapter Three

Still four weeks since Joseph dumped me, and an unknown number of minutes or hours since he stood in my lobby.

'Are we going to be staring at it all night, and if so can we at least open a bottle of wine?' asks Sian.

I haven't taken my eyes off the box since she picked it up and deposited it in the corner of my living room. It's my last link to Joseph and I'm afraid if I look away from it it'll disappear.

'I think there's half a bottle in the fridge,' I say, waving her in the direction of my kitchen area.

I hear her opening the fridge door, before she starts chinking glasses together as she takes them down off the shelf. There's a satisfying glug-glug-glug noise as she pours, before I'm handed a glass.

'Here you go,' she says.

'Thanks,' I say, taking it as I continue to stare at the box. I take a large sip. I hadn't realised until then that my hands are shaking.

'Are you at least going to open it?' Sian sits down on the sofa next to me.

'I don't think so, or at least not yet.'

If I don't open it I can imagine that it might contain a heart-felt letter where Joseph reveals he's made a mistake and begs for me back, or at the very least gives me an explanation as to why he broke up with me. His whole 'we're too different and we don't want the same things in life' is such bollocks. How does he know what I want? He never asked me whether I wanted a white picket fence and 2.4 kids, or whether I wanted to move to the big smoke and live in some flashy apartment *sans* children.

'Right. Well, if you don't mind, I've had enough of box-staring so I'm going to stare at this mark on your wall instead. At least with that I can try and guess what exactly it is. Hmmm, are you a splash of red wine? A bit of chocolate? The mind boggles,' says Sian sarcastically.

Grudgingly, I smile. 'Very funny, it's spag bol.'

'Seriously, Abi, it's Saturday night. I'm not staying in looking at a cardboard bloody box.'

'I just don't think I can go out now, not after coming home to that.'

For a split second I'd been looking forward to getting all dolled up and going out, but the thought of Joseph having been in my building has unnerved me. Did he ring my doorbell or drop it straight off without checking whether I was in? What if I'd been here when he'd dropped it off?

My mind's racing so fast, thinking of what we might have been, that I can't keep up with all the hypothetical situations.

It just seems so unjust that I've been in my flat almost 24/7 since we broke up, and the moment that I emerge from my hibernation he comes here.

'But what about your new dress, and your hair? The box is still going to be here when you get back. In fact, you can spend all day tomorrow staring at it.'

I'd already planned to do that anyway.

'I'm not in the mood to go out any more. You go. I'm sure that Ashley and Becca will be out somewhere.'

'I've got a better idea,' says Sian, practically downing her whole glass of wine.

I watch her as she walks over to the box and opens the flaps.

'Don't!' I screech, getting off the sofa to stop her, but I'm too late. The box is open and she's started to pull things out of it.

I settle by her side to help. It feels like she's opened Pandora's box and now there's no going back.

'Oh, I love this jumper of yours, and this top – you'll be glad of that when the weather perks up a bit,' she says, making a messy pile of clothes on my coffee table.

My eyes track every item that she pulls out. Each piece triggering a memory. The jumper I wore when we went on our trip to Cheltenham to watch the horse racing. The pair of thick wool socks I'd taken up to London with us to go ice skating at Somerset House, only we'd never made it past the cocktails at Las Iguanas on the South Bank. The black cocktail dress I'd worn to his work Christmas do.

'You left a lot of stuff there,' says Sian.

She's stopped pulling everything out and is now poking around it.

'I know,' I say, looking at the large box. 'I thought I'd only left a couple of tops and the odd CD. I didn't realise it was a whole box full of stuff. Do you think that's why he dumped me?'

'Yes, that was it. I'm sure one cardboard box worth of stuff was taking up far too much room in his three-bedroom town house. Either that or he took one look at this jumper and wondered if he was actually dating Gyles Brandreth.'

'Hey,' I say, grabbing it from Sian and clutching it protectively to my chest. 'It's a reindeer and they're very in.'

'Yeah, the ones which you buy in the shops are. This one looks like my blind nan made it. Did you knit it yourself?'

'Might have done,' I say sulkily. A lot of blood, sweat and tears went into that. 'It was a present for Joseph.'

It had seemed like such a good idea at the time. My gran had taught me to knit when I was little and I'd thought I'd been all right at it. The idea had hit me when I'd been watching *Bridget Jones's Diary* and seen Colin Firth at the Christmas party wearing his reindeer jumper, and instead of cringing like Bridget, I'd thought how cute he looked. And Joseph looks a little Colin-Firth-like. They've got the same wavy hair and softly spoken, posh voice.

I thought he could wear it to the little pre-Christmas drinks party I was hosting, only he'd come straight from work and hadn't had time to change into it. I hadn't expected him to give it back, it was a gift.

I slip it on, breathing in the smell of aftershave that's lingering on it, presumably from when I'd made him try it on. One arm is slightly longer than the other and, looking down at it, the nose is quite wonky. There's more than a few dropped stitches that have created little holes in it. Oh, God. What was I thinking giving that to him? I must have truly been under his spell, believing anything is acceptable when you're in love.

'Suits you,' says Sian, trying not to laugh at me.

I stick my tongue out at her. 'Well, I won't be making you one this Christmas then.'

'I'm devastated. I'll have to make do with my usual smellies. Ooh, is this some kind of headband?'

She pulls out something black and silky. She wrinkles her face as she stretches the elastic and turns it round, trying to figure out which way it goes.

'Oh, God,' I say. 'Put it back! Put it back!'

But it's too late. Her face changes from a look of curiosity to terror as she stretches the little silky number out into a knicker shape and realises what she's holding.

'Yuck,' she says throwing them at my head. 'What the hell are they?'

'Nothing,' I say tucking them safely under my jumper.

'They certainly are nothing. Oh, God, are they crotchless pants? And I touched them. Ick!'

She jumps up and goes over to the sink to wash her hands.

I shift my bum cheeks uncomfortably on the floor. It's bad enough that thanks to Joseph I own a pair, but now Sian knows I'll never hear the end of it.

'They are, aren't they? You kinky little minx. I feel slightly responsible having lent you *Fifty Shades*,' she says, walking back over and sitting down on the floor again.

'Actually, Joseph bought them for me. In fact, maybe you should stop going through that box as he bought me other stuff too.'

Sian had put her hand back into the box, but she snaps it back out quickly.

'I have to say I'm a bit surprised. I would have thought of him as the kind of man that has sex with his socks on and you in a long nightie.'

'Oh, no,' I say, my cheeks warming at the memories. I have to admit when I'd first met him I'd thought he'd be quite straight-laced in that department too, but it turned out he was into quite kinky lace. 'Joseph liked me to wear things.'

'What kind of things?' asks Sian, her eyes widening.

I peek into the box to see what he's put in there. I pull out a red suspender belt with matching fish-net stockings, followed by a see-through cami and a PVC French maid's outfit.

'Abi Martin!' she shrieks. 'I didn't know you had it in you.'

I shrug, laughing. She's right, it's not really my kind of thing. I'd always wanted a boyfriend to buy me fancy lingerie and when I'd seen the first Agent Provocateur bag I'd been really excited, but then he'd pulled out underwear that didn't leave anything to the imagination. Far from making me feel sexy it had actually made me feel a bit tacky.

'What are you going to do with them?' asks Sian. 'You can't keep them, surely?'

I look down at the sheer-fabric items. What do you do with naughty undies that your ex gave you? 'I don't know. It's not like I could wear them for anyone else. They'd always make me think of Joseph.'

'Throw them in the bin,' says Sian, drinking more of her wine.

'I can't. What if we get back together?'

'Abs,' she says, sighing and rolling her eyes, 'he's given you your stuff back now. Surely that's a pretty big sign that it's over.'

'No,' I say, shaking my head. I can't entertain the thought that we won't get back together.

'He was pretty specific when you broke up,' she says, focusing on her wine glass and not looking me in the eye. 'He said that he thought you were different people. It's not like you're going to wake up tomorrow having changed completely.'

'But opposites attract, don't they? The past year was the best of my life and we had so many amazing times, I can't believe that they didn't mean anything to him.'

I drain my glass and look over at my kitchen to see if I've got any bottles stacked in my wine rack, but it's empty. It's taken a bit of a beating over the last few weeks.

'I'm sure they meant something, but he was probably looking at the long-term picture. He's older than us, don't forget.'

'He's only six years older than me.'

'Still, he's probably thinking of settling down.'

'So am I. See, we don't want different things after all. Maybe I just didn't show him the real me.'

'In a year?'

I sigh. 'If I could just have another chance to show him what I'm really like.'

'Oh, Abs,' says Sian, as she notices the tear that's escaped and run down my face. She puts her arm round my shoulder and gives me a squeeze. 'You'll get through this and find someone else, I promise you. Someone with better taste in underwear.'

I wipe the tear away from my face and try and stop the floodgates from opening. It took three weeks to close them the last time, I can't go through that again.

Sian lets go of me and finishes her wine. 'Have you got another bottle?'

'No, it was the last one.'

'How about I do a Co-op run? There's no way I'm going to be discovering more of your boudoir secrets without more wine. Is there anything else you need?'

'Maybe some Kettle Chips. Oh, and some chocolate fingers,' I say. My diet went out the window when the box arrived.

'How about something for dinner?'

As if on cue my stomach growls. 'Oh, that might be a good idea.'

'OK, I'll grab us a pizza.'

She gets up and I hand her my keys so that she can let herself back in.

'I'll see you in a bit,' she says as she walks out.

I pull the crotchless panties out from under my jumper and look at them. They really don't leave any room for modesty.

I gather up the rest of the underwear and not knowing what to do with it, I shove it in the cupboard of my sideboard along with all my other junk. I can't throw them out – just in case Joseph comes back to me. Make that *when* Joseph comes back to me. I've got to think positively about these things. Or as positively as I can about the prospect that I'm going to have to wear those crotchless panties again. They gave me a double wedgie.

I go back into my lounge and root through the last of the items in the box. There's my Ed Sheeran CD, a Michael Bublé one and a few books I'd lent him. I take the books out and go over to my bookshelf to stack them neatly away when I realise there's one that I don't recognise. I turn it over to read the blurb on the back – it doesn't seem familiar. The spine's bent and it's clearly been read. I flick through the pages, as if I'm trying to absorb the essence of Joseph, when a piece of paper falls out.

I unfold it to a reveal an A4 sheet of white paper, with a hand-written list.

I recognise the handwriting instantly as Joseph's and I trace my fingers over the letters as I read it.

THINGS TO DO BEFORE I'M 40

1. Have tea at the Ritz
2. Learn a language
3. Go wine tasting at an actual vineyard
4. Do Paris in a day
5. Go to Glastonbury
6. Cycle round the Isle of Wight
7. Hike the UK's Four Peaks
8. Learn to windsurf
9. Do a half marathon
10. Abseil down the Spinnaker Tower

I read through the list twice before it starts to sink in. I can picture Joseph sitting down at the antique desk in his study to write it. It's written with a fountain pen in his perfectly neat handwriting.

I wonder when he wrote it? He's thirty-six now, so he's got plenty of time left to finish it, which is a good job too, as to my knowledge he hasn't done any of these things.

I vaguely remember him buying trainers, with the ambition to start running, but I don't think they ever made it out of the box.

If he'd told me about his bucket list, I could have helped him tick off the items. I'm sure it wouldn't be too much of a hardship going to the Ritz, you know, if I had to. And whilst I know nothing about wines I do know that I like tasting them.

It just makes me even madder about our break-up. If these are things he wants to do in life, then I can't understand why he thinks we're really that different, as I would have happily done them with him.

OK, so I might think that windsurfing combines the worst elements of outdoor pursuits – strong winds, freezing cold sea and unflattering wetsuits – but Glasto looks awesome, or least it does when I watch it from the comfort of my home where I'm warm and dry. Even though I'm not known for my camping skills, I can't imagine it would be *that* bad for a one-off. Just imagine how good my skin would be after a few days caked in mud.

The only one that fills me with absolute dread is the abseiling. We're currently putting together a bid to do the Spinnaker Tower's marketing materials, and I know for a fact after perusing their old ones, that it's 560 feet high. That's 559 feet higher up than I like to be. I've never made it past the bar on the ground level, so Joseph might have had to do that one on his own, but the rest of them I'd have attempted.

What if I tell him that I've found his list and that I'll help him do it?

I shake my head. That wouldn't work. I tried pretty hard when we broke up to convince him that he had made a mistake, but he was adamant that he'd made up his mind and he wouldn't change it.

If only I could prove to him he was wrong. Make him see that I was the right woman for him.

I can feel my heart starting to beat quicker and thoughts begin to whizz round my mind as a plan starts to form.

I could do his bucket list!

I could complete the tasks and then put pictures and updates on Facebook in the hope that he sees them.

I read one to ten again and my spine tingles as I look at the abseiling. If I do that one last then maybe he'll have already come running back, and I won't have to go through with it.

'I'm back,' calls Sian.

I hurriedly fold up the piece of paper and throw it back into the box.

'Everything OK?' she asks.

'Fine,' I reply, trying to look as innocent as I can. I can't tell her about my idea, she'll only try and talk me out of it. She hasn't exactly been enthusiastic when I've talked about trying to get Joseph back.

She's about to open the bottle of wine she's just bought, but I can't let her do that. If she opens it, there'll be nothing to stop her going near the box.

'I've changed my mind,' I say quickly. 'I want to go out.'

'You do?' says Sian, putting down the corkscrew.

'Uh-huh. If you're still up for it.'

'Of course I am. Blimey, what did you find in the box to make you change your tune?'

'Nothing,' I say, closing the flaps and pushing it into the corner. 'I finished going through it and realised that you're right – I can't look at it all night.'

Sian pauses and stares at the box, and for a moment I think I'm busted.

'OK, then,' she says. 'Let's go get ready.'

I breathe a sigh of relief that the list is still my little secret. We walk towards my bedroom to get ready and it takes all my resolve not to reach into the box and sneak the list into my pocket. It'll still be there when I get back.

My hands are practically shaking when I'm reunited with the white piece of paper three hours later.

How I made it through our night out without telling Sian about the list I'll never know. She thought my sudden transformation was down to her getting me out to a bar rather than the discovery I'd made before we left.

The night at the bar was better than I thought it would be. I may have even enjoyed myself a teeny tiny bit, but I couldn't wait to make it home as soon as it was acceptable so that I could get back to the box.

I slip the dodgy woollen reindeer jumper over my PJs and pick up the piece of paper as I climb into bed.

There's something about reading the list in the dim light of the lamp that adds to the air of monumental importance that surrounds it. It's as if I've found the Holy Grail; a blueprint to getting Joseph back.

I couldn't concentrate on anything Sian was saying at the bar. She was trying to get me involved in her usual prowling for men, and whilst there were some good-looking guys, none of them held a candle to Joseph. It made me feel a bit funny watching the men downing drinks and ogling the girls in short skirts. It reminded me how refined and grown-up my ex-boyfriend was.

I don't want a boy, I want a *man*. And not any old man – I want Joseph.

The more I think about it, the more I believe that this list is going to help make that happen.

Things to do before he's forty. Is that what our break-up was about? Is he having a mid-life crisis? I think back over our relationship and maybe we had got into a bit of a rut. The timetabled nature of our nights together: Monday, Wednesday, Friday nights and alternate Saturdays pencilled into the diary. The rotation between his town house and my flat. The inevitable visit to the American-style diner for Sunday brunch if he'd stayed at mine or the trendy gastro-pub down his road if I'd stayed at his. Perhaps he'd got fed up with the predictable and there was me thinking that this had been the foundation of our stability.

I start to pull a hoop of loose wool on the jumper and a chunk of the arm starts to unravel – it's as if it's a metaphor for mine and Joseph's relationship.

If only I'd mixed things up. Shown up unannounced on a Tuesday, wearing nothing but a mac and bedroom heels. Or taken him to the all-you-can-eat Thai buffet instead of the diner. But I didn't. I hate to say it, but I liked the familiarity and the habitual way Joseph organised our lives. I knew exactly where I was, or at least I thought I did.

I look back at the piece of paper resting on my bed, its corners already wrinkled from where I've been handling it so much. Could I really do everything on it?

A niggle of doubt begins to creep in as I try and imagine myself gliding out to sea on a windsurfer, the thought of the howling wind and the wet sea spray is making goosebumps appear on my arms.

What if I do everything and Joseph doesn't notice? I'll have put myself through hell for nothing. I'll still have lost the love of my life, and probably my sanity too.

I close my eyes and it's his face that I see. I breathe in and I can smell his aftershave wafting off the jumper, and for once I'm glad that he used to drown himself in it as at least it's still lingering on the wool after all this time.

I have to get him back, or at least attempt to.

I open my eyes. *I can do this,* I say out loud as I reread the list. I have to show him that there's more to me than he thought.

I hug the piece of paper to my chest, and close my eyes to summon Joseph's face once more. I can only hope I've found the key to how I'm going to get him back, because if this doesn't work I'm all out of ideas.

Chapter Four

Four weeks, one day since Joseph and I broke up, but hopefully less than three months until we're back together (if this list works out …).

My mouth is aching from having to force my smile into a more neutral facial expression. I don't want Sian to get suspicious about my newfound happiness.

I'm still amazed that I managed to make it through our trip to the bar last night without mentioning the list, or even uttering Joseph's name. I'm absolutely dying to tell her about my idea to complete a bucket list, and yet I've been biting my tongue, trying to leave it a respectable amount of time before I bring it up. I don't want her to realise that my list is designed to get Joseph back, so I want to drop it casually into the conversation with my cover story that I'm doing it to get over him. Not only is she anti-romance and anti-Joseph, but she's also got pretty strong feminist views and would never approve of me changing myself for a man.

'So who are we meeting again?' she asks as we climb out of her car and look out over the estuary towards Hayling Island.

'My work colleague, Giles – who I think you met last Christmas – and his wife Laura and a few of his mates who I don't know.'

Giles sent me a text message this morning in case I'd changed my mind about doing the cycle ride, and whilst I didn't wake up having had a complete personality transplant or discovering that I actually owned a bike, I said I'd join them at the pub after. I roped Sian into coming with me, and instead of cycling our epic journey is going to entail about five minutes on the ferry.

'So where's this ferry then?' I say, scanning the horizon.

I've lived in Portsmouth for years and I've not made this journey before. I'm a little bit excited as it feels like we're going on a proper day trip.

'It's just coming in.'

'Where?' I say squinting.

'There.'

I follow her pointed finger, but I'm clearly not seeing what she is.

'I can only see that little boat.'

'That's the ferry,' says Sian, heading down towards the jetty that it's attaching itself to.

I stand stock-still, staring at it.

'That's it?' I say in disbelief.

In my mind a ferry's a large boat with different tiers and plenty of space, not a little thing that could be mistaken for a fishing boat.

'Come on, we don't want to miss it,' she calls over her shoulder.

It's not that I'm afraid of boats, it's just that the last booze cruise crossing I did was in pretty choppy weather and I spent the whole journey being as sick as a dog. I'm slightly concerned that I'm going to go green around the gills after the two bottles of wine that we drank last night.

'Abi.'

'I'm coming,' I say, reluctantly following her.

We walk up to the man who's taking the money and hand him our fare. Sian walks along the wooden gangplank onto the boat, and I have no choice but to follow her as she's got the car keys.

I sit down next to her and pray I keep this morning's bacon sarnie down.

I decide to distract myself from the smallness of the vessel and tell Sian about the list.

'So this morning I was doing some research on the Internet about how to get over a break-up.'

I casually look round the boat to downplay the significance.

'And what did it say?'

Sian's giving me one of her trademark looks. Her head's tilted to the side and her mouth is twisting. She's raised her eyebrows and it's like she's subconsciously trying to tell me that she thinks I'm a moron.

'Well …' I say, pausing, trying to get my fake story straight in my head. 'It suggested creating a bucket list of things that you want to achieve in the short term. You know, stuff to do before you die. Going swimming with dolphins, learning Mandarin, sleeping in the ice hotel.'

'You want to go swimming with Flipper and learn Chinese? That's supposed to mend your broken heart?'

'Oh, no, they'd be way too difficult. They're just examples, but apparently focusing on your goals helps with the process of getting over an ex.'

I Googled it this morning and there was a BuzzFeed article about it – proof it must be true.

'I sort of prefer the old if-you-want-to-get-over-someone-you-get-under-someone rule,' says Sian.

'Well, you would,' I say, laughing. 'But I think I like this bucket list idea – less risk of an STD.'

'What are you trying to say?' she says, smiling.

I smile back – I'm saying nothing.

The ferry grinds to a halt and I look round to see that we've reached our destination. I'd barely noticed we'd got going, and it seems my belly hadn't either as I don't feel the remotest bit sick. We stand up and find our way back onto dry land.

The pub is almost straight in front of us. I can already see Giles's head over a table of people in the garden. In the garden, *in March*?

'Seriously, what's on your bucket list, then?' asks Sian, as we start walking towards the pub.

I take a deep breath and try to remain calm. I know if she's going to believe me I've got to pass each of these ideas off as if they're my own.

'I want to go and have afternoon tea at one of the fancy places in London, like Claridge's or Harrods or the Ritz,' I say, trying to sound like I haven't got it set in stone. 'And then, I thought, I could go wine tasting at an actual vineyard. Um, learning a language – I've always wanted to learn Spanish.'

That much is true. I adore Spanish food and would love to be able to pronounce items off a tapas menu properly rather than making up my own like 'al-bing-bongs' for meatballs.

I pause and watch her reaction closely. I expect her to laugh, but she doesn't and I grow more confident about telling her the rest of the list. But before I can broach the big ones – the things that are going to test if my cover has been blown – we arrive at Giles's table.

He looks up at us, and then does a double take.

'Hey, Abi! I almost didn't recognise you with your haircut.'

'Hi,' I say, putting my hand up to it, still surprised that it's so short. 'I thought it was time for a change.'

'Well, it suits you,' says Giles.

'It certainly does,' agrees his wife, Laura.

'Thank you,' I say smiling at them both.

Sian coughs and I remember my manners.

'This is my friend Sian.'

'Nice to see you again,' says Giles, grinning. 'This is my wife Laura, and my mates, Doug and Ben and Ben's girlfriend Tammy.'

We all smile at each other and mumble our 'nice to meet yous'.

'I'll get you guys a drink. What do you want?' he asks, standing up.

'I'll have a Coke,' I reply, thinking that it might help to settle my stomach after the wine last night.

'Make that two,' says Sian. 'I'm driving.'

Giles goes off to the bar, and we sit down at the table.

For a second there's an awkward silence as we realise that the person binding us together has just left.

'How was the ride over, then?' I say, attempting to break the ice.

'It was pretty good,' says Laura. 'Although I think these guys could have done it in their sleep it was so easy for them.'

'But it's a nice day for a blast,' replies one of the boys.

I look at him, forcing my mind to remember what Giles said his name was, but I've forgotten it already – I'm so rubbish. I hadn't noticed before that he's actually quite cute. I self-consciously tuck my hair behind my ear and wonder how I didn't notice when I sat down. I feel my cheeks start to burn a little, before it hits me – he reminds me of Joseph – that's obviously why I'm finding him attractive.

I start to really study him and the more I look, the more I realise they're nothing alike. All they've got in common is their curly hair. But this guy's is messier and he's got what looks like a few days of stubble on his cheeks, whereas Joseph would never have been seen in public any way but perfectly groomed.

See this is what this break-up has done to me. It's making me have the horn for anyone who fleetingly looks like Joseph.

'Yeah, you've been lucky with the weather,' I say, taking off my scarf in the hope it will calm my hot cheeks.

The silence descends once more, and I'm beginning to regret coming. We all look around nervously and I'm half expecting the tumbleweed to roll over the table at any moment.

'So, Abi was just telling me that she's created a bucket list,' says Sian.

I shoot her a look, but she ignores me.

'You know, one of these twenty-things-to-do-before-you-pop-your-clogs lists. She was just telling me what she's picked.'

'Oh, that sounds exciting,' says Laura. 'What's on it?'

All the eyes around the table focus on me and I begin to feel self-conscious. It was bad enough plucking up the courage to tell Sian about the list, but now I feel like I've got a whole panel judging me. And not to mention that Giles's friends are all probably pretty adventurous and I'm sure they'd be able to tick off all the challenges before breakfast.

Laura's smiling warmly, but the other woman, Tammy, is watching me with great interest. I feel a bit funny talking about the list in front of her because, whereas I look like I repel adventure and exercise, she looks like a magnet for it. She's super tall and skinny, with high cheekbones and a naturally tanned complexion that comes from being outside rather than a bottle of St Tropez like mine does. I'm worried I'm going to open my mouth and she'll howl with laughter at how pathetic the list is.

'Um, it's a bit silly,' I say, feeling downhearted.

'Go on, what's on it?' says Tammy enthusiastically. It's as if she's sensed what I'm thinking and is trying to put me at ease.

Giles comes back over to the table with our drinks, and Laura fills him in on our topic of conversation.

'I've already told Sian about afternoon tea at a fancy London spot, wine tasting at a vineyard and learning Spanish, but I'd also like to run a half marathon.'

I'm waiting for someone to point out that I'm not really the shape of a natural runner, with curvy hips and large boobs, but no one says anything. They're just staring at me, interested.

'Um, I want to go to Paris and do all the sights in a day … and also cycle round the Isle of Wight.'

'Ah, now today would have been a perfect training ride,' says Laura, interrupting me.

'I think I need to do pre-training training,' I say. I need to remember how to ride a bike first.

'You won't have to do that much, it's pretty flat and I'd say pretty doable for a novice,' says Tammy, smiling at me in encouragement.

'If you don't have a bike you should go and see Ben,' says Giles, pointing at his friend with the messy curls. 'He's got a shop.'

I look over at his friend, making an effort to commit his name to memory.

'That would be good. I'm going to have to get some practice in before I do the ride.'

Ben reaches into his wallet and pulls out a card.

'Here you go – the address for the shop's on the card. We'll sort you out with something.'

'Thanks,' I say, slipping it into my handbag.

'So what else is on the list?' asks Sian, clearly bored of the biking interlude.

'Um, go to Glastonbury, learn to windsurf and hike one of the UK's four peaks.'

I've already decided that there's no way I can hike all four in the timeframe that I'm setting myself. I have to do the things quickly to get Joseph back before he has time to replace me with a new girlfriend, and men like Joseph don't tend to hang around on the singles' market for long.

Hiking all four peaks would take me a whole month of weekends. I did discover there's some charity event where you can do three peaks in twenty-four hours, but I'd be the one needing the charity after that as I'm not fit enough to survive it.

'Four peaks?' asks Sian.

'Yep.' I still need to find out what the mysterious fourth one is.

'Aren't there only three?' she says.

'No, no, I'm quite sure there are four.' Joseph says there are. He's right about most things.

'Um, the fourth one is Slieve Donard,' says Ben's girlfriend with a generous helping of incredulity and eye-rolling.

Sian responds by sitting up a little straighter and pursing her lips, the two of them are locking eyes with each other as if they're bucks squaring up to lock horns.

It's not the first time I've witnessed this attitude from women towards Sian. I think they can almost sense that she's a no-strings-attached-man-eater type and they're worried about their boyfriends. But Sian's being very restrained today. She's not in prowling mode, and I can't say I'm surprised. Neither

Giles, Doug nor Ben are her type – too rough and ready with a hint of geek. Sian's all about the suited and booted, smooth-talking charmer. Tammy really has nothing to worry about with her boyfriend.

'It's in Northern Ireland,' says Ben, staring at his girlfriend before turning his attention back to me.

'I've always wanted to go to Northern Ireland,' I say, nodding. Or at least I have since getting mildly obsessed with *Game of Thrones*. Maybe I'll do that one.

'It's a good one to do, as it isn't very steep,' says Tammy, smiling at me like she's just had a personality transplant in the thirty seconds since she last spoke. 'I went riding round there last year as a warm-up for an off-road challenge I was doing.'

Whatever it was about Sian that rattled Tammy's cage, I clearly haven't. I'm almost offended that she doesn't see me as a threat. She's probably right though because despite my hair giving me a boost of confidence, I've still got the panda eyes and muffin top, and I don't exactly give off an Angelina Jolie, man-stealer vibe.

'We're doing a trip to Snowdon next month if you want to come with us and have that as your peak,' says Giles.

'Oh, yes, Abi, please come. Always nice to have another woman along. Are you able to make it, Tammy?'

'No, I'm doing a race in Cumbria that weekend,' she replies.

'Ah, that means you've got to come, Abi. Save me from being the token female.'

'Oh, um, next month,' I stutter.

I wonder if I'll be fit enough by then. Snowdon is a mountain and whilst I do a lot of walking, the flat pavements of Portsmouth aren't really in the same league. I'm torn between the idea of having the trip organised and handed to me on a plate and the fact that I'm woefully unfit and unprepared.

Sod it. I need to get this list done quickly.

'OK then, if you don't mind me tagging along and slowing you down,' I say.

'We'd love to have you,' says Laura, looking pleased.

'So that's everything on the list, is it?' asks Sian.

I'm fantasising about sipping a drink in a nice cosy pub after the hike, when a dark cloud descends as I recall the last task.

'Um, and I want to abseil down the Spinnaker Tower,' I add, looking down at the table.

If there's one thing that's going to flash warning lights at Sian, this is it. She knows my fear of heights all too well. She once convinced me to go on the London Eye, and her hand still bears the scars from where my nails dug into her as I was clinging on for dear life. It was the longest thirty minutes of both our lives.

'You want to abseil down Spinnaker? Like from the top?' she says.

I can see her eyes narrowing as they burn into me.

'Uh-huh,' I reply nonchalantly, as if it's the kind of thing I'd do every day.

'You, that's scared of heights?' she says.

I try to avoid looking at anyone round the table. I know everyone will probably think I'm ridiculous. I hate being acrophobic, it makes me feel so pathetic.

'You're scared of heights and you still want to do the abseil?' says Giles. 'Flipping heck, Abi, I don't mind heights but even I'd struggle with that. The way the wind rushes around that tower. Isn't that why the outside lift doesn't work? Because it used to get pushed around in the wind?'

My stomach lurches at the thought and my heart's starting to pound. I try and keep Joseph's face in my mind to remind myself why I want to do the list. All I can hope is that he comes back to me before I get to the Spinnaker, because I'm just as sceptical as those two about the chances of me completing it.

'It could be a way to conquer your fear once and for all,' says Laura, shrugging her shoulders.

'I have to say I wouldn't have picked you as a windsurfer,' says Giles.

'Nor me,' says Sian. She's intensely staring at me again and I feel like I'm under extreme scrutiny.

'Well, I spent a lot of time reading bucket list websites and they all said learn to surf, but Portsmouth isn't really known for surfing, but it is known for windsurfing.'

'You haven't got many things abroad on that list,' says Sian, looking pensive. 'What about putting New York on? Haven't you always wanted to go?'

Sian doesn't realise that the list is closed to additions. I guess if I did have to do something fake to convince her that the list was real, then I could think of much worse things.

'Um, perhaps,' I say, trying to sound vague.

'What about places off the beaten track?' says Tammy, glaring in Sian's direction and causing Sian to flare her nostrils in response. It's like handbags at dawn.

'Yeah,' says Ben joining in. 'A lot of people have travelling on their bucket lists. Why don't you add trekking to Machu Picchu or climbing Kilimanjaro?'

New York's one thing, but places in the back of beyond are quite another.

'That's a good call. They'd definitely be on mine,' says Giles.

'I don't know if they're really my kind of thing,' I say, not entirely sure where either are. I didn't pay that much attention to Geography at school.

'Oh, man, there's nothing that beats arriving at Machu Picchu to see the sun rise over the top of it,' says the man whose name I think is Doug.

'Yeah, except I really wish I hadn't drunk so much the night before when I went. I felt as sick as a dog on that last stretch of the trail,' says Ben.

'Is that the Inca trail?' asks Sian.

'Yeah,' both men reply, nodding sagely as if they're thousands of miles away back in Peru.

'I think that's definitely out for Abi – she hates camping.'

'Yet you've got Glastonbury on the list,' says Laura, her face wrinkling in confusion.

'I, er …' All eyes are on me and I begin to stutter. 'I'm sure I could glamp at Glastonbury.'

'That spoils the fun of it. Trying to find a toilet with the least amount of shit around the side, and having to hear the people in the tent next to yours talking absolute bollocks when you're trying to sleep is all part of the experience,' says Doug.

I'm sure the colour must be draining from my face. I hate Portaloos at the best of times, but the thought of using them at a music festival ... I'm starting to wonder if I've taken on this challenge too lightly. The only thing giving me hope is that my sister goes to Glastonbury, so maybe I've got festival-goer genes in me somewhere.

'You could add clubbing in Ibiza,' says Sian. 'That's something that everyone should do once.'

'Or trekking in the Himalayas,' says Tammy, as if she's competing with Sian.

'How about going to see the Northern Lights?' suggests Giles.

'Oh, learning to dive,' adds Doug.

My head's turning back and forth trying to keep up with the suggestions. I keep trying to get a word in edgeways to protest but the suggestions keep coming.

'Skydiving over Christ the Redeemer in Rio,' says Giles.

'Or climbing the Sydney Harbour Bridge,' says Laura.

'What about learning to do burlesque dancing?' says Sian, lifting an eyebrow seductively.

The image of me wearing nipple tassels and parading around in my pants flashes through my mind. Whilst I'm sure that would be right up Joseph's street, I can't see how I could put that on Facebook without having most people unfriend me for scarring their eyes.

Poor Joseph, his list is taking a bit of a beating. There was me thinking he was all Action Man, but the others have made the tasks sound more like a Ken doll day out.

'I think I'll just stick to what I've got, for now,' I say. 'I mean, I want it to be achievable as I want to tick off the items as quickly as I can.'

The quicker I can do the list, the quicker I'll have Joseph back and the less likely he'll have been snapped up by someone else.

'If I was doing one of those lists, I'd start with a bungee jump off the Tees Transporter Bridge,' says Doug.

'Oh, I'd be so up for that,' says Tammy, nodding her head.

'I'd want to go in one of those planes that simulates zero gravity,' says Giles.

I'm relieved that Joseph isn't as adventurous as either of them or I'd be waving goodbye to him once and for all.

I let everyone get lost in their thoughts about what they'd put on their own bucket lists. The more they think about theirs, the less they're thinking about mine.

'Well, Abi, here's to you. Good luck with your list,' says Giles, raising his pint.

'To Abi's list,' seconds Sian, raising her Coke.

The rest of the table join in and they all chink my glass before we drink the toast.

I feel a sense of elation that I've passed the first test: convincing Sian that the list was my idea. Now all I need to do is actually start ticking things off, and soon.

Images of the list's contents flash through my mind like a film montage and I'm wondering what I've let myself in for. The lasting image is of me dangling from the Spinnaker Tower, and the flesh on my arms starts to get goosebumps. Now that I've told everyone, I can't back out. I'm doing this list, and getting Joseph back – even if it kills me.

Chapter Five

~~Four weeks, three days since Joseph and I broke up.~~
Three months and counting to get Joseph back before
he replaces me.

I can't help but be the tiniest bit offended by how much everyone loves my new hair. Yes, it's great that people think that I look like I've just stepped off the pages of a photo shoot, I'm sure it's also a huge compliment that I now look a bit like Alexa Chung and Caroline Flack, but every coo and compliment makes me wonder just how bad everyone thought I looked before.

It's day three of the new haircut at work and instead of people accepting it and moving on, my colleagues keep saying that they can't believe it's me.

I'm walking over to the communal office printer, and if I get one more hair comment then I'm going to hide it under my woolly beanie for the rest of the week.

I'm only a few steps away from the printer when I see Lindsey, sorry, 'Linz' with a Z as I keep overhearing her telling people on the phone, get there first. I'm about to try and pretend that I'm on my way to the kitchenette, when I see she's holding my printout and looking bemused.

'That's mine,' I say, resisting the urge to snatch it away from her. I don't know what it is about her that's got my back up, but I guess I'm suspicious of naturally bubbly people.

She looks up at me and flashes her perfect pearly-white teeth. With her blond hair tied up high in a ponytail and sun-kissed skin, she looks like she'd be more at home in California than Portsmouth.

'Hi, Abi,' she says, still grinning and not handing over the paper.

'Linz,' I reply, putting my hand out.

Instead of giving it to me she looks down at it once more.

'The Eiffel Tower?' she says.

Ten out of ten for identifying one of the most easily recognisable buildings on the planet.

'That's right, it's for a mood board,' I say.

Which is true. It just happens to be for the mood board I'm creating at home of all the challenges on Joseph's bucket list. We've got a super-dooper colour printer at work and I've been sneakily, or at least up until now, printing off pictures for it.

'Oh, right, what account's it for?'

Why won't she give me my bloody bit of paper!

I stare, mentally willing her to hand it over to me.

She can only be in her early twenties, not long out of university. She's got that fresh-faced, eager-beaver look that I used to have when I started my career. The sort of enthusiasm that comes from the naivety of not calculating how many days of your life you've got to work before you draw your pension.

'For the Spinnaker account. I thought it might be helpful to remind myself of other iconic towers.'

Sometimes I scare myself with how quickly I can come up with lies.

'That's such a good idea. And I love the idea of making actual physical mood boards. That's so old school.'

As if I needed another reason not to like this girl.

'I'm just a bit confused, though. I got the impression from Rick that I was going to do the design for it.'

I turn back to face her and she gives me that sweet and innocent smile that she seems to have down to a tee.

'Um, when we first got word of the tendering process last month, *before* you started, Rick assigned it to me, so I'm not sure what gave you that idea ...'

She shakes her head.

'Of course,' she says handing me my Eiffel Tower picture. 'That was only when we were in the pub after work on Friday. Rick had mentioned that it might be a good project to build up my portfolio, but I'm sure he was only being nice. He's obviously invited me to the meeting this morning just to show me how things are done here.'

She bats her eyelashes at me like Road Runner used to do to a stunned Coyote, then turns and walks off with her printouts leaving me standing alone.

After-work drinks on Friday with Rick sounds a little bit cosy for my liking.

I'm reminded of what Giles said to me last week, about her getting her feet under the table. I must get him to elaborate.

I walk back to my desk wishing that Hayley would come back soon. But, given that her baby was only born last week, I know I've got to put up with Linz for the foreseeable future.

I settle back into my chair and tuck my Eiffel Tower picture safely in my bag. I've now got nearly all the photos for my mood board, which means the next step might actually be to attempt to do one of the tasks on the list.

It's been a whole four days since the arrival of the box that started me down the journey of trying to complete Joseph's bucket list. And so far, I haven't managed to tick off a single thing.

When I'd looked at his list, I'd thought that I'd whip through it in no time. But I've been researching the activities, and nearly all of them are going to take time and preparation. No wonder Joseph hadn't completed any himself. There are hurdles and obstacles everywhere I look.

Take having afternoon tea at the Ritz. I'd imagined I'd tip up, eat my monthly quota of cakes and put a big fat tick on the list. Sian had agreed to take a day off with me, and we were going to go up later this week. Only when I checked the website I realised that it wasn't as easy as I'd imagined. I had to book and after a lot of searching on the online booking facility, I just about managed to find a slot that Sian, the Ritz and I could all do. We're going next Tuesday.

Then there was the Spanish. At first I thought I'd try teaching myself, but that proved a lot harder than I thought. I had got a Michel Thomas CD out from the library on Monday night, but I'd fallen asleep listening to it. I found the sultry tone of his voice so soothing. And, disappointingly, I didn't manage to learn Spanish by osmosis. So I've booked myself onto a course.

I'm just bringing up Facebook to scan Joseph's page to see if there's been any activity that might indicate a new female companion, when my phone rings, the number's withheld, and I cross my fingers, hoping it's one of my outstanding enquiries, rather than some call centre ringing to tell me that I'm eligible to switch phone companies.

'Hello.'

'Hi, is that Abi? It's Jenny here from the Outdoor Centre.'

'Oh, hello. Thanks for calling me back.'

'No problem. So you said in your message that you wanted to learn to windsurf?'

I have to fight the instinct to shout no at the top of my voice, but instead I hear myself squeaking a yes. Why anyone would want to sail out to sea standing on a wedge of foam with a flimsy plastic sail is beyond me. Whenever I've seen windsurfers in Portsmouth it's always on those foul, stinking days where they're getting bashed around by the howling wind and rain. It's not the best advert for the sport.

'Well, the best way to start is to do an introduction to windsurfing day. Then from there you can do a weekend beginners' course, then an intermediate and before you know it you'll be riding the waves on your own.'

I stifle a laugh. Yeah, right.

'Will the introductory thing teach me to stop and go?'

'Um, yeah, there's hopefully a little more to it than that, but essentially that's it.'

'Perfect,' I say. The list said learn to windsurf, so that will be it – job done. I'll have my photo for Facebook. If only I could do it without getting wet. 'Do you supply the boards?'

I'm desperately hoping the answer will be yes, as not only do I not want to fork out for one when I've already got to buy a bike, but I can't imagine where I'd possibly store it in my shoe-box flat.

'Yes, we lend you everything. Wetsuits, board and sail and buoyancy aids.'

'Great.'

'So, we've got room on our course on Saturday.'

'This Saturday?'

Now, I know I've been banging on about whipping through the challenges, but this Saturday? That only gives me three days to stress, stew and psych myself up. I was hoping to dip my toe into this list with the easy stuff first before I prepared to battle one of man's most dangerous adversaries: the sea.

'Yes, or we've got another one running the last weekend of the month, if you'd prefer.'

'Um, yes, that sounds better,' I say, exhaling.

That gives me three weeks to get my confidence up. By then I'll probably be some adrenaline junkie pro. Or I've got three weeks to get myself some Valium to get me through it.

'Great. So the course, including hire, costs seventy-five pounds. You can pay a deposit of fifty pounds now and the rest on the day.'

This list is getting more expensive by the minute. So far, afternoon tea at the Ritz is costing me fifty pounds (plus travel expenses and inevitable cocktails after), a ten-week beginner's Spanish course that starts next week is costing me seventy pounds, and I've entered a 10k Race for Life (which is almost a half marathon – right?) at sixteen pounds. And that's before I buy proper running shoes and a decent sports bra to strap the puppies into. I'd worked out that doing those three challenges alone was going to cost me about £250.

This is probably why people do their bucket lists over a few years rather than a few months. I'm beginning to wonder if I'm losing my mind – as well as my hard-earned pounds – doing this.

With my rent going up, my savings can't really afford to take such a hit, but I can't put a cost on love, can I? I mean, at the end of it I'll be poor, but I'll have Joseph back, and surely that'll be all that matters. That and when we get back together this time I might bring up moving in with him and then I'll save money. If you think about it, it's just a short-term investment.

I rattle off my card details, officially booking my place, and say my goodbyes to Jenny. As I put my credit card back into my wallet, I spot the card that Giles's friend Ben gave me last week. I ought to pay him a visit at the bike shop because the sooner I start practising how to ride on two wheels, the sooner I'll be able to tick it off my list. I look at the address and realise it's not that far from the office. I could probably go in my lunch hour tomorrow.

'That sounded exciting,' says my colleague Fran, leaning between the crack in the partition that separates our desks.

'Oh, um, yes, should be.'

I hadn't realised that anyone would overhear. I don't like to make personal calls at work.

'Are you coming to the meeting?' asks Giles before Fran can ask any more questions.

I glance at the clock behind his head and I see that it's ten o'clock already. I've been at work an hour and so far all I've done is sort out my extracurricular activities. I was meant to be doing some initial designs for a museum client, but I'll have to do it after lunch now.

'Yep,' I say, standing up and rummaging around my desk for a pad and pens.

'So that was fun at the pub the other day,' he says as we make our way to our meeting room.

'Yes, thanks for inviting me. I had a lovely time.'

'Us too. Laura's really excited about you coming to Wales.'

'Well, that makes one of us,' I say, before realising how awful that sounds. 'I mean it's not that I'm not excited about going with you lot, but I'm pretty nervous about the hike. I'm worried that I'm never going to make it to the top.'

I'm desperately trying to dig my way out of the hole I found myself in as Giles pushes open the door to our meeting.

'You'll be fine,' he says quietly as he holds the door open for me.

We take our seats opposite Rick and Linz, who barely seem to have noticed we've arrived – too lost in their own conversation.

I clear my throat noisily.

'Hey,' says Rick, snapping his head to face forward. He still can't look me in the eye, after the whole trampoline-boob-grabbing incident. I fold my arms protectively over my chest as if to hide the offenders. 'Now you're both here we'll get started. I've asked Linz along as she's new to the business and the tendering process, so I thought this would be a good way to walk her through it.

'Right, as you know Spinnaker are considering changing marketing agencies, and their head office in York has put it out to tender. We're competing with national as well as local firms. I'm hoping what gives us an edge is our local knowledge, so let's bear that in mind when we work up a concept. They want us to give them a glimpse of the design and what they'd expect from us, so I'm hoping we'll be able to come up with something fresh and innovative that they'll like. Giles, at this stage we don't need you to build a website, but could you liaise with Abi about ideas for it, as it might influence the branding and design Abi puts together. Also, Abi, if you could bring Linz into that design process that would be great. I think it's good to get some fresh, young blood on this.'

Between that and Linz's earlier comment about my mood boards being old school, I'm beginning to think that I should be reaching for my Zimmer frame.

'Whilst I'm going to make sure that I make the figures as competitive as possible, I think it's really going to come down to how we impress them with the concept. So have you had any ideas so far?'

Rick looks between me and Giles and I'm about to open my mouth when Linz pipes up.

'I thought a good starting point might be to consider other iconic towers, you know the Eiffel Tower, the Shard, the Empire State Building. We've got to think of the Spinnaker being Portsmouth's version of one of those,' she says in a confident tone.

My mouth's dropped open and I'm staring at her in disbelief. She's stolen my idea. Or at least my fake idea. I'd fudged that as a cover story to hide my printing motivations, but of course Linz doesn't know that. In her head, she thinks she's pre-empting what I was going to say.

'That's an interesting take,' says Rick. 'And how would you translate that into a design idea?'

'Um, well, I guess … it would be about making it seem large and impressive.'

Any feeling of annoyance at her poaching my idea fades away as it seems that given a little bit of rope Linz will hang herself.

'OK,' says Rick, smiling at her politely. 'So, Abi, Giles, any ideas?'

'Well, I think we should concentrate on the USPs – I mean it's all about the view. The nearest equivalent experience would be somewhere in London. I think the fact that it's located on the seafront is a key component that could be reflected in the design,' I say.

'I think that's heading along the right lines,' says Rick, nodding.

'We could have the tower as part of the letters in the logo,' says Linz, like an animated puppy. 'You know the 'p' could be a picture of the tower.'

I watch as she starts to doodle on a pad and I'm a little gutted to say that it looks pretty good.

'That's great,' says Rick, nodding enthusiastically. 'Abi, could you work with Linz further to mock that up.'

Linz gives me a flash of her bright whites and I smile back through gritted teeth.

'I've had an idea,' says Giles. 'Or, at least, Abi's given me an idea. She was telling me how she wants to abseil down the tower …'

Oh no. I snap my head round and widen my eyes to get Giles to stop, but I can't get his attention. I see Rick's eyes are twinkling – his interest piqued.

'I was thinking,' continues Giles, 'why don't we do it as a team event? Show that the agency is up to the challenge?'

Oh, God. There it is. He's laid down the gauntlet for the bloody king of crazy challenges.

I was hoping that I'd never have to do the Spinnaker abseil. It was supposed to be the finale that would never come because my leading man would show up at the end of Act One.

'I love that idea. What better way to prove that we understand the attraction than experiencing it in a way that no other agency would,' says Rick, slamming his hand down on the table in triumph.

I'm starting to hyperventilate. I feel Linz staring at me, her eyes narrowing, as if she's a dog smelling my fear.

'I'm so up for that,' she says looking directly at me. 'I love abseiling. I did loads of it at university.'

'Excellent,' says Rick. 'Us four will obviously do it, but we can open it to the wider office to see if anyone else wants to take part.'

'But, Giles,' I say, 'weren't you saying the other day that you couldn't imagine doing it?'

'Well, if you're going to, then I'd be pretty wimpy not doing it myself,' he says, shrugging his shoulders.

'That settles it. The pitch for the tender is at the end of May, so if we could do it before then. Abi, are you all right to organise it?' says Rick.

'Of course,' I say, rehearsing in my head the little white lie I'll tell this afternoon – that sadly every date between now and the end of May is full.

'I can do it,' says Linz, putting her hand up as if she is still at school. 'I mean, Abi's so busy with all her existing account work, I'll happily coordinate a day we can all do.'

'OK, then. Thanks, Linz,' says Rick.

Linz raises a satisfied eyebrow, and gives me a smile that only a woman would understand. I'm sure neither of the boys will realise it has all the hallmarks of a bitchy move.

'So, let's get cracking on some concepts, and we'll meet back in two weeks to see what we've come up with. And hopefully Linz will have some news for us on the abseil. Excellent idea, Abi – I hadn't picked you as the adventurous type. I'm impressed,' says Rick as we stand up to leave.

I see Linz's face fall as he praises me, and I can't help feeling a little swell of pride. No one's ever called me adventurous before.

Although I'm sure he won't be calling me that when I back out, unable to even go up the tower, let alone abseil down it.

I watch Linz as she bounds out of the meeting room, energetic and hungry for the job. I can't shake the feeling that she was deliberately trying to steal my thunder at the meeting. I wonder if that's what Giles meant the other day. That while I was at home brooding, she was here getting cosy and muscling in on my job.

It's bad enough that I'm having to up my game thanks to my written warning, but now I'm going to have to keep up with some eager-beaver newbie who's showing me up.

How am I going to get out of the abseil now? There was me thinking that I wouldn't actually have to go through with this, but now everyone at work will be expecting me to do it. I've not only got to get Joseph back before the end of May, but I also need to come up with a good enough excuse to wriggle out of the abseil. One that's less disturbing than Fran's fake baby. I thought I had enough on my plate trying to do this list, but now the pressure is really on.

Chapter Six

Sod having three months to get Joseph back – I've got under eight weeks until the Spinnaker Tower abseil, which now gives me less than eight weeks to get him back and think of an excuse to actually get out of it ...

I'm wandering down Marmion Road, a pretty little shopping street in Southsea, trying not to get sucked into the quirky shops that line the route. I'm looking down the side streets for Ben's bike shop. I've only got an hour for lunch and whilst the shop is only a ten-minute walk from my work, I haven't got time to get distracted by window displays or the treasure-trove of beautiful things in the interior design shop. Focus, Abi. Focus.

I find the street and spot Ben's shop immediately with its bikes chained up outside. I've never noticed it before, but that's probably because there's a chocolate shop on the other side of the main road, and I've usually crossed over by this point to drool through the window.

I turn up the narrow street that would just about fit one car. On one side of the road there is a row of cute, colourfully painted terraced houses, all with hanging baskets or window boxes outside that will be brimming with flowers in the next month or two, which will add to the cottagey feel. On the other side is the back of the hardware store that fronts onto the main road, and next to that is Ben's bike shop – On the Rivet.

I push open the door and the bell jangles noisily. I'm surprised that it's such a big shop as from the outside it looked narrow and pokey. Inside it seems to stretch back and is much more open than I expected. It's positively Tardis-like. It's also surprisingly light and airy with wooden floors and bikes hanging from shiny chrome fittings. Not at all how I imagined it would be.

'Be there in a second,' calls a voice that I recognise to be Ben's.

I look around at all the bikes and a wall full of clothes and accessories. There's a lot of stock and, as the only customer, I wonder how he can get enough footfall to run this place.

Too scared to look at the bikes by myself, I start browsing the clothes instead. I'm squinting at what looks like a Borat mankini when Ben pops out from the back.

'Hello,' he says as he walks over to me.

I turn to face him and he breaks out into a smile.

'Abi?'

He wrinkles his eyes at me as if checking that he's got my name right. I give him a quick nod as I reply, 'Hi, Ben.'

His smile is infectious and I smile back. He runs a hand through his messy hair but it does little to tame it. He's also got more facial hair than last week – he's practically got a beard now.

'So, you were serious about needing a bike then?'

'Yeah – there's no way round it. I need a bike if I'm going to cycle the Isle of Wight.'

'Wow, most people that say they're going to do those kind of lists talk about them for ages before they actually do anything about it. So have you started it yet?' he asks.

'Not exactly. I had no idea it would all take so much planning. But I've got things booked – tea at the Ritz, a 10k run, a windsurfing course. Oh, and the abseil.'

My stomach lurches at the thought. I got an email from Linz this morning to say that our team abseil has been booked for the beginning of May. I've got eight weeks to come up with an excuse. Hot favourite at the moment is a tumble down Snowdon resulting in a twisted ankle. Although, with me being so uncoordinated that's a pretty likely outcome whether I need an excuse or not.

'Gosh, you're really going for it,' he says. 'That's some determination.'

I smile and nod. Joseph's worth being determined for.

We stand there awkwardly for a moment, before I turn towards the bikes as if to remind him of why I'm there.

'Right,' he says, taking the hint. 'So what type of bike are you used to?'

'Well,' I say thinking back to my childhood bikes, 'I had a Muddyfox mountain bike when I was little.'

Although I should have added the disclaimer that, much to my parents' annoyance, it was more of a decorative feature of our garage, residing there without disturbance and playing home to a number of spider families.

'Oh, didn't every girl? My sister had one of those too. OK, so mountain bikes. Hmm, are you going to do much off-roading then?'

'Only if I can't steer properly,' I say with a nervous laugh. 'But no, I don't know what it's like circumnavigating the Isle of Wight, but I imagine it's roads most of the way.'

'Yeah, it is, but do you not need a bike for after? I mean, I'm surprised living in Pompey you don't have one.'

'Oh, God, no. I don't know what's worse in this city, the bikes that don't think the Highway Code applies to them, or the car drivers that jump all the red lights. I don't think I know anyone who rides a bike down here that hasn't been hit by a car.'

Ben's looking at the floor and I get the feeling he's avoiding eye contact.

'I mean, I bet you've been hit by a car in Portsmouth?' I ask.

'Well, yes. A couple of times,' he mutters.

'I rest my case. No, I think the Isle of Wight will do me. And I guess I'll have to do a bit of training beforehand. It'll take a few days to do the challenge, won't it? I still don't know where I'm going to stay overnight, or who I'm going to get to drive the support van behind me,' I say, thinking about what I've read so far about cycle challenges. 'There's just so much to organise with this bucket list.'

Ben looks like he's biting his lip and I get the impression that he's trying hard not to laugh.

'What's so funny?'

'Sorry,' he says laughing. 'It's just I've never heard of anyone having a support van for it before. It's not like you're doing

London to Paris. Then you might have needed some help, but most people do the Isle of Wight in a day.'

'They do?' I say in disbelief. 'One day?'

It still seems like an awful lot of cycling to me, but instead of scaring me, Ben's revelation has the opposite effect. This challenge is suddenly sounding achievable.

'Yep, that's why I assumed you'd put it on your list. It's often in those must-do cycle-ride lists that they have in magazines and newspapers because it's relatively easy and doable in a day. I mean, not that I don't think it's a challenge,' he says in reaction to my fallen face. 'If you're not a cyclist then it will be hard for you.'

'Don't say that,' I say, trying to smile. 'I don't want you to put me off.'

'No, sorry. I forget that for some people getting on a bike is hard. Usually we only get die-hard bike nuts in here. Most amateurs go to Halfords.'

The way he says that makes me feel like that's where I should have gone.

'Oh, God, Abi. I didn't mean it like that. I just meant that most people that don't know anything about bikes go there as it's easy. A lot of people find this kind of place intimidating.'

I look around the shop and realise it's actually one of the least intimidating specialist shops I've ever been in. It looks fresh and modern and everything's bathed in a warm glow. There's a cosy feel to the place that makes it almost homely.

'I mean, how I could intimidate anyone, I don't know.' He laughs abruptly and it startles me.

He shakes his head before he rolls up his long sleeves and walks towards a rack of bikes. 'Let's get you a bike then, before I talk myself out of a sale.'

Judging by the empty shop, he definitely couldn't afford to do that.

I follow him over and stroke the handlebars of a mountain bike. It looks a lot more hard core than my old Muddyfox and there are certainly no pastel pink or purple hues in sight.

'Now, these are our second-hand bikes. I'm guessing you really don't want a brand new one. I've refurbished all these myself and they'll be fine for what you need.'

I see the second-hand sign hanging over them and glance longingly over at the new ones – my inner child rearing her head like a magpie. They are so shiny.

'How much are the new ones?'

'They start from a thousand pounds.'

I try and swallow the lump that's appeared in my throat and my eyes almost pop out of my head.

'A thousand pounds?' I repeat.

'Yeah, but as I said our market is serious cyclists. We customise most of the components, so you're looking at spending upwards of one to two thousand if you want something decent.'

'So, the second-hand ones,' I say turning my attention back to them.

They might not be as shiny, but I'm sure it's like a new car, once it's off the forecourt and a little muddy you'll never know the difference.

Ben smiles and pulls one out. 'This one's probably the right kind of thing for you. It's a hybrid, so you can ride it on and off the road. I'm hoping that you'll get the cycling bug and want to use it after your challenge. I mean, that's what I hope for with every customer,' he says and coughs. 'So it's got decent brakes, it's had new tyres put on and the suspension's pretty decent. Do you want to hop on and see how it feels?'

'OK,' I say, swinging my leg over the bike. I notice the price tag of £200. That's more than I'd budgeted for, but still, my poor savings.

I wriggle my bum into the seat and try and get comfy, which I would have thought would have been a bit easier thanks to the extra pounds I've put on lately. I grip the handlebars tightly and squeeze the brakes. I put one of my feet on a pedal and swing it a little.

'Seems OK,' I say, not really having a clue what it's supposed to feel like.

'Hop off for a second.'

I do as I'm told and Ben bends over the bike and makes an adjustment to the seat.

'OK, get back on.'

I mount the bike once more and it feels a lot better. I'm no longer on tiptoes trying to reach the floor.

'That's better,' says Ben. As he leans over me and changes a dial by the handlebar I can smell his aftershave. It's not one I recognise, but it's got a lovely, fresh smell and I want to breathe it in more. I have to stop myself leaning into him like I'm in one of those ridiculous Lynx adverts. I have to remind myself that it's just a chemical reaction.

'So, take it for a spin,' says Ben, moving away and taking his nice scent with him.

'I'm sorry,' I say, thinking that I've misheard.

'Go for a blast, if you turn right out of the shop you can do a little loop and that way you'll find your stride before you hit Marmion Road and have pedestrians to contend with.'

'You want me to go for a ride?'

'Um, yeah. You wouldn't buy a car without a test drive, would you?'

'No,' I say glumly. If I'd known I was going to have to ride a bike I might have prepared myself.

'You should be OK in what you're wearing. It's not like you've got heels on.'

I look down and curse the fact that I'm wearing practical skinny jeans and flat boots.

Ben's looking at me expectantly and I don't want to tell him that I'm scared. I mean, what thirty-year-old can't ride a bike? I swing my leg off the bike and go to push it out of the shop.

Ben opens the door for me and I lift the front wheel up over the threshold. I have to admit it's nice and light – at least I can steer it while I walk. I wonder how long it would take me to walk around the Isle of Wight pushing a bike? I could hop on the bike for the photos, and Joseph wouldn't be any the wiser.

'Off you go then,' says Ben.

'But I don't have a helmet on, or anything,' I say, desperately trying to think of an excuse. It's bad enough having to ride a bike for the first time in about twenty years, without Ben the expert watching me do it. I'm scared I'm going to wobble into one of the many parked cars, or fall off into the road. They say that you never forget how to ride a bike, but what if I'm the exception to the rule?

Ben's disappeared into the shop. I sigh with relief. Perhaps he's giving me some space. I'm taking a deep breath to try and compose myself before I set off, when he returns with a helmet in his hands. He gives it to me with one hand and takes the bike with his other.

I reluctantly take the helmet and put it on, defeated. I'm not going to be able to get out of this. I adjust the chin strap before clipping it together. At least if I fall off now I'll be protected.

'You're all set,' he says, taking his hand away as I put mine on the handlebars.

'I'm on my lunch break, you know. I've got to get back in half an hour,' I say, clutching at straws.

'Abi, I'm asking you to go once round the block, not once round Portsmouth. It takes most people about a minute max.'

I'm not most people …

I sense that he's not going to let me buy this without riding it.

I take another deep breath, swing my leg over once more and balance a foot on the pedal. I can feel my legs quivering beneath me. I push off with my other foot and desperately look down, trying to find the other pedal. The handlebars are turning left and right and the front wheel is wobbling out of control.

'Whoa,' says Ben, running after me, grabbing the handlebars and steering me away from a parked car.

'Sorry,' I say as he steadies me and lets go. I try to steer in as straight a line as I can, this time keeping my eyes forward.

I manage to make it a few metres down the road, cycling at about the pace of a snail. I'll bet Ben didn't take that into consideration when he said it would take a day to do the Isle of Wight.

'Abi, stop!' shouts Ben.

I squeeze the brake and put my left foot down. I feel the bike lurch, throwing me forward a little. Thank goodness I wasn't going any faster, I might have had use for my helmet.

I look round at him, trying to calm my pounding heart. 'What's wrong, wasn't I doing it right?' I say.

'Yes, you were. It's just you were going to turn the corner, and the pavement on that road is a little uneven. I thought it might throw you – literally.'

What a loser. I feel like I'm back in my garden when I was seven being shoved off down towards my house after my dad removed my stabilisers much against my will. That time I'd ended up in a pile of recently raked leaves with a bruised shin. Now it might only have been my pride that was bruised, but somehow that seems worse.

I get off the bike and turn it round.

'I'm the worst rider you've ever seen,' I say glumly.

'Not the worst rider,' he says, taking control of the handlebars and lifting the bike back over the doorway into the shop. 'But one of them.'

'Oi,' I say, folding my arms over my chest defensively.

He laughs and I notice a little dimple on his left cheek that's in danger of being swallowed up completely if his beard grows any more.

'You'll get there. You just need a little bit of practice somewhere with a few less obstacles,' he says.

'So you don't think that I'm going to be able to ride around the Isle of Wight next week then?'

'Not next week, and maybe not the week after. But you'll get there.'

I sigh. This bucket list is getting harder and harder every day. Instead of getting closer to achieving anything I'm getting further away.

'I tell you what, how about I take you out on a training ride? Get your confidence up,' he says, as if he's sensing my deflated mood.

'That would be really great.'

'It would have to be a Sunday though, if that's OK?' he says.

'Yes, that's great with me. I don't suppose you can do this week, can you?'

I feel like I've got a bit of momentum and don't want to lose it.

'Oh, no, I can't, sorry. I'm going to see Tammy race. But I can do the one after.'

I think back to her and her comments about cycling down mountains at the pub.

'I'm sure she'd laugh if she knew that I couldn't even cycle down a road,' I say.

'Not everyone's a natural like her,' he says, before wiping away a bit of dirt that's found its way onto the bike's frame with his sleeve. 'It was like she was born on two wheels.'

'What kind of racing does she do?'

'She races road bikes.'

'Right,' I say, nodding. Still none the wiser.

'You know, like they did in the Olympics round Surrey and into London? She did the women's equivalent of the Tour de France last year.'

'Cool.'

No wonder she looks so bloody skinny and super-fit. I can see how she and Ben are totally made for each other.

'I better get going as my lunch break is almost over. But I'll see you a week on Sunday?' I say, thinking I'm out of my depth in this conversation.

'Great. Shall I keep the bike until then?'

'Yes, that would be great. Save me having to push it all the way home.' I open my bag and pull out my wallet.

'Don't worry about that,' says Ben. 'You can sort it out next week if you meet me here.'

'OK, are you sure?' I say.

'Yep, just in case you change your mind. Think of it as a cooling-off period.'

I smile. The old me definitely would have cooled off and changed her mind, but not the new Abi – the one who's determined to win back Joseph.

'I'll see you next week, then. Thanks for everything.'

'No problem, take it easy,' he says.

I turn and walk out of the shop. I'm so pleased I made the effort to come and see Ben. I give him a wave as I walk past the window and he waves back.

With Ben helping me with the bike ride and the Ritz almost ticked off, maybe this crazy plan will work after all. Maybe I'll have this bucket list done and Joseph back before I know it, and, more importantly, before he has time to find a new girlfriend.

Chapter Seven

Six weeks and four days until the Tower of Terror and the first item off my list is about to be completed ...

I can't quite believe it, but ten days after deciding to live out Joseph's bucket list, I'm finally ticking something off. Sian and I are sitting down to afternoon tea in the Palm Court at the Ritz.

'This is swanky,' whispers Sian as she slips off her coat and hands it to the person seating us.

'Isn't it?' I say.

It was hard to know what to expect before I arrived, but it's certainly more opulent than I imagined it would be. I study the room as subtly as I can, but wherever I look, my mouth keeps dropping open in wonder. Birdcage chandeliers hang imposingly from the gilded ceiling and statues seem to leap out of the alcoves. And, as if the surroundings aren't fancy enough, the tables are decked out with starched white linen with delicate chinaware laid on top. Once I sit down, I'm scared to move in case I knock something over. All in all, it oozes five-star sumptuousness.

After handing us menus the man tells us our waiter will be with us straightaway.

'Oh, this sounds amazing,' I say as I read what courses we've got coming up. Although the sandwiches all sound nice, it's the scones and cakes I'm most looking forward to.

'It really does. Good choice, Abi.'

Distracted by a cake stand full of the most exquisite-looking petits fours I've ever seen that's being carried past our table, I'm about to say that I can't take credit for it, with it being Joseph's idea. Luckily I stop myself, remembering that Sian thinks this is one of my dreams.

'I can't believe I haven't thought of doing it before,' I say in all honesty. I mean, I might have needed Joseph to plant the idea in my mind, but it really is up my street. Tea and cake are two of my favourite things.

Our waiter comes over with a box of tea and asks us which we want. I order the Rose Congou and Sian the Russian Caravan, and after complimenting us on our selection he disappears.

'That woman over there looks like that presenter off *The One Show*,' says Sian, gasping.

I crane my neck, instantly seeing who Sian's talking about. She does look like the woman off *The One Show*, but I don't think it is her as I doubt she'd be taking selfies in quite such an obvious way. I think she's just another tourist like us. Slightly disappointed, I snap my head back round again, trying to pretend that I come to fancy places like this all the time and I have no need to gawp at strangers or the surroundings.

Our waiter comes back over and delivers our individual tea pots, before another waiter arrives with our three-tiered sandwich-and-cake stand. I'm practically salivating as the waiter explains the fillings of the sandwiches and describes all the cakes. If I wasn't in such a fancy-pants place I'd have been rude and dived straight in whilst he was talking.

'Thank you,' says Sian, as the waiter finishes.

We pause and smile up at him, and as he turns to go we're both in there like a rocket. I desperately want to start on the scones, but I've paid fifty pounds for this so I've got to get my money's worth and that means eating everything. I bite into a smoked-salmon sandwich and I can't help closing my eyes – the meeting of the salmon and the lemon butter is delicious.

Taste buds satisfied with a mouthful of food, it's time to get down to business; the all important prove-I-was-here photo.

I self-consciously pull the camera out of my handbag. I'd love to snap a quick selfie, but I'm always left with double chins and a ginormous face that would leave little room for Joseph to take in our surroundings. I'll have to find someone else to take our photo. Perhaps I can ask a passing waiter. I try to catch one of their eyes as they go past, lifting my hand and whispering an excuse me. As usual when I try and get waiting staff's attention, they don't hear my meek, terribly polite, terribly apologetic voice.

'What are you trying to do?' asks Sian, stuffing a second sandwich finger into her mouth in one bite.

'I want to get a photo of us here,' I say feebly. I know we've got the whole of our afternoon tea slot to get our photo, but it's the main reason we're here. It's not only to tick it off the list, but to flaunt it in Joseph's face. I don't think I'm going to be able to fully relax until it's done.

Sian looks at me before looking back at the cake stand as if I've lost all sense of priorities.

'I wanted a nice photo of us to pin on my mood board,' I say, shrugging. 'You know, to spur me on for the rest of the list.'

'Excuse me,' she says leaning over to the couple next to us. 'Would you mind taking a photo of me and my friend?'

I shoot her an I-can't-believe-you-just-did-that look.

The middle-aged woman looks at us and gives us a small smile.

'Of course,' she says, leaning in towards our table, 'but only if you'll take one of my husband and me with our camera after. We've been dying to ask a waiter but didn't dare.'

'No problem,' says Sian, pulling a face at me and reaching over to take my camera.

OK, perhaps she didn't deserve my death stare, after all.

I smooth my hair down and push my shoulders back, before I hold up a tea cup and Sian theatrically puts a third sandwich finger into her mouth. The flash goes off and I get those multi-coloured lights flickering in front of my eyes.

Sian reaches over and takes the couple's camera and, as she gets them to pose, I review our photo and feel relieved that the shot is perfect. Perhaps not quite how I'd have framed it, but for once I don't mind that we're not centred as you can see a lot of the room behind us. There's no doubting that we're some-where fancy.

Photo out of the way, I start to catch up on my sandwich allocation. We barely talk other than to 'um and ooh' through our food. We manage to decline an extra helping of sandwiches from our waiter – as delicious as they are, we're saving room for cake.

I pick up a mini millefeuille and I feel like I've died and gone to heaven.

'Can we do this every week?' I ask.

'I wish we could. It almost makes me want to learn to bake so I can do these myself,' says Sian, examining her mini Bakewell tart intently.

'I know. I watch those people on *Bake Off* and I can't work out how they're not the size of houses. I mean, if I could bake like that I'd be eating cakes for breakfast, lunch and tea.'

'Me too. Perhaps it's good for the waistline that I can only be arsed to bake a cake once in a blue moon.'

We finish the cakes we've got in our hands and peer curiously into the cake stand, trying to work out which to go for next. I select what looks like an orange iced ball, and Sian goes for some type of tiered sponge cake.

'So Giles was asking if you were going to come along on the Snowdon trip.'

'Me?' she says, spraying a few crumbs of cake across the table-cloth. She immediately wipes them into her hand and sprinkles them onto her plate.

'Yeah, it could be fun.'

'Me, walk up a mountain? I don't even have walking boots.'

'Neither do I. We could go shopping for them together.'

I try to appeal to Sian's passion for shoe shopping, but I doubt somehow that visiting outdoor shops is going to be as tempting as scouring our local Kurt Geiger outlet.

She raises an eyebrow at me and I realise I've got to try another approach.

'It'll be fun. We're all staying in a bunkhouse at the bottom of the mountain and apparently there's a log fire, and they're all bringing lots of booze for the evening.'

I omit the part that I'll probably have passed out in bed from exhaustion as soon as we walk through the door.

'When is it?' she asks.

'The weekend of the tenth and eleventh of April.'

I don't mention she'd have to take the Monday off work to travel back. Sian's a local reporter and pretty much a workaholic. It's difficult enough getting her to take time off at the weekend sometimes, and during the week it can be almost impossible. That's why we're here on a Tuesday, as they tend to be slow news days.

'I think I might be covering the comedy festival, but I'll check,' she says.

'Oh, is that that weekend?'

I feel momentarily torn between the hiking and the festival. Sian usually gives me her plus one tickets for events like that. They're pretty much always VIP, meaning we can get up close and personal with the performers. I'm mentally weighing up being wet and muddy, climbing what might as well be Everest for all my mountaineering experience, versus hobnobbing with famous funny men. The scales are tipping in favour of the comedy, and I'm about to say bugger it, but I catch sight of a man who looks like Joseph and I'm reminded why I want to go to Wales in the first place.

'I hope you can come,' I say, mourning my potential loss of the free tickets if she can't.

I dab the corner of my mouth with my napkin, before I go to stand up.

'I'm going to pay a visit to the little girls' room.'

'See you in a minute,' says Sian.

I watch as she takes another cake, and I take a mental snapshot of what's left on the stand. Ever since an incident with a pack of chocolate fingers that went down very quickly when I was out of the room, I pay close attention to what food I'm leaving her with.

I'm trying to look subtly for the toilet, too scared to ask a waiter, when I spot another woman who looks like she knows where she's going. I follow her into the pastel pink toilets and am reminded of a fondant fancy.

With cakes on the brain, I hurry through my visit, not wanting to leave Sian for any longer than necessary. I apply a quick coat of lip gloss and ruffle my hair to encourage a little bit of volume into it.

I take a moment before heading out the door to make sure that I'm not committing any heinous faux pas. Skirt not tucked into knickers – check. Tights pulled up sufficiently so as to not cause Nora Batty wrinkles – check. No toilet paper hanging from anywhere – check.

Confident that I'm good to go, I throw my hair back and walk out. I'm striding purposefully across the salon, noticing that Sian's reaching into the cake stand again, when I catch sight of the man that looks like Joseph. I turn to look at him properly. My eyes must be playing tricks on me, but he really does look like him. In fact, the way he's laughing and tipping his head back is uncanny. A waiter comes up to him and he rests his elbows on the table and folds his hands together. His signature move.

Oh, my God, it's him! I come to an abrupt halt as a wave of panic hits me. Joseph is sitting a few metres away from where I'm standing.

As if sensing me he looks up, but despite having been desperate to see him for weeks, I'm too flustered to talk to him and I hurry back towards my table, crashing into someone as I go.

I realise that it's a waiter – *of course it is*. And not only a waiter, but one carrying a silver tray of used teacups. He stumbles slightly and the cups rattle noisily on the tray. I watch in horror as he lunges like a juggler on a unicycle, trying to keep everything balanced. I close my eyes, bracing myself for the sound of smashing china, but it doesn't come. Instead, the waiter coughs slightly before walking off back towards the kitchen. What a pro.

I feel hot with embarrassment at the scene I almost caused. I look over at Joseph to check if he's seen the commotion and he's looking straight at me. My muscles stiffen, waiting for the look of recognition, but he turns back to the woman he's with and carries on his conversation.

I'm almost too shocked to move, but another waiter coming towards me with two cake stands is a good motivator. I might have avoided causing a scene like a Greek wedding a moment ago, but I'm not lucky enough to do it twice.

How did I not notice him sitting so close to me before? Damn my fear of looking round in case I looked like a tourist. But more to the point, what's he doing here? His Facebook page gave me no indication that he was in the vicinity, not that I checked his page on my phone on the train on the way up or anything ...

As I sit down, Sian places a scone on my plate without asking.

'I got another round ordered whilst you were in the loo – without raisins, especially for you.'

I stare at the scone like my life depends on it, not fully appreciating Sian's kind gesture. I'm not a particularly fussy eater but I hate raisins with a passion. I'm all for grapes, but there's something about eating a fruit that's been left out to shrivel and die that's not right.

'What's wrong with you? You look like you've seen a ghost.'

I'm still not speaking and I'm not even preparing my scone.

'Abi?'

'Joseph's here,' I say in a whisper.

'Joseph? What, your Joseph?' says Sian, leaning into the table conspiratorially.

'Yep,' I say, sighing.

I can't believe he's here. I mean, I know that we're only here because of him, but of all the times for him to come.

'Where?' she says, looking round like a meerkat surveying the desert.

I put my hand up to the side of my face as if to shield me. 'There. Look. Behind you, to the right.'

We're treated to a view of the back of his head, and unfortunately for me, that means we're facing his female companion, who I get to see in all her glory.

She, unlike me, looks like she belongs in the Ritz. Her brown hair is wrapped and pinned neatly on top of her head, with a grown-up fringe that frames her face perfectly. She's dressed in a long-sleeved black dress overlaid with lace. Her ears sparkle from the diamond earrings dropping from her delicate earlobes and there's a matching bracelet dangling off her wrist.

I look down at my electric-blue skater dress that I'd matched with tights and a black cardigan. I feel bright and showy rather than elegant and classy like her. I start to feel foolish for being here at all. Maybe it's not enough to simply be here. Maybe I'm just not that type of woman.

'Did he see you?' says Sian, turning her head round to face me.

'That's the weird thing, I'm sure he looked right at me, but he didn't even flinch. It's not even like he was pretending not to have seen me, more like he didn't.'

'Maybe he didn't recognise you with your new haircut.'

My hand instinctively goes up to my bob and I run my fingers through it.

'Surely I can't look that different?'

'You do – it's completely changed your look.'

My mind's in a maelstrom as I try and work out if I'm going to be able to continue to sit here with Joseph so close to me.

'Do you think I should go and speak to him? Thank him for bringing my box back?'

'Ordinarily I'd say no, but it seems such a shame not to when you're looking so good. I mean, how many times do you get to run into your ex after a break-up when you're dressed to impress?' says Sian, echoing what I'm thinking.

Only he's with a woman. I stare absentmindedly at the cakes in front of me. My appetite has disappeared.

'But look at his new girlfriend – she's stunning and I don't want to make an idiot of myself.'

If he wasn't with whoever she is, then I might have gone up to him, but I couldn't guarantee that it wouldn't reduce me to a weeping mess and I have too much pride to let that happen in front of her.

'She's not all that,' says Sian, turning her nose up.

I'm lost in the thought that I might be too late with this bucket list as the position of Joseph Small's girlfriend might already have been filled, when I notice a shadow fall over the table.

'Abi?' he asks in his distinctive posh voice.

'Hello, Joseph,' I say as I look up and our eyes lock. How my voice is so calm and collected I'll never know. I've managed to make it sound like bumping into him was completely normal, and not something I've fantasised about nearly every hour since he dumped me.

'I can't believe it's really you. Your hair,' he says as if questioning it.

'Ah, yes, I had it cut last week. Fancied a change,' I say, shrugging my shoulders, still trying to be as cool as a cucumber despite the fact I'm shaking like a leaf.

'I didn't recognise you when I first saw you, but I caught another glimpse of you and I thought it was you. Of course, then I had to come over and check. And here you are.'

Is he rambling? He's usually so measured, but I'm getting the impression I've unnerved him.

'Here I am,' I repeat.

'Thanks for dropping off my stuff last week,' I say in a bid to take the attention away from my hair.

'Oh, that was no problem. I was in the area, and I thought I'd pop it in. I did buzz but you didn't answer. I hope you don't mind me leaving it in the lobby.'

'Not at all.'

There's another pause and the conversation grinds to a halt. It all feels horribly formal and stiff. It's so unnatural. We were once so intimate with each other and now we're talking like we're casual acquaintances. I can feel the tears prickling behind my eyes at the thought of what we'd once been.

'So what brings you here, Joseph?' *Apart from your top-secret bucket list.*

'I've always fancied coming, and it's my sister Bianca's birthday so I thought I'd treat her.'

I catch Sian stifling a giggle at the way he pronounces his sister's name – *Bee-arn-ka*. His accent makes the name sound as far from the *EastEnders* character as it could possibly get.

Then I register what he's said: his sister. Not his new girl-friend. I try to fight against the instinct to break out into a huge smile.

'That's nice of you,' I say.

'Yes, I should probably be getting back to her. It was really nice to see you, Abi. You're looking ... well, really well.'

'Thanks,' I say, feeling my cheeks flushing at the compliment.

He holds my gaze for a moment more before he turns and walks back over to his sister.

'Not his new girlfriend after all,' says Sian, 'just his sister Be-arn-kaaaaa.'

I laugh at Sian's impression. I'd forgotten quite how posh he could sound.

'I know,' I say.

Inside I'm secretly air punching in victory. All is not lost yet.

'I bet he's definitely kicking himself for letting you go now,' says Sian.

'Do you think?' I say, my breath catching in my throat.

'Absolutely. Did you see the way he was looking at you? He was practically drooling into my tea cup.'

I smile at the thought. Maybe I'm not crazy for trying to get him back after all. I knew that I hadn't imagined the connection Joseph and I had.

'So, do you think I should follow up with a chatty Facebook message? You know, get the ball rolling again.'

'Wait. Do you still honestly want him back? What about your list and all the things you've planned to do to get over him?' asks Sian.

If only I'd told her my real motivation behind the bucket list.

'I know, but I wasn't expecting to see him.' *So soon.*

'Well,' she says, taking yet another cake, I've lost count of how many she's had. 'You know what I think about you trying to get him back, and I can't stop you, but I do think that you should wait for him to come to you. I mean, he was the one that broke up with you. You shouldn't be the one to make the first move. Just because you saw him doesn't change anything.'

I sigh. She's right. If I message him it makes me look pathetic and desperate, which defeats the whole purpose of me doing the bucket list in the first place.

I see Joseph and his sister push back their chairs and stand up. As Bianca turns to walk out the door I see the striking family resemblance and wonder how I didn't notice it before. Joseph follows behind her and glances over his shoulder in my direction as he goes. He gives me a small smile before he disappears out of the room.

My stomach feels like fireworks are exploding inside it.

'Now that he's gone, are we going to get back to the business of finishing the cakes?' asks Sian.

'Oh, yes,' I say, suddenly feeling ravenous. 'Let's order some more.'

After all, I'm going to be burning plenty of calories with all the cycling, running and hiking on the list. Seeing Joseph has made me more focused and reminded me what the end prize is.

I'm looking forward to my cycling lesson on Sunday. I can't wait to get riding and pedal my way right back into Joseph's heart.

I might only have one challenge under my belt, but nothing, not even my fear, is going to stand in the way of me doing the other nine. Seeing him has made me realise how important it is to get him back, and I'm more convinced than ever that this list is the key to doing that.

Chapter Eight

Five weeks, six days until D-Day, aka the abseil. One item ticked off my list, another nine to go ...

'This isn't so bad,' I say, turning my head to shout over my shoulder. I don't know why I didn't trust Ben before when he said I should start pedalling quicker.

I see his eyes widen as he watches me with horror.

'Look out!' he shouts, raising his arm.

I snap my head back and realise that I'm heading straight for a partition hedge.

'Oh, crap!'

I turn at the last minute and my tyres bump the curb. I brake hard and put a foot down, my heart racing nineteen to the dozen, but somehow I manage to keep the bike upright.

'Who put that there? Stupid hedge,' I say, kicking it.

Trust me to find one of the only obstacles in this empty car park.

I've been riding my new bike for the best part of an hour and it's safe to say that I'm not a natural. Ben's brought me to a deserted office car park on the outskirts of the city, and I've been riding so slowly that he's been able to keep up by walking behind me. But of course, just when he gets me to go faster and I think I've cracked it, I go and practically throw myself into a bush.

'You were doing really well,' he says, bending down to examine my wheel, presumably to make sure that I haven't done any lasting damage. 'You just need to keep looking forward. Think of it as if you were driving a car. You wouldn't turn round to talk to me then, would you?'

'Wouldn't I? It's a good job you drove.'

He smiles and exposes his dimple. It's doing less hiding today as the stubble's been trimmed since our last encounter. 'Do you want to keep on going for a bit longer, or take a break? I brought some tea.'

'Tea?' I say in disbelief, climbing off my bike. It's like he's said the magic word.

He takes his backpack off and digs around inside, before pulling out a flask and two tin mugs. He sits down on the curb that I bumped into and begins to pour me a cup.

'Hope you don't mind it white, and I didn't bring any sugar,' he says a little apologetically as I sit down beside him and take the cup.

'It's perfect. Thank you. It's exactly what I need.'

I curl my hands around the metal mug, liking the fact that it's instantly warm.

'I can't believe you came so prepared.' I take a sip and sigh in satisfaction like they do in tea adverts.

'It isn't a proper bike ride without tea and oh ...' Ben digs into his bag again and pulls out two Mini Rolls. 'Cake.'

I look dubiously at the Mini Rolls. After eating what felt like my body weight in cakes at the Ritz on Tuesday, my diet to shift my post-break-up pounds hasn't got off to a very good start. But one little Mini Roll isn't going to hurt, is it? And besides, I've been cycling for at least an hour. Surely that's got to have burnt some calories, despite my tortoise-like speed.

I pop my mug down on the floor and take the cake from Ben.

'Doesn't this go against the whole healthy bike-riding stuff? Isn't your body supposed to be a temple?' I say, unwrapping my cake.

'Ha, mine's not. You have to let yourself have a treat on a ride – it's the highlight. I actually bought some chocolates from the chocolatiers near the shop, but unfortunately, I, um, ate them last night.'

'I've always wanted to go in there but never trusted myself.'

'Probably wise. I have an addiction to the marshmallow and honeycomb chocolates. They're to die for.'

'Now you're making me want them.'

'Sorry, but Mini Rolls are the next best thing, honestly.'

He puts the cake in his mouth in one go. He gets another one out of his bag and offers it to me. I shake my head, before he opens his and eats it, again in almost one bite. I look at his skinny frame and think that maybe he's onto something with all this cycling. Maybe if I nailed this riding thing I'd be able to eat all the cake in the world ...

'So is the riding getting any easier?'

'A little bit, but I thought it might come back a little quicker. I still feel like I could be lapped by a toddler.'

'Maybe it would help if you started riding to work to build up your confidence.'

'Um.' I'm not convinced. Although it wouldn't take that long there are junctions that scare me as a pedestrian and I only cross with the aid of a little green man, let alone launching myself into the traffic on a rickety metal frame that I can barely control.

'You do seem to be getting better. You got up to a decent speed in the end. I mean, it would still take you quite a while to get round the Isle of Wight like this, but it was definitely quicker than walking pace. I think at this rate you'll be ready to do it by the end of the year.'

My heart sinks. That's not quite in keeping with the time-frame that I have to win Joseph back.

'I was thinking more next month.'

'Well, that's ... um ... ambitious. You'll have to do a lot more practising between now and then.'

I nod eagerly, pleased that he didn't laugh.

'I was a bit worried earlier that I might have to hike round the island with you as you ride,' he says, smiling.

'Watch, it,' I say, laughing, picturing him walking in front of me with a big flag like they used to do in front of trains in the olden days.

I'm just relieved that he offered to come with me on the big challenge. It's relaxed me no end to know that I'm going to be in expert company if it all goes wrong. 'It's not my fault that I'm the world's crappiest cyclist.'

'Um, actually it is. You know how to ride a bike, and you're not woefully unfit, so really there's no reason why you can't do it.'

'Except the fear that I'm going to go flying over the handlebars.'

'Oh, you're one of those worst-case-scenario people,' he says, raising his eyebrows and nodding his head.

'No, I'm not. I'm quite an optimist. Well, I am until it's a life-and-death situation. Look at the hedge incident. If you hadn't been behind me, then I wouldn't have had any warning and would have gone head first into it.'

'If I hadn't been behind you, you wouldn't have been turning round to talk to me and you'd have been looking where you were going. And is that what you really think – that this is a life-and-death situation? Here in a car park with no cars and barely any obstacles?'

I can see the dimple making an appearance.

'I know I sound ridiculous,' I say, sipping my tea.

'I don't get what you're so scared of. You've got the fundamentals down, but something's holding you back.'

'Fear,' I say more to my drink than Ben.

'Of what?'

'Of falling. Of going so fast that I can't stop.'

'It's funny, but that's usually what gives me a buzz. When I'm mountain biking down big slopes, it's that fear that gives me the rush. You know that heady adrenaline that makes you feel a bit sick and like you want to wee, but at the same time you want to do it again as soon as you stop. Do you know?'

I shake my head. I don't know.

'To be honest, I usually stop anything before I get to that stage.'

'Then, Abi, you're missing out. Perhaps after we do the Isle of Wight, you'll come mountain biking with me and Tammy.'

I splutter a laugh that causes my hand to judder, splashing tea down my leg.

I don't know what's more unlikely, me voluntarily mountain biking or getting on a bike in front of Tammy, the pro-cycler. It's one thing to make a fool of myself in front of someone like Ben, who clearly doesn't have a judgemental bone in his body – but Tammy's a different kettle of fish all together.

'Me, mountain biking? I think I'd rather do the abseil down the Spinnaker than voluntarily biking off-road and down a hill.'

'Giles told me last week that you'd all decided to do it as a work thing.'

I think back to the team meeting with Rick and Linz, and I still don't know how I'm going to get out of it.

A cool breeze blows over us, and Ben pulls down the sleeves of his hoodie.

'Yeah, he suggested it.' A chill runs over my body, and it's got nothing to do with the wind.

He looks at me for a minute and opens his mouth to say something, but seems to change his mind.

'What?' I say.

He wrinkles his brow as if something's weighing heavily on his mind.

'It's just I don't get you. If it terrifies you so much, why did you put it on your list? Bucket lists are supposed to be about doing things you've always dreamt about, not torturing yourself.'

I wish someone had told that to Joseph.

'I thought I'd challenge myself,' I say weakly. I've rehearsed these stock answers in case Sian interrogates me.

'I'm sure there are plenty of ways that you could have challenged yourself which wouldn't make you look like you're about to have a heart attack whenever a task is mentioned. I mean, it's like this riding a bike round the Isle of Wight – it doesn't seem like the type of thing you'd naturally want to do.'

I shrug my shoulders and concentrate on my tea.

'Are you sure you've given this list proper thought?'

I hug my near-empty cup of tea into my chest. I seem to have thought of little else since I found Joseph's piece of paper.

'Uh-huh,' I say, not even convincing myself.

'I mean, why don't you change it? It's your list. It's not going to matter if you stick to things you'll enjoy.'

'I'm trying to get over a break-up and I have to do this list.'

'No you don't,' says Ben, scratching his head. 'There are plenty of other ways to mend a broken heart, and doing some list full of stuff that you don't want to do doesn't have to be one of them.'

'But how else will I get Joseph back?'

I've blurted it out before I realise what I've said.

'Get Joseph back?' repeats Ben.

I scrunch my eyes up, too embarrassed to look at him.

'You're trying to get your ex back by doing tasks that scare you?'

I finally open my eyes and see that Ben's turned his head and is looking straight at me, studying my face. I turn to meet his gaze and I know that I'm hiding nothing in my eyes.

'It's pathetic, I know,' I say, sighing.

People seem to accept the bucket list when they think it's to get over someone. I knew it would be different if anyone found out it was a plan to get someone back.

'Abi, is it his list that you're doing?'

I nod my head slowly and shut my eyes.

Ben whistles through his teeth. 'And suddenly it all makes sense. I couldn't understand why you'd be putting yourself through all these things that terrified you. Is there anything on the list that you actually want to do?'

'Tea at the Ritz, going to Paris and the wine tasting sound all right. And I'm looking forward to the Spanish lessons that I'm starting next week.'

Even if listening to Shakira's Spanish songs has done nothing to improve my language skills.

'But let me guess, the four peaks hiking, the cycling and the abseiling wouldn't have made your own list?'

'Or the windsurfing,' I say, my whole body shivering at the thought of the sea.

I'm expecting a lecture. It's what Sian would do. First she'd be mad at me for lying to her and passing the list off as my own. Then she'd be pissed off that I was trying to change myself for a man.

I tense my muscles, waiting for a full-on assault about my stupidity, but instead Ben laughs.

'What?' It's not funny. Sad, pathetic, maybe, but not laugh-out-loud funny.

He smiles at me, and shakes his head a little. 'Nothing. It's just that's almost the most ridiculous thing I've ever heard someone do to try to win someone back.'

I look at him incredulously. It's not the worst thing I could have done. I could have 'accidentally' turned up at all the same places as him. Or tried to date one of his friends to make him jealous. Before I found the list I came up with 101 crazy schemes to win him back, and this sounded like the most sane.

'I'm sorry, Abi. But you've got to admit it's a little bit extreme. What are you expecting him to do when he finds out?'

'When he finds out what? That I've done some things on his list?'

'That you've been acting out his *exact* list. Don't you think it'll freak him out?'

I shrug again. 'I'm hoping he never finds out that I found it in the first place. And it's not his exact list, I've modified it a bit. I'm only running a 10k rather than a half marathon.'

'Right,' says Ben. I can see the dimple, which I've learnt means that he's laughing on the inside.

'Oh, come on. Men never notice what's going on under their noses. Besides, if he did find out what I'm doing, I'm sure he'd find it endearing. Wouldn't you be flattered if someone went to all that trouble doing death-defying stunts that scared the bejesus out of them just to get you back?'

The dimple disappears and Ben looks serious for a moment.

'I mean, what if you and Tammy broke up and she did something like this for you. Surely it would show you how much she cared?'

'I can't imagine she'd even notice we weren't together,' mutters Ben under his breath. 'Besides, what are you expecting to happen? That he'll be so impressed with your list that you get back together and live happily ever after?'

'That's pretty much the gist of it.'

'There are no such things as happy endings in real life, Abi. You might as well save yourself the time and effort.' He shakes his head.

'I know it sounds ridiculous,' I say, sighing. 'It's just I couldn't think of another way to get him back. I'm not crazy, I just really love him. You don't have to keep helping me if you don't want to. I'll understand if you change your mind about coming to the Isle of Wight, but you can't talk me out of it. I'm doing this list.'

'I'm not going to talk you out of it, even though I think you'd be better off doing a list for yourself. In my experience sometimes if you love someone it's better to let them go, as you're only going to get hurt. The more you love someone, the more your heart breaks when it ends.'

Boy, talk about cynical.

'Are you sure your ex is worth all the effort?'

I think of Joseph, a fresh memory of him at the Ritz, looking all groomed in his neatly-pressed shirt and Ralph Lauren jumper draped over his shoulders as he left.

'Absolutely,' I say without hesitation.

'Well, then, who am I to stand in your way?'

'You won't tell Giles, will you?'

He looks at me and I see him frown.

'Not if you don't want me to. Although, I think you should tell him and your friend Sian too. I don't think they'd like being lied to. Besides, they'll probably understand better than you think.'

'Oh, no,' I say, shaking my head defiantly. 'Sian definitely won't get it. She'd be furious. She's all about girl power and she'll think I'm committing a crime against feminism. No, we've got to keep this our little secret, if that's OK?'

He continues to look at me open-mouthed.

'I know it's silly,' I say.

'It's not silly. You're getting over a heartbreak. Believe me, I know all about it.'

'You do?'

I look at Ben and realise that I've told him one of the biggest secrets I've ever kept, and yet I know nothing about him. I don't have any idea of his relationship history or how long he's been with Tammy.

'I do.'

I raise my eyebrow to indicate that I want him to elaborate.

'After I broke up with my first proper girlfriend, I tried quite hard to get her back.'

'What did you do?'

'Well, I might have flown around the world to track her down on her gap year in Thailand, Vietnam, then Australia.'

'Oh, my God. You were a stalker.'

'Well, I wasn't a stalker as such. I just happened to be doing a similar route to her around South East Asia and Australia. I popped up every couple of months. I did do my own travelling in between.'

'And what happened? Did you get her back?'

'Not exactly. I bumped into her in Thailand, and she was travelling with this guy. Then by the time I saw her in Vietnam, she was with another guy and then when I saw her again in Oz and was about to declare my undying love, she was with someone else. That was when I realised that I was on the other side of the world chasing someone who didn't want me. If she didn't fall at my feet when I saw her thousands of miles away in Thailand, then she never would.'

'Wow. So you're almost as much of a nutter as me.'

No wonder Ben didn't believe in happy endings.

'Well, I did say your list was almost the craziest thing I'd ever heard of. But, in my defence, I was only eighteen. You should know better by now. You're over thirty, right?'

'Oi. Watch it,' I say digging him in the ribs with my elbow. 'I'm only just.'

I know that Ben's made a joke, but there's still a sadness in his eyes as if he's still nursing a broken heart. He smiles weakly as he gets to his feet.

'Come on, let's get you back on this bike, otherwise you'll be nearing forty by the time you complete the Isle of Wight challenge.'

I stand up and reluctantly put the helmet back on my head.

'Thanks, Ben,' I say, picking up my bike. 'For doing this, even though you now know I'm a complete loser.'

'That's all right. I mean, I already knew you were a bit of a loser. What woman your age can't ride a bike?'

With that, Ben swings his leg over his own bike that he's been pushing around all morning and cycles off.

I can feel my cheeks colouring and I desperately want to shout at him and give him another dig in the ribs. There's only one thing for it.

'I'm going to get you, Ben,' I shout as I mount my bike and pedal as fast as my fear will let me.

As I pedal after him, I realise that I feel a sense of relief. I might have been embarrassed initially sharing my secret, but somehow confiding in Ben has made my shoulders feel lighter. There's something about him that makes me feel comfortable talking about something so personal, even though he's practically a stranger.

And he didn't think it was *that* terrible an idea, and he didn't talk me out of it. And look, I'm actually cycling properly. All I need is for Ben to make me angry and I'll get round the Isle of Wight no problem.

The wheels are really flying round now and my legs are almost burning with how quickly I'm pedalling. Maybe I haven't forgotten how to ride a bike after all.

For a split second I believe that I can do this and, unlike Ben's story of his lost love, my crazy plan is going to work.

Chapter Nine

Five weeks and two days left to do this list, but I feel like I need five years at this rate...

'What's wrong with you today? You look like you've been slapped round the face by a wet trout,' says Giles as we get our handlebars tangled on the pavement again. It seems pushing a bike is just as difficult as riding it.

I feel a bit bad as I've dragged him north of where we work to go to a specialist running shop and spent the whole time being grumpy.

It's all the list's fault. It's not going well.

I sigh heavily again. I don't want to talk about it, but I feel I owe him an explanation.

'My Spanish lesson last night was abysmal. Then, if it wasn't bad enough having to spend the morning at the printer with Linz shadowing me, I tried to buy Glastonbury tickets during the spring re-release only to find that I was meant to have registered in October. *October*!' I say incredulously.

I mean what a bloody stupid system. You have to commit to wanting to go to a festival almost a full year in advance.

Giles nods his head. 'If it makes you feel any better, the chances of getting tickets anyway were pretty slim, even if you had registered. And there's always next year.'

I almost laugh out loud. Of course there would be next year if this was any normal person's bucket list, but it's not. I'm in a race against time to get Joseph back.

'I even asked my sister if she or any of her friends had any spare tickets, and she laughed in my face. Apparently you have to apply using a photo and it's mega strict.'

'What about going to another festival? Glastonbury's great, but it's so big. You spend most of your time walking the site rather than seeing anything. Why don't you try one of the other ones – maybe V Festival? They usually have plenty of commercial artists too, which might be more to your taste.'

'More to my taste?' I say, my nostrils flaring.

Giles clocks my look and widens his eyes in panic. 'No, I didn't mean it like that. It's just, I know your playlist at work.'

'What's wrong with my playlist?'

'Nothing. If you like Taylor Swift and Beyoncé.'

'Hey, I've got some Imagine Dragons on there and maybe a Foo Fighters track,' I say, trying to raise my music cred. But in truth, he's right – my playlist is cheesier than a French fromagerie. Damn the fact that everyone at work can access each other's iTunes.

I know I'm overreacting. Giles has only insinuated that I'm more of a *Now That's What I Call Music* girl than an *NME* one, but it's as if he's siding with Joseph. It's like saying that

I'm deluded in thinking I could be cool enough to go to Glastonbury.

'OK, well, why not try a different festival then? A less commercial one. There are loads of really cool ones that are smaller and less overrated. What about the Big Chill or Bestival?'

I scrunch up my face as I try to imagine what Joseph would do. Would he be impressed with any festival or would it have to be Glastonbury? I think of him trotting around a muddy field, and I mentally picture him in his Hunter wellies and wax jacket, like the Monarch of the Glen. I try and put him into cool festival clothes but fail miserably. In fact, I can't see Joseph there at all. He's no more a camper than I am. When I saw him packing for work trips away he used to interleave tissue paper between his clothes to stop them from creasing.

Maybe it wouldn't matter what festival I went to. Maybe I'm getting too bogged down in the details.

'At least Bestival is close,' I say, thinking of another trip to the Isle of Wight.

'There you go. And Laura and I would be up for going if you wanted to get a group of people together. We went about five years ago and it was a right laugh. Everyone dresses in fancy dress for this big competition.'

He had me until fancy dress.

'I'll look into it,' I say despondently.

'*Digame sobre tu español clase.*'

'Excuse me?' I say, a sweat breaking out on my forehead as I remember how I felt last night in my Spanish class. Within thirty seconds after we finished saying *hola*, the only Spanish word I know, I was lost.

'I said, tell me about your Spanish lesson.'

'Right. It was a fricking disaster. It's supposed to be a beginner's class but there were people there that seemed to be practically fluent. And they were all doing this perfect *Three Amigos* type accent. I felt like a right plonker. I couldn't even get "my name is Abi" right.'

'What were you saying? That your name was Fred?'

I shoot Giles a death stare. Today is not the day to have a joke at my expense. I am suffering from major sense of humour failure.

'Give it a go.'

I'm really not in the mood.

'Come on,' he says, with bounding enthusiasm.

'*Me la-mo* Abi.'

'*Me llamo* – it's pronounced ya-mo,' says Giles.

'See,' I say, shaking my head. 'I've had it written down and I've been practising it all day at work and I still get it wrong.'

'It's just a pronunciation thing. Don't be so hard on yourself. At least you added the reflexive bit – that's impressive.'

'The what bit? Oh, God, don't confuse me any more than I already am.'

The mere mention of anything that sounds like grammar is sending shivers down my spine and making me think back to French at school – the GCSE that blemishes my CV with a D.

All I wanted to be able to do was order meatballs, not reawaken my teenage fears.

'Sorry. Look, if you need a hand I did Spanish at school. *Podríamos practicar hablar español en el trabajo.*'

Now I'm really starting to hate him.

He holds up his hands to fight off the inevitable death stare that he knows is coming his way.

'I just said we could practise at work, but you know, once you've had a few more lessons and you're ready for it.'

'I'm never going to be ready for it. But thanks.'

God, today has been a disaster. I should have taken it as an omen and gone straight home rather than going to the trainer shop. My pockets are now ninety pounds lighter and the woman gave me a copy of an introductory training plan. Who knew there'd be so much training to do for a 10k? I might as well be doing the half marathon.

The windsurfing course this weekend is creeping ever closer and any enthusiasm I had for it is waning rapidly. With every-thing else going wrong at the moment I dread to think what's going to happen when I'm out at sea.

'At least your bike-riding plans are going well,' he says waving his hand at my bike. 'Ben says you're making progress.'

'Ben's being kind,' I say, thinking back to my snail-paced riding session.

'Well, with him helping you with that one, at least you'll have one thing ticked off your list.'

I bloody hope so, but I'm still sulky. Two out of ten tasks completed is hardly going to get Joseph running back to me with open arms.

We're about to cross a main road when I spot a familiar car.

I put my arm out in front of Giles to stop him from walking and I back up a few steps.

'Look.'

I stop as I watch our boss Rick's BMW park across the road a little further down from us. I wonder what he's doing here. But it's not where we are that's so shocking: it's who's in his passenger seat that has stopped me in my tracks. I'd recognise that swinging ponytail anywhere.

The door opens, and out climbs Linz.

I watch in disbelief as she bounds round to Rick's door and the two of them walk into a nearby pub together.

'Did you see that?' I say, gasping.

My whole body prickles with goosebumps. This can't mean good things.

'Yeah, so they're grabbing a drink after work. We do it all the time. Well, not all the time, but it's not unheard of.'

'Um, yeah we do, but we're allowed to. We're underlings that have to get together to bitch about work, and besides we don't often go alone – it's usually an open invitation to the office. I mean, have you ever gone to a pub with Rick alone?'

'Only when we were out visiting a client around lunchtime.'

'Exactly,' I say, as if building my case.

'Maybe they're meeting some other people in there?'

'I don't think so. If there were others from work going we would have heard, wouldn't we? And why would they come all the way up here if it wasn't to be discreet. Oh, God, what if they're dating?'

What's worse than merely working with Linz? Working with Linz when she's the boss's girlfriend, that's what.

'Chill out, so what if they are? It wouldn't change anything,' says Giles as we cross the road, Rick and Linz now safely out of sight.

I roll my eyes. 'It would change everything.'

Boys really are clueless. Despite the fact that the age gap is creepy enough in itself, it would be an absolute disaster work wise.

'Take this morning when we went to the printer. She was flirting with Jim the print guy so much that he gave her a key ring. A key ring! I've been going there for years and never even got so much as a pen, let alone a key ring.'

Giles raises an eyebrow at me. OK, so I know I'm overreacting, but I feel at the moment like wherever I turn at work Linz is there, and she's doing a better job than me. Whether it's smooth-talking clients or having stellar design ideas. It's like she's the new improved me, and now with her potentially dating Rick, she's not just getting her feet under the table, she's been given the keys to the whole bloody dining room.

'Let's go see what they're up to,' I say, pacing off towards the pub.

Giles grabs me by my coat hood.

I pull another cross face to add to my ever-growing library of disdain. This guy is really pissing me off.

'Easy there, tiger. If we're going to spy, we at least need to be inconspicuous.'

My frown turns upside down and I watch as Giles chains up his bike to a nearby lamp post and I follow suit.

'Right, then,' he says, after securing the bikes. 'Let's go, Bond.'

We approach the pub and do what any good spy would do – a couple of walk-bys with casual glances. This gets us nowhere, though, as the windows are opaque and covered with old-fashioned beer adverts. Instead, we have to peak through the tiny gap at the edge of the windows.

'There they are,' I whisper, for reasons unknown. It's not like they'd hear us from here. 'At the bar.'

I watch as they take their drinks to a corner table.

'See, it's a date. She's drinking wine. If it were work-related she'd be drinking a Coke or a J2O. And they're sitting in the corner. Oh, God.'

I've practically married them off in my mind.

'Calm down, Abi. If it was a date I'm sure they'd be going somewhere a little bit more fancy than the Thistle at five thirty in the evening. And look, Linz has got a pen and paper out. Maybe it is work after all.'

I stare at them and wish I was better at lip reading.

'Do you think we should go in? Say that we saw them when we were passing,' I ask, desperate to be a fly on the wall.

'Oh, yes, we saw them all the way in the corner through the windows that are almost impossible to see through.'

'Well, we could pretend that we were coming here for a drink anyway and just casually bumped into them. We could have been thirsty on the way back from the running shop.'

'I probably shouldn't. I've got to get back. Laura and I do salsa on a Thursday night.'

He's kept that quiet. I can't quite imagine him and his lanky frame doing salsa.

'I'm sure whatever is going on it's all completely innocent. You've never pulled out a pen and paper on a date with someone, have you?'

'No,' I say, racking my brains. I've done some pretty strange things on dates – pretended I was someone else, been sick on my date's shoes, had an egg thrown at me, but never taken notes.

'Well, there you go. Why don't you just ask Linz tomorrow what she did last night.'

'Oh, like that won't be suspicious. I barely speak to her – surely she'd smell a rat.'

'Listen, Abi, I know you don't like her, but it looks innocent to me.'

I squint through the window and watch as Linz pulls her ponytail over her shoulder and runs her hands through it. I recognise those moves. She's flirting. OK, so they're not my flirting moves – mine are more clumsy and involve some drooling – but they're girlie-girl moves.

Giles doesn't get it.

I turn back to him and bat my eyelashes, trying to summon a bit of what Linz has in order to convince him that we need to go in.

He sighs loudly. 'One drink. Then I'm leaving,' he says, pulling the door open before I know what's happening.

I try and act as cool as I can, but Giles has forged ahead to the bar and I barely have time to collect my thoughts. He balances an arm on the bar, with his back to Linz and Rick. I know he's trying to look casual, but with his height he sticks out like a sore thumb. I go and stand next to him, facing straight ahead, not wanting to make eye contact with the love birds. If we're going to bump into them, they'll need to notice us, not the other way round.

We order our drinks, and I try to come up with a plan.

'Where are we going to sit?' I say, my mouth barely moving and my gaze unfaltering.

'I don't know. What about down there,' says Giles, pointing to the other end of the rectangular pub.

I look down at the little table near the toilets and shake my head. 'We'll never hear anything from over there.'

This is why Giles shouldn't have been so hasty coming inside. We should have come up with a plan beforehand – worked out where we were going to sit or stand, planned a cover story. Now we're here and more clueless than Alicia Silverstone.

I try and take deep calming breaths and my eyelids flicker, matching the speed of my mind as it desperately tries to formulate a plan.

As the barman places our pints in front of us, I feel a hand pat me on the back. I turn and see Rick.

'Hey, guys,' says our boss.

Part of me melts with relief and the other part is trying to stop myself from weeing in fear. I guess this is ultimately what we wanted to happen, but I feel like we've been caught red-handed.

'Hi, Rick,' I say in an exaggerated squeal. 'What are you doing here?'

I would try to look cool and sip my pint, but my hands are far too shaky.

'I'm just here with Linz, talking her through the history of the company. That girl's a real keen one,' he says, smiling.

That girl's a real clever one, I think to myself. Rick has an ego the size of Australia – incidentally the place from where he hails – and he loves nothing more than having it massaged.

'Come and join us,' he says, gesturing over to his table.

'OK, thanks,' says Giles, without so much as a pause. He could have at least pretended that this wasn't part of the grand plan.

Giles turns round and for a minute I think he's blown it as he expertly navigates his way to Rick and Linz's table.

Linz looks up at us and gives us what I can see is a fake smile.

'Giles, Abi, how great to see you.'

'Linz.'

'This is nice, isn't it? Getting together outside the office,' says Rick.

'Isn't it?' says Giles, looking between Linz and Rick in an incredibly unsubtle way. I'm surprised he's not raising his eyebrow and getting out a magnifying glass to examine them more carefully.

'It's a good opportunity to talk about T-shirts for the abseil,' says Linz, looking directly at me. It's like she's sniffed out my secret and is trying to call my bluff. 'I thought we should all have matching ones with some sort of slogan.'

'I love that idea,' says Rick, his eyes gleaming. 'I'll have to think up a strap line.'

'And then I'll design them,' says Linz hurriedly. As if I would want that pleasure when I'm trying to do my utmost to forget about the whole thing. 'I'm sure Jim at the print shop would give us a good deal. He seemed very keen this morning to have a closer working relationship.

'He's going to send me over a new sample of this material called Ultra Board that they now print on. It's a lightweight cardboard rigid enough for display panels but fully recyclable. I think it would fit perfectly with your vision for offering a green marketing package.'

I look at her, stunned. What green marketing package? Since when is Rick discussing strategy with her? She's only been with the company five minutes. And, more importantly, why isn't Jim sending me that sample? I'm the senior designer.

'I don't remember him showing us that,' I say, thinking that I must have been doing some serious daydreaming.

'Oh, he didn't. We just got chatting when I phoned him to thank him for taking the time to show us round.'

I shift uncomfortably in my seat. Of course she phoned him. I'm beginning to understand how she operates.

'Brilliant, Linz. Sounds just like what I was after. I can't wait to see it.'

'So how many people are doing the abseil?' asks Giles. He throws me a look and I know he's deliberately changing the subject. He's clearly uncomfortable with the Linz appreciation society too.

'There's now eight of us doing it. Us four, then Fran, Greg, Isla from accounts and Pat,' replies Rick.

I can't believe anyone else volunteered to do it. Greg and Isla are quite adventurous, as is Pat the office manager, who's in her sixties and is totally putting me to shame, but it does surprise me that Fran's volunteered. It doesn't seem like her type of thing at all, especially after she wriggled out of the trampoline because of her fake pregnancy. I wonder if she'll come up with anything equally ridiculous to get out of this.

'It's going to look fantastic at our Spinnaker pitch. Abi, I can't thank you enough for inspiring it,' says Rick.

I forget about my shaky hands and lunge for my pint of cider and down it, my brow breaking out in a cold sweat at the thought of the abseil.

'I never pictured you as an adrenaline junkie,' he continues.

'Oh, Abi's turning over a new leaf. She's learning how to wind-surf at the weekend.'

I shoot Giles a look. That's it. I've got to stop telling him about the list.

'You are? Well, I've got a couple of boards if you want to go out for a blast on the water after?'

I'd rather poke my eyes out with skewers.

'I love windsurfing,' says Linz, practically purring. 'I did it a couple of times in France. Where do you go round here?'

'Usually Hayling or the Witterings.'

'Wow. I bet it's great sailing out to sea. I've only ever been on a lake before.'

I bite my lip. I think that she believes she lives on the West Coast of the US, rather than on the South Coast of England, which is bombarded with a fierce sea breeze strong enough to knock your socks off nearly all year round.

'Why don't you do the course with Abi?' says Rick. 'And then you could always come out with me on one of my boards.'

'That's a fab idea,' says Linz, grinning.

'It's such short notice. I think they'll probably be full already.'

It's bad enough that I'm having to put up with her five days a week at work, let alone seeing her on a weekend. Especially when I'm doing something as important as one of the tasks off my list.

'I could phone them to check. Can you text me the number of the centre?'

'Of course,' I say, thinking that I'll give her a fake number.

'It might be too late for you to hire a wetsuit and things,' I say, lying.

'Oh,' says Linz. Her face falls.

'Don't worry about that. I've got loads of my ex-wife's wetsuits kicking about the house. I'm sure one would fit. She was petite like you.'

I can't be sure but it sounds like Rick is flirting. He's old enough to be her dad – well, if he had been an extremely sexually active eleven-year-old, but still, it's physiologically possible and therefore gross.

'Ah, thanks, Rick, that would be fantastic,' she says, batting her eyelashes. 'I can't wait. It'll be the start of my nautical adventures living here by the sea.'

'Look at us all, bonding as a team,' says Rick.

I grit my teeth and try to smile.

'Abi, I love the fact that you're making Linz feel so welcome by taking her windsurfing with you. It's so hard when you move to a new city and don't know anyone. I remember when I first came over to England. It wasn't easy not knowing anyone down here. Especially when I didn't move to London with the rest of the Antipodeans.'

Now I feel like a bitch. Rick's right. Maybe Linz isn't being intentionally annoying. Maybe she's just new to Portsmouth and lonely.

I forget sometimes that I have it relatively easy, having stayed here after university. It was surprising the number of us that hung around the area, so I know quite a lot of people. But Linz is brand new.

I dig out my phone and find the number for the outdoor centre and read it off to Linz.

'Thanks. Fingers crossed they have some space,' she says, smiling and holding up her fingers.

'Fingers crossed,' I mutter into my pint.

Perhaps there's no great secret romance after all. I should probably just feel sorry for her, rather than letting my imagination run away with itself.

After all, I've got enough to worry about doing my bucket list, without worrying about Linz too.

Chapter Ten

Five weeks until the abseil – that's if I don't get swept out to sea during my windsurfing challenge ... or is that wishful thinking?

'Morning, morning!' calls Linz as she strides across the entrance hall of the outdoor centre.

She's still unnaturally happy despite the fact we're up earlier than should be legal on a Saturday morning. Instead of looking knackered from the week at work and too many vinos on a Friday night like me, she looks all bright-eyed and bushy-tailed. What it must be to still have that young skin which doesn't show the daily wear and tear so badly.

I wave at her. It's about as enthusiastic as I can get at this time in the morning, especially when I'm preoccupied with the fact that any minute now we're going to be plunged into icy water.

I've lived in Portsmouth for over ten years and I can count the number of times I've been in the sea on one hand. It's always freezing, even if it's a blistering hot day at the end of summer. Going into the choppy sea in March when it's so cold that I had to put on a winter coat this morning is not something I'm relishing.

'All right, guys,' says a man who's surely still a teenager, if not in body then in mind. He's got bright blond shoulder-length surfer hair and he's wearing shorts and flip-flops. His nod to the fact that it's nippy out is a hoodie … because that's going to keep his toes warm.

The motley crew of aspiring windsurfers assemble in front of him. All four of us, of whom I'm the oldest and most out of shape.

'All up for getting blown away?' He flashes his big grin at us and his eyes settle for longer than necessary on Linz, who giggles appreciatively.

Everyone replies enthusiastically, apart from me, and we're led through into a little classroom which has rows of those desks with flippy-down tables that you can never balance paper on properly, and a whiteboard at the front.

'Now, I know you're all eager to get wet,' he says, winking at Linz. 'But we've got to understand the basics first. I'm going to go through how you essentially sail a windsurf and some of the key concepts like jibing and tacking that I'll be teaching you later on. So are we ready to learn?' he says, dishing out some little books.

'Yes,' I say eagerly. I notice that everyone else is sighing, but I'm relieved to get a few more moments snuggled up in my hoodie and trackie bottoms. In fact, if only the whole course was desk-based. That would be ideal.

Unfortunately for me, the whole course is not desk-based. What I am hoping will be a long and lengthy windsurfing 101 is in reality a twenty-minute lecture with stick men drawn on the board. By the end, I know as little as I did before the lesson and I still think that tacking is something to do with horses.

'Let's get you all kitted out then,' he says, eyeing us up and handing out wetsuits. 'Abi, I think you might get away with a medium, but I'll give you a large too to be on the safe side.'

'Thanks,' I say, my cheeks colouring. There was me hoping I'd lost some post-break-up pounds with my cycling to work, but clearly not.

'Here you go, Linz – you'll be a small,' he says, handing a wetsuit to her.

She flashes him a big smile before heading into the female changing room. I sigh and follow her.

I hate wetsuits with a passion, but the only thing worse than having to put on a wetsuit is going into the freezing cold sea without one.

I catch a glimpse of Linz in her itsy-bitsy teenie-weenie blue almost polka-dot bikini and I sigh again. I look down at my own black Speedo swimming costume, chosen to attract the minimum amount of attention, and I can't help but notice the thick belly protruding from it.

Where did my toned stomach go? OK, so I might not have had a super-toned stomach for a number of years, but before I got together with Joseph I'd been able to look over my stomach line and see the waist band of my low-rise jeans. Now there's a roll of fat in the way. All those contented pub lunches and meals out plus the post-break-up Chinese did me no favours.

I look between the medium and the large suit and back down at my thighs. I guess it can't hurt to try the smaller one first. I do want it to be tight to help keep warm.

I step into the wetsuit and I immediately cringe that it's ever so slightly damp. I daren't think about the fact that means someone else was recently wearing it. I pull it up over my thighs and start to jump it up. My boobs go flying as I try and wriggle to get myself in.

I'm starting to think I should have gone for large, but I'm too invested to give up now.

I see out of the corner of my eye that Linz seems to pull hers on like a glove and she has no problem getting it up over her chest and then pulling the long strap up at the back to fasten it.

I curse under my breath and put my hands through the arms. This'll be the test of whether it really is too small.

To my sheer amazement, I get my arms in and the fabric pulls tight across my chest. I practically break my arm trying to grab the strap at the back, before Linz bounds over and helps me.

'Let me grab that for you.'

She zips me up, and I yelp as a little bit of back skin gets stuck in the zip.

'Oops, hang on,' she says poking at my flesh and trying once more.

This time it does up and I windmill my arms to make sure I can move around. The fabric stretches a little bit and I think I'm going to be OK.

'Shall we go?' asks Linz enthusiastically as she leaves the room.

I try not to look at her skinny little behind as she walks out of the changing room in her wetsuit and flip-flops. I pad behind her, my wetsuit shoes flapping noisily on the tiles. I catch a glimpse of myself in a mirror and instantly wish I hadn't. This wetsuit is the least flattering thing I think I've ever worn. They're clearly not designed for women with hour-glass figures. My boobs still look massive despite being compressed in neoprene and my thighs look like tree trunks.

Any sense of glee that I felt at squeezing into the medium disappears as I waddle out feeling like an overweight walrus.

'Let's get this show on the road,' says Brett, as we meet him and the other two guys in the lobby. We follow him outside, where there's a windsurfing board fixed to the floor.

'So, I'm going to run you through what you're going to do when you get out on your boards,' he says, jumping on and masterfully spinning the board around with his legs. I find myself being impressed and suddenly Brett's become that little bit more attractive. Down, cougar, down.

He takes us through what we're supposed to do at breakneck speed. And then he calls for us to have a go one by one.

When it's my turn, I climb onto the board, and push myself up to stand. The board swivels underneath me, instantly making me nervous. What on earth possessed Joseph to put this on his list?

The thought of him in a wetsuit with wet curls running out of the surf, à la *Baywatch*, suddenly makes my knees buckle and I'm reminded why I'm doing this.

I gain control of my legs once more and push my arms out rigid. *I can do this.* I chant.

I mean, what's the worst that could happen? I could fall the three inches from the board – and probably face plant into the concrete floor below …

'That's it, Abi. Strong legs. Now, gently pull the rope of the sail up and lean back whilst grabbing the bar.'

I take a deep breath and do as he says. The wind begins to take the sail and I pull it up. I can sense Brett hovering behind me and from watching the others I know he'll have his hands outstretched, so with that in mind I lean back and allow myself to get in the position.

'Sweet, Abi, sweet,' says Brett. 'OK, you can hop on down.'

I stand back upright and almost immediately let go of the sail. It crashes noisily to the ground.

'Sorry,' I say, wincing as it hits the concrete below.

Brett tries to smile through his own wince. 'That's OK, just go careful.'

The last of our group takes to the fake board and I start to think that this windsurfing malarkey might be quite easy after all. I can already stand on the board and pull the sail up, and Brett says from there the wind will carry us, so really I can practically do it already.

Maybe I should just get Linz to take the prove-I-was-here photo and then I can call it a day.

'Right, guys, let's grab our boards and get in the water. I've already attached the sails and I'll teach you about connecting the rig after lunch.'

Brett has deposited our windsurfers on the edge of a concrete slipway and he helps each of us carry ours into the water.

I can't help but try and tiptoe as the water starts to run over my ankles and into my wetsuit shoe.

The coldness of the water takes my breath away and I can't believe that I'm voluntarily wading into it.

We all hang onto our boards like seals, with our torsos resting on them.

'Right, guys, push away and have a go.'

Brett brings a motorised orange dinghy down the slipway. 'When you need towing back to the shore, just give me a wave and I'll bring you back. Don't go any further than that orange buoy.'

I look out onto the horizon and just about see the orange dot he's talking about. I almost laugh. There's no chance of that, it looks like it's miles away. I'm going to be hugging the shore as much as possible.

'Come on then, guys – mount your windsurfers.'

I slide my chest off the board and my feet sink into the muddy sand below. I place my hands flat on top of it and go to push myself up like you would getting in and out of a swimming pool.

I instantly tip the board backwards and fall into the water.

It was a whole lot easier when the board was on concrete.

'Almost, Abi,' calls Brett.

I look over and see that everyone else has made it onto their boards, and I'm the only one splashing about.

It takes me three attempts to get on all fours on the board, and I've already got my hair wet. The water is so cold that my head feels like I just took part in the ice bucket challenge.

I stay for a moment in crawling toddler pose and watch the others as they shakily get up. One guy stands up for a second before tumbling backwards. He's so tall that he makes it look as if he's just stepped off his board – as he's still waist deep in the water that comes up to my shoulders.

Linz stands up first time and without the sail up she looks like she's surfing.

'Way to go, Linz,' says Brett circling her in his dinghy.

Her flirtatious cackle catches in the wind and I feel like it's taunting me.

I try and block her out and think of Joseph instead. I imagine him standing astride a board with his hands on his hips and it spurs me on as I get lost in a fantasy of the two of us windsurfing off into the sunset.

Before I know it I'm standing on my own two feet.

'I'm up!' I shout, involuntarily. 'I'm up.'

Or at least I am for about a second before in my celebration I lose my balance and topple backwards.

I land clumsily in the water and my knees buckle from the impact of the mud.

I'm now the only one in the water. Everyone else is standing and attempting to pull up their sails. They remind me of snake charmers slowly coaxing the snakes up out of a basket.

'Come on, Abi, hop on,' says Brett, waving at me.

I fight the urge to stick my finger up at him, and instead smile through gritted teeth. I practically bellyflop onto the board and push myself up. At least I'm perfecting the beached whale to crawl pose. This time I make it up to stand and I attempt to balance, putting myself into the rope-pull position.

'Here goes nothing,' I mutter under my breath.

The sail's much heavier than it was on dry land. The water's fighting against it, and I'm struggling with all my might to pull it out gently whilst keeping my balance. It's touch and go as it emerges out of the water, and I just manage to correct my balance in time, and before I know it, I've got the sail up level with me in the neutral position.

I take a deep breath and close my eyes momentarily, trying to remember what comes next.

'Turn it round and off you go, Abi.'

I try and remember how to turn the sail, crisscrossing my hands over one another like I've been shown.

'Lean back into it,' shouts Brett.

I wobble as I try and take his advice, but I push through my legs, like we were taught, and hey presto, I'm actually moving.

There's a light breeze and as I move the sail slightly the wind catches it, and I find myself cruising along. Maybe I'm a natural after all.

'All right, Abi!' says Brett, whooping.

I want to do a victory air punch, but I daren't let go.

The wind picks up and I start to gain speed and suddenly I'm going pretty fast and the shore is disappearing behind me at a rate of knots.

I look back at Brett to see if he can help me, but he's circling Linz, who's managed to turn her sail and is heading back to the shore.

How did she do that? I can't remember what Brett said to do, and the orange buoy is getting ever closer.

I vaguely remember that I have to move the sail round, and as I go to move it out of the wind I lose my balance and not knowing what to do I drop it. The next thing I know I'm crashing into the water. Only this time I'm far from the shore and I plunge straight under.

I pop back up a second later and throw my arms over the board, spluttering from the mouthful of water. I can confirm it tastes as bad as it smells.

I wipe my soaking wet hair out of my eyes and wonder what to do.

I'm contemplating how I'm going to get back on the board now that my feet aren't touching the ground, when a small two-person sailboat floats by. The couple, who are wearing matching orange life jackets, give me a small smile of pity as they glide past. Why couldn't Joseph have put that on his list instead? Look how lovely and romantic that looks. The lady's got a little cap and sunglasses on (despite a lack of sun), and her hair's nice and dry. That's more like it.

I get boat envy as I watch them navigate to shore, twisting their hand this way and that to move the sail. No wetsuits that make you feel like a whale or arm- and leg-workouts required.

The more time I spend in the sea, the more I realise how cold it is, wetsuit or no wetsuit. I've got to make it back to the others.

I try to climb on my board. My first attempt sees me tip the board backwards and plunge down to the icy depths. The second sees me do the same manoeuvre, only this time I wallop my nose on the board in the process. Third time lucky I make it up on, and I'm standing within no time. What do I do now? I'm drifting along and the orange buoy is only a metre or two away and beyond it is what looks like a giant industrial ship. What if I bring my sail up and I can't turn it and I crash head first into it? What if I don't stop and I drift across the water and I find myself landing on Hayling Island? Or worse, I hit a current and I'm swept out into the sea and lost for evermore.

I'm practically hyperventilating as I try and wave to catch Brett's attention so he can rescue me, only he's still sailing round Linz as she wiggles around on her windsurfer.

'Help!' I shout. Only the wind is blowing in the wrong direction and not one person hears me.

By now I'm panicking. I'm not a strong enough swimmer to drag the windsurfer behind me, and with the sail dragging in the water I doubt I'd be able to paddle it back like a surfboard.

I curse Joseph and try and conjure up my best memory of him, the one where he first told me he loved me. If I'm going to die doing this stupid list, I might as well die with a good memory in mind.

Brett's still perving on Linz as she demonstrates her ability to turn her windsurfer. I knew letting her come was a mistake. If she hadn't been here, I might actually have been rescued.

I watch her with annoyance as she drops the sail and leans it round the wind, turning herself in the process.

'That's it,' I say to myself. 'That's what I need to do.'

I look once more at the orange buoy that's coming perilously close. I lift the sail, trying to lean into it to counter-balance. Somehow I manage to do what Linz did and my sail swings, turning my board around. I find myself facing the shore and I cling on for dear life as the wind catches the sail and propels me towards safety.

For once I don't mind that I'm moving pretty fast. I'm just relieved to be heading towards dry land.

'Hey, Abi,' says Brett. 'What kept you?'

Steam practically comes out of my ears.

'Right, guys, let's head back into the centre and we'll get a hot chocolate and I'll teach you the next step.'

Next step? Isn't this it?

I let the sail down gently and dismount as gracefully as I can into the waist-deep water. I pull the board behind me and just as I'm congratulating myself I slip onto the concrete slipway and bash my knee.

'Ouch!' I cry.

'Yeah, you have to be careful coming up onto here. The seaweed can make it slippery.'

'Thanks,' I mumble. I'm not particularly reassured that he's making today any safer for me.

He helps me heave the board out and I collapse on the ground for a moment, allowing myself to breathe deeply.

I can't believe I did that. I look at the orange dot in the distance and a sudden burst of pride washes over me. I, Abi Martin, have managed to windsurf. I don't think I'll be sailing off into the sunset any time soon, but I feel like I can almost tick it off my list. All I've got to do is get through the rest of the day without too many more injuries, snap that all-important photo and not get swept out to sea. Sounds like a breeze ...

Chapter Eleven

Four weeks, six days until the end of the list, and at this rate, my muscles might just be operational again after the windsurfing…

'Seriously!' I shout as my door buzzes for the third time. Unless it's Joseph standing there naked with a rose up his bum like James Nesbitt in *Cold Feet* I don't want to know. It's Sunday morning, pure lie-in territory, and whoever it is has obviously not got the memo.

I pull my pillow over my head in an attempt to block out the mechanical din, but the goose feathers aren't dense enough and I can still hear it.

I sigh loudly as I get up, not that whoever's buzzing can hear me because there are two fire doors between me and the main entrance, but at least it makes me feel better.

I shove a hoodie over my PJs and sigh again when I notice my clock and see that it's not even ten o'clock yet.

'Quarter to bloody ten,' I mutter as I attempt to walk to the hallway to pick up the intercom. I make pretty slow progress as the windsurfing yesterday has left me walking like John Wayne due to the muscle aches. Not to mention the fact that I'm black and blue with bruises.

'Yes,' I snap into it the intercom as I pick it up.

'Abi, it's Ben. I've been out for a ride and I was passing and thought we could talk about next week.'

It takes me a minute to compute.

'Do you want to come in?'

'Yeah, if that's convenient? But if it's not I can give you a shout later.'

'No, I'm up now,' I say, perhaps a little more tersely than I meant to.

I buzz him in and unlock my door, before going and poking my head out of the main corridor to direct him through to my flat.

He wheels his bike inside the lobby.

'You can bring it in if you like. Probably safer than leaving it there.'

'OK,' he says. I blush slightly as his skin-tight lycra is leaving nothing to the imagination.

I try and hide my blushes by focusing on finding somewhere to put the bike. There's just about enough room for it next to my shoe rack.

'You're up early,' I say, yawning.

'Yeah, I'm an early riser. Sorry, did I wake you?'

'I was awake, I was just refusing to get out of bed. Cup of tea or coffee?' I say, automatically filling up the kettle. I need a caffeine fix even if he doesn't.

'Coffee, if it's going, please. I should have texted you before buzzing, I didn't think as I've been up for hours. I went out to the Witterings and watched the sunrise.'

'The Witterings? Blimey, they're miles away.'

'As I said, I was up early, and it was worth it. Have you ever been to see the sunrise there?'

'I've never been to see a sunrise anywhere.'

'What?'

Ben's wrinkling his face like I've said that I've never eaten chocolate. I'm surely not the only person in the world that hasn't seen one.

'How can you never have seen a sunrise?'

'Because I'm in bed, like normal people. You can sit down, you know,' I say pointing over to the sofa. His hovering about is making me nervous. Not to mention, I keep staring at his skinny bones in his lycra and finding my eyes drawn to his crotch as if there are flashing neon lights down there. Seriously, why do they have to wear such clingy stuff? He might as well be naked, and that's before we even discuss the fact that part of his leg fabric looks see-through.

'I'm a bit sweaty.'

'Don't worry, it's only faux leather, and my mum's Labrador sits on it when he comes.'

'Good to know that you hold me in the same esteem as a dog.'

I bite my lip. That came out all wrong.

'You know what I mean,' I say, turning round to face him and realising he's grinning.

He digs into his backpack and pulls out a pair of tracksuit bottoms and slips them on.

I breathe a sigh of relief – at least that's put crotch-gate to bed.

I dig out a cafetiere from the back of the cupboard where it's stayed since Joseph last used it. As much as I like proper coffee, I can never be bothered to get rid of the coffee grains after. But I've got company so I don't break out the Asda Gold Blend knock-off.

'Well, one morning you should go over to the Witterings. On a clear day, there's nothing more magical.'

Maybe when Joseph and I get back together we could go there and do it. I can imagine sitting on the sand watching the sunrise with him curled up around me.

The kettle boils loudly and snaps me out of my fantasy. I fill up the cafetiere and leave it to brew.

'I ride out there quite a lot to see it. You could tag along one day, if you like.'

I laugh out loud. 'How long do you think that would take me?'

Ben shrugs. 'OK, so maybe it would be better to go and see the sunset on West Wittering. That way you'd have all day to get there.'

'That sounds a bit more like it. Although I have to say that I think after yesterday I'm going to be a bit of a speed demon. I actually went pretty fast on the windsurfer and enjoyed it,' I say proudly.

'So it went well then?'

'Yeah, it did. Amazingly.'

I bring the coffee and a two pinter of milk over to the table, before I return with two mugs and some sugar.

'Help yourself,' I say waving my hand over. I'm sure my mum would mark me down for not pouring the milk into a jug and the sugar into a sugar bowl, but seeing as how I own neither, Ben'll have to take it as it comes.

'So you can now windsurf?'

'Yep,' I say, sitting down on the other end of the couch and instantly curling my legs underneath me. 'I can stop and go. And I even turned a couple of times without falling off.'

'That's pretty good.'

'I know. I impressed myself. The only thing is, my thighs are burning. I feel like I've been put through my paces in the bedroom by Christian Grey.'

Ben's hand spasms and he shakes the spoonful of sugar he's holding all over the table.

I can see his cheeks go a little pink under his stubble. I think I crossed a line, forgetting that he's not one of my girlfriends.

'I mean, I'm not used to my inner thighs having such a work out,' I say hurriedly.

'You're not making it any better,' says Ben. He's managed to recover his steady hands and is now stirring his coffee. 'So, aside from the thighs, you managed to do it?'

'Yeah, I did. It was weird, but with Linz, my annoying work colleague, there, I felt like I had to prove something, and then once I started I was off.'

'Maybe that's the problem you've had with the bike: you're going so slowly that it's easy to put your foot down and stop yourself before you pick up speed. Maybe we need to build you up some momentum so you're forced to go faster.'

I don't think I like the sound of momentum. It conjures up the image of metal balls smacking into one another in a Newton's cradle.

'How about we go and grab a bacon sarnie and do some bike riding?'

I screw my face up. 'How about bacon sarnie and no bike riding. My thighs, remember.'

'How could we forget your bow-legged thighs. Seriously, it will help to stretch them out.'

I pull a face.

'Come on, lazy bones. We won't go all day. Just for the morning. It's gorgeous out there and it's actually warm.'

I'm not convinced. I had already planned a busy morning of squeezing as many episodes of *Unbreakable Kimmy Schmidt* from Netflix as I could.

'Look, you can come back and have a nice relaxing hot bath after. But I promise you, it will make you feel so much better. Plus, it's great training for the Isle of Wight next week.'

I'd been trying to banish any thoughts of that until after my windsurfing, as I don't know how my legs are going to recover in time.

'Do we have to?' I say, pouting like a sulky teenager.

'No, we don't have to. But I think we should. It will be fun, plus I want to see how much of an improvement you've made from riding to work.

'I'll ride home and pick up the car and that should give you time to get ready.'

'I'm not going to be able to convince you that I should stay at home all day, am I?'

'Nope. Get your arse in gear. Or else next week is going to be a whole lot harder.'

'At least then it will be over,' I say. 'Then I might get my Sunday morning lie-ins back.'

Ben drains his coffee cup, stands up and deposits it on my kitchen sideboard.

'No chance. Once the Isle of Wight is out the way, we've got a mountain to hike.'

I groan and curse Joseph in my head. His bloody list. I bet he's lying in bed still, or lazing about reading the Sunday papers in his kitchen, Radio Two blasting, his expensive coffee machine whirring away in the background. For a split second I wonder if he's there alone. I close my eyes. I can't think that he's replaced me yet, not when I'm going to all this trouble to get him back.

'So I'll be back in twenty minutes. Wear something tight.'

'What?' I say, thinking I've heard him wrong.

'I mean wear something like leggings – nothing that'll get caught in the wheels.'

This is just getting worse by the minute. My thighs in leggings have got to be three times the size of Ben's chicken legs.

'See you soon,' he says as he wheels his bike back out.

My Sunday morning is panning out dramatically differently to how I'd planned. But I guess there's no use fighting it.

I quickly pick up my phone to check Facebook, scrolling through my notifications, before I jump in the shower. A few people have liked my windsurfing pictures, but not Joseph. I bring up his page, just to see if he's been up to anything, but all he's got is a check-in at his local pub on a Saturday night, which is hardly a shocker, being that he's a creature of habit. The only good thing is that he checked in with Marcus, which gives me a kernel of hope that he's still single, and that spurs me on to get ready for my cycling adventure with Ben.

'There's no way in hell I'm doing that,' I say, crossing my arms defiantly.

Wearing leggings and exposing my thighs is one thing, but hurtling down a hill on a mountain bike is quite another.

'It's not as bad as it looks. It's barely a slope.'

I should have twigged that what goes up must come down. Ben's brought me to the Queen Elizabeth Country Park. A lovely wooded hilly area, perfect for a stroll and a coffee and cake after. But what I hadn't realised is that it's also home to a labyrinth of cycle paths that seem to propel the riders down sheer sides of muddy hills. Surely they aren't health and safety approved?

'It's practically a cliff face,' I say dramatically.

OK, I'm exaggerating, it's not a cliff face, but it is a hill. And it is steep.

'You're just going to ride down and pick up a little extra speed, that's all. But see how the path levels out there at the bottom? Any speed you have will disappear quickly when you get there.'

'But what if I hit a tree root? Or my wheel doesn't grip the mud? Or I go over the handlebars?'

'Or you get hit by a falling meteorite,' says Ben laughing. 'Yes, Abi, all those things could happen. But you could trip over when you're walking on a pavement, or you could roll out of bed and land on the floor. But usually it doesn't happen, and if it does it's an accident. By the way you talk, sometimes I think it's a miracle you leave your house at all.'

I'm momentarily winded. Ben is laughing and smiling at me and I do try and smile back, but I can feel the tears building up. He doesn't realise it, but he's hit a nerve. I know I'm a wimp. I know I don't take risks. He doesn't need to point out that I'm scared of more things than is rational, but that's who I am. I blink my eyes a little to try and get them to stop from turning into full-on tears.

'Oh, Abi,' says Ben, his tone changing, and his expression turning to concern. He reaches his hand out and squeezes my arm. 'I didn't mean anything by it. I was just joking.'

'I know,' I say, trying with all my might to force a smile on my face. I feel pathetic enough as it is without adding to it.

'Look, we can walk down with the bikes if you like? And stick to flatter paths. You are doing much better today as it is.'

'No,' I say firmly. 'Let's do this. You're right. I could injure myself in everyday life. I practically take my life into my hands when I go out drinking in my high-heels. You go first though.'

'Are you sure? You don't have to.'

'I'm sure,' I say, nodding my head and mounting my bike.

'OK,' says Ben, climbing onto his and giving me a look to make sure I'm serious before he sets off down the hill. 'Just make sure if you do brake that you do it gently and squeeze the back one first.'

I nod and wave him off.

I watch as Ben descends and I wonder if I can actually go through with it. I know he must be braking more than he usually does as he's not hurtling down like I thought he would.

He makes it to the bottom, and I know it's now or never.

I want to be the kind of woman who would do this. I try and pretend for a moment that Ben is Joseph. If he was here in front of me, there's no way I'd let him leave me behind up here and no way I would want him to know that I'm too much of a wimp to do it.

I put my feet on the pedals and grip the handlebars hard so that my arms go rigid and I'm afraid they might snap.

I concentrate with all my might to make sure that I stay in a straight line and don't go off the path, trying to stay in Ben's track line. My speed picks up and I begin to feel that dizzy somersault feeling in my belly and the wind whistling through my hair.

I'm terrified, but as I start to level out and slow down, I realise it wasn't that bad. Yes, I may have peed myself a little bit, and my heart is racing, but I'm smiling. I'm actually proper cheek-achingly smiling.

'You survived, then,' says Ben as I come to a halt next to him.

'I did.'

'And you're grinning. I'm going to take that as a sign that you actually enjoyed yourself?'

'Steady on. Enjoy might be bit strong. But it definitely wasn't as bad as I thought it was going to be.'

'So, do you want to do the same slope again?'

'No.'

I watch Ben's face fall.

'I want to go higher,' I say before I can change my mind.

'Really?'

'Careful or I'll chicken out.'

Ben grabs hold of his handlebars, 'Come on, then. I know just the one.'

I follow Ben as the path climbs higher. My legs are crying out in pain, and I'm tempted to get off and push, but I don't. Ben gets smaller and smaller in the distance until he reaches the top. I'm a bit behind him, but I eventually make it to the top, huffing and puffing, and I see we're on the edge of another hill.

Now, with my fear of heights I'm generally OK if the ground is solidly beneath me. Towers, bridges, open stairs – all give me the heebie-jeebies, but as long as the hill I'm on has a wide path and I don't have to peer off the edge, I'm OK.

But this one is quite steep and it goes on and on and on.

'Still OK? We can go back the way we came if you like – it's not as steep,' says Ben, as if he's reading my mind.

I shake my head. 'What's to fear?' I say, banishing all thoughts of tree roots, flying over handlebars and broken limbs.

'That's the spirit. See you at the bottom.'

Ben pushes off and I'm left in a cloud of dust. He's clearly going faster this time.

I take one last look over my shoulder at what, in comparison, looks like a gentle incline (although my thighs would disagree), and go for it.

I can't stop the little wail that escapes my lips as I whizz down the hill. My hand hovers over the brake and whilst every instinct is shouting for me to squeeze it, a little voice in my head tells me not to. My heart begins to pound so loudly that I can hear it pulsing in my ears, and the wail I'm emitting is getting louder. I'm going so fast now that I don't know how I'm ever going to stop. But the funny thing is, it's OK. Yes, I'm terrified. Yes, I fear I'm in imminent danger, but I've gone all light-headed and stomach-flippy and I feel fan-bloody-tastic!

I reach the end of the slope and, as the path goes uphill again, I naturally slow down. Ben's waiting up ahead where the track has levelled out near some open woodland with picnic benches. He's got a stunned look on his face.

'Blimey, you weren't hanging around there, were you?'

He climbs off his bike and takes off his helmet, before hanging it off his handlebars and leading his bike over to a picnic table. I follow him over and unclip my helmet. My hands are shaking so hard that I can't get the catch, and Ben leans over to help me.

'Are you OK?' he asks, as I take off the helmet. He hasn't moved back since he helped me with the clasp and he's so close that I can feel his breath on my cheek. I look up at him and find myself staring straight into his eyes. For a second they're locked in and I almost want to reach up and kiss him. But I don't. Instead I look away and take a step backwards. It's just the adrenaline from the ride.

'That was some rush,' I say. 'Is it always like that?'

'Most of the time,' says Ben. 'But the more you do it, the more you need to up the ante to beat it. Like going off-trail and going down sheer drops.' He raises an eyebrow as if suggesting that we try that.

'I think I'll stick with this for now.'

I laugh as Ben gets out his flask.

'What? I don't go anywhere without tea? Don't tell me you don't want a cup?'

'Of course I do.' I wince as I sit down on the bench, still sore from yesterday's adventures. Although Ben was annoyingly right, the riding has loosened me up a bit.

Ben pours the tea and hands me a cup.

'Thank you. Don't suppose you've got a sneaky cake in there too, have you?' I say peering into the top of his rucksack and thinking that I've earned it with today's ride and yesterday's windsurfing.

'Always,' says Ben, throwing me a Mr Kipling cake bar.

He truly is a man after my own heart.

'I can't believe I did that,' I say biting into the cake bar.

'I know. I'm so proud of you. Last week you could barely go in a straight line and now you're hurtling yourself down hills. What's changed?'

I shrug my shoulders and begin to pick at my cake. What has changed?

'I don't know. I think it helped going windsurfing yesterday. I mean, I know I was shockingly bad at it, but I kept falling in that freezing water and I kept getting back up and at some point something pinged in my head and said, look at you, you can do this. And I guess when we were on that hill earlier I realised that I'm so blindsided by what could go wrong that I don't think about what could go right. And it just hit me, it's only fear.'

Ben drinks his tea and nods.

'I mean, I definitely don't want to go up any steeper hills or narrower tracks, and I still have no idea how I'm going to abseil the Spinnaker Tower, but I've got to learn to trust myself and my abilities more. God, I sound cheesy,' I say blushing.

Ben's so easy to talk to that I sometimes forget that we barely know each other. He probably thinks I'm such a loser. I only cycled a path a five-year-old could do blindfolded. It's not like I tightrope walked over the Grand Canyon or anything.

'No, you don't. You sound honest. I'm usually around such adrenaline junkies that sometimes I forget that things like this can be a big deal.'

'You mean, I'm a loser for thinking it's a big deal?'

'No, I mean it – it's refreshing. I'm caught up in a world where it's always who can do the steepest run or the craziest ride and sometimes you forget that it's not always about what other people are doing, it's about your own personal journey and what you feel.'

'Deep, man,' I say, taking the last bite of the cake.

'Totally,' he says, laughing. 'Oh, I forgot, I took a photo of you on my phone during that last run,' he says.

'You did?'

'Yeah,' says Ben, pulling his phone out and after tapping away he hands it over.

'Oh, wow.'

I'm pulling a weird face that looks like I'm having a tooth extracted, but there's no denying the rest of it is all action.

'Can you send it to me? I want to put it on Facebook. That's a perfect try-to-win-Joseph-back photo.'

Ben frowns and opens his mouth as if to say something, but he's interrupted as a set of bike brakes screeches near us and I instinctively flinch as dust heads our way.

'Hiya,' says a woman, stepping off her bike and unclipping her helmet.

She goes over and kisses Ben on the lips and I realise that it's his girlfriend, Tammy.

'Hey, I didn't realise you were up here,' he says in surprise.

'Yeah, I was supposed to be going to Steyning but I overslept. I was just setting up my GPS to map my route, and saw that you were here too.'

She looks over at me as if she's only just noticed I'm there. At first she looks a little unsure of who I am and what I'm doing with her boyfriend.

'Abi,' she says after a second, breaking into a smile. 'How nice to see you. And out on a bike too, huh? Ben and his bike-bullying strikes again.'

'Hi, Tammy,' I say. 'Just giving it a go.'

'Are you getting on any better than you were before? Ben said you were a little nervous.'

My cheeks flush and I suddenly wonder what else Ben has told her. What if he's told her about my real motivation behind the bucket list?

'She's improving in leaps and bounds,' he says.

'Excellent – well Ben is a very patient teacher. Right, I'll let you get back to your lesson. I'm just on a warm-up so better keep moving. But I'll drop by yours this afternoon, shall I? Are you going to be in?'

'Yeah. We'll be heading back to Portsmouth soon. Abi's got a busy afternoon of TV-watching planned,' laughs Ben.

'OK, great. Perhaps we could go for a run along the seafront.'

'Yeah, OK.'

My cheeks flush as I feel even more like a couch potato. These two really are the polar opposite of me and the way I spend my downtime. They also seem really laid back as a couple – dropping in if they're free. Totally different to the super-committed, diary-dated relationship I had with Joseph.

Tammy's got her helmet back on and she's ready to go.

'Good luck with the Isle of Wight next week, Abi.'

'Thanks, I'm going to need it,' I reply, waving.

With a whoosh she's off, flying back up the hill we came down earlier, probably at the same speed that I cycled down it. She has to be one of the fittest people I've ever seen.

'Right,' says Ben taking the cake wrappers. 'We should get going again as well. Before our muscles seize up. Now, there're a couple more gentle slopes down and then we'll be at the car. Then you can get back to your TV.'

'Great,' I say, suddenly, and just for a second, a little disappointed that I'm going to be in my flat alone this afternoon. I begin to wonder if I should go for a run, train for the 10k.

I slowly stand up and my legs buckle at the pain. On second thoughts maybe an afternoon lounging in the bath with a book might be in order. I'll leave the running to Ben and Tammy.

'Thanks, Ben,' I say as we mount our bikes again.

'For what? The cake bars?'

'No, for everything. I couldn't have done this challenge without your help.'

'Don't mention it,' he says, putting on his helmet.

'I mean it. Thank you.'

I really do mean it. If it wasn't for Ben I'd be sitting at home still feeling sorry for myself instead of having Lara Croft-esque photos taken of me to post on Facebook and woo Joseph back.

Suddenly spending an afternoon alone doesn't seem like such a dull prospect. At least I'll have time to craft the perfect Facebook status updates.

I'm going to get Joseph back, I can feel it in my bones. OK, so that might be aches from yesterday's windsurfing, but something in my head has changed. It's like for the first time I'm confident that I can do this list, and that means I'm getting ever closer to getting back the love of my life.

Chapter Twelve

Four weeks to get Joseph back before the abseil, and after tomorrow's cycle ride I'll be four challenges in. Ain't no stopping me now ...

'It can't be a big night tonight,' I say as I answer the door to Sian. Tomorrow is the Isle of Wight bike ride. It's going to be rough enough going over on the hovercraft at seven in the morning; I can't imagine doing it with a hangover.

The fact that she's shown up at five in the afternoon worries me as that usually means a few drinks before we go out.

'That's fine. I just wanted to get out of my house. Angela is driving me insane.'

Ah, Angela, Sian's note-writing, rule-setting housemate.

'Do you know she left me a note to tell me that I had accumulated too many wine bottles and I needed to go to the bottle bank. How does she even know they're all mine?'

'Are they?' I ask as we walk into my little lounge.

'Well, probably, because she's like a saint who takes about three weeks to finish one bottle of rosé and Hannah only drinks gin. But still. It's like living with my mother. Except worse, as at least my mother drinks as much wine as me.'

Sian collapses onto the sofa and huffs loudly.

'I don't know why you don't just move out. Get somewhere of your own. I'm sure you could afford it.'

I sit down opposite her in my wicker rocking chair.

'I could, but then I'd be tied into a six-month or year-long lease. And what if *the* job came up?'

I nod. I'd forgotten about *the* job. Ever since I've known Sian she's been desperate to become a reporter in London at one of the Nationals. She's chomping at the bit to be a tabloid journalist. She made the transition from uni newspaper, to small-town newspaper and now she's working at the city newspaper here in Portsmouth. It's a pretty big paper, but it's not quite big enough for Sian, and at every opportunity she's trying for the next step up.

The problem is, she's been trying for more years than I think she cares to remember, and if she doesn't make the move soon I think she'll be stuck in local news for ever. Not that that would be a bad thing. She's brilliant at keeping her finger on the pulse of the city and I think she'd miss the community buzz and the relationships she's established if she left.

'Surely even if you got the job, you could commute for a few months whilst you finished your rental? You can't keep your life on hold indefinitely – your housemates are going to drive you round the bend before that.'

'I know, it's a risk that I might flip out and kill them, becoming the subject of the very headline I'd love to write.'

'It's a shame I don't have a spare room here,' I say. That would solve her housemate problems and some of my money worries too. But although my bank balance might be healthier, my liver certainly would not. Sian and I lived with each other for a year at uni and I think I was in a perpetual state of hair of the dog.

'I know. Right, well enough with all that, let's talk about tonight,' she says before downing the wine that I've just given her.

'So where do you fancy? The White Horse? Barley Mow?' I say thinking of quiet-night-approved pubs in the vicinity.

'Actually, I've got something that's going to make you happy.'

She pulls open her handbag.

'I've got us tickets,' she says, smiling.

'What are they for?' I ask, hoping that they're for the cinema, as there aren't many other types of tickets that scream early night.

'I'm helping with your bucket list. You've got Glastonbury on your list, yes?'

'Uh-huh,' I say, very confused. Glastonbury isn't for another couple of months or so and it's sold out.

'Well, they're having a festival over on the common tonight, and I got us free tickets.'

She pulls out two brightly coloured passes hanging on neon pink lanyards and waves them around.

'Great,' I say through gritted teeth.

I can't be mad, as it's actually really sweet and supportive.

'You don't have to drink a lot. We can just bop about to the bands and it's practically on your doorstep so you can come home when you want.'

I'm not convinced.

'I know it's not a camping type of festival, but there's a number of different bands on, and there'll be Portaloos, so that has to count for something, right? And the passes cover tomorrow too, so if you fancy it after the bike ride ...'

'Um ...'

'Come on, Abs. When else are you going to get free festival tickets? Plus, they're VIP.'

My eyes shoot up and meet Sian's. She knows I'm a sucker for the word VIP. I'm still yet to spot an actual celeb at one of these events, but VIP isn't only synonymous with famous peeps, it usually means freebies.

'Do I need to change?' I say, sighing. I can't be arsed to change out of my jeans and vest top.

'No, just grab a hoodie. It's bound to get cold later on.'

At least that's a result – no dressing up required.

'So, get your stuff and we'll go.'

'What? Now?'

'Uh-huh. It started at three, so we're already a bit late.'

I groan. 'OK, but if I go out now, I'm coming back early. I need to get some proper sleep before tomorrow.'

'Deal,' says Sian, as I rock myself up from my chair and go in search of a hoodie from my bedroom.

I reappear moments later having found one, and tie it round my waist. I look in the mirror and I can still see remnants of today's mascara and I figure that will be good enough make-up for standing around outside.

I notice Sian's eyes are lined with dark and broody liquid eyeliner, and she's wearing denim shorts over leggings. Much more festival-ready than I am. If only I could be arsed to do the same.

'So what time are you setting off tomorrow, then?' asks Sian.

I open my back door and the faint sound of rock music drifts over to us.

'We're catching the seven-fifteen hovercraft.'

'Ooh, the hovercraft. You are being brave.'

'I know,' I say, wincing.

The hovercraft alone would usually be enough to keep me this side of the water. Yet tomorrow that's going to be just the start of my pain.

I try to block the thought of the ride out of my mind. At least I know from last week with the downhill riding that I can actually ride a bike now, and my muscles have finally recovered from the windsurfing. I've also just worked out that with tonight's cheat festival and tomorrow's cycle ride, I'm going to be halfway through the list. We'll just gloss over the fact that I still can't speak much Spanish other than saying *hola*. I'm still going to the classes, so I am at least trying to learn a language – that counts, right?

Halfway through the list. That's halfway to getting Joseph back. Or halfway to failing to get Joseph back. I've been posting my pictures up on Facebook, and attracting lots of likes from my friends, but Joseph hasn't been one of them. You'd think nowadays Facebook would be able to tell you who's viewed your profile page. What if he's blocked me from his newsfeed? What if he never sees that I've done any of these amazing things? What if it's all for nothing?

I sigh loudly at the thought.

'What was that for?' asks Sian.

I was so lost in my thoughts that I'd almost forgotten she was there. For a moment I wonder if I should be honest and tell her about my true motivation behind completing the list. After all, she is my best friend, and I've felt crappy lying to her, but I don't want her to be mad.

'Just nerves about tomorrow,' I say, lying again.

'You'll be fine. You've got that Ben guy to help you. You said you'd been making progress in your practice rides, didn't you?'

'Yes, but my fifteen-minute rides to work are a tad different to a ten-hour bike ride. I mean, what if I don't have the stamina to do it?'

'I'm sure you'll be fine.'

I start to feel my breathing getting more strained. 'What if I get halfway round and I'm too knackered to get back?'

'Then you'll get the train or the bus back. And you'll try again another day. I don't know why you're in such a desperate hurry to get this list done so quickly.'

So I get Joseph back before he gets another girlfriend.

'If it was me then I'd be spreading it over the year. What are you going to do with yourself when it all comes to an end?' asks Sian.

Spend my days with Joseph who's going to come back to me of course. Duh.

'I'm sure I'll think of other things to do. It's just I need to push myself to do the tasks or they'll just stay on the list for ever.'

We cross the road and enter the common. The festival itself is easy to spot as there's a large fenced-off area in one corner. I know Sian said it's a pretty small festival, but it doesn't look it from here.

As we approach the music gets louder and I begin to feel quite excited. I can't remember the last time I went to a gig and I've never really been to anything like this. I'm a true festival virgin.

We have our passes scanned, our bags searched and ourselves patted down as we enter. All the while the burly security lady gives me an evil eye and I can't help feeling I'm guilty of something. She slaps a wristband on my wrist so tight that I think it's going to cut off my circulation, but she's way too scary to ask to get it loosened.

'Blimey, she wasn't taking any prisoners, was she?' I say as we walk away.

'She certainly wasn't.'

I pull off my lanyard and flip through the attached cards, looking at the line-up.

'Who shall we watch first? In the dance tent is some dance DJ that I've never heard of, on the local stage there's a band called the Passion Peaches who I've never heard of and on the main stage there's a band called the Stay who again, shockingly, I've never heard of.'

'Sorry that it's not quite the Glasto line-up, but the Flaming Lips are headlining here tonight.'

'Another band I've never heard of.'

'What? You must have. They were big when we were at uni.'

'What did they sing?'

'Well … I don't know,' says Sian, practically scratching her head in recollection. 'But they're supposed to be really good live.'

I look around the common that's been transformed into a festival. It's packed with people wandering about drinking from oversized paper cups. There's a tent in one corner that looks like it would be at home at a circus, a white beer tent in the opposite corner, and a large open stage at the front.

I glance longingly at the giant paper cups.

'How about we get a drink first?' I say pointing to a bar next to us.

'Great idea,' says Sian, linking her arm through mine and pulling me towards it.

'This will be my only drink.'

It's probably all right to have a couple of beers now as it's still early. I can sober up later on and still get an early night.

'Yeah, whatever,' says Sian, as we shuffle round the queue. When we finally make it to one of the many bar people she orders us the double-pint cups. She pays and we walk back into the throng of people.

'So, who are we going to go and see first?' I say.

'How about we check out the VIP area at the main stage?'

'Sounds good.'

We follow the signs for the VIP area and find ourselves in a small tent to the left of the main stage. Not only do we have a brilliant view of the band, but there is also a quiet-looking bar in the corner. It's sponsored by my favourite fruit cider company, and it has signs saying it's a free cider bar.

'Oh, my God, look,' I say pointing at the sign and salivating.

'I wish I'd known that before I spent fifteen pounds on crappy, flat beer.'

'I wish I'd known that before I agreed to come. What a test of willpower.'

They could have been sponsored by any alcohol brand, but oh, no, they had to be sponsored by them.

I pop my cardboard cup down and go and get myself some strawberry-flavoured cider. I decide that I'm only going to have this one, but as I sip it I know I'm kidding myself.

The VIP tent is quite busy, yet it's small enough to have an intimate feel. It's got high tables scattered throughout to lean on/park the copious amounts of free drink, and it's decorated with twinkly fairy lights.

I look round at the other VIPs and I suddenly feel woefully underdressed. Whilst my no-make-up, teenager-in-a-hoodie look was perfect for the rest of the festival, the women in here are more rock chick trendy. They're all dolled up in mini-skirts and shorts, cropped leather jackets and T-shirts with band logos.

I look down at the plain black vest top that I think I bought during my weekly shop at Tesco and stand further back against the black canvas in the hope that I blend into the background.

At least from here we've got a very good vantage point of the band and they're actually pretty good, even though we've never heard of them.

Sian has managed to perch herself up against a table and she's exhibiting all the signs of meerkatting around the tent. It's a classic Sian move where she scans the room for potential men. She'll already have identified if there are any eligible bachelors and has probably started to make eyes at them.

I can't imagine who she would have picked. Everyone's a bit too young and hipster for my liking.

'This cider is so good,' says Sian, downing the rest of her bottle.

'Whoa, slow down, appreciate the flavour,' I say, taking another tiny sip. My resolve weakening with each one.

I watch Sian as she suddenly stands up a little straighter, and shakes her hair back. I follow her gaze towards the man that's just walked into the tent.

My heart starts to beat faster as I realise it's Joseph's best friend Marcus. I brace myself in case Joseph walks in behind him, but he seems to be alone. He scans the room briefly before seeing a woman standing at one of the tables in the middle, and he goes and brushes her cheek with a gentle kiss.

'Typical,' says Sian, shaking her head. 'The good ones are always taken.'

I purse my lips. As Sian wasn't Joseph's biggest fan, we'd never mixed our friends so she's not met Marcus before.

'I don't think he's necessarily a good one,' I say, sighing. 'He's Joseph's best friend.'

'What?' says Sian, her head snapping round for another look. 'Why an earth didn't you introduce me to him before? He's gorgeous.'

'He's also a bit of a player. Changes his girlfriends more than most people change their knickers.'

'I wouldn't mind him changing my knickers.'

How much cider has she had?

I see Marcus looking round the tent and I try and hide behind Sian. It's so small in here that it would be almost impossible for him not to see me. I instinctively reach for my bottle and down it. So much for self-restraint. Seeing him has unnerved me and I need some Dutch courage. There's no way that Marcus won't mention to Joseph that he's seen me. And it would be bloody typical that I'm here dressed in a plain top with jeans, looking like I've made zero effort. Although I guess it could be worse – Joseph could be here too.

'Slow down, aren't you supposed to taste it,' says Sian, mocking me.

'Very funny,' I say. 'I was thirsty.'

I honestly couldn't tell her what I've just drunk – my mouth was numb to the taste.

'Do you want to go perch at that table?' says Sian, pointing to one that some people have vacated closer to the stage.

'No,' I say rather too quickly. 'I'm happy here.'

The black canvas of the tent and the shadows are my friend at the moment.

'But we'd have a much better view of the band over there. And we'd be more part of the action.'

I'm about to protest that it's not the proximity to the band that's putting me off, it's the fact that we'd only be one table away from Marcus and his friend, but before I get a chance, Sian has swanned off towards it.

I have no real choice but to follow her. I try to keep my head down, hiding my face with the side of my hair.

Sian is already in conversation with a man before I get there. He's not her usual type. He's young, and wearing a faded Led-Zeppelin T-shirt and skinny jeans. He's got his curly hair tamed in a hairband and a checked shirt round his waist. He looks like he could be auditioning for One Direction.

'So tell me about the rationale behind the festival,' says Sian.

Ah, that explains it. She's in work mode rather than cougar mode. Her iPhone is out and she's nodding away as the young man starts talking about local talent and promoting the city.

I start to relax as I look around and realise that perhaps my boring outfit has done me some favours. I simply blend into the background whether I'm at the edge of the tent or in the centre, which means maybe I'll be able to hide from Marcus in plain sight.

I've turned my attention to the band and I'm tapping away with my foot when I hear my name.

'Abi,' he says in his familiar commanding voice.

I look up and our eyes meet.

'Marcus,' I say, downing Sian's bottle of cider that she'd put down to conduct her interview, my shaking hand just about allowing me.

'I saw the photos of your new hair on Facebook – it really suits you.'

I instinctively raise a hand to my hair before jolting at the mention of Facebook. I'd forgotten I was friends with him. A flutter of an idea flies through my mind – if he's seen the photos of me with new hair doing the challenges, does that mean that Joseph has seen them too?

'Thanks. And how are you?'

'Good, thanks,' he replies. 'What brings you to the VIP area then?'

'My friend Sian is a local journalist,' I say, pointing to her interviewing the Harry Styles wannabe. 'How about you?'

There's a loud cough to our left and Marcus's companion seems to have been doing the hacking. 'I'm sorry,' he says, turning towards her before looking back at me. 'You know Bianca, don't you? Joseph's sister. She's the one that got us the tickets. She was involved with the PR for the festival.'

I'm really glad that the table is high up as I manage to grab hold of it to steady myself.

I hadn't recognised her. Her hair is a completely different colour from when we were at the Ritz and it's plaited round the top of her head, with the rest of it spilling out in surfer waves that hang halfway down her back. From her pretty white dress, teamed with faded denim jacket and cowboy boots, you'd think she was attending Coachella rather than a tiny festival in Portsmouth.

'We never actually met,' I say, weakly, feeling a bit pathetic that I dated Joseph for practically a whole year and I never met his sister. 'I'm Abi, pleased to meet you.'

'Abi,' she says as if running it through a mental Rolodex. 'Joseph's Abi?'

I feel my heart pang at the description. It sounds so right, so perfect.

She looks at Marcus who nods at her in confirmation before she snaps her head back to me, cocking it to the side, studying me curiously as if I am an exhibit in a museum.

'Well, well, well,' she says in her uber-posh voice. 'It's nice to finally meet you.'

'Likewise,' I say, searching for one of the women with the trays of drinks.

'Joseph's always so secretive when it comes to his girlfriends. He seems to think me and my mother will scare them off. I mean, it's preposterous, how could little old me intimidate anyone?'

She laughs with a cackle and Marcus politely joins in, but even though she means it light-heartedly there's a seriousness to her voice. Despite the cider fog that's descending on my brain, it hasn't gone unnoticed that she's been eyeing me up and down suspiciously and even glancing at the handbag I have over my shoulder. From the Fendi that's dangling off hers, something tells me that she wouldn't be impressed with my New Look accessory.

I look round at Sian for reinforcement, but I've lost her for the moment. She's nodding like a Churchill dog, a hand resting on the arm of the young man. Not only is she preparing her story, it looks like she's preparing to get close to him too. Perhaps I was wrong; perhaps she's on the cougar prowl after all.

'So how are you, Abi? Since, you know,' says Marcus in a low whisper.

'Fine, really,' I lie. He doesn't need to know about the hibernation. 'I've been keeping busy. I've started to windsurf and I've got quite into cycling.'

'Right, I think I saw the photos. That's great, keeping busy.'

'Yes,' I say, thinking about how busy this list is making me. 'In fact, I'm off tomorrow with my friend Ben to cycle round the Isle of Wight.'

'What, like on a bike?' says Bianca, her nose wrinkling.

'Yep. Should be fun. I haven't been over to the island for years.'

'Me neither,' says Marcus. 'I used to love it as a kid, though. Will it take you long?'

'Hopefully about ten hours,' I say, a little optimistically.

'That's fantastic. Well, good luck with that. I'll be thinking of you when I'm at home nursing my hangover from tonight,' he says, raising a bottle.

There's a slight lull in the conversation and I really want to jump in and quiz him about Joseph and whether he's still single, but I know that will make me look desperate, exactly what I'm trying to avoid.

'Excuse me for interrupting,' says Sian. 'Do you mind if I take a photo of you lot chatting for the *News*? I'm covering the event for them.'

Bianca fluffs up her hair.

'Of course,' she says, turning to face Sian and pouting.

'Great.'

She turns her iPhone sideways and directs us to squash in, before taking a few snaps.

I can't believe it. This couldn't be more perfect. Sian is the queen of Facebook and tagging. It'll be posted up there within minutes and all I need to do is tag Marcus. Even if Joseph isn't seeing my posts, I'm sure he won't miss this one – his ex, his best friend and his sister all in the same shot.

I must look like a demented guppy as I try to force my mouth muscles not to smile so hard. I don't want to scare anyone with quite how excited I've become.

'I don't like this band,' says Bianca, turning her nose up once the photo is taken. 'It's a bit rocky for me. Shall we go and see who's in the acoustic tent?'

'Yes, OK. It was lovely to see you again,' says Marcus, in his charming tones. It's no wonder he gets women falling at his feet.

'You too. Give my best to Joseph.'

'Will do,' he calls over his shoulder as he walks away.

I grab hold of the table to steady myself and take a deep breath. That encounter was nowhere near as bad as it could have been. Hopefully Joseph will not only see me on Facebook, but Marcus might report back that I'm going on a cycling adventure with another man.

'Has he gone?' asks Sian, suddenly appearing by my side.

'Marcus? Yes.'

'Damn it. What happened?'

'We just chatted. He's here with Joseph's sister Bianca.'

'The one from the Ritz?' she says, not so subtly looking round at her as they leave. 'Blimey, she looks different.'

'I know. She's positively chameleonesque.'

'So how was it? What was she like? Are they dating? Is he single?'

'Wow, one at a time, Sparky,' I say, raising my hands. I feel like Sian hasn't slipped back out of reporter mode yet.

'OK, the important one. Is that guy single?'

'Didn't ask. Probably. He dates at a rate of knots so even if he was in a relationship when he walked in, he won't be by the time he leaves.'

'Perhaps we should go and see another band too.'

'Perhaps you should leave him alone. Trust me. As charming as he is, he's a heartbreaker.'

Sian pouts. I know that she can usually take care of herself with men, and she's not Mrs Commitment herself, but he's the type that would chew her up and spit her out. He's not for the faint-hearted.

'I'm doing you a favour, honestly.'

'Doing me a favour would be getting me to a position where I take him home with me for a wicked evening of naughty sex. But I will, on this occasion, take your word for it. Although I have had enough of this band. Can we go to another stage? No sexual motivations, I promise.'

'OK, then.'

At least I know where Marcus and Bianca are headed, and I can steer Sian away to the opposite side of the festival.

By the time the headline act comes on to the main stage, I've all but forgotten my vow to get an early night and not drink too much. After downing those bottles when I saw Marcus, my resolve weakened.

I'm now on the wrong side of tipsy. My speech slightly slurred, my confidence soaring, and my ability to walk in a straight line – despite being in trainers – compromised. I'm leaning on to the bar in the VIP tent more for support than because I actually want a drink, when I spot that I've got a massive ketchup stain on my hoodie. I try and suck it out in the hope that it won't have dried in the half-hour since I ate a hot dog.

I hear a snort beside me and I'm about to snap and ask the person what they're staring at, when I see it's Bianca.

Despite the fact that it's been a few hours since our last encounter, and that it's started to rain outside, she still has the immaculate waves in her hair and her bright white dress is still bright white and clean with no ketchup spillages.

She gives me a wry smile. Of all the people to catch me when I'm sucking on my jumper like a messy toddler.

'You know, I must say, you're doing remarkably well for someone that's been dumped by my brother.'

Is that supposed to be ironic? Unlike hers, my hair is a frizz-ball mess, and I'm wearing dirty clothes.

She pulls out a Chanel lip gloss from her bag and begins to apply it expertly to her lips.

'Well, it's been a couple of months,' I say, my heart panging at the thought that it's been so long since we were together.

'But, still. You would not believe the girls he's dated in the past. I'll never forget the ones that used to practically camp outside our house, or the one who, when I was staying with him a few years ago, used to come round daily to beg for him back. It was pathetic. But you don't seem to be bothered.

'Of course, it's always his own fault. It's always the same with Joseph. He falls in love at the drop of a hat, and whisks the poor women off their feet. He's always been Mr Serial Relationship. In a committed relationship before he's even learnt their name. Then, after a while, when he gets to know the girl, he realises she isn't the future Mrs Small and he breaks her heart. Always the same old story. I'm sure it was no different with you.'

She gives me a look up and down as if to reinforce the inference that I'm not special enough to have hung onto someone like him.

'No,' she says, popping her lip gloss back into her bag and gesturing to the barman. 'Until he finds the one, he'll not change.'

With that she raises an eyebrow, villain-style, takes the two bottles of cider that the barman hands her and struts away.

I'm left at the bar wondering what just happened. I strengthen my grip on it to steady myself, feeling like I've had the wind knocked out of me.

Her words fly round my mind as I try and process what she's said. I might be a bit drunk, but I know she's wrong. I know I was the one. I'm certain of it.

The barman asks me what I want and I shake my head. I'd almost forgotten that that's what I was waiting for, but all of a sudden I'm not in the mood to drink.

'Are you ready to go?' asks Sian as I approach her.

I nod my head. I definitely need some fresh air.

'You need to get your beauty sleep before the big cycle ride tomorrow.'

I sigh loudly. Right now, tomorrow's bike ride is the last thing on my mind.

Chapter Thirteen

No idea how long it is until the tower, or what day or time it is. The only thing I know is that my head is killing me . . .

I sit bolt upright at the shock of the noise, and instantly regret it. My head is spinning wildly out of control and I think I'm going to be sick. Why an earth is my phone making such an evil sound? I find it by the side of my bed and hit snooze on the aggressive alarm that's all noise and vibration.

I double-check the time. Six a.m. Why on earth have I set my alarm so early?

'Six a.m.,' I say, cursing and pulling a pillow over my head.

I'm trying not to use my brain too much, but I can't help it as I try to remember why there's a punishing Slipknot concert going on inside my head.

My ears seem to be ringing with tinnitus and an image flashes through my mind as my stomach conjures up the taste of cider in my mouth. I feel a familiar rumble and know what's going to happen.

Despite the room spinning around me, I run to the bathroom and just about make it to the toilet bowl before the sickness floods through me in waves.

I didn't think I'd had that much to drink, did I?

After I've emptied the contents of my stomach I sit back against the bathroom wall and reflect while my head pounds. I'm hoping that soon there will be a momentary window where I'll feel well enough to attempt to swallow some ibuprofen.

Then it hits me. Today's Sunday: the day of the cycle ride.

Ben's supposed to be coming over at twenty to seven so that we can ride over to the hovercraft together.

I stand up slowly and test out my wobbly legs. They buckle slightly under my weight, causing me to hit the sides of my narrow corridor as I walk into my living area. If I'm this unbalanced walking, what am I going to be like on two wheels?

I open one of my kitchen cupboards and locate some ibuprofen before pulling out one of the many Lucozade Sports that I bought for today's epic journey from the fridge. I swallow the pills and for an instant the sweetness of the drink makes me feel better. But only for a second. A wave of nausea soon washes over me again.

I glance up at my kitchen clock, I've got half an hour before Ben arrives. How do I get rid of a hangover in half an hour?

I open my fridge for inspiration, but the sight and smell of food flips my stomach.

Maybe a shower will sort me out. Hopefully by the time I get out of it the pills might have kicked in and magically taken away the hangover.

I manage to make it through the shower, only getting out to be sick once. Not bad, but not good. I still feel like I'm knocking at death's door and I have about five minutes to get dressed before Ben arrives.

I go over to my chest of drawers, my head at a sixty-degree angle which seems to ease the pain slightly. I'm not entirely sure it'll be an angle conducive to cycling, but I'll soon find out.

I manage to pull out the necessary undies and socks before I throw on one of the new cycling shirts I bought from Ben's shop and some old gym leggings. I check myself out in the mirror; I look like I don't belong in the cycling top. I just needed something to look the part, and as there's never anyone in Ben's shop when I go, I felt like it was a nice way to give something back to him after everything he's done for me.

Before I can get too hung up on how ridiculous I look, my mobile buzzes. I throw a hoodie over my head and pick it up.

'Hello,' I croak. My voice has that husky, alcohol-strained tone.

'Morning! I'm at the back gate. Thought it would be easier just to come out the back way, seeing as that's where your bike is. Will you let me in?'

'Sure,' I say, thinking how much easier it would be to keep him penned up outside so that I could crawl back into bed … 'I'll just put my trainers on.'

I retch twice as I slip on my shoes and tie my laces. I can't possibly cycle in this state. I'm feeling that bad. The trouble is that Ben has been giving up so much of his precious free time on his days off that I don't feel I can let him down.

I unlock my back door and the fresh air hits me like a slap in the face. It is actually helping my hangover as it keeps me in a type of stasis. I'm not feeling any worse and the cold wind seems to be distracting my body from falling apart. Maybe there's hope after all.

'Morning,' calls Ben cheerily as I pull open the gate. I'm not in the mood for shiny, happy people this morning.

'Morning.'

'Oh, dear. Someone a bit nervous about today?'

'Not so much nervous,' I mutter as we walk back to my garden, where Ben deposits his bike against the wall.

I walk up the small set of stairs and through my back door.

'So what's going on?' asks Ben as he hands me a paper bag with a Danish pastry sticking out of it.

I cover my mouth with one hand at the sight of the pastry. Definitely not what I need right now.

I don't feel I can tell Ben that I'm hungover. I mean, I'm thirty, not nineteen. I should have the willpower to go out without getting absolutely hammered. It's all Joseph's fault. If Marcus hadn't been there last night, then I wouldn't have had to get drunk.

'Abi?' asks Ben. He's got a look of genuine concern on his face. He's clearly registered that I'm as pale as a ghost and look like I could be Morticia's stunt double.

'I went out last night with Sian. I only meant to have one or two, but I guess I had more than I thought. I've got a bit of a hangover.'

'Oh, is that all? I thought something was actually up,' says Ben, munching his pastry. 'Right, is your bag all packed? We should get going soon.'

I look at him as if he hasn't heard me properly.

'But I'm really hungover.'

'Yeah,' says Ben nodding. 'We've all been there, but the bike ride will sort you out.'

'I very much doubt that,' I say with a laugh of disbelief. 'A fry-up, a pint of Coke, a packet of Nurofen and my bed – that's what'll sort me out.'

'Well, it's too bad that that ain't going to happen, isn't it? Now, have you packed your drinks and snacks?'

I sigh loudly before stomping over to the fridge.

'Whenever I go away for bike tours or races, there's usually one night where things get out of control and I wake up the next day feeling like shit. But an hour or two into the ride and all that fresh air makes it better. I promise. Just pack some plastic bags in case you're sick on the hovercraft.'

Ben's smiling at me, but I don't think he realises how close to the mark he might be.

I stuff my drinks and high-energy snacks that sound disgusting into my bag, along with some emergency Snickers bars, the rest of my ibuprofen and a handful of Tesco's plastic bags.

'That's the spirit. You'll feel better before you know it.'

I bare my teeth like an agitated dog and follow him out of the door.

A couple of minutes later, I've uncovered and unlocked my bike and I'm climbing onto it.

I'm wobblier than usual, which is quite a feat, but amazingly I manage to ride the short distance to the hovercraft terminal a stone's throw away from my flat.

'I don't think I can get on it,' I say, as we watch the inflatable boat slide into its landing spot. The air cushion deflates and we watch as the people disembark.

'You'll be fine,' says Ben. 'I was only joking about being sick. It's not that choppy out there today and it's so quick, we'll be there before you know it.'

'But I'm not very good on the water at the best of times,' I say. I can feel my skin turning green at the thought.

The doors are open and it's time for us to get on board.

'Come on, what's the worst that could happen?'

If my life was a movie, right now they'd cut away to a clip of the hovercraft being thrown around on the sea and everyone inside being theatrically thrown from one side to the other, while I'm being sick and it's landing all over the other, very disgruntled, passengers.

I don't reply. I'm too hungover even to give him one of my infamous death stares.

He starts laughing at me. 'Come on, Abi.'

He walks off, pushing his bike, and I know I've got to follow him.

I curse Joseph for the second time this morning. It's his fault that I'm doing this bloody cycle ride instead of being tucked up in bed.

'So what did you get up to last night, anyway? You went out with Sian?'

I nod my head as we prop our bikes in the bike rack and take a seat nearby.

'We went to the festival on the common. Sian thought it would help tick "do a festival" off my list.'

'Was it as good as it sounded? I could hear it from my flat.'

'It was great. Or at least most of it was,' I say, thinking back to the run-in at the end with Bianca.

The hovercraft air cushions start to inflate, a sign of our impending departure, and my stomach lurches.

'Here we go. We're all doomed,' says Ben, laughing theatrically.

I give him a playful punch for taking the piss out of my irrational hovercraft fears.

'Hey,' he says rubbing his arm. 'I was only trying to lighten the mood.'

'I know. Sorry. I haven't got much of a sense of humour this morning.'

'Oh, great. I'm so glad I'm going to be stuck on an island with you for ten hours.'

I pull what I can only imagine is a very unattractive face.

The hovercraft ramp tips up and it's propelled into the sea. I bite my lip, hoping everything stays down.

By the time we make it back onto dry land I feel worse than I did when I left the house. I might have managed not to be sick on the hovercraft, but I feel so dizzy now that I can barely stand up. I sit on the nearest bench and hang my head over my bike frame.

'You feeling that rough?' asks Ben.

For a minute I can't answer him. I'm too busy taking deep breaths.

Eventually I mutter a yes and I feel a tear roll down my face.

'I know you said I'll feel better when I get going, but I just can't see how I'm going to,' I say, feeling pathetic.

Ben sits down next to me and places his arm around me, pulling me into him.

'Abi, there's no need to cry about it. It's a bike ride. It's no big deal.'

'But it is a big deal,' I say, the tears flowing freely now. 'You gave up your Sunday to do it, and we made it all the way over here. I'm not doing a very good job of doing this list. It feels as if I'm cheating left, right and centre. I mean my Spanish is still almost *nada*. Saying I can windsurf is a bit of a stretch of the imagination as I could only get up and stand on the board and bring the sail up one in three attempts, I'm only doing one peak rather than four, I didn't do the whole festival staying-over thing and I'm only doing a 10k race rather than a half marathon. I'm just not cut out for this bucket list. Joseph was right. We're not compatible. I can't do any of the things he wants to do.'

I hate hangovers – they always make you feel like shit, both physically and mentally.

Ben squeezes my arm. 'Abi, you're beating yourself up over nothing. You've been doing the list for about a month. Most people take years to do their lists. Joseph, as far as you can tell, has barely started it. At least you tried the windsurfing, and from what you said you got better by the end of the day. And look at you last week on the bike. You totally nailed those hills. The Abi I first met never would have entertained the thought of doing that.'

I wipe away my tears and sniff a little.

'And besides, you've already ticked off the Ritz, and you definitely did that right.'

I splutter and hiccup as I try not to laugh.

'That's great. If only all the challenges were to eat cake and drink tea, then I'd be laughing.'

'Well, you know me, that pretty much sounds like all my bike rides.'

I smile and wipe away the rest of my tears and Ben pulls his arm away from me.

'Look, we don't have to do this today, if you really don't want to.'

I'm about to tell him that I don't want to, only the thought of going back on that hovercraft ... 'But, I think seeing as you're here we might as well attempt it. We don't have to do it quickly and if you want we could even cheat a little. There are a couple of stretches we could get the bus between, if it's really that bad.'

'Ben,' I say, shocked. He's never struck me as the type who'd suggest cheating.

'Just a thought. I feel like it would be better to do something than nothing.'

'No,' I say defiantly. 'If I'm going to do this thing, I'm going to do it all. I want to do at least one thing properly.'

'That's the spirit,' says Ben.

I've really got to work on his chirpiness.

'I just don't think I can go right now,' I say.

'OK, you want to sit here for a bit?'

'No, I think I want to go in there.'

I point to a small cafe that has all the hallmarks of a greasy spoon.

'A fry-up? Not your usual energy-boosting pre-ride breakfast, but a bloody good idea.'

'And we can even sit outside,' I say. I'm still lapping up the sea breeze like a dog hanging his head out of the window of a moving car.

'Perfect, always good to keep an eye on the bikes,' says Ben.

Of course, that's what I was thinking too.

We walk across the road and find a lamp post to lock the bikes to.

'You know I could help you with the other challenges too.'

'What do you mean?' I ask. Unsurprisingly my mind isn't the sharpest this morning.

'Well, the other challenges. Like the Spanish. I spent a year backpacking round Central and South America, so I'm pretty hot on the old lingo.'

'Are you now?'

Ben's one of those people who seems to be full of surprises. I knew he'd done Asia and Oz, but I didn't realise he'd been to Latin America too.

'*Sí, señorita.*'

We sit down on the cold metal chairs and I try to pull my hoodie down so it's as much under my bum as I can get it.

'That would be great,' I say. 'But I feel so bad. You're already allowing me to gatecrash your Snowdon trip and you've been so good with all this biking stuff.'

Ben shrugs his shoulders. 'It's nice watching someone still discovering stuff. I think thirty's the kind of age when people seem to be slowing down and settling down. In our twenties me and the guys were always off hiking or biking somewhere far flung at the weekend, but now we have to plan our rare weekends away months in advance around girlfriends and babysitting duties. I kind of like that you're still in that whole exploration phase. It's like I'm seeing all these things with new eyes.'

'I've always been a bit of late bloomer,' I say with a weak smile.

'It's refreshing. So what else have you got outstanding on the list?'

'I need to train for the Race for Life,' I say, thinking that I still haven't worn my new, expensive running shoes anywhere other than my flat. 'Then there's Paris. That's an easy one. I've got to do Paris in a day.'

'There you go. That's what you should do next. Get on the Eurostar, head on over and get ticking it off your list. What would you have to see – Arc de Triomphe, shop on the Champs-Élysées, Notre Dame and the Eiffel Tower.'

I gulp at the mention of the Eiffel Tower. I've seen the little caged lift in movies.

Ben narrows his eyes as if he's trying to work out what's going on in my mind.

'The Eiffel Tower,' I say, by way of explanation. 'My fear of heights …'

'Ah,' he says, nodding his head slowly. 'If it makes you feel any better, it's not that high. Nothing like the Empire State or what they used to call the Sears Tower.'

'It doesn't matter how high it is, it's the fact it's high at all. I've seen it on TV and films, the floor's made of that mesh and you can see right down.'

'Yeah, but you don't look down. Besides, you don't have to go up the tower, if you really don't want to. That's not specifically on the list, is it? All it says is do Paris in a day. For all you know Joseph wanted to put Mickey Mouse ears on and go round Disneyland all day.'

I laugh. The thought of Joseph in novelty headwear is too much.

'He's not really your dressing-up type of a guy. And I couldn't imagine anyone less likely to go to Disney.'

'Really? Who wouldn't want to go to Disney?' says Ben, sounding like an overgrown kid. 'It's the happiest place on earth.'

Of course he would say that. He could be one of those happy dolls singing 'It's a Small World' all day.

'It's not really Joseph's thing. But sitting in a cafe in the Latin Quarter, that I can imagine. I guess I hadn't really thought about Paris, but you're right, it's one of the easiest things to tick off the list.'

A waitress comes outside and takes our order. We both plump for artery-clogging breakfasts as I'm suddenly starving. Even if by some miracle it cures my hangover, I'm sure the big breakfast isn't going to be very conducive to cycling.

'I just wish that Sian could come with me to Paris, but she's such a nightmare to pin down for a day off. She's always so busy and then last-minute stories crop up. I was amazed that we made it to the Ritz.'

'I can go with you if you like. I usually take Tuesdays off from the shop if you wanted to go then. I mean, if you wanted to go with me. I know it's Paris, and it's a whole day trip, so I'll understand if you want to go with someone else,' he says, fiddling with the little packets of sugar in the pot on the table.

'I'd love to go with you,' I say, realising that I sound a little too eager. 'It would be nice to go with you. In fact, it could be my treat, my way of thanking you for helping me with everything.'

'You don't have to do that.'

No, you don't, screams the logical part of my brain that's thinking about my bank balance.

'I do, and I insist.'

'Well, thank you,' says Ben. 'I'm looking forward to it already. It's been years since I've been to Paris.'

'Me too,' I say. 'I went on a school trip when we were on a French exchange, but we spent most of the time in the Louvre.'

The waitress deposits our coffee in front of us, and promises to bring our breakfasts right out. My stomach seems to hear her and lets out a gigantic rumble.

'But what about Tammy? Do you think she would mind you coming to Paris with me? I mean, it is the most romantic city in the world.'

I stir in more sugar than I'd usually put in a coffee, still desperate for a hangover cure.

'Tammy? She wouldn't bat an eyelid,' says Ben, sipping his coffee with what must be Teflon lips. 'We don't have that kind of relationship.'

Those two really are weird. I'd hate it if my boyfriend went off with another woman to Paris for the day, even if it was purely platonic. But Ben seems to be really happy with the way their relationship works and besides, he's Mr Anti-romance not believing in happy endings. Paris probably isn't the romance mecca for him that it is for me.

Before I can dig any deeper, the waitress brings us our breakfasts. I look down at the sausages, beans, hash browns, bacon and eggs; either this will make me feel worse or it will cure my hangover. I hope it's the latter, as now that we're here on the island it would be a shame to fail on another bucket list adventure.

I give myself a mental pep-talk. I've got to start thinking positive. This is going to kick that hangover to the curb, and I'm going to have another photo to add to Facebook tonight.

Hangover or no hangover, I'm going to focus on the fact that when I'm finished with this I'll be halfway through the list, and hopefully halfway to winning back Joseph.

Chapter Fourteen

*Hurrah! Halfway through the list, which means I've got
three weeks and six days to do the last four items and
win Joseph back. All before I have to do (get out of)
the final task – the abseil.*

If I thought my muscles were broken after the windsurfing day,
then I was seriously deluded. *Now they are broken.* I'm sitting
on my sofa and I feel like I've got rigor mortis. I'm ridiculously
uncomfortable; even the tiniest of movements sends shock-
waves of pain around my body.

It's no longer my hangover causing me pain – that disappeared long ago – instead it's the fact that I rode for ten hours
and thirty-nine minutes around the Isle of Wight. That's right,
folks – without so much as a short cut. I well and truly ticked
something off the bucket list without cheating.

So I might have to sleep on the couch as I won't be able to
make it to my bed tonight, and I might have to work from home
tomorrow, but the feeling of accomplishment is worth it.

I'm now officially halfway through my list. Now that I'm not
hungover I've got some perspective back and Ben was right, it's

a huge achievement that I've managed to accomplish so much in such a short space of time. I know I may have cut some corners, but kudos to me for actually trying to do them.

'Here we are,' says Ben, walking in from my hallway. He's carrying two white plastic bags full of yummy Chinese food and despite me eating what seemed like my weekly quota of calories this morning at breakfast, I'm starving.

He pops the bag down on the coffee table in front of the sofa and goes over to the kitchen, navigating it seamlessly, finding plates and cutlery.

I just about manage to heave myself forward on the sofa and reach out to open the little paper and foil cartons. Taking a plate from Ben, I start to scoop out some food.

'I got a bit carried away and ordered some prawn toast and chicken satay too. Probably a bit greedy,' says Ben. 'But I am so hungry, and everything on the menu sounded so good.'

I survey the number of cartons. It does look like it would easily feed six people, but I don't think I've ever been so ravenous. Not even Ben's emergency cakes or super-disgusting energy bars that we ate while we were riding had managed to fill the void.

'I reckon I'll eat it,' I say, shovelling an entire bit of prawn toast into my mouth at once.

We settle into the sofa with our fully-laden plates and watch the *Antiques Roadshow*, which is about all my brain can cope with. Neither of us talks, but it's not an awkward silence. It's obviously what comes from spending thirteen hours with someone.

We probably look like an old married couple sitting here in companionable silence with our TV dinners. It's funny because during my whole relationship with Joseph, we never hung out like this. Our dates were always so structured. I can't imagine sitting here with him dressed in tatty tracksuit bottoms, not caring that I probably have sweet-and-sour sauce splatters around my chin.

'I'm stuffed,' I say eventually, putting my plate down and trying to ease myself gently back onto the sofa. My belly is well and truly full and feeling happy.

'I think I can finish the rest off,' says Ben, scooping the last of the assortment of dishes onto his plate.

'You must have hollow legs,' I say, laughing. 'I have never known anyone to eat so much, especially someone so skinny.'

'I do in fact have hollow legs and arms. It comes in handy for occasions like this. Plus, I've still got to cycle home. And I don't fancy bonking on the way back.'

'Um, good to know,' I say, raising my eyebrows and thinking that he doesn't need to tell me about his and Tammy's sex life.

'You know, you bonked on the bike earlier?'

'Um, no I didn't,' I say. Believe me, I would have remembered a bit of bonking – it's been over two months since I broke up with Joseph and therefore two months since I had any sexy time. I know there was that moment that I almost passed out, but surely I wouldn't have forgotten doing something like that, would I?

'Don't you remember when you started hallucinating and almost fell off your bike?'

Oh, God. That was when I almost passed out. Maybe cycling's like some sort of date-rape drug. My lady bits are sore, but I put that down to ten-and-a-half hours in the saddle.

'Abi, don't look so alarmed,' says Ben, finally cottoning on to my look of horror. 'Bonking's a cycling term, for when you hit the energy wall and your muscles can't take any more.'

'Oh, phew,' I say, the relief probably evident in my voice. 'You made it sound so dirty.'

'I think it's more that you've got a dirty mind, jumping to the wrong conclusion.'

'I still think it sounds wrong,' I say.

'Yeah, you know I wanted to call the shop Bonk and Chains but my bank manager thought it would give people the wrong idea.'

'Think it might have done ... but you never know, you might have had some people interested in your tight lycra.'

'Yeah, I think he was right, even though it would have been a great marketing tool.'

'Speaking of marketing tools,' I say, choosing my words carefully. 'If you ever need any help in that department, Giles and I could help with your company. You know, if you wanted to try and get the word out about the shop.'

'Ah, thanks, but I don't think I could cope with it being any busier.'

I laugh, thinking that he's made a joke, but he looks deadpan serious.

'Sorry,' I say, coughing.

'You've never been to the shop on a Saturday, have you?' says Ben, smiling. 'I know what you're thinking – that the shop's as dead as a morgue. Which it is during the week. But Saturdays are manic.'

'But don't you want the other days to be that busy too?' I say, thinking that he can't need the whole week to recover.

'No, that's when I do the mail order stuff.'

'Mail order?' I say, confused.

'Yeah, that's where a lot of my business comes from. Sending bike parts here there and everywhere. In fact, that side of the shop is doing so well that I'm going to have to move to bigger premises later in the year to accommodate the stock.'

'Right,' I say, nodding and raising my eyebrows. I'd completely underestimated On the Rivet. I guess I never asked.

'So, shall we sort out this Paris trip?' he says, clearly not offended that I accused his business of failing.

'OK. But are you really sure you're all right to come with me?'

'It's Paris, not a trip to the dump.'

'I know, but are you sure you don't need to check with Tammy first?'

'We're going to Paris as friends, so unless you're planning to seduce me, then she's got nothing to worry about.'

'Um, I think you're safe on that score. I haven't morphed into Sian or anything.'

'Good. So shall we look at dates?'

'OK. Can you pass me the laptop?'

I point to the laptop that's on the shelf underneath my coffee table. There's no way that I'm going to be able to pull myself off the sofa to get that. My muscles are still locked in place.

Luckily Ben, being the polite gentleman he is, obliges and pops it on the armrest of the sofa next to me.

I pull up the Eurostar website, and get stuck into the calendar.

'They've got returns for seventy-two pounds. Blimey, that's good,' I exclaim.

There was me putting this off as I thought it was going to be one of the more expensive elements of my trip.

'That's great. Have they got any available on a Tuesday?'

'Um.' I scan the calendar for the next month. 'Here we are – two weeks on Tuesday. A week after the Snowdon weekend? Would you be sick of me?'

'Probably,' says Ben, nodding. 'But at least it would get it all out of the way in one go.'

'Very funny. OK, so we'd have to leave at five forty in the morning to get the good rate, and that gets us in at nine thirty, but we'd never be able to get the train from here to get there in time. What time is the first train?'

I'm rattling this off whilst I bring up the timetable for Portsmouth to London.

'I think the first train's at five, isn't it?' says Ben.

'Um, four thirty. Gets us in at six thirty. Which means we wouldn't make the seven, so we'd have to go at eight, which is a bit more expensive and doesn't get us in until eleven thirty. Is that going to be a bit late to do the sights?'

'Probably. What about if we stayed over in London the night before so we could get the early one?'

There's no way I can afford to pay for Ben's Eurostar ticket and a hotel in London the night before – not with the prices they charge.

'We could stay with my sister Jill and her boyfriend. They live in Islington,' I say.

'Would they mind?'

'Don't think so. They usually use mine as a base before they go to the Isle of Wight Festival. Theirs isn't the world's biggest flat, but they've got a couple of couches that we could crash on.'

'Sounds perfect.'

I pick up my phone and bang her a quick text to double-check.

'Now for the return we can get the last train at nine o'clock. That gets us back into London at half past ten, so we should make the last train back to Pompey.'

'Great.'

I sigh. 'Do you think it's a bit much? I mean, it's going to be one hell of a long day.'

'But that's the fun of the challenge, isn't it?'

'I guess so.'

'Come on, Abi, it'll be an easy one to tick off.'

My phone buzzes and I've got my reply from Jill with a yes to letting us crash.

'Looks like we've got a bed for the night before. So shall I book it?'

'Do it!'

I select the trains and hit continue – booking it before I can change my mind.

'Done,' I say, hitting return on the final screen. The booking reference comes up and a wave of excitement passes over me.

I know it's not really a holiday and it's not going to be relaxing, but anywhere you need to take a passport to get in brings out the inner child in me.

A little part of me wishes that it was Joseph and me going on the Eurostar together for a romantic trip. I could see us now having a cheeky bottle of champers on the train to start the trip off.

We'd stroll hand in hand along the Seine and eat our body weight in crêpes. Then he'd lean over and shower me with kisses before getting down on one knee and bringing out a tiny ring box ... I almost shout *I do* out loud before I realise that I'm lost in a ridiculous fantasy.

Thinking of Joseph reminds me that I still need to post the pictures of our cycle ride on Facebook.

'Ben,' I say, using a voice that my dad always calls my little-girl voice. It's reserved for when I'm feeling a bit pathetic and need someone to do something for me.

'Abi,' he says in a low voice.

'I don't suppose you'd get my camera out of my bag, would you?'

He shakes his head at me. 'You know you'll never be able to move if you don't get up soon.'

'I know, but it hurts so bad.'

Ben stands up. 'This is the last time I'm getting up. So is there anything else you need?'

'The lead to plug it into my laptop – it's in that dresser over there. And maybe some chocolate,' I say eyeing up the big bag of Maltesers on the side that has appeared, presumably from Ben.

Ben hands me my camera and crouches down to peer into the dresser.

'Whereabouts is the lead?'

'I don't know, somewhere in there – have a poke about,' I say, knowing I should get off my lazy bum and try and help him rather than letting him sort through my mess. It's where I stash things when I want the place to look tidy, and it's in desperate need of being cleared out.

It suddenly dawns on me what I've put in there recently. I jump off the sofa, hoping to wrestle him out of the cupboard before he comes across the stash of sexy lingerie that Joseph bought me.

'You're a secretly messy person, aren't you?' says Ben, pulling out a random DVD and an old digital camera.

'I'll take those,' I say, peering into the dresser by his side, but as I go to throw them back in, I disturb the pile of underwear and it comes tumbling out on to the floor.

It's a jumble of lace and silk and I recoil in horror, but amazingly Ben hasn't noticed. He's still focused on his mission of finding the wire. I desperately want to get him out the way without drawing attention to what's on the floor.

'I'd forgotten how messy it is in there. I'll have a look instead,' I say, pushing him out the way a little more forcefully than I'd planned, and he lands on his bum right next to the underwear.

He lunges for it in a way that scares me, but then I see what he's spotted.

'Is this the wire we're looking for?'

He's holding the camera wire that is indeed the one we're after, only it's hanging through a faux-leather basque.

I try and snatch it away, but Ben lifts up the basque, and I see it dawn on him what he's holding.

'Oh, that's, um, interesting, is that …?' His cheeks are colouring and he's looking a bit perplexed.

I take the basque off him and Ben, still clutching the wire, tries to pull it out of the fabric. Only it's stuck.

'Lift it up a little,' says Ben.

I want to shove it under my jumper, but I do as I'm told. I lift the basque in front of my face, hoping it will hide my embarrassment.

'OK, it seems to be stuck here in this hole. What the hell is this hole?' he says, looking at me with confusion.

I lift it to the side to see what he's talking about.

'It's a peephole,' I say in almost a whisper.

'A peephole?'

He's squinting in a bemused fashion. I get the impression that Ben doesn't have the same taste in lingerie as Joseph.

'What's that for?' Ben tilts his head to one side trying to work out exactly what he's looking at and quickly tugs at the lead before standing up.

Oh, dear. I'm going to have to spell it out for him.

'It's for the . . . um, nipples to show through,' I say, my voice squeaking.

His eyes widen and I quickly scrunch the basque up.

'Right … um …' he says, coughing and standing up quite abruptly. 'So, chocolate then.'

He turns and walks straight into the fridge.

'Who put that there?'

His cheeks are the reddest I've ever seen. They're practically the same colour as beetroot.

'You all right?' I ask as Ben drops the bag of Maltesers on the floor. I shove the basque back in the dresser and watch the newly clumsy Ben navigating his way back to the sofa.

'Uh-huh, fine. It's just I never pictured you as being the kind of girl to wear stuff like that.'

'What, you've never imagined me in sexy underwear? I'm heartbroken,' I say, knowing I'm being mean, but I've never seen the usually cool-as-a-cucumber Ben so flustered. It's actually nice to see him looking uncomfortable for a change.

'Oh, God. That came out really wrong. I just meant that it's always the ones you'd least expect.'

'How about we open the chocolate,' I say, standing up. As much as I'm enjoying seeing Ben squirm, I'm very aware that we're still discussing my underwear.

'What a great idea,' he says, retrieving the packet off the floor and sitting back down on the sofa. I sit next to him and plug the offending lead into my camera and connect it to my laptop.

'How good are you at blowing?' asks Ben.

My mouth falls open, before I hastily snap it shut. Just because I own kinky underwear does not mean to say I'm that kind of girl.

I turn to him about to give him a piece of my mind when I see that he's blowing a Malteser a few centimetres in the air.

'How do you do that?' I say in shock as I try and get my mind out of the gutter. In all my Malteser-eating years I've never seen anything like that.

Ben laughs and the chocolate falls. He catches it on his chin and puts it back on his lips before blowing again.

I can't resist trying to do the same, only my Malteser isn't going anywhere.

'It's not working,' I say, keeping my head tilted because now that I've moved it, it's as stiff as a board, just like every other part of my body. That sudden run off the sofa to dive for the underwear did not do me any favours.

'You've got to pout more, really push your lips together,' says Ben, demonstrating again before letting the Malteser drop and swallowing it.

I better perfect this before Ben eats all of the chocolate.

I try again, this time pouting like Victoria Beckham and blowing as hard as I can. But nothing. I truly am a failure. I can't even blow a light chocolate a millimetre into the air. I'd be at this all night if my neck wasn't so bloody sore.

Ben blows his next one really high as if to rub in the fact that I'm so inept.

'I can't believe you've never done this.'

'I don't think I'm ever going to be able to eat a Malteser normally again now.'

I yank my neck forward using my hand for support and see that the photos have loaded on the computer.

'Oh, my, I look so rough.'

There on the screen is me in all my hungover glory. I've got bags under my eyes the size of Tote bags and I look as green as the witch in *Wicked*.

'I think that was just after breakfast,' says Ben.

I can see that he's trying hard not to laugh.

I squint my way through the next few photos. I'm going to be struggling to find the perfect Facebook photo. One that might make Joseph jealous, rather than thankful that he dodged a bullet dating someone that looked like they were an extra from *The Walking Dead*.

'What's that one?' I say stopping the flicking and going back. There's a photo that I took. I'm not known for my great photography skills, but I'd been trying to get the famous Needles and Lighthouse into the shot. But what I seem to have captured in the bottom left-hand corner is Ben having a sneaky wee.

'Are you doing what I think you're doing?'

'Is that some sort of panoramic picture? I thought you were well occupied and would never notice.'

'That's one for Facebook then,' I say, rubbing my hands together like it's some sort of master criminal plan.

'You can't. I'm friends with my nan on Facebook – she'd never forgive me.'

'You're friends with your nan?'

The shock is clearly evident in my voice as Ben gives me a look.

'Why wouldn't I be? It's not like I'm eighteen any more and getting wasted all the time. There's not a lot to hide in my life.'

I would never even entertain the thought of being Facebook friends with my nan. Even if she did know what the Internet was. I won't even accept my mum's Facebook request.

'It's not like I have anything to hide,' I say, thinking my life is pretty dull in comparison to some of my Facebook friends. 'But I feel like it's a line that shouldn't be crossed.'

Ben shrugs. 'Most of my posts are bike-related so it probably sends my nan off to sleep anyway.'

'And everyone else,' I say laughing.

'Oi. I thought I'd converted you to the lycra life.'

'That doesn't sound dodgy in the slightest.'

'We all know you've got a dirty mind now that I've seen your taste in underwear.'

I cringe. He's never going to let me live that down. First Sian, now Ben. Perhaps I should get rid of that underwear, or at least hide it better.

'You have converted me in the sense that the bike might not live out the rest of its life chained to my balcony railings. I may actually use it again.'

'Then my work here is done, Daniel-San.'

'And without any need to use wax.'

'Well, we haven't got round to talking about how cyclists wax their leg hair off,' says Ben, totally deadpan. 'I can't believe you got my *Karate Kid* reference.'

'I can't believe you just told me you wax your legs,' I say, wrinkling my nose. 'How do women cope with that? The pressure for the woman to keep her legs stubble-free, you wouldn't want your man with less stubble than you.'

Ben lifts up his leg and rolls up his trouser leg.

'Look, hair. Gone are my racing days when I used to remove it.'

For some reason I stroke his leg hair as if to check that it's real, before I realise that that's totally weird. There have been a lot of boundaries overstepped tonight.

I quickly remove my hand and go back to the photos.

'What about this one?' I say, changing the subject as quickly as possible so that we don't dwell on the stroking incident.

'What for?' asks Ben.

'For the Facebook post. I thought perhaps this one, and maybe the one of the Needles – the one that doesn't feature the peeing – and one of me at the finish.'

'They're as good as any of them.'

I login to Facebook and I see my notification tab is red. I click on it and my stomach instantly flips. One new notification from Joseph Small. My fingers begin to shake as I double click on it. The photo that Sian took last night of Marcus, Bianca and me at the festival comes up and there is a grand total of fifteen likes. I hover over the list of names, and there amongst them is Joseph's.

He's seen the photo.

He's liked the photo.

Bloody hell.

My heart's racing and I'm having difficulty breathing. I try and tell myself that it's just a like. Yesterday I liked that my old school friend Becky had granola and berries for breakfast. It doesn't mean anything.

It's not a declaration of love, but I can't help the corners of my mouth creeping into a smile. It's confirmation that he's actually looked at one of my photos. He's seen me out socialising.

And, unlike today's photos, I don't look too bad. I'm ignoring my glassy-eyed stare and smudged mascara, but my cleavage looks amazing – that's all he'll notice, right? It's screaming at him to look at what he's missing. And he's bloody seen it! And liked it!

'Everything OK?' asks Ben.

I'd forgotten he was here. I'm so lost in my Facebook bubble where Joseph liking the photo is as good as a step away from him proposing marriage.

'More than OK. Look, Joseph liked my photo,' I say, grinning like I've got a coat hanger jammed down my throat.

'That's, um, great,' says Ben.

He doesn't sound like he thinks it's great. He clearly doesn't understand the significance of a like and its relation to the impending rekindling of romance. Or maybe his cynical heart is prohibiting excitement.

I get to work uploading the photos from today's trip, hoping that now I'm on Joseph's radar he'll be wowed by my cycling feat.

The music of the *Antiques Roadshow* fills the air and Ben stands up.

'Right, then, I think I'm going to head off.'

'What, now?' I say, barely taking my eyes off the screen.

'Yep. I'm beat.'

'Oh, really? I thought we were going to watch *The Blacklist*?'

'Yeah, but I think the early start has caught up with me. Another time,' he says, slipping his backpack over his shoulder and unlocking my back door.

He's practically out of the door before I can put my laptop down and prise myself off the sofa.

'Thanks for everything, Ben,' I say, leaning on the door for balance as he walks down the stairs into my garden.

'That's OK, I had a great time,' he says, without looking back.

He unlocks his bike and I can't help thinking that something's changed. Where's the easy-going Malteser-blowing Ben that was here half an hour ago?

'See you later,' he says, wheeling his bike out of the gate.

'See you,' I repeat, waving to him as he leaves. He's already swung his leg over his bike and ridden out into the alley.

I hear a ping and know instantly it's a Facebook notification. I manage to forget about my aching limbs and rush over to the laptop as quickly as they'll allow me.

It's a comment from Sian.

'*I can't believe you did that after last night! Well done you! I still feel rough.*'

I bet she does – she had loads more cider than me.

I wonder if Joseph's seen my new photos yet. He's not on Facebook 24/7 like Sian seems to be, but you never know. I could have posted at the exact same time that he was on.

A ripple of excitement passes over me. He could be looking at the photos right now. I put the laptop back on the table and let my imagination run wild.

I might not be able to move properly, but this plan to get Joseph back just might be working after all. And right now that kernel of hope is enough to make me want to finish the rest of the list as quickly as I can.

Chapter Fifteen

Three weeks and three days until D-Day. Three days since Joseph liked my photo at the festival, but no more likes or comments since.

'I think they're going to look fantastic,' says Linz as we walk back into the office.

I'm designing exhibition panels for a local museum and we've just come back from a client meeting there. I'd taken Linz along at Rick's insistence, but for once I didn't mind. Unlike our time at the printer, she stayed in the background and seemed to actually understand her role as a shadow.

'Thanks. I'm really pleased that they liked the designs.'

'How could they not,' says Linz, trowelling it on thick.

It's a bit unnerving because she's done nothing but compliment me all day. She hasn't tried to suggest any improvements or cast her young, fresh eye on anything, and it feels a little unnatural.

It pains me to say, but I'm actually finding her quite likeable today.

'Hi, ladies,' says Fran, as I get back to my desk.

'Hey, Fran, all right?' I say.

'Oh, yes, I'm fine. How was the museum?'

'Good, thank you. They liked the designs, and they've finally finished working out their layout so I've got the final measurements for the panels. In just a few tweaks I'll have the final drafts done today.'

I can't help feeling pretty upbeat.

For the first time in I can't remember how long, I feel on top of my work. My enthusiasm doesn't seem to be limited to when I'm in a client meeting; I'm genuinely enjoying it.

I don't know whether it's because I'm still buzzing from my cycle ride at the weekend or whether it's because Joseph liked the photo of me, but either way it's good for business.

I unpack my iPad and the notes from the meeting before picking up my phone and walking over to the coffee station.

As I wait for the kettle to boil I bring up Facebook. I wait for it to update itself, holding my breath as the notification button turns red. Ever since Joseph liked the photo of the festival at the weekend I've been checking to see if he's liked any more of my photos.

Two notifications. My heart races as I close my eyes and wish that it'll be him. But alas, it's my cousin and an old school friend liking my cycling photos.

I click on Joseph's page, to see if there is any evidence that he's replaced me. I hate the not knowing – I'm worried that I could be doing this for nothing.

He was tagged at a pub for lunch yesterday with Marcus. No surprise there, we often went to the same one on a Sunday for lunch. He really is a creature of habit.

My mind suddenly goes into overdrive as I wonder if there's a way I could speed up my plan. Maybe I could use his habitual nature to my advantage and bump into him. It couldn't hurt, could it?

'Boo,' says Giles, bringing me back to the office with a jolt.

'Oh,' I say, looking up and trying to work out where I am. Damn Facebook app.

I shove the phone into my pocket and make a cup of tea.

I'm walking back to my desk, when I see Rick bounding across to our table.

'Abi, have you uploaded those files from the meeting yesterday yet?'

My cheeks immediately burn as I realise that I'd completely forgotten.

Rick and I had a meeting with the council events department yesterday and they gave us a memory stick with the project information on. I was supposed to put it on the shared drive. I'd put the stick in my desk drawer before lunch and then completely forgotten about it. The lure of the duck wrap from the sandwich shop down the road had been too hard to ignore.

'I didn't,' I say honestly. Rick is a fan of honesty. 'I'll do it now.'

I slide open my drawer and look for it.

I dig through the tangled mess of elastic bands, Blu-tack and paperclips. I really must tidy this up, I think to myself as I find odd change and biro lids.

I can feel Rick impatiently looking over my shoulder.

'It was right here,' I say, confused about where it could have gone. I haven't opened the drawer since.

I pull open the paperwork drawer beneath it, in case it somehow fell through the solid bottom, but with that being tidier it's easy to see that there are no memory sticks in there.

'I hope you haven't lost it,' he says, sighing. 'It took us ages to get a meeting with them and I can't go back and ask for them to give us the files again.'

'Well, it can't be lost. It has to be here.'

'What's going on?' asks Linz, walking over. 'Hi, Rick.'

Even in my flustered state I don't fail to notice the eyelash-flutter she gives our boss.

'Hi, Linz. Abi here has lost an important memory stick.'

'I haven't lost it,' I say grumpily. 'It's got to be here somewhere.' I remember so vividly putting it away. I sigh.

I've scoured the drawer and it's definitely not there. I'm so worried, I can't even get excited that I've found half a packet of Starburst at the back.

I look around my desk in desperation, lifting files and notes to look underneath, just in case I'd absentmindedly taken the memory stick out to transfer the files.

'Is this what you're looking for?' asks Linz.

I look at where she's reaching down to the floor. She comes back up in what looks like a version of the *Legally Blonde* bend and snap move. But for once Rick doesn't seem to have noticed. He snatches the memory stick out of her hand.

There's no denying it's the right one as it has the council logo on it.

'You really should be more careful with these types of files.'

'I don't know how it got on the floor,' I say, scratching my head. Was I really too busy thinking about the duck wrap that I didn't put it away securely? 'I'll pop it on the drive now.'

I hold my hand out, but Rick snaps his fingers protectively around it.

'It's all right. I'll do it. Wouldn't want it to go missing again. Thank you, Linz, for finding it.'

Rick walks off and I'm left with Linz standing beside me, beaming, like an expectant puppy waiting for her reward.

But I've got no treats coming her way. I growl slightly in her direction and she goes off, ponytail swinging, to her desk.

'Could have happened to anyone,' says Fran, poking her head through the gap in our partition. 'Maybe one of the cleaners knocked it off your desk.'

I bite my tongue. It wasn't on my desk. I know it wasn't.

'Although it would have to be Linz that found it,' says Fran. 'As if she's not the golden child already in Rick's eyes. She's now playing the hero.'

I nod. She's got a point – of all the people to find it.

So much for my good mood. I was just starting to feel like I was getting back on Rick's good side after my working from home letter, but now he's pissed off at me again.

My phone rings and I sigh as I answer it.

'Hello, Design Works, Abi speaking.'

'Abi, hi, it's Lucinda here,' says a woman whose voice I don't recognise. I mentally flip through my work Rolodex but I can't think of any Lucinda.

'You know, from Spanish class?'

'Oh, Lucinda,' I say. I do know. 'How are you?'

'Fine, thanks.'

'Been practising?' I say, feeling guilty that I haven't picked up my textbook since last Wednesday's class.

'I made Thomas have a Spanish evening. I cooked my best tapas to get us in the mood, but to be honest, we ran out of conversation after about five minutes. It was fun at first – we made up new identities, but after hello, what's your name, where do you come from and what do you do, we sort of exhausted our vocabulary.'

I laugh. Lucinda's one of the absolute beginners like me.

'You're doing a lot better than I am,' I say, feeling relief that the college is having an open evening tonight and therefore we don't have a lesson.

'So,' says Lucinda, snapping into what sounds like professional mode. 'I'm calling about the design work we talked about last week. I think I've persuaded Thomas to go ahead.'

'That's great news,' I say. I'd forgotten all about that chat. We'd been talking in the break about the boutique hotel she and her husband run on the seafront, and how they'd just finished a big refurbishment. She'd casually mentioned that they were going to need to remarket it, and I'd passed her my business card. I hadn't given it another thought. I'd mainly done it because I'm always desperate to get rid of my cards – I don't want to be that sad loser with a massive stack of them if I ever leave.

'How do we go about it then?' she asks. 'It's all a bit new for us – the last time we did leaflets I did them myself at Pronto Printers.'

I cringe, glad that she can't see my wrinkled expression. I know that Pronto Printers do a perfectly good job of design templates and I can't blame businesses for using them, because they are very cost-effective, but that doesn't mean that it doesn't grate on me a bit.

'Right, well here we do things a little differently. We'd have to set up an initial meeting to establish your brief and talk through what you want. You know, if it's just leaflet design or whether you want us to do a whole package including rebranding and website.'

I try to remember the sales patter that the account managers would come out with, as it's not my usual forte.

'OK, right. Lots to think about then. So how soon can we meet? I don't want Thomas changing his mind.'

'I'll talk to Rick, our director, and see who he'll assign on accounts, then I'll get back to you ASAP about a meeting. It would probably be helpful for it to take place at the hotel so we can see the refurb and get ideas for the design. And seeing as you're not far away, I'm sure we can schedule something in for the next couple of days.'

'Great, that would be perfect. If Thomas doesn't have to go anywhere he'll be even happier.'

'Perfect, then. I'll go and have a chat with Rick now and get back to you.'

'Thanks, Abi. Speak soon.'

I can't wait to jump out of my chair and go and tell Rick the good news.

I tap on his door, still a bit nervous after the memory stick debacle.

'Come in,' he calls.

I push the door open and poke my head in nervously. He doesn't look very pleased to see me.

'What can I do for you now?' he says, sighing.

'Well,' I say, hovering in the doorway. 'I have a new client for us. I've just taken a phone call from a hotel on the seafront about doing their new leaflets. They're a little boutique hotel that's just had a refurb. I go to Spanish classes with the owners and you'll be pleased to know I gave them a business card when they said they might need some marketing done.'

I thought Rick would at least have smiled, but I'm clearly still in the bad books.

'Anyway,' I continue, 'they want to arrange a meeting with us to discuss a plan of action. They'd ideally like to do it as soon as possible.'

'OK. Give me their number and I'll call them.'

'OK. It's just I said I'd call them quite quickly to let them know about a meeting.'

I don't want to tell Rick that Lucinda stressed that she didn't want Thomas to have time to change his mind. I don't want him to think that they're going to be flaky clients.

'Fine. I'll call them now.'

'OK, great.'

I sense that he doesn't want me to hang around today and I walk back over to my desk.

'Everything all right?' asks Fran as I sit down.

'Yes, fine,' I say, still feeling slightly deflated.

All I want to do in this mood is go on Facebook and do some Joseph stalking, to see if I can plan my bumping into him, but instead, like the trouper I am, I pick up the notes that I took from the museum and start to enter the dimensions into the design files.

I don't notice the shadow fall over my desk at first, but I get the sense that someone is standing there.

'Hi, Rick,' I say with trepidation.

'Abi, great work with the Vista Hotel. We've had a quick chat and they want a complete rebranding operation. New leaflets, business cards, adverts, websites.'

His smile is infectious, and I feel my frown turning upside down.

'I've set up a meeting with them for tomorrow afternoon. They're keen to get the ball rolling before the summer season.'

'Perfect.'

'I've got Pat to put it on the calendar for us.'

I'm pleased to hear the word us, after the memory stick debacle I'd half thought that he'd take the account away from me and give it to Linz.

Speaking of whom, she's come up behind us.

'Ah, Linz,' says Rick. 'You can come to the meeting tomorrow too. There's going to be a lot of work with this new client and I'm sure that Abi's going to need a hand with the workload as I think it's going to be quite a quick turnaround.'

Linz flashes her pearly whites at Rick.

'Who's the client?'

'A boutique hotel on the seafront. Abi brought them in. See, you should always network as you never know where your next client is coming from.'

He walks off, and I don't think I'm imagining that he's got a spring to his step.

'Well done, Abi,' says Fran, leaning between the partition.

'Thank you.' My cheeks colour at the praise.

'Yes, well done you,' says Linz. Her tone is less flattering than before.

I turn back to my Mac and try to channel the buzz and enthusiasm I had this morning. I seem to have been forgiven for my earlier office faux pas.

It just shows you what you get if you take matters into your own hands. If I hadn't given out the business card I would still be in the bad books. Maybe that's what I need to do with the list too – dangle a carrot in Joseph's face, or in this case, me. It couldn't hurt, could it?

Chapter Sixteen

Three weeks, two days until the abseil and possibly only hours until I get back together with Joseph if the stalking plan works …

Since I decided to try and see if I could help the list along a bit quicker by bumping into Joseph, I haven't been able to think of anything else. I've got a busy weekend ahead of me. It's the big Snowdon adventure, and having convinced Sian to come, I've got to go on an emergency trip to an outlet shopping centre tomorrow night after work so she can buy walking boots. Which only leaves me with tonight to put my hasty plan into action.

It's Thursday evening, and luckily for me I know exactly where he will be: his local Waitrose. I'd much rather have tried to run into him somewhere more glamorous that sold alcohol that you could drink in situ, but beggars can't be choosers.

The only slight spanner in the works is that I don't know exactly what time he'll be here. He'll be coming after work, which could mean anywhere from six o'clock until about seven thirty, depending on how busy he is at the office. Which means potentially I've got to make my shop last an hour and a half. It's either that or hang around outside on a bench and wait, but somehow I don't think that will give off the same air of casually bumping into one another.

I decide to start my trip with a familiarisation of the supermarket, walking round every aisle with an empty trolley to get the lie of the land, trying to work out if there are any good spots to bump into him. So far the wine aisles are looking the best, as they're fairly near the entrance and in a semi-circular area that means you get a good vantage point of at least three other aisles. Also, I know that Joseph can't resist walking past a wine shop any more than I can resist walking down the confectionery aisle.

Now to try and make this look like a real shopping expedition. I wander down the sweet aisle, filling my trolley with bits for Snowdon. I stock up on emergency chocolate rations and sugary sweets that are going to glue my teeth together, but might give me a much needed sugar rush when I'm halfway up a mountain. I'm not sure if you bonk when hiking, but I don't want to find out.

I throw in some giant packs of crisps for everyone to share whilst I'm at it – although part of me wonders if they won't make it past the car journey up with Sian.

I make sure that I don't get too focused on the shopping, and keep scanning for Joseph, I don't want to come all this way and accidentally miss him.

I head down the cosmetics aisle and put in different foot lotions and blister plasters, and then remember that I probably should stock up on some tampons whilst I'm here. See, this is a really useful shop after all, and totally not just stalking.

I've just thrown the box of tampons into my trolley before I look at it from Joseph's perspective. My trolley looks like it belongs to a teenage girl who has a severe case of manky feet and is about to have a sleepover. There's no way I can bump into him with this crap in my trolley, necessities for the weekend or not.

I break out into a cold sweat, and start to go into *Supermarket Sweep* mode, as I hastily try to replenish the shelves with what I've taken.

I'm just putting back a packet of chocolate fingers when I hear my name being called.

'Abi. I thought it was you.'

I look up in surprise to see Ben's girlfriend Tammy in front of me.

'Hiya,' I say, as enthusiastically as possible. I push the chocolate fingers back onto the shelf a little too forcefully making the rest of the packets clatter noisily onto the floor.

I bend down to pick them up, and hastily shove them back in embarrassment.

'What are you doing out here?' I say to Tammy. I got the impression that she lived in Portsmouth too.

'I work round the corner – how about you?'

'I had a client meeting near here,' I say, in a very parroted voice. I've been rehearsing it in the car on the way over to make it sound natural, but it still sounds robotic.

'Oh, right. Having a bit of a binge, are we?' she says, peering into my trolley, which is solely full of chocolate.

'Just getting some bits for the Snowdon weekend – you know, for everyone to share.'

I look into her basket and notice it's all bean sprouts and fresh vegetables. Of course it is.

'Oh, right, yes, I forgot you were going to that. It's a shame I'm racing. I had a really good time when we went last year. The bunkhouse is a little rough around the edges, but it just adds to the fun of it.'

'Can't wait.'

I'm lying. I'd been really looking forward to it, but the closer I get to it and the more I find out about the rustic charm from Giles, the more I'm starting to worry.

'So your little list should be finished soon.'

Hopefully even sooner if it goes well in the supermarket tonight.

'Yes, after Snowdon, it will just be wine tasting, a 10k run, the trip to Paris and the abseil.'

It makes it sound like I've still got loads left, but with the 10k and Paris booked for the week after next I'm really ploughing through it at a rate of knots. My stomach sinks at the thought of the abseil. At this rate if I'm not careful I'm going to be dangling off that tower before I know it.

'Ben mentioned that he was going to Paris with you,' she says, nodding.

I suddenly feel a little awkward. 'Um, yes, I do hope you don't mind me borrowing your boyfriend for the day.'

To go to the most romantic city in the world.

'Why should I mind? Besides, Ben says that it's the last task he's helping you with as then you'll have practically finished your list. Then I'll get my boyfriend back all to myself. Without the list you'll have no reason to spend time with him any more, will you?'

I'm taken aback as the words sink in. I'm pretty sure she's just weed on her territory by telling me that I'm not allowed to spend time with her boyfriend once the list is finished. She's got a polite smile on her face, but her tone's changed. It's more like the one she used when talking to Sian.

'I think he felt sorry for you. Thinking you're out of your depth with the challenges, but then once they're done, they're done, aren't they?' She raises an eyebrow in such a way that I'm left in no doubt that she's warning me off spending time with Ben.

I haven't really thought about what will happen when I finish doing my list, but I guess I'd assumed we'd stay friends. We get on really well and it's refreshing to have a male friend that's purely platonic, but clearly Tammy's got other ideas.

'I guess so – no reason at all,' I say, looking her in the eye to indicate that I've understood her warning.

'Great. Well, I best get on. I'm off to Ben's tonight. Good luck with Snowdon!' she says, the cheer entering her voice once more.

For a moment I'm too stunned to move. I knew from the way she acted with Sian that she could be a little bitchy, but on the couple of occasions I've met her she's been nothing but nice to me. Maybe Ben got it wrong and she's more bothered about Paris than he realises.

But I don't have time to dwell on Ben and Tammy's relationship when I've got my own to sort out.

I look back down at the crap in my trolley and continue repacking the aisles. I glance at my watch – it's half past six already. Wow. I've managed to burn half an hour and have nothing in my trolley to show for it. Not bad.

I stare at the entrance again, this time using Tammy's example and stocking up on fresh items. I have to be slightly careful as I'm away for the weekend so I don't want to buy too much, but I guess I could always make a soup with them when I get home. If I get home, that is. Imagine how amazing it would be if Joseph swept me off my feet *An Officer and a Gentleman* style and walked me out of the supermarket, abandoning our trolleys and taking me back to his house …

I snap myself out of the fantasy. I wonder what goes into a soup?

A thought pops into my head as I remember reading an article about supermarket dating, where single people filled their trolley with green produce to advertise that they were available. Maybe if I had lots of green veg in my trolley it would subliminally give Joseph the idea that I'm still up for grabs.

I quickly peruse the veg aisle and by the time I'm finished I have nearly every green vegetable known to man. Pak choi and fennel soup? I'm sure that's a thing.

I look proudly at my trolley and start to think about what else would look impressive to Joseph. Perhaps some nice wine? I spend the next ten minutes agonising over two Riojas and in the end plump for one that's fifteen pounds. It's way over my usual budget, but I guess it'll be worth every penny if it helps to convince Joseph that I learnt a thing or two about wines when I was with him.

I look round frantically, realising that I haven't been looking out for him, when I catch the eye of the security guard. He looks at me intently for what feels like minutes. In the end, I hastily push my trolley along to the next aisle.

I end up in the dessert aisle and ponder whether to put one in my trolley. I want to make it look like I'm going to cook a nice meal, but I don't want it to look like I'm cooking for two. Yet, if I choose a dessert for one then I feel that looks a little sad. Why is this so bloody difficult?

I take a quick look around me in the hope of spotting Joseph, but instead I see a security guard hovering a few feet away from me.

'Um, is there something you wanted?'

'No, no. You carry on,' he says, waving his hand.

I turn back round but get the feeling he's still watching me closely.

'Have you never seen anyone shopping before?' I say grumpily, turning to face him.

'Funnily enough, it's what I spend my day doing.'

'Well, then, I don't know why you're taking such a great interest in me.'

'Um, maybe it's because you packed one trolley full of items, dashed round like you were on speed to put it back, then packed another full of completely different items. Not to mention you seem to be wandering round in circles.'

'I'm just keeping an eye out, that's all.' My cheeks puff red. Has he never seen someone trying to stalk their ex in a supermarket before? 'As far as I know none of that is a crime.'

'No, no, and neither is me standing here doing my job.'

I turn back to the desserts. OK, so this is going to look totally normal. I'm sure Joseph won't think anything of the fact that I'm being trailed by the security guard. It just adds to the easy, breezy tone I'm trying to set.

I hastily shove in a box with two cheesecakes and skulk off.

I speed up my shop a little, to please my new security guard BFF and end up with a trolley stuffed full of fresh pasta and worldly breads, and things that I hope make me look exciting and extravagant. I want it to scream, look how over you I am, I'm no longer surviving on a diet of pure crap.

Bob, the security guard (I checked out his name tag), and I head back to the wine aisle. If I don't bump into Joseph soon, I'll have to give up, because even I'm beginning to realise how crazy and desperate I look.

I've just found what I think is a bargain gem of a Chablis to take to Snowdon when I hear Joseph call my name.

'Abi?'

I'm bent right over with my arse in the air, hardly my best angle, and I hastily bring myself up to standing and try to pretend that I'm shocked to see him.

'Joseph, how nice to see you.' My voice becoming suddenly posh and a bit waif-like.

'Yeah, nice to see you too,' he says, nodding. 'What brings you to Havant?'

'Oh, I had a client meeting here, and then thought I'd miss the traffic going back into Portsmouth.'

He nods, and I'm relieved he bought it. As unpleasant as it was to bump into Tammy, maybe it was useful for something because the cover story sounded much more natural second time around.

There's a pause and we're both smiling politely at each other, and I'm wondering what to say. I've spent so much time working out what to put in my sodding trolley, but maybe my time would have been better spent thinking about what I was going to actually say.

'So, what have you been up to?' I say, clutching at straws. The real question I want to ask him is whether he's dating again yet.

'Oh, this and that,' he says, running a hand through his curls. 'You know, the usual. Work, work and more work. Nothing exciting.'

I nod. He hasn't started his list then …

I take a cursory glance into his trolley and try to guess his status. There's a worrying amount of red peppers and tomatoes in there – is that the red stop sign à la supermarket dating?

'Did I see on Facebook that you've taken up cycling?'

I look back at him in surprise. Ding, ding, ding! Jackpot!

'Yes, I have. Thought it was about time that I owned a bike. Everyone else in Portsmouth seems to. Plus, it's a great way to get fit.'

I try and suck in my tummy in a bid to make it look like I've at least made some dent in shifting the post-break-up pounds. But it seems to have become more attached to me than ever and it doesn't seem to be going anywhere, despite my almost ten-fold increase in exercise.

'It looks like you were doing some tough rides.'

Inside I'm lit up like a flipping Christmas tree. I love the way he started off like he wasn't sure it was me that was doing the cycling and yet now he's getting specific about individual photos.

'Yeah, it was up at Queen Elizabeth Country Park – they've got some really good trails up there.'

'Looks it,' he says, nodding.

I take another sneaky peak in his trolley, but it looks like he's only at the start of his shop and apart from the abundance of red veg there are no clues about his status.

There's another pause and it seems like he wants to say something else. He's got a look in his eyes that I can't read. I used to think that I knew what he was thinking, but after he dumped me out of the blue, I realised that I didn't.

'That's a nice bottle of wine you've got there,' he says, pointing to the one in my trolley that I proudly put alone in the end bit exactly for this purpose.

'Is it? That's good to know. I'm off to Snowdon with friends this weekend and thought we'd jolly well deserve a little treat after the hike.'

Why am I talking like I'm in *Downton Abbey*?

'Sounds impressive. I think I'm working all weekend. Dull, huh?'

I want to swoon and say that he could never be dull in my eyes, but I manage a little coquettish laugh instead.

I clock Bob the security guard out of the corner of my eye and he's shaking his head at me as if the penny's dropped at what I was doing. He slumps off out of my view, disappointed that I'm no longer on Havant's Most Wanted List.

'Right, well I best be going,' I say, thinking that I should perhaps leave him wanting more. My main objective was to find out if he'd seen me on Facebook – which he has.

'OK, well, it was nice to see you again,' he says. He opens his mouth to say something else before a quick shake of the head. 'I'll see you around again, then?'

There's a hint of a question to his voice and my stomach fills with butterflies.

'Yes, take care,' I say, hurrying away whilst my legs are still working. I wheel all the way to the checkout before I let out a deep breath and consider what I've done.

It might have been one small step for man, but it was a giant leap for me. As I very cheerily (and very un-me-like) unpack and pack my shopping again, I can't help hoping that I've nudged Joseph along a little more. Reminded him in person what he's missing.

'That'll be £110.57, please,' says the cashier.

The smile instantly falls off my face. How the bloody hell did that happen?

I hastily shove my credit card into the chip and pin machine and wince. It better have nudged Joseph along as at this rate I'm going to be broke before the list is up.

Chapter Seventeen

Three weeks until completion, and another challenge bites the dust ... well, almost.

'Here we are,' I say as I park next to what looks like a derelict barn.

'Here we are where?' says Sian. 'You're not telling me that we're staying in there?'

I look up and shiver. The barn has crumbling brickwork and one wall missing, exposing it to the elements that sweep across the valley. It's my idea of holiday hell.

'No, we've just got to park the car here. Look, there's Giles's Ford Focus. We've got to get to the bunkhouse on foot.'

Sian's jaw drops; it's as if I've told her that we've got to walk barefoot over hot coals. I hadn't told her until now as I desperately wanted her to come and not change her mind.

'We have to walk?' she asks, her eyebrows practically lodging themselves in her hairline.

'We are on a walking holiday. Let's boot up,' I say, trying to rally some enthusiasm.

To be honest I had the same reaction, but Giles told me to man up, after all it's just a half-kilometre walk across a field, and, as he pointed out, tomorrow we're going to walk God knows how many kilometres up a mountain.

'I thought the whole point of going on this type of walking holiday was so that you stayed next to a pub.'

'There are definitely no pubs around here,' I say as we move away from the barn and start walking through the boggy field.

The little bunkhouse we're walking towards is acting like a beacon in the distance – it seems a lot further away than half a kilometre. Thank goodness Giles lent me one of his old backpacks. There's no way my trusty suitcase would have made it.

I just hope the others have done a good job with the food and booze. Because of the access issue the boys had suggested doing a food kitty and stocking up. Apparently the owner said she'd quad bike the supplies in when they arrived.

'Are we nearly there yet?' asks Sian.

'I don't think so,' I say; we've been going for all of about five minutes and the bunkhouse seems to be getting further away with each step. It must be some type of optical illusion due to its sunken position in the field.

I'm mildly concerned that we're going the wrong way. But there's only a narrow path of beaten-down grass and I don't fancy traipsing through the waist-deep stuff. It's the kind of wild grass that you know would be all tickly if it caught bare flesh, and goodness knows what lives in it.

'So you never did finish telling me about the Isle of Wight,' says Sian.

'I don't think there's much more to tell.'

In the car on the way to Snowdonia I gave her a brief overview of the hangover start, and duly reprimanded her for her part in it, and then I described our day as best I could. It's hard to condense a ten-hour ride into a concise conversation.

'Right. So you spent the whole day with Ben, during which he agreed to go to Paris with you, and there's nothing else to tell.'

I don't like where this line of questioning is heading.

'No, not really. You'll see this weekend. Ben's a really nice guy. He's simply trying to help me achieve my bucket list.'

'Uh-huh,' says Sian.

I can't see her face because we're walking single file and she's behind me, but I can picture exactly what it will look like. Her left eyebrow will be arched right up to the sky and she'll have her lips pursed together smugly.

'Really, he's just being nice.'

'Mm-hmm.'

I can tell the look is getting smugger and I spin round so Sian nearly comes crashing into me.

'What are you doing?' she says, laughing.

'There's nothing going on with me and Ben,' I say, looking her deep in the eye. 'He's got a girlfriend, who made it perfectly clear to me that my friendship with Ben ends when the list does.'

'When did you see her again?'

Oh, crap. I hadn't told Sian about my trip to the supermarket on Thursday. I knew she would smell a rat if I trotted out my excuse that I bumped into Joseph there by accident.

'I ran into her when I was food shopping the other day.'

'Right, well, I thought they weren't that serious anyway.'

'Sian,' I say, and this time it's my turn to raise an eyebrow. 'Some people take relationships seriously.'

I turn back round and continue walking.

'It's just that you did say that you were doing your bucket list to mend your broken heart, and what better way than finding someone else.'

'That sort of defeats the object.'

Of course the object is to win Joseph back, but Sian doesn't know that.

'I know that a bucket list is all about finding yourself and all that deep shit, but what if it's not yourself you're supposed to find.'

'For someone that doesn't really believe in love, you're sounding increasingly like a hopeless romantic.'

'Hey,' says Sian. 'You take that back.'

I feel like I'm getting my own back and pushing Sian's buttons.

She'd had one of those incredibly serious boyfriends in her latter teen years, and they'd been engaged when she'd arrived at uni. He'd gone to nearby Southampton so that they could continue seeing each other, but she found out that he'd cheated on her in Freshers' Week and that's when the Sian that I know – the kick-ass, take-no-crap-from-men girl – was born.

She didn't hole herself up inside eating Chinese takeaways and feeling sorry for herself. Oh, no, Sian threw herself into uni life and soon cemented her position on the party scene. Flings were as common as hangovers in her life.

Whatever really happened with that boy scarred Sian for life in the romance stakes, and I've given up trying to fix her. If she used to be a romantic, she's buried it so far inside you would need a miner to extract it.

'Hello there!' shouts a voice.

I look up and see Laura standing in front of the bunkhouse.

'Hiya,' I wave as enthusiastically as I can, but it's a bit half-hearted because I'm knackered. I might have been doing a lot of exercise on the bike lately, but I'm not used to walking with a heavy pack on my back.

'Giles is just putting the kettle on.'

'Now that's music to my ears,' says Sian.

We eventually arrive outside the little bunkhouse. It's a one-storey stone building set in a little dip in the fields.

'This is lovely,' I say taking in the surroundings, and for the first time since getting out of the car, appreciating the scenery. The green rolling hills look like something out of the Wales Tourist Board brochure. I love the little stone walls dotted around the landscape, breaking up the view. It's a view that screams we're properly in the middle of nowhere.

'Did you get stuck in traffic on the way up?' says Laura.

I bet they were here hours ago. The truth is that we had stopped for a long leisurely lunch somewhere past Birmingham.

And we had a lie-in. Something that early bird Ben wouldn't know anything about.

'No, we were really lucky, weren't we, Sian?'

'Yeah, really lucky.'

We follow Laura into the bunkhouse and it's just as beautiful on the inside. Heavy stone walls, and dark slate-coloured floor tiles. She shows us to a room where we can dump our bags. It's not quite the Ritz – just bunk beds and a rail to hang your clothes on.

The kitchen isn't any more luxurious. A hob and a kettle sit on an empty worktop. It's the most Spartan place I've ever stayed. I guess it's only one step up from camping, but at least there's a flushing loo inside. Or at least I hope there is.

'Hey, guys,' says Giles, turning round from the kettle. He hands me a steaming cup of tea and it instantly warms my hands. The stone walls and floors might look pretty, but they add a certain chill to the air. 'How do you take your tea, Sian?'

As she tells him, we're joined in the kitchen by Ben, Doug and another man.

'Hi, Abi,' Ben beams.

'Hiya,' I say, trying not to be as enthusiastic as I want to be because I can tell that I'm being scrutinised by Sian.

'This is my friend, Pete,' he says gesturing to the man beside him.

'Nice to meet you, Pete. I'm Abi.'

He nods a hello back.

'And I'm Sian.'

Uh-oh, I don't fail to notice the sparkle that has just appeared in her eyes.

'Nice to meet you both.'

'And you remember Doug from Hayling Island?'

We nod, and I smile my hello. Sian barely gives him a passing glance. She seems to have eyes only for Pete.

To be fair, he's almost her type. He's not suited and booted, but he's clean-shaven, with neatly-styled dark hair. He's wearing tight walking trousers and a fitted charcoal fleece that matches his eyes.

For an awkward minute we're all standing on ceremony in the kitchen. I'm too busy worrying that Sian's going to end up sleeping in someone else's bunk. With only seven of us here, that has the potential to be very awkward.

'Shall we go through to the lounge? I've got the fire going,' says Ben.

My body responds by shivering. 'That sounds perfect,' I say, realising that I'm actually quite cold.

I follow Ben into the lounge, and I don't know what I was expecting but in my head I was visualising curling up in a comfy armchair and dozing off in front of the fire. In reality the Spartan house strikes again, and the square room is lined with wooden church pews along three of the walls with a large coffee table in the middle. The other wall is given over to the fire. There's not even a cosy rug on the floor.

'Wow, this is rustic,' says Sian.

'Yep, it's really geared up for muddy walkers – absolutely no soft furnishings.'

'Just what I need after a long drive,' mutters Sian.

'Believe me, it will get worse after tomorrow's walk,' laughs Ben. 'The trick is to grab some of the duvets and pillows from the rooms and put them on the benches.'

'I'll get them,' says Pete.

'I'll help,' says Sian.

I raise an eyebrow at her as she leaves. She's not usually known for her willingness to volunteer. She's a bit like the Queen and usually waits for things to be brought to her.

'You know all the tips and tricks,' I say, thankful that at least someone knows what they're doing. If it was left to me I would have had a sore bum after hours sitting on the wooden benches.

'We stayed here last year,' says Ben.

The sound of what I can only describe as cackling rattles down the hallway. Sian's charm offensive has clearly begun.

When they return Pete and Sian distribute the bare duvets and pillows and we line the wooden benches the best we can.

'That's better,' says Laura.

We all sit down in the imposing room and the silence falls upon us once again.

'So,' I say. 'What now?'

I realise that soft furnishings aren't the only thing missing. There's no TV and no stereo. Is this going to be the longest weekend ever?

I wonder how Joseph would have done this. I'm sure he would have rented a luxury cottage or stayed in one of the five-star B&Bs that we drove past en route. All soft bedding and waterfall showers.

The more I think about this list, the more I can't picture Joseph doing any of it. Maybe it's because the way I'm approaching it is so different to how he would have done it. But I just can't imagine him donning a cagoule and hiking boots.

'Well, it'll be getting dark soon, so we could start doing dinner,' says Laura, smiling and snapping me out of my thoughts once again.

'Right, and then after dinner?'

'Have a few beers and chill out ready for tomorrow's early start,' says Ben.

'Right,' I say, nodding.

'Don't sound so thrilled at the prospect of actually having to talk to us,' he says, turning to me as the others start to talk amongst themselves.

'Well, come on. A whole weekend of having to make conversation, it's going to be a big ask.'

'Believe me, some of the best nights I've had were in these kind of bunkhouses. It's much better when there's no TV. By tomorrow night you won't even miss it.'

I'm about to argue that criticising the judges on *The Voice* is my usual Saturday night warm-up act, but he's right, it's not going to kill me.

'I bet once the cards come out, you'll change your tune. Unless you're as bad at cards as you were at riding bikes.'

'I'll have you know I'm an excellent poker player.'

'Did someone say poker?' calls Sian from the other side of the room, where she's sitting very close to Pete. 'I love poker, although I'm best at the strip variety.'

Ben raises an eyebrow.

'Don't get any ideas,' I say to him.

'No,' says Laura, 'that's not a game to be playing when you've got a married couple in your midst.'

Or when I've bought my frumpiest underwear. There is nothing attractive about my old Marks and Spencer's sports bra, but I don't want the puppies bounding all up and down the mountains.

'We could play shithead,' I say, offering a fully-clothed alternative.

'Now you're talking,' says Ben.

'Why don't I get the pasta on?' says Laura. 'And then we can start the evening's festivities.'

'Great plan,' I say, suddenly excited rather than miserable about the night ahead. 'I'll give you a hand.'

'Shithead!' I shout into Ben's face, laying the card down and standing up from his bench to do a victory dance.

The boys are not happy. That's the third game in a row that either Laura or I have won.

I collapse back down on to the folded duvet that's acting as a cushion and watch the rest of the game unfold.

'I can't believe you won again,' mutters Ben. He's still holding a large hand of cards, and if he's not careful he's going to end up shithead again. A position he's held to my king status twice now, and both times I've had him running round the bunkhouse doing my errands. A cup of tea here. A beer there.

'So what is it this time?' he says, throwing down the last of his cards when he narrowly loses out to Giles who has a smug look on his face. 'Beer, tea, a grape peeled for you?'

'Do we have any grapes?'

'Alas, no,' he says, shaking his head.

'Hmm, well, I've still got tea, and I'm not hungry,' I say, looking round for inspiration. It seems like a bit of a waste not to get him to get me anything. 'Oh, I know. You could get me my foot cream. It's in my make-up bag, in one of the side pockets in my backpack.'

Ben gives me a mock salute, and goes off out of the room.

'Why can't I win with you as the shithead,' says Laura to Giles. 'I'd love for you to be my bitch.'

'But I'm always your bitch, sweetie.' Giles leans over and gives her a quick squeeze on the arm.

There's a real intimacy between those two that's lovely to see. She brings out a whole different side to him to the one I usually see in the office. There he's all gangly limbs and goofy jokes.

'Right, then, here you go,' says Ben, handing me the foot cream.

I'm about to take it when he sighs.

'I'm guessing you're going to make me rub it on your feet too, aren't you?'

That wasn't what I had in mind, but now that he's mentioned it, a little foot rub would be quite nice. It would be good to give my feet some pampering before they trek up those hills, and we did walk all that way from the car.

I open my mouth to say what a wonderful idea, when I catch Sian's expression out of the corner of my eye. I know that smug, I-told-you-so look.

Instead I reach over and take the cream. 'You're OK. Maybe if I win again.'

'Something to look forward to,' says Giles, raising his eyebrows. 'I sit on the opposite side of the office and I can still smell those bad boys.'

'Oi,' I say, reaching under my bum and grabbing the pillow I'm sitting on and playfully beating him round the head.

'Not that I'm put off by the thought of stinky feet, but I think I'm going to head to bed,' says Ben, trying to hide a yawn behind his hand. 'I want to get up early tomorrow and go for a blast on the bike before we set off.'

'Are you mad?' I say, thinking there is something seriously wrong with this man. Surely that much exercise isn't good for anyone.

'I can't miss having a ride on these hills. Besides, it's not like we're climbing a mountain or anything tomorrow. Oh, wait ...' He gets up, smiling, and Laura stands up too.

'We probably should get to bed too,' she says, rubbing Giles's shoulders. 'That early start this morning did me no favours.'

We all slowly stand up. All except Sian, who's looking up at us.

'But we can't go now, I haven't won yet,' she says a little grumpily. 'Plus, there's still wine to drink.' She shakes the half-full bottle of red at us.

'We can pop the cork back in and have it tomorrow,' I say.

I'm instantly hit with a look of death.

I shrug. I'm too sleepy to respond to telepathic death threats.

Everyone starts to drift towards the door and I hold my hand out to Sian, who ignores it.

'Pete, you'll stay and have a night cap with me, won't you?'

He looks between Sian and me and then back at the others who are disappearing out of the door.

'Um, I think we should probably call it a night. You don't want to be hungover for the walk.'

I shudder at the thought. I'm not doing two of my challenges feeling like I'm knocking at death's door.

Sian sighs loudly, and folds her arms like a petulant schoolgirl.

'Look, we don't have to get up early on Monday so we can stay up later tomorrow night,' says Pete, a slight twinkle appearing in his eye.

'You promise?' asks Sian.

'I promise.'

Oh, boy, I think, he's on a promise all right.

Ignoring my previous efforts to help her up, she reaches her hand out to Pete and allows him to pull her to standing. It doesn't escape my attention that they continue to hold hands until they're almost out of the room.

Tomorrow's supposed to be all about me ticking mountain hiking off my bucket list, and I selfishly hope that Sian and Pete wait until they are back in the safety of the bunkhouse before anything happens. Sian's not averse to al fresco fornication and I don't want to have to worry about them nipping off to some crofter's hut for a quickie. It's going to be hard enough getting up that mountain without keeping tabs on my best friend when she's acting like a horny teenager.

Getting up the mountain. I'd almost forgotten with all the fun and frivolity tonight that we were here for that reason.

Tomorrow I'll be conquering my personal Everest. I try and tell myself that it can't be worse than cycling the Isle of Wight with a hangover, but I'm not entirely convinced.

One thing's for sure: I'm here now and I'm going to do it, by hook or by crook.

Chapter Eighteen

Two weeks, six days of the list to go, and the end is nigh. After today there'll only be three more challenges to do ...

Something weird is happening to me. I don't really know how to explain it. I'm standing on a plateau of rock, looking out at the mist-shrouded valley below. I've got my cagoule pulled tightly round my face with only my eyes visible, and I look like I'm doing an impression of Kenny from *South Park*. Despite the Gore-Tex waterproofs my body feels damp and my hair is starting to go frizzy. My calves are aching in that freshly used way and I could really do with a sit-down and a cuppa. But you know what? I'm enjoying myself.

At fourteen fifty-six this afternoon I, Abi Martin, reached the summit of Mount Snowdon. There might not have been fixed ropes, crampons or oxygen, but by golly I stood on my first mountain top. There wasn't a right lot to see, thanks to the mist, but I know I was there, and I got my all-important photo.

It was actually surprisingly easy. We took a vote this morning and because of the weather we opted to go for one of the easier routes up. No one fancied scrambling up damp rock with limited visibility. Despite the rain, it was all quite civilised – there was even a tea shop at the top, and I treated myself to a scone laden with clotted cream and strawberry jam, and a hot chocolate with whipped cream and marshmallows. Well, I must have burned off a lot of calories on the hike.

And, to my amazement, Sian has been very well behaved. It seems that the rain has dampened her horn. She can be as naughty as she wants tonight now that I've achieved my objective – the photo of me on top of Snowdon.

'Did you ever wonder what the magic words were?' says Ben, walking up behind me.

For a second it takes me a moment to register what he's talking about, before I remember our last conversation had been about *SuperTed*.

'I can't remember there being magic words. Didn't he just rip off his fur and there was his SuperTed outfit?' I say, trying to remember the beloved eighties cartoon.

'Yes, but only after he said something.'

'No,' I say, shaking my head. 'I don't remember that. Or what Bananaman said either, come to think of it.'

'I don't think he said anything, did he? Didn't he just eat a banana?'

'Oh, right, that would make sense,' I say, laughing. This trip down memory lane has distracted me almost all the way down the mountain.

'What are you two talking about?' asks Sian, catching us up.

'*Bananaman* and *SuperTed*.'

'Right,' she says. I can hear her rolling her eyes, even if I can't see it. 'This weather is seriously pissing me off now. My feet are all soggy.'

'We're nearly back at the bunkhouse,' says Ben. 'And then you can have a nice lukewarm shower.'

Sian lets out a humph. Ben takes it as a sign to leave us alone and walks a little faster to catch up with Giles.

'So, it's nice watching you two together. Clearly just platonic friends,' says Sian with a sarcastic tone to her voice.

'Well, that's what we are.'

'Yeah, really looks like it. You obviously can't see what's in front of your nose. I mean you've been talking to each other non-stop all the way up and all the way down this bloody mountain.'

I think over the day, and she's right – I haven't really spoken to anyone else. I suddenly feel a bit bad that I begged Sian to come and I've left her on her own the whole time.

'I'm so sorry. I've been neglecting you.'

'Don't be daft. I've really enjoyed getting to know Laura and Giles. They're really sweet.'

I feel a moment of relief that she's not having a terrible time.

'But, really, you and Ben – I haven't seen you laugh this much in ages.'

'We've been talking about children's TV programmes, and he does the best impressions,' I say, trying not to laugh at the memory of his *Rugrats* one.

'Well, I never saw Joseph make your face crease up like that.'

'Joking around isn't his style,' I say. Joseph is one of those people who always smiles but never really seems to laugh. In fact, in our whole relationship I don't think I ever heard him do a proper belly laugh once.

'And yet you thought he was the one? Imagine a lifetime without laughter.'

I want to defend mine and Joseph's relationship. There's a serious side to love too. It's not all fun and games.

'It's not just the laughing,' says Sian, before I get a chance. 'You've been really tactile with Ben all day.'

'No, I haven't,' I say, folding my arms over my chest defensively.

'Um, I think you'll find you have. There's been shoves and arm hits, not to mention the hug when Laura took your picture.'

'It wasn't a hug – he was a putting his arm round me in a friendly mates' way.'

'Uh-huh.'

I'm suddenly hit with a wave of embarrassment. 'Oh, God, do you think it looks like I'm coming on to him?'

I'm wondering if it wasn't Sian's mood that scared him off earlier, but more a desperate attempt to break away from me. Maybe he's been trying to get away from me all day and I haven't noticed. This was supposed to be his trip away with his friends and I totally gatecrashed it.

'Far from it. I think he's giving as good as he's getting. In fact, I'd say he's pretty into you.'

'Um, whatever,' I say, turning into an American teenager.

'Come on. He looks at you with his puppy-dog eyes. When we were eating lunch I caught him just staring at you.'

'But he's got a girlfriend.'

'I get the impression from Laura that it's an on/off relationship. If it's not serious ...'

I look up at Ben bounding down the mountain. He's talking to Giles, his arms waving around as he explains something. I catch a glimpse of his profile – his dark messy hair, his overgrown beard. He's so not my type. Yet, at the same time, he's not unattractive. Not in the slightest.

'Maybe you should ask him out on a date. I mean, what's stopping you?'

Tammy for starters. She made her position very clear on Thursday.

Then there's the more important fact that he's not Joseph. Seeing Joseph on Thursday night at the supermarket seemed to cement in my mind why I was doing this crazy list.

And anyway, Sian's wrong about Ben having any feelings for me. He knows that I'm trying to win back the love of my life. If there was even so much as the remotest hint that he fancied me then why would he be helping me to do it? And, even if he did like me and I liked him, he's hardly boyfriend material – he's banged on enough about how doomed love is. He's even more pessimistic than Sian.

'I'm just saying, think about it,' she says, walking a little quicker so we can catch up with Ben who's now walking with Pete.

Ben turns to me and smiles and I can't help smiling back, but it's only because he's got one of those magnetic smiles – nothing else.

'So, Pete, what games are we going to play tonight then?' asks Sian as she weaves her way between him and Ben.

I inwardly groan. It seems the closer we get to the bunkhouse, the more Sian's libido wakes up.

'I'm not sure. My mind's just on getting showered and changed into dry clothes at the moment.'

'In the nice lukewarm showers,' says Sian, turning towards Ben. 'As I've been reminded.'

He looks at me, smiling.

'I was only saying. It's not my fault there's no water pressure or hot water.'

'Are you sure it wasn't because you were having a long shower this morning primping and preening all your curls?' I say, giggling.

'Well, they do get dehydrated otherwise,' says Ben, laughing.

I don't care about the dribbly shower, I'd settle for towelling myself down and getting out of these damp clothes and into my trackie bottoms and hoodie. I can picture myself being curled up by the fire (on a duvet on the floor) with a cuppa.

'I thought she was more outdoorsy than you,' says Ben.

'I thought so too. She's always trying to get me to go camping.'

'You know you're only one step away from camping in that bunkhouse.'

'Probably, but it's the thought of not having a toilet, and being able to hear everything outside that gets me. The lumps that you feel through the floor, and the fact that you always get mud inside the tent, no matter how hard you try. And it always gets so messy as there's never enough room to put everything.' I shudder at the thought of camping holidays when I was little.

'So, you have camped before?'

'Not by choice, only when I was too young to refuse.'

'Camping's changed a lot since we were kids.'

'Are there now tents with flushing toilets?'

'Well, no.'

'Do you still have to put the tents up yourself and wrestle to get them down again?'

'There are the little pop-up tents that you can throw up.'

'But aren't they super small? And I take it you can't also throw them to put them away again.'

'No.'

'I rest my case. No camping for me.'

'I still think you're missing out. Some of the best memories I have are from camping.'

'Seems like some of your best memories are from anything that doesn't involve creature comforts.'

Ben thinks for a moment, before nodding. 'You know that's pretty true. I'm at my happiest when I'm outdoors doing stuff like this. Don't get me wrong, I don't want to live in a hut in the woods, and I love my TV as much as the next guy, but sometimes the most fun things are the most simple and basic.

'I've done the whole staying in five-star hotels thing. When I went backpacking round South East Asia I used to treat myself every so often and stay somewhere super-swanky. I'm not saying it wasn't nice. Hot baths. Beds that had comfortable duvets and you knew wouldn't have lice. But, once I was clean and lying in bed, all I did was watch telly. Something I could have done at home. Whereas in the flea-ridden backpackers' bungalow on the beach your tiny wooden hut wasn't conducive for chilling out, so you'd always hang out in the communal areas on the triangular floor cushions, drinking cold beers and chewing the fat with other travellers.'

The laid-back traveller retreats that Ben's talking about sound pretty alluring. I'm not going to ask him about the toilet situation, though. I don't want to ruin my romantic impression of his hippy hang-outs.

'I have to admit, I'd settle for a five-star hotel now, though. Wouldn't you? Just imagine how nice it would be to slip out of these wet clothes, and into a lavender-infused bubble bath,' I say.

I tried with his roughing-it vision, I really did. But a bath, fluffy robe and free flip-flop slippers are exactly what I fancy. I bet Joseph would be climbing into one right now if he'd done this challenge. In fact, I bet he would have caught the train back down the mountain and been all clean, tucking into a pint in one of the many village pubs by now.

I look at the bunkhouse that's coming into view and try not to feel bitter that it's my home for the night. Honestly.

'So, are you pleased that you're rapidly ticking off the things on your list? I mean, you're well and truly over halfway through now.'

'I know,' I say.

'You don't sound particularly pleased about it.'

'It's just that I'm over halfway through now, and I still worry that it might be all be for nothing. What if I don't get Joseph back?'

'If Joseph isn't impressed with what you've been up to then he's not worthy of you. Besides, you know I don't believe in happy endings.'

I'm about to reply when he gives a low whistle.

'Blimey, what's she doing here?' he says, the confusion evident in his voice.

I look closer at the bunkhouse and I can see the tiny figure of a woman sitting on the doorstep playing with a phone.

There's no mistaking that it's Tammy.

Our last one hundred metres are spent in silence as Ben stares at his girlfriend in disbelief.

I can't help but feel disappointed that she's here. I know she's his girlfriend and she has every right to be here, but I've enjoyed having Ben almost to myself this weekend – all banter and easy conversation. She made it perfectly clear that I wasn't to continue my friendship with Ben after this list is complete, and I wanted to make the most of our time together while I could. It's only going to feel awkward with her here.

I deliberately distance myself from Ben as we approach, wary about her warning, and I watch as he goes over to her. Sian was well and truly barking up the wrong tree – he couldn't seem to get to her quickly enough.

'What are you doing here?' he says, his hands resting on his hips.

'There was some problem with my race entry,' she says, holding her hands out for him to pull her up. 'Aren't you pleased to see me?'

He looks around at the rest of us, who have come up behind him, and seems a little self-conscious. 'Just surprised.'

She leans over and kisses him on the lips before turning to the rest of us.

'Laura,' she says, going over and giving her a hug. 'Giles, Pete, Doug.'

She does a roll call and smiles at each of the boys. I don't know if I'm imagining it but they don't seem that thrilled to see her either.

'Hello,' she says, turning to me and Sian. 'Nice to see you two again.'

I see Sian's nostrils flare, the tension from their first meeting still there.

'So, you all look like you need to get warm, and I'm dying for a drink,' she says going over to retrieve her backpack.

Laura hurries forward and opens the front door.

We all pull our waterproofs and boots off and make our way to the drying room to hang them up. I'm desperately trying not to step in any of the damp patches that we've made all over the floor as, miraculously, my super-comfy thick hiking socks are the only things that remained dry.

'I'll put the kettle on,' calls Laura as she hands her wet gear to Giles.

'That sounds like heaven,' I say. I could think of nothing better right now than a nice cup of tea.

'Dibs I get first shower,' says Sian. 'Is that OK?'

'Fine with me,' I say. 'I'm just going to get changed and towel dry my hair.'

I'm sure that piddly shower will only make me colder.

'Now, get your bits together,' Tammy says to Ben. 'I've booked us into a B&B in town so we can have some proper time alone.'

It suddenly feels a bit crowded in the drying room.

'Um, really?' says Ben. 'But we're all here together. We've got some wine, and we were going to have dinner.'

'But you've done your walk. Wasn't that the important thing? You said you had to do that, but you didn't say anything about the socialising afterwards.'

Tammy's voice seems to be echoing around the walls, and if she hadn't been blocking the door I'd be legging it out of there. It's the most uncomfortable I've been all day, which is saying something as my knickers have been damp from the rain for the last hour.

'Can we talk about this somewhere else?' says Ben, trying to push Tammy out into the corridor.

'Fine, but we're going to the B&B. I've already got my stuff there.'

Ben looks round at us, and we all look away, embarrassed at the scene playing out.

'But these are my friends.'

'And what am I supposed to be? Now come on, let's get your stuff.' She turns on her heel and walks towards the bedrooms.

For a minute Ben stands there motionless and none of the rest of us leave either. It seems there is safety in numbers as Tammy is pretty scary in her current mood.

'Ben!' she shrieks from down the corridor.

He turns to us once more.

'I'm really sorry, guys. I don't know what to say. I wasn't expecting her. I wasn't expecting this.'

He's so apologetic, I feel ridiculously sorry for him. He seems genuinely torn between his friends and his girlfriend, but I know who he's going to choose. He has to, after all. She's his girlfriend.

'Don't worry, mate,' says Giles, slapping him on the back. 'Go enjoy your comfy bed and your bubble bath.'

For a moment I'm lost in the thought of luxury and want to suggest that I take Ben's place. But then Tammy shrieks again, and there's no bubble bath in the world that would be good enough to want to spend any more time near her in that mood.

'Well done, Abi. I'm proud of you for conquering your first mountain. We'll toast to it in Paris,' says Ben, deliberately lowering his voice.

I smile. 'You bet.'

At least we'll always have Paris. Our last hurrah as friends. After seeing Tammy in action today she's shown that she's not a woman to be crossed.

'So, that's interesting,' says Sian, as I walk into our room.

'Wasn't it?' I say, my voice sounding a little deflated.

'I thought it was just me that brought out the worst in her, but she was spitting venom at everyone. It's a shame Ben's going. You can't tell me that you're not a little gutted,' says Sian.

I look up but am too slow to correct her.

'I knew it. You can deny it all you want, but there's something between you and Ben.'

I start to pull off my soggy clothes. 'It's not that,' I say, sighing. 'It's more that I've enjoyed having him to myself. Does that sound nuts?'

'Not really.'

She's gathering up her shower stuff to go and brave the luke-warm drizzle.

'I mean, we've had such a lovely few weeks of doing my challenges, and then this weekend it's been so fun, but as soon as he saw her he changed.'

'Maybe it was just shock. He did seem caught off guard that she was here.'

'Maybe,' I say, putting on my clean, dry clothes. Pulling my old comfy hoodie over my head feels as if someone's giving me a really nice hug.

'But, honestly, I thought he was into you.'

'Told you you were wrong,' I say, sliding my feet into my slippers and following Sian as she walks out of the bedroom.

We walk into the corridor and bump straight into Tammy and Ben. She's got her arms wrapped around his neck, stroking the nape of his neck. She's giving him a look that's so seductive that I don't think even Sian the man-eater could pull it off.

Ben looks up and takes a step back from her and she turns and gives me a sly look. It's a territory thing and whatever Sian and I might have thought, Ben is Tammy's property. She made her feelings more than clear on Thursday, and it's as if she's shown up today to flex her muscles and show me how serious she was.

It dawns on me that I've been using Ben as my surrogate boyfriend, but he was never mine to use.

I try and focus my mind on this weekend's objective. It wasn't to spend time with Ben – it was to climb Snowdon and I've done that. I've ticked another item off my list and that will hopefully lead me one step closer to Joseph. Although, right now, not even the thought of us reuniting is cheering me up.

Chapter Nineteen

Two weeks, four days left, and I'm trying to come up with an excuse to get out of this abseil, but my mind is blank. Maybe Fran was onto something with the baby bump after all . . .

'It was a shame that Ben bailed on Sunday night. Wasn't the same after he left,' says Giles as he puts a capsule into the Nespresso machine.

'It certainly wasn't.'

With Ben out of the way, there was an even number of men to women and it made the rest of the weekend feel a bit couply. Obviously Giles and Laura were their adorable selves – the more wine they drank the more canoodling they did – and Sian did her best impression of a bitch on heat in her unsuccessful pursuit of Pete. But poor old Doug and I were left giving each other looks of sympathy, like a mismatched couple at a dinner party.

'I mean, it just changed the dynamics. And what with Sian throwing herself at Pete.'

'Hmmm,' says Giles, raising his eyebrows.

Sian had really ramped it up a gear on Sunday night. She had kept Pete's wine glass permanently topped up and worn a spaghetti-strapped vest top that didn't leave much to the imagination, and at one point she was practically sitting on Pete's lap. But all to no avail.

Pete did seem into her, but whereas she was all about the night, he seemed to be in no rush to get it on. As a consequence, Sian's been hounding me about him ever since.

'She was certainly forward,' says Giles, grinning.

'She was so forward she was practically in fifth gear driving down a motorway.'

Giles lets out a little laugh and stirs his coffee. 'It was a shame Ben missed it all.'

'Oh, well,' I say shrugging. 'I'm sure he had a nice time in his luxury B&B.'

'I spoke to him last night and he was gutted to have left the bunkhouse.'

'Really? Didn't he want to spend time with Tammy?'

'I think he needed to spend time with her, but I think he felt like she'd railroaded his weekend. He'd planned to spend it with us and all of a sudden she was there.'

'I guess it was a bit *Fatal Attraction*.'

'Yeah, it's a good job Ben doesn't have any pets as she is definitely leaning towards the bunny boiler.'

A laugh escapes my lips, and I catch Linz's eye across the office. I cough as I try to get my giggles under control. I have to remind myself that I'm at work.

I quickly busy myself making a cup of coffee to legitimise my water-cooler chat.

'I always got the impression that she was supposed to be this laid-back type of woman, but she was something quite different on Sunday,' I say, dipping my toe into the water. I've been dying to ask Giles about their relationship but never dared in case it's breaking some unspoken bro code.

'Yeah, Tammy is …' Giles pauses as if he's trying to find the right word. 'Well, to be honest, she's perplexing. I've known her since she and Ben first got together about three years ago and I still don't feel like I know her. One minute she's so laid-back she's horizontal and the next she's like she was on Sunday.'

'They've been together three years?' I don't know why but I assumed that they hadn't been together for very long. Three years doesn't scream casual.

'Yeah, but it's always on and off with those two, one month they're together, the next they're on a break. It's not like a normal relationship.'

I pretend that I'm concentrating on stirring my coffee instead of hanging off Giles's every word.

'I couldn't do that,' I say, honestly. 'I'm one of those people that when I'm in a relationship then I'm really in one. Perhaps that's where I went wrong with Joseph – maybe I was too into it. Scared him off.'

'I doubt it, Abs. As a happily married man, believe me, if the right woman is into you, you can't get enough of them. It's only the crazy ones that can scare you off.' Giles's mouth drops open for a second. 'I don't mean that you were crazy in your relationship with Joseph. I just mean that if he was the one, he wouldn't care that you were too into him. In fact, he would have loved it.'

I think for a moment about whether that's true. I hope it isn't or else I'm well and truly wasting my time with this list and trying to get him back.

'But you're right, I couldn't do it either,' he says, continuing with the Ben and Tammy conversation.

'Then why do you think he puts up with it?'

I know I should be doing my work. I've got a huge meeting later on this morning and I still need to print off stuff for it, but now that I've opened this can of worms with Giles, I don't feel like I can close it again. Not until I've got the dirt.

'Well, there was this ex of his that messed him up pretty badly, and since then he's not really committed to anyone.'

I think of Sian and how damaged she is for the same reason, and I think of my own pathetic break-up. For a minute I wonder why we ever try this love game when a heartbreak can have that effect on the rest of your life. Maybe Ben's got a point, saving himself the heartache.

'He told me about her,' I say, nodding. 'Sounds like he really lost someone he loved.'

'Yeah, and then there's everything that happened with his mum. So when he met Tammy at some biking event they started dating and it quickly became apparent that she wasn't the type of girl to settle down. She was never at home, always off somewhere at a race and it didn't take long for Ben to real-ise that she blew hot and cold like the wind. But much to our amazement, he put up with it. It's a shame as we'd like nothing more than to see Ben settle down with someone nice – he deserves it.'

Giles gives me a fleeting look, before opening a cupboard and pulling out the biscuit tin.

'I'm not saying that Tammy isn't nice,' he says quickly. 'She's usually all right. It's just that none of us like the way she walks in and out of Ben's life.'

'None of you like her? Not Pete, not Doug?'

'Don't like is probably a bit strong, but no, none of us are impressed with how she treats him. Please don't say anything to him, though. He'd hate to know how we feel.'

'Of course not,' I say. 'Your secret's safe with me.'

He grabs a handful of biscuits and offers me the tub, but there are only Garabaldis filled with evil raisins left, so I shake my head. He slams the lid shut, putting it back in the cupboard.

I can't help thinking him shutting the lid like that is a metaphor for our conversation about Ben and Tammy – firmly closed. Whether Giles feels guilty about going behind his best friend's back, I don't know, but suddenly it's as if there's a super-injunction on the topic and Giles goes stony silent.

'I better get ready for this meeting,' I say, taking my cue to leave.

I settle myself at my desk and pull up my to-do list. But before I can get stuck into it, my phone buzzes.

I see it's a text message from Sian.

Have you texted Ben yet about Sunday? x

I sigh. This is probably my third text of the day from her, all along the same lines. On the long, long drive back from Snowdonia, where the topic of conversation was pretty much exclusively about Pete, Sian came up with a plan. We'd all go and visit a vineyard in West Sussex on Sunday to tick wine tasting off my list.

I did try to point out that it would seem like I was suggesting a double date with Ben, Pete, Sian and me, but I was overruled. It seemed that my list was the perfect excuse for Sian to legitimise seeing Pete again. I pointed out that I could just get his number from Ben and she could call and ask him out herself, but she was having none of it. His cool response to her friskiness at the weekend had made her doubt her mojo and she wanted to engineer an informal outing to see what would happen between them.

I had wanted to keep Sunday free as Sian and I have got the Race for Life on Saturday and Ben and I are off to Paris on Tuesday. I was looking forward to having some downtime, but then I reasoned that wandering round a vineyard in the spring sunshine would be quite relaxing and I've only got two more weeks to tick it off my list before the abseil.

Besides, I don't think she's going to give me any peace until I get it organised. So I fire off a quick text to Ben, using the words that Sian had so carefully crafted between Birmingham and Oxford. Apparently it needs to seem casual, but also be clear that it would work best if it was only the four of us. I can imagine Tammy's wrath now ...

'Hey, Abi.'

I finish sending a quick text to Sian with the word 'done'. I look up and see Fran peering through the partition.

'Hiya, you all right?' I say, thinking that I don't need any more interruptions this morning.

'Yeah, just checking you were all set for the meeting with Vista later.'

'More or less,' I say, lying. Fran's a real organised cookie who always has a neatly prepared folder for every meeting she attends.

'Great. I was speaking to Rick about it and he was waxing lyrical about you landing the account. It seems you've earned yourself a lot of brownie points.'

I'm still pleased as punch that I managed to snag my own client. It's usually the account execs that bring in the business, not us designers.

'I'm glad he noticed,' I say, looking over at him in the far corner with Linz.

Fran follows my gaze.

'Quite,' she says. 'When does Hayley get back from maternity leave?'

We share a smile in solidarity.

'I better get back to the preparation for this meeting,' I say to Fran, when in reality I'm scanning Facebook to check if there has been any new Joseph activity.

'Great, well, let me know if you need any help,' she says as she disappears from the gap.

'Thanks,' I call, but I shouldn't need any help. For once I feel in control.

I finished my designs late last week and I was ridiculously happy with them. I often like to tinker with work right up until the last moment, but something about these designs just clicked.

I hope that Lucinda and Thomas, the clients from my Spanish class, love them as much as I do.

I open InDesign to load up my files and I can't stop the grin exploding on my face. I'm still brimming with enthusiasm for my job and I really can't help thanking the list.

For the first time in what feels like months, my life seems on the up. My job's going well, my boss is pleased with me, I've done amazing feats that I never thought I'd be brave enough to do, and I'm hopefully starting to impress Joseph and am therefore closer to getting him back.

I'm practically whistling with joy as I navigate finder looking for my client folder. I open it up and am gobsmacked to find it's empty.

'It can't be,' I say, clicking out of the folder and back in.

I might be messy in the real world, but in my virtual world I'm a total neat freak.

I start to look at folders either side in case I've accidentally dragged or dropped the files somewhere else. But there's nothing – only what's supposed to be in there.

My heart starts to race and I'm finding it difficult to breathe.

I know the files have to be here somewhere. They couldn't have just disappeared, could they?

Think, Abi, think.

It's not only my designs that are missing from the folder but the initial client brief isn't there either, and neither is the outline of my work I'd sent to Rick at the beginning.

I can feel the beads of sweat starting to collect on my forehead.

I try and think logically, or as logically as my brain will let me.

I bring up the search button and type in the file name.

The wheel of death appears on my Mac for a moment and I close my eyes, unable to watch its progress.

When the search comes up empty I start to inwardly panic.

'Hi, Abi, everything ready for the meeting?' says Rick.

Why is everyone asking me that question today?

'Um, doing the last-minute changes now,' I lie.

There's no point in worrying him unnecessarily. They're going to turn up – they have to.

'Perfect. Well, I'll see you in the meeting room in twenty minutes then.'

Twenty minutes!

I look up in shock at the clock and realise the time. Why on earth did I leave the printing so late in the first place? It was so late last Friday when I finished them and I couldn't face waiting for the printer to warm up and do its slow-time printing. I should have printed them when I came into the office first thing this morning, instead of grilling Giles about Ben or trying to tackle the mountain of emails from when I took yesterday off travelling back from Snowdon.

I pick up the phone and wonder who I'm going to call. I don't really want anyone else in the office to get a whiff of what's going on, but at the same time my technical knowledge in the field of locating missing work is pretty non-existent.

I look over to Giles's side of the office as he's a computer whizz kid, but it's empty.

I stare up at the big clock hanging on the office wall and the second hand seems to tick loudly, reminding me that I'm ever closer to my impending doom. I can't go to this big client meeting empty-handed and it's way too late to postpone it.

The dial tone makes that funny noise and reminds me that I've had the phone off the hook too long. I replace the receiver before picking it up again in a moment of clarity. I can phone our IT people. They'll be able to help.

We outsource our IT work to a company who I'm pretty sure work out of their bedrooms. I'm always convinced that I can hear *Game of Thrones* on in the background.

'Hello, Abi.'

'Hello,' I say, not knowing whether I'm speaking to Greg or Adam. The two are the same person in my head. Too much skill and glasses to tell the difference.

'What can I do for you?'

'I'm trying to locate some files. I did some work last Friday and now the files are gone. When I open InDesign and try and open the source files from there it says the files no longer exist in their location.

'OK, I'll just take control of your machine.'

I panic for a second as I check my screen to make sure I don't have Facebook still up.

Having someone else remotely manipulate my computer freaks me out. In a matter of seconds my curser moves across the screen like it's being controlled by a poltergeist. It always makes me feel violated.

'What are the file names?'

I list them off and I watch as he does the same search I did five minutes ago. So much for the genius of the IT department.

I can see Pat the office manager taking the hot flasks of water into the conference room as the meeting time gets ever closer.

My cheeks are starting to burn and I know without looking in a mirror that they'll have gone all red and blotchy.

'They don't appear to be on the system, either in your personal or the shared drives,' says the IT guru.

'Well, can't you fix it? Can't you track them down?' I ask, thinking about the stories I'm always reading about the police taking away hard drives and retrieving files that criminals wanted hidden. I've always been under the impression that it's super hard to actually get rid of things permanently from your computer.

'I'm sure we can. When did you say you last edited them?'

'Friday night, just before I left.'

'OK, well the files are backed up every night, so I can just go to the backup files and find them.'

'Great,' I say, releasing the biggest breath and fighting the urge to tell him how much I love him.

The relief is immense. And it's not a moment too soon. Pat's just walked into the meeting room with the fancy biscuits and the clock says it's five minutes until meeting o'clock.

'If you leave it with me, I'll retrieve them and send them over this afternoon.'

'This afternoon!' I cough. 'But my meeting is in five minutes. I need them now.'

Greg/Adam sucks air through his lips. 'No can do. I have to access the server computer and then find Friday's directories and I guess if I did it quickly it would take half an hour at the very least, but usually when we recover design files because of their size they can take an hour.'

'What?' I say gulping. 'This is supposed to be the twenty-first century.'

'And that's if the files are there.'

'What do you mean if the files are there? Why wouldn't they be there?'

'Well, they were obviously deleted, so if they were deleted before the back up happened at midnight then there's no hope of getting them back.'

I'm back to the hyperventilating.

'Look, Abi. I'll give it a go right now and get them to you if they're there as soon as I can.'

'Thank you,' I say, mumbling, and hang up the phone.

What the hell happened to my files? It sounds like we've ruled out the idea that me or someone else has accidentally moved them. They've been deleted. What sort of a moron would do that?

I see Rick striding through the office on his way to reception. He gives me a nod of the head which he does when he's off to welcome clients from reception.

That's usually my cue to position myself in the conference room and put my boards up ready. Only today I've got no boards. I've got no designs. I've got nothing. I don't even have my Word file of ideas. I've never been so unprepared for a meeting in all my life.

I rise to my feet and look over to the back fire escape. I've probably got time to hot foot it down those stairs and out on to the street. But I can't do that. These are *my* clients. The first clients that I've bought to the agency.

I'm going to have to wing it. I know what the designs looked like, I'm going to have to try and describe them.

I force my legs to walk over to the conference room, but they've gone limp and jelly-like.

'You all right, Abi?' asks Linz, her perfect white teeth gleaming as she smiles.

'Fine,' I say, even though I'm anything but.

'I'm looking forward to seeing your final designs.'

I stop for a second and stare into her eyes. There was something about the way she said that that makes me suspicious.

What if Linz deliberately deleted my files? I tell myself I'm being ridiculous. She might be a peppy pain in the arse, but she's not evil.

She pushes the door open and takes a seat at the large round table.

I'm studying her face to look for clues about my predicament when Rick walks in with the clients.

'Hello,' I say, standing up and planting a fake smile on my face, hoping I can make up for my lack of designs with my winning personality.

'Nice to see you again, Abi,' says Lucinda, walking in, followed by Thomas who smiles warmly.

Linz bounces up immediately, introducing herself and offering coffee.

She does have her uses after all, because there's no way I'd be able to hold a coffee cup straight enough to get any liquid into it as my hands are shaking worse than a jelly in an earthquake. I'm sitting on them to try and numb them in a bid to stop the quaking.

'Right, then, shall we hand over to Abi who will talk you through the designs. I'm sure you'll be eager to see them.'

I see him looking round the room, noticing that neither the whiteboard is on nor the easel loaded with boards. I can tell he's clicked that there are no designs present.

'Thanks, Rick,' I say as best I can. My mouth has gone so dry that my tongue is getting stuck to the roof of it.

I stand up, hoping that it will make whatever I have to say seem more authoritative, as if it was all part of my grand plan.

'So, I know you are all dying to see what I've come up with.' I laugh nervously. They're not the only ones. My hands haven't been so clammy since I slow danced with Russell Thomson at the year nine disco. I try and rub them on my jeans as discreetly as I can, but it only makes them quiver more.

'Well, I'm going to be honest with you. I had done designs for today. Brilliant ones, even perfect ones, but we've had a tiny problem with our IT system.'

I hear Rick gasp, and I know it's going to be downhill from here.

'So, I'm going to have to explain my concept as best I can, and then email you the files this afternoon.'

The look of hope on Lucinda's face has fallen, and Thomas shifts in his chair. Rick looks like he's going to throw the fancy biscuit he's just picked up at my head, and Linz has that stupid inane grin on her face that makes me want to punch her even more than usual.

'So,' I say, realising that I'm starting to ramble, 'the idea for the concept is to subtly rebrand your logo. You want to position yourself in the luxury hotel market, which obviously your refurbishment allows you to, but your logo is currently a little out of date. We think that whilst you want to hang on to the word Vista, it would be worth rebranding as the Vista Boutique Hotel.'

Thomas and Lucinda look at each other.

'Do you think we should really change our name? That would mean changing everything – all our leaflets, our website,' says Thomas, sighing.

I can't point out that that's why they're at our design agency, as I'm supposed to be on a charm offensive to make up for the lack of designs.

'Yes, but I think if we get the branding right, it would be worth it. You've already done the hard work with the refurb, and the rooms and hotel are looking fantastic. What you want is a design that really reflects the changes you've made. And as you'll be able to charge more for the rooms, you'll hopefully be able to recoup the marketing costs easily.'

'And the refurb costs,' says Thomas, looking at Lucinda.

I get the impression that he didn't really want to make the changes to the hotel, but Lucinda was right to do it. She's transformed what was a tired old seafront hotel with pink floral carpets and peeling wallpaper and made it modern and fresh, with Farrow-and-Ball-painted rooms, Egyptian cotton bedding and twenty-first-century carpet.

'We've been through this,' says Lucinda. 'In two years' time everything, including these marketing costs, will be paid off.'

He sighs loudly and rubs his hand through his hair.

'I like the name, but what would the logo look like?' she says.

'Well,' I say, feeling like an idiot having to describe my designs rather than show them. 'I'd taken the colours from your new rooms. The deep grey, turquoise and the fuchsia. They work really well in combination. The word Vista is large in fuchsia, with the boutique hotel written in grey below. The turquoise is used to highlight it and to give the impression of waves to represent what that vista is.'

I see the confused looks on their faces. Even I could barely follow that description and I can see it like a photograph in my mind.

Linz reaches into her bag and pulls out a bag of felt tip pens. She walks calmly over to the flip chart beside me.

'I saw Abi's designs last week,' she says. 'They go a bit like this.'

In the space of two minutes she manages to draw on the flip chart a pretty accurate rough sketch of what my design looks like.

'OK,' says Lucinda, 'I think that could work. And you're going to send us over the designs today?'

'Yes,' I say, hoping that Adam or Greg will come through. 'IT are working on it as we speak. Hopefully I can send you something by the time you get back to the hotel.'

'OK, great,' she says, nodding.

'Good work, Linz,' says Rick, patting her on the back as she sits down.

'So that's it. We're changing the name, just like that? Based on some felt-tip-pen drawing,' says Thomas.

'Yes,' replies Lucinda. The discussion seems to be over and we're left without any doubt as to who wears the trousers in their relationship.

'Right then, so once you've seen the designs and approved or amended them, we'll hand them over to Giles to get started on the website design, and Abi was going to mock up the leaflets.'

He gives me a look as if there's some doubt as to whether I'll be able to handle it.

'Absolutely,' I say.

'Right,' says Rick, almost through gritted teeth. 'We will arrange for our photographer to come round and take photos of your new rooms and the views, and could you supply us with the text you want to use. I've highlighted a number of key words from your project brief for you to incorporate.'

He hands over a piece of paper to Lucinda, who takes it, nodding.

'Perfect. It sounds as if it's all on the right lines, and I can't wait to see this logo. Such a shame about the IT,' she says, giving me a small smile.

'Isn't it?' I say, looking Linz in the eye. It's all very convenient that she was here, with her pens and her quick sketching, to save the day. I remember her coming over last week and peering over my shoulder, asking me questions about the colours, but now I wonder if there was more to it.

We say our goodbyes to Lucinda and Thomas as Rick ushers them out of the conference room. 'Abi, you wait here,' he hisses as he leaves.

Linz packs away her pens and pops them back in her bag, before slipping it over her shoulder.

'IT problems can happen to anyone,' she says with a sympathetic look.

'Yes, it was very strange that all my files were deleted.'

'Deleted?' she repeats, a look of shock appearing on her face. I hadn't realised that she'd be quite such a good actress.

'Yes, they are all missing.'

'Are you sure they weren't put in the wrong folder by mistake?'

I love the fact that everyone thinks I'm some type of moron that would have done that or that that wouldn't have been the first thing that I checked.

'No, quite sure they've been wiped off the system. Luckily IT are probably going to be able to restore them from Friday night's back up.'

'That is lucky,' she says. 'Just a shame that you couldn't do that in time for the meeting.'

She's back to smug, smiling Linz.

'Yes. Good job you were here with your pens though.'

She shrugs. 'I thought you needed a little help. Right, I'm going to get myself a coffee. Do you want me to put one on your desk? Sounds like you might need it after Rick is finished with you.'

'No, thanks,' I say, starting to really believe that she's to blame for my files going missing. 'I'll get my own later.'

She smiles and walks off, wiggling her hips as she goes.

I watch through the glass window as she bumps into Rick and he rubs her arm as if congratulating her.

'Right, Abi. What the hell happened?' he says as he walks through the door. It's like he rubbed his good mood off on Linz's arm. His face is like thunder and I have no idea how I'm going to get through this.

Today started off so well. I was buzzing after conquering Snowdon, and hugely excited about wowing the clients I'd managed to bring in. And now look at the mess I'm in. Rick looks like he's about to throw me to the wolves, and the clients probably think I'm an incompetent idiot. The only reason that I didn't fall flat on my face is that I was rescued by someone who is fast becoming my office nemesis.

I take a deep breath before launching into my spiel of the deleted files. It's going to sound like I'm telling him the equivalent of the dog ate my homework tale. I was just starting to get back on an even keel at work after the disciplinary letter about my working from home stint, and things like this and the memory stick keep putting me back. It's not like I've got any more clients I can magically pull out of my sleeve to put me back in favour.

I've only got myself to blame. If only I'd been more organised and printed my designs off this morning rather than faffing about on Facebook. I've got to leave Joseph and my list with my personal life at the door. From now on I've got to put work Abi first.

Chapter Twenty

*One week and six days until the abseil. I can't even get
excited that I'm ticking two items off my list this weekend,
as the more I tick off the closer I am to having to dangle
from that thread ...*

'And you have no idea where they went?' says Ben, whistling air through his teeth.

'None. Thank God for IT and their back-ups. I'm just glad I was working later than Linz on Friday night, because if she'd deleted them before the back-up then I would have had to start from scratch and I would have been in even more trouble with Rick and the clients for delaying the designs.'

The train that had been rocketing through the West Sussex countryside begins to slow, signalling the approach into our station.

'You're sure that it's Linz that did it?' he asks.

'Absolutely. I spent the rest of the week watching her, and she kept looking at me and giving me these small, telling smiles. And she's all over Rick like a rash. It's disgusting.'

'Have you told him about your suspicions?' asks Sian.

I look up, surprised for a second that she'd joined the conversation. I hadn't realised she'd been listening. Ever since we'd met Ben and Pete at the train station, she's only had eyes and ears for Pete. I'd almost forgotten that they were with us.

'No, I felt pathetic enough saying I'd lost the files, I didn't want to risk accusing the golden child.'

'So what are you going to do?' asks Ben.

'I don't know. I'm being extra careful and saving everything to my personal Dropbox account as well as on the office folder. There's not really a lot I can do. It's not like I can prove who did it.'

'Can't your IT department tell who deleted the files? You would think in this day and age that would be possible,' says Pete.

I hadn't even thought to ask them. I was just so grateful that they were able to find the files.

'I don't know. I guess I can ring them on Monday.'

It's a long shot, but if I could prove that it was Linz that did it, I could go to Rick and show him what she's really like.

The train grinds to a halt and we hurry off it.

'Where did this rain come from?' I say, wishing I'd bought my cagoule instead of my silly lightweight military jacket – it's barely warming, let alone waterproof.

Yesterday, when I'd sweated my way through the Race for Life, it had been unseasonably hot for April, but today, when we actually want to feel like we're on the Med, it pisses down. Typical bloody English weather.

Pete starts singing 'Why Does it Always Rain on Me?' and Sian giggles.

'Right, shall we wait for the rain to ease off a bit,' says Ben. 'It looks like it's just a shower, and the vineyard is supposed to be a half-hour walk from here.'

'What about getting a taxi?' asks Sian.

'That would get us there dry,' I say. 'But I think you have to walk around a lot of the vineyard to get to the bit where they do the tasting anyway. There's a pub over there. Why don't we get a quick drink and wait for the rain to pass?'

The pub is all cute and villagey and looks inviting. It's one of those crooked white-washed buildings with a thatched roof.

'Sounds good to me. I don't think I've dried out from last week yet,' says Pete.

He links arms with Sian and they make a run for it out of the station and across the road to the pub.

'Seems like they're getting on well,' says Ben, raising his eyebrow at me.

'Yes, well, you missed the warm-up act last Sunday.'

He nods slowly. 'I'm sorry about that. I had no idea that Tammy was going to show up and I really needed to talk to her, so I couldn't not go.'

'It's fine,' I say, waving my hand around like I wasn't in the slightest bit bothered. 'Right, let's go.'

We do a fast walk out of the station and a slight jog across the road.

I push open the heavy door and barely get over the threshold, when Sian calls over to ask me what I'm drinking.

I take in the surroundings – it's exactly as I imagined it would be from the outside. There's the log fire at one end and low, dark wooden beams decorated with horse brasses and tankards.

'I'll have a G&T.' This doesn't look like the type of pub you drink wine in and my real-ale days are well and truly behind me.

I go into scout mode, looking for somewhere to sit. It's not very busy – just a few people tucked around the tables by the fire. I soon come across a snug at the back of the pub. There's a large round table, and a wooden bench that runs around it lined with cushions.

'This is perfect,' says Sian, squeezing round and Pete shimmies in next to her. I go round the other way to sit next to her and Ben sits next to me.

'Well, cheers,' says Pete, and we all chink glasses.

'This is really cute,' says Sian, looking around.

'I know, isn't it?' I say.

'I've been here before,' says Pete, 'When I was walking the South Downs. There's actually a few more pubs in the village that are really quaint too. It's a village that's big with the walkers.'

I sip my drink and realise that it's going down rather nicely.

'It's a shame we're not going on a village pub crawl, instead of the wine tasting,' I say.

I can just see myself sipping G&Ts at the other pubs. Maybe having some Scampi Fries in one of them and a fat home-cooked pie in another. If I'm honest I don't really feel like swilling wine around my mouth and spitting it out, trying to pretend I can taste the hint of pine or blackberries that are supposedly there.

'We've got to get your list done somehow,' says Ben.

Ah, yes, the list. It all comes down to the list. He's right. It might not impress Joseph to see pictures of me in the pub where he'd probably expect me to be, but walking through vineyards and sipping wine with barrels behind me might. Only in my head I think I'd imagined some French vineyard in the boiling hot sunshine. I hardly think walking in the countryside being pelted by the rain, my hair all frizzy and the vines obscured by the drizzle, is going to conjure the same image.

'I was thinking of you this week,' says Ben.

We've lost Sian and Pete to the board game Mastermind.

'You were?'

'Yes, I got an email about a colour run in Brighton, and I thought you and Sian might want to enter. I know you've ticked the run off your list, but they're pretty cool. I thought after yesterday's race you might have caught the running bug.'

As my Rudolph the Reindeer-coloured nose will testify, the only thing I caught yesterday was the sun. I honestly thought at times on the course that I was going to have a heart attack. By the end I was little more than speed marching and even that was tough. I don't want to put myself through that again, especially if it wasn't even for the sake of the list.

'What's a colour run?' I ask out of politeness.

'Oh, it's like this running event where everyone wears white and then at various points of the course people throw coloured powder at you.'

'Right,' I say, thinking that it sounds like one of the weirdest things I've ever heard of. Not only do you have the torture of running, but you get stuff thrown at you to boot.

'It was fun when I did it. You end up all coloured and they have really good music pumping round. The atmosphere is electric and you barely realise you've run anywhere. Thought it might be the kind of thing you'd like now.'

'Um.' I'm still not convinced.

'I'll forward you the email, just in case,' he says, shrugging.

I feel a hint of sadness that he's suggested that I do it with Sian and not him. It really does sound like when this list is over we won't be seeing each other again.

'Anyone want another drink?' asks Pete, standing up.

'Wouldn't say no,' says Ben. 'Is it still raining?'

Pete leans round the edge of the snug. 'Seems to be.'

'OK, then, I'll have another pint.'

'And I'll have another G&T,' I say, looking down at my almost empty glass.

'I'll give you a hand,' says Sian, getting up to join Pete.

'I don't think this beer is doing my palate any good for the wine tasting,' says Ben.

'Like you'd be such an expert anyway.'

'I'll have you know I'm a wine taster extraordinaire.'

'Oh, really,' I say, laughing.

I know I haven't been in that many drinking situations with Ben, but I've never seen or heard him talk about wine. I've only seen him drink beer.

'Oh, yes, when I was at university I was quite the expert.'

'Uh-huh.'

'Yep, we lived near a Netto, and I think I tried every wine they sold for under four pounds. I'm pretty good at telling what's drinkable and what's essentially vinegar.'

'Sounds sophisticated,' I say.

I don't want to tell him that I'm not much better. I still pick my wines based on what's on special offer.

'To be honest, I may drink a lot of wine, and despite Joseph trying to educate me, I don't have much of a clue what I'm talking about. I usually play it safe with a Pinot Grigio for a white and a Shiraz for red.'

At least I can pronounce them, unlike *Chi*anti . . .

'Well, that's probably more than I know. I got told off by a girlfriend once for pouring her wine into a mug and ever since then I've given it a wide berth.'

'You never heard of glasses?' I say, laughing.

'Of course, but I lived with four other blokes at uni. There was no way we'd own actual wine glasses. She wasn't impressed and refused to drink it. But really, what difference is there between a mug and a glass?'

'She sounds like she was high maintenance.' I nod in consolation.

'Yeah, the mug probably did me a favour.'

'Well, I have to say I've never drunk wine from a mug before.'

'Then you've never lived. I did offer her the bottle so she could swig it straight from that, but she wasn't having any of that either.'

'Another thing I've never done.'

'And you went to university? Things must have been different at yours than they were at mine. I drank alcohol from anything that hadn't been piled up on the kitchen side for more than a week. I once drank shots from an egg cup and beer from a saucepan.'

'Yuck, that's gross. It definitely wasn't like that in our shared house. We had a dishwasher.'

'What? That's cheating. Were you like the poshest students ever?'

'No, probably just cleaner than you were. I remember going round to some of the houses of the guys that we knew. They were disgusting. I used to pray that I never had to use the loo. They were worse than the ones from when I went camping as a kid.'

Ben lets out a belly laugh.

'Yeah, I remember my mum coming to visit once a month and bringing her Marigolds. I'm sure she even had one of those funny SARS face masks too.'

I get a mental picture of his mum dressing up in a floral pinny and slipping on industrial rubber gloves before going in to tackle the unknown.

'Now that's best-mum-in-the-world material right there.'

'Absolutely. None of us understood what bleach was. I think she probably stopped us from getting dysentery or some other godawful disease.'

'Does your mum still come and do your cleaning for you?'

I haven't been to Ben's flat. I know he lives above the shop, but I can't imagine it being anything like Joseph's grown-up bachelor pad. Even though it's a long time since Ben was a student, I still imagine him living like one. I can visualise the dishes piled up in the sink and the floor covered in oily bike parts. I'm sure his mum nips round every few weeks to give it a blast.

'She actually passed away a few years ago, so no.'

'Oh, God. Ben, I'm so sorry,' I say. Instantly the smile falls off my face and I sober up a notch. 'I didn't mean to put my foot in it.'

'You didn't and you weren't to know. Besides, it's fine, I can talk about it without being a total crumbling mess. Well, most of the time anyway.'

'What happened?' I ask, unsure if he'll want to talk about it.

I'm suddenly glad that we're in the snug and away from the hustle and the bustle of the rest of the pub as this has suddenly turned into an intimate conversation.

'She had a brain tumour. It was all quite sudden, although I think the symptoms had been there for a while but we hadn't put them all together. She went through a round of treatment and they thought they'd got it, but then it came back more aggressively and there was nothing they could do.'

'That's awful.' I instinctively reach over and rub his arm.

'It was awful, there's no denying it, but at the same time, she knew she was going. A few weeks before she died, we went up to her favourite holiday cottage in the Lake District for two weeks – we'd been there when we were kids. We played board games, read books to her, spent time on the water. It was some of the best family time we'd ever had.

'That's how I remember her. Sitting on the deck of a boat in the pissing rain, all wrapped up in waterproofs, giggling away. She'd never looked so happy.'

I share Ben's smile, but my heart aches for him. It's one of those awful fears that you have as you get older. You know your parents are getting closer to death, and there's nothing you can do to stop it.

I can't imagine a world without my parents. They drive me crazy, and we're not that close, but I like to think they'd be at the end of a phone line if I needed them.

'I'm lucky that I've still got my dad. It hit him really hard when she died. They'd been teenage sweethearts and they were that couple that was really in love, you know?'

I can't imagine the pain you must get from losing your soulmate like that.

'I see a lot of him, though, as he helps out in the shop once a week.'

'That's really nice. Does he live locally?'

The more I talk to Ben the more I realise how little I know about him. We've spent all this time together and I never knew about his mum or that his dad worked at the shop. It makes me realise how self-obsessed I've been – talking about myself and my petty love-life problems.

'He lives in Winchester, so not far. He hops on the train, and comes down for the day. We usually go out for a bite to eat and watch a footie game if there's one on and then he goes back that night.'

'That's really nice.'

'Yeah. But, wow, I didn't mean to put such a downer on the conversation.' He coughs. 'We should talk about something more upbeat. Like kids' TV again or the trip to Paris.'

Ben's looking at me, his brow still furrowed. He looks so vulnerable and I just want to hold him tight and tell him that everything's going to be OK. I've still got my arm resting on his and I desperately want to pull him into me.

Something pings in the back of my mind and I'm reminded of the chat I had with Giles about Ben and Tammy's relationship. He said that his mum was one of the reasons that he wanted things casual.

'Your parents' love,' I say. 'Is that what you meant when you said the more you love a person the harder your heart breaks?'

It's all starting to make sense now. The love story and heart-break he witnessed wasn't his own but his parents'.

'It's difficult to see what grief from that kind of love can do to a person and still go in search of it.' His voice catches in his throat and for a fleeting second he looks like he's going to cry.

My eyes meet his and I give him a look as if to show him how much his conversation has touched me. I just want to wrap him in a big hug to comfort him.

'Here you go,' says Sian, bustling into the snug.

I let go of Ben's arm and we shuffle apart.

Pete follows closely behind and puts Ben's pint down in front of him.

'Thanks,' I say, blushing.

Sian is looking between me and Ben as if she's sensed that she's interrupted something. She hesitates for a second before sitting down.

'So, this rain doesn't seem like it's going to stop any time soon,' says Pete as he sits down, oblivious to the change of atmosphere.

'Actually, if no one minds, I thought we could stay in the pub,' I say, looking nervously at everyone. After that conversation with Ben I don't really fancy going all pretentious and wine-snobby. I feel like I'm finally getting to understand him and I want to know more.

'That sounds good to me,' says Sian.

I don't think she cares as long as she's near Pete. It wasn't so much about the vineyard for her as it was an excuse to see him again.

'Me too,' says Pete. 'I didn't fancy being out in the rain again this weekend. We could always do a pub crawl round the village. There's no more than a five-minute walk between each of them.'

'That sounds perfect,' I say.

'Rematch,' asks Sian, raising her eyes at Pete and pushing the Mastermind box in front of him.

'Are you sure you don't want to do the wine tasting?' asks Ben, whilst the others get their competitive groove on.

'Absolutely. I can do it another day.'

The list-obsessed part of me is jumping up and down and tapping the schedule, but I don't care about her right now – there are more important things in life.

'I'm guessing after your uni confessions that you don't mind giving it a miss.'

'No, I'm pretty happy. It's just that I know how you were trying to do the list as quickly as you could.'

He knows that Sian doesn't know about Joseph and I know that he's hinting at it subtly.

'It doesn't matter,' I say. 'I mean, maybe I could substitute it with a country pub crawl.'

That's almost as adventurous as wine tasting, right? I mean Joseph and I never did one of those.

'Maybe you should shake things up on the list more often, or add some new things to it.'

I know we're talking in code, but I wish we weren't talking about this in such close proximity to Sian. I feel so guilty that Ben knows things my best friend doesn't. It breaks my heart a little that I'm keeping such a big secret from her.

'I think I will one day, but now I'm happy doing what I'm doing.'

'Right,' says Ben, nodding.

'I have to admit, though, it is nice doing something spontaneous. It feels like so much of my life has been planned lately and all my weekends taken up by the list and previously by Joseph, that blowing off a task feels a bit naughty, but really good. When I was dating Joseph, he always liked everything ordered and routine. Not that it was a bad thing, I'm one of those people that needs pushing into gear sometimes, as you might have gathered. But it's nice to do something spur of the moment once in a while.'

I look at Ben expectantly.

'And aren't you going to say that your best memories come from you being spontaneous?'

'I wasn't going to,' says Ben laughing. 'Although thinking about it, those spontaneous camping trips in the middle of nowhere ...'

Him and his bloody camping.

'But seriously, once this list is done, you'll have to start doing more of these types of things.'

He's right. This list has opened my eyes to what I've been missing out on all these years and I really should be experiencing more.

All this talk of the end of the list is making me nervous. If I'm officially changing the wine tasting to a country pub crawl, then I've only got Paris and the abseil left to do. What if I get through the list and I still don't have Joseph back? I know it won't have all been for nothing, but I'll still be right where I am now. Single. And I won't even have Ben to hang out with.

I'm not ready to think about that just yet.

'So, after your B&B experience, can you honestly tell me that you'd rather have stayed in the bunkhouse?' I say, changing the subject away from me and the list.

'Honestly?' He runs his hands through his messy hair. 'Yes, I would have much rather stayed in the bunkhouse. Although they did have this wet room at the B&B that almost converted me. It had those little jets that spurted down the shower wall so that it massaged your back and kept you warm.'

'Are you sure that didn't beat the bunkhouse?'

Ben nods, but I'm not convinced.

I know one thing for sure: if I was his girlfriend I wouldn't be too impressed to hear him talk like that. I know he's only being loyal to his friends, and that he felt bad bailing on everyone, but I'd like to think if I'd surprised my boyfriend that it would have been the ultimate good surprise.

I suddenly notice that it's gone quiet at the other end of the table, and I turn to see Sian and Pete kissing.

I gesture with my head to Ben, and he raises his eyebrows.

'Shall we go?' I mouth to him, and he nods.

We slide out from the table as quietly as possible, but the two lovebirds don't seem to have noticed.

'Darts?' says Ben, pointing at the board in the corner.

'Why not?'

It doesn't look like we're going anywhere any time soon. And for once, when Sian's getting her claws into a man, and I'm stuck with the guy's mate, I don't mind. I could think of a million worse ways to spend an afternoon than hanging out in a pub with Ben. Especially when I finally feel like I'm starting to get to know the real him.

Chapter Twenty-One

One week, four days, and after today, no more tasks to hide behind. I better come up with an excuse and fast ...

'I don't think I've ever been so excited to get out of bed at such an ungodly hour,' I say as we walk into the carriage of our Eurostar train.

I've got those butterflies I used to get when I went on a school trip. That feeling of being let loose in an unknown environment whilst filled with the excitement of what might happen.

'You know me, I like mornings.'

Before I met Ben I thought it was an urban myth that anyone liked mornings.

We find our seats – two together without a table. We thought that would be nicer than having to make small talk with anyone else. It's bad enough I'm going to have to talk to Ben at seven a.m., let alone to strangers.

I settle in by the window and look out over the station platform. I can't believe in a matter of hours we'll be stepping off the other side in Gay Paree. I rub my hands together in glee and Ben laughs at me.

'What, can't a girl be happy that she's on her way to Paris?'

'It's just – it's the first time that I've seen you happy about anything we've done on the list. I was thinking I'd have to drag you kicking and screaming from your bed.'

'And there was me bringing you a cup of tea.'

The train announcement crackles through the intercom and tells of our imminent departure.

Ben opens his rucksack and I'm hedging my bets that he's going to pull out his trusty flask of tea to go with the Danish pastries we've brought along for the journey, but to my surprise he pulls out a little half bottle of Veuve Clicquot.

It's the kind of thing that I would have expected Joseph to do, not Ben.

'Thought it was that kind of trip,' he says, almost apologetically, as I realise that I'm staring at him open-mouthed.

'That's a lovely touch.'

He smiles and his little dimple endearingly appears in his cheek.

'I've got some orange juice too,' he says, pulling out a bottle of Tropicana, and two plastic flutes.

'Flutes,' I say, laughing. 'Wow, you really are pushing the boat out.'

'Well, I know how you feel about drinking wine from mugs, so I figured that Champagne from anything other than a flute would be heresy.'

'It absolutely would,' I say, putting on my poshest voice and taking the glasses so that Ben can undo the champers.

He pops the cork and we have that immediate moment of scrambling to get the drink in the glasses and not over our laps, forgetting to leave room for the orange juice.

'Ah well,' I say shrugging. 'Next one's a Buck's Fizz.'

'To Paris.' Ben holds his glass up towards mine.

'To Paris,' I repeat, and as I catch his eye for a moment I go all warm and fuzzy inside.

'To Paris,' I mumble to myself again as I avert my eyes and try to break the spell. I quickly sip my drink and look out the window as the train lurches into action.

'We're here,' says Ben, nudging my side.

I snap my head up with a jolt and subtly try to wipe away the drool that's formed in the corner of my mouth.

Judging from the smirk on Ben's face, it wasn't that subtle.

'How long was I asleep?' I ask, thinking that I barely remember going past Ashford. It seems that the Champagne and early start didn't really agree with me.

'Most of the way. Good job I had my Kindle to keep me company.'

'Sorry,' I mumble.

'No worries, I'm sure Dave Gorman is much more interesting than you would have been at this time in the morning anyway.'

'Oi,' I say, nudging him back and then smoothing down my hair.

'Well, here we are, Gare du Nord.'

'So much for us making a plan of action on the train,' I say, tucking my unopened guidebook away into my rucksack.

'I think we wing it, except I did book the tickets for the Eiffel Tower lifts for us at –'

'Don't tell me when.'

'What?'

We gather up our things and start walking towards the doors of the train.

'Don't tell me what time. I'm going to be panicking enough as it is that we're going up that thing, I don't want to know the time of D-Day. I'd rather be surprised and that way I don't have time to get worked up about it.'

Ben rolls his eyes at me in a jokey way.

'All right, crazy lady. Whatever you want. So, aside from the mystery of the Eiffel Tower, what do you want to do? Did you actually want to go inside the Louvre, because if you do that should probably be our starting point.'

'Not really – I've been before,' I say, squinting. 'Is that bad? I know it's got all those wonderful paintings, but I'd much rather soak up the other delicacies Paris has to offer.'

'Like?'

'Coffee and croissants.'

'In that case, let's start with getting a proper breakfast. We can head to the Ile de la Cité, that way we can tick off going to see Notre Dame and the Seine at the same time. There are loads of little cute cafes and –'

'– and we can sit outside on one of those iron chairs and watch the glamorous people walk by.'

'Yeah, I was going to say, and have overpriced coffee and crois-sants, but sure. Your version sounds better.'

Half an hour later we're sat in La Place Dauphine, a pretty, tree-lined square surrounded by Parisian-looking buildings with little cafes at the bottom of them.

It's everything I imagined it would be – uncomfortable iron chairs that are cold on your bum, overpriced tourist menu and impatient waiting staff that scoff at my poor GCSE French skills – but I love it.

Our waiter brings out our grands cafés crèmes and the croque-madame I've ordered. Not traditional breakfast fare, but I couldn't resist that oozy egg and cheese combo.

The weather's being kind to us and it's a perfect spring morning – bright, with only a few clouds in the sky. There's still a slight chill in the air, so I wrap my light jacket round me and pull my patterned White Stuff scarf higher around my neck.

It took me ages to select an outfit worthy of a day trip to the fashion capital of the world. In the end I settled on skinny jeans, a Breton-style blue-and-white-striped jumper, my navy military jacket and my navy-and-red floral scarf. I deliberated at length about the shoes, and plumped for a pair of tatty Con-verse which don't really go, but I thought they'd be infinitely more comfortable than my red ballet pumps that would have been my first choice.

'So, should I take your picture?' asks Ben picking up his cam-era just as I tuck into my sandwich and have a giant mouthful of food.

I try to smile, but imagine I look like a hamster with puffy cheeks. Ben looks at the viewfinder and pulls a face.

'Perhaps I'll wait until you've finished.'

'What? Am I not an attractive eater?' I ask, finally swallowing.

'You're one of the most attractive eaters I've ever known,' he says, laughing.

I blush a little even though I know he's only joking.

'OK, let's try again,' I say picking up my coffee cup to hide my cheeks.

Ben picks up his camera again and snaps away.

'So, we're off to see Notre Dame after this then?'

I'm trying to rack my brains to remember the story of the Hunchback from the Disney movie, but it's all a bit foggy in my mind.

'Yes, it's not very far from here. Then we can go and see City Hall – that's pretty impressive – and then we could hop on the metro and go to the Champs-Élysées and get your all-important photo of the Arc de Triomphe.'

'Wowsers. That's a pretty detailed list for winging it.'

I sip my coffee and it hits all the right spots. It's exactly what I needed to pep me up after that little catnap on the train.

'I may have looked at the guidebook whilst you were sleeping.'

'I knew it,' I say, smiling. 'You like to paint this picture that you're this easy, breezy spontaneous guy, but deep down you're a guidebook follower.'

'I feel wounded,' he says, putting his hand across his chest. 'You've insulted my inner traveller.'

'It's true though, isn't it?' I squint my eyes as if I'm trying to scrutinise his soul.

'OK, I'll admit it – whenever I've backpacked I've always taken the bible, otherwise known as the *Lonely Planet*. I don't follow it to the letter, but they are bloody useful in making sure you don't miss bits. I learnt that lesson when I was seventeen and interrailed round Europe. I didn't do the guidebook thing, and only read about places as I left a city. I missed out on an awful lot just traipsing around trying to soak up the atmosphere. So now I try and do a bit of both. Wandering around a little aimlessly but still seeing the famous sights. They're usually famous for a reason.'

'I guess that's true,' I say, secretly pleased that Ben has taken control. We're not here for very long and it's a tall order to do Paris in a day, so at least with him taking charge we might actually get to see more than a few cafes, which is what I'd probably have spent the day doing otherwise.

We finish our food and drink and pay the grumpy waiter, before walking along the Seine in the direction of Notre Dame.

I feel like I'm walking in a postcard scene; everything from the weather to the scenery looks so perfect. I turn to Ben and for a moment I almost scoop up his hand in mine so we can walk along swinging our arms. It just feels like it's the thing to do. I know Paris is supposed to the city of love but I didn't expect it to make me all doe-eyed while I was here with Ben. Maybe when Joseph and I get back together we should come to Paris if this is the effect the city can have on me.

'How about a photo?' I say, realising we've got the perfect backdrop as you can see the Eiffel Tower and other picturesque Parisian buildings on the other side of the Seine.

'OK,' says Ben, digging out his camera and standing back.

'No, you've got to be in the photo too. I reckon your arms are long enough for a selfie.'

'Are you saying I'm gangly?'

'No, they're just a bit longer than mine,' I say, getting the giggles.

Ben looks behind us at the view and positions me next to the concrete balustrade before standing next to me.

'I think we're going to have to get in close,' he says, putting his arm around me and stretching out the one holding the camera.

It feels cosy being nestled in with Ben. Instead of feeling awkward and as if I'm invading his personal space, it feels natural.

He takes the photo and for a minute we stay wrapped up together as he reviews the picture on the viewfinder.

'That's not bad,' I say.

It really isn't. Not only do I not have a double chin or giant bags under my eyes, but I look kind of pretty. Ben looks like, well, Ben. A mess of curls on his head and his stubbly beard. We actually make a cute couple.

What is it with this damn city, are they pumping pheromones out somewhere?

'So,' says Ben, releasing his arm with a little cough as if he's embarrassed that we've stayed that way for longer than necessary.

'I should probably take a photo just of you, as I'm sure you don't want to put that photo on Facebook – it might give Joseph the wrong idea.'

'Joseph, right,' I say nodding. I'd temporarily forgotten about him. My mind has been stuck on that hug and that photo. 'Although a photo of the two of us might make him jealous.'

A number of photos of me and Ben looking starry-eyed in Paris might rile him up enough to get him back.

'I hardly think he'll be jealous of me, if your descriptions of him are anything to go by.'

We start to slowly meander along the river bank once more. Despite being on a tight schedule, it seems neither of us are in the mood to hurry.

'I think he'd have every reason to be jealous of you,' I say without thinking.

This city has got right under my skin and suddenly all I want to do is kiss him. Where did that come from? It's like I got out of the train station and accidentally inhaled a love potion.

I can feel Ben looking at me and I can't turn to meet his eyes, in case he's thinking the same as me.

I try and fix an image of Joseph in my mind to remind myself why we're in this city in the first place.

Ben doesn't say anything and after a little while I sense that he's looked away again.

'Oh, wow,' I say involuntarily as I realise we've made it to the cathedral. It's the perfect thing to distract me from the crazy thoughts about Ben that keep interrupting my Joseph pining.

'I had no idea this place was so impressive,' I say, gaping at the building like a proper tourist.

There's a swarm of people milling about snapping photos and craning their necks to get a better view, and I can't help but join them.

'When I came here on the school trip they were doing restoration work on it,' I say. 'It had those big canopy sheets over the scaffolding with a painted scene of what it looked like, but it did not do it justice.'

I start snapping away like I'm David Bailey – I honestly don't think I've seen anything like it. The architecture is extraordinary.

I look back at Ben, who's standing on the pavement smiling.

'What?'

I tuck my hair behind my ear, suddenly feeling slightly self-conscious.

'Nothing. It's just nice to see you like this.'

'What, happy?'

'No, excited and passionate about something.'

'Ah, well, don't forget you've probably seen me at my worst, doing things that I'd rather not do. Whereas this, this is totally up my street. I did a history of architecture module at university and I actually really enjoyed it.'

'So you've got an inner geek in you too.'

'Oh, yes, she's not buried that deep. I was torn between doing art history and graphic design at university.'

'Do you think you made the right choice?' asks Ben as we start to circle the outside of the building.

'Definitely. As soon as I started my course I knew it was the right decision. I love being creative every day in my job. I can't imagine now that I'd have been happy studying someone else's creativity.'

'It's nice, isn't it? Doing a job you love.'

'Yeah, I often forget how lucky I am to enjoy what I do. I guess I take it for granted.'

'I think we're all a little guilty of that.'

'And you, you love working in the shop?'

'I do.'

'What did you do at uni?'

Ben coughs and mutters something.

'I'm sorry, I didn't quite hear.'

'Forensic science,' he repeats before sighing.

'Forensic science? Like CSI, white-suit type stuff?'

Ben nods.

'And you ended up with a bike shop? How did that happen?'

'I worked in a specialist bike shop when I was at uni. Then I came down to Portsmouth to start a master's, but after a few weeks I realised it wasn't for me. I ended up doing some temping work in a call centre and working part-time at a bike shop. One day the owner told me he was looking to sell and I thought, what the hell.'

'Wow. You just bought it?'

'Uh-huh. It sounds pretty crazy now, but the guy hadn't done a very good job with it, and it didn't cost that much. I had some inheritance money from my granddad and I managed to make a pretty good business case and got a bank loan. Of course, that was before the recession when they handed out loans willy-nilly.'

'That's still pretty impressive.'

'Well, I'd had the idea for supporting the shop with the mail-order side, and luckily over the years that's kept the shop afloat.'

'Would you ever consider just going mail-order? If that's where the money is?'

Ben shakes his head. 'Nah, I'd miss the people in the shop. There's something really satisfying about seeing people find their perfect bike.'

'You're a really cheesy guy at heart, aren't you?'

'Absolutely.'

For a minute we lock eyes and I feel that thing between us again. I'm getting the impression that it's got nothing to do with the city and its romantic vibe and everything to do with the man standing in front of me. It's as if I'm looking at him for the first time and really seeing him.

I can't believe that I've never noticed the way his hazel eyes twinkle in the light, or the way his messy waves of hair sprout off in such different directions. He's got an air of Patrick Dempsey about him and for the first time I see him as my own McDreamy.

Oh, McDreamy – RIP.

I want to reach up and run my hand over his stubbly cheek and pull his face into mine. And I want more than anything to kiss him. I take a deep breath and wonder if I'm brave enough, but before I get the chance we're interrupted by his mobile ringing.

The moment is gone and I look away as he scrambles around in his bag for it.

'It's Tammy,' he says looking at the caller ID.

He answers the phone and walks away towards the river as I watch him go.

I feel foolish. There was me about to kiss someone who has a girlfriend. I shake my head. I may be in the most romantic city in the world, but I have to remember I'm with someone else's boyfriend.

And not only that, I'm here to win back my ex-boyfriend. The man who's supposed to be the love of my life. This is no time to be distracted just because there's a cute guy here in front of me.

I sigh and look up at the building once more and suddenly remember the story of the unrequited love of Quasimodo in *The Hunchback of Notre-Dame*. It's an omen of doomed love if ever I saw one, and a reminder that things with Ben are not meant to be.

I look at my watch. I've got just under ten hours to spend in Paris with Ben, and I'm going to have to keep my emerging feelings under wraps and remind myself that Joseph's the man I want to be with, not Ben.

As he strolls towards me, I try and compose myself, putting on the best smile I can muster.

'So,' I say, 'ready for the Champs-Élysées.'

Nothing kills romance like shopping.

'*On y va*,' says Ben.

He doesn't explain his conversation with Tammy and I don't ask. I don't want to know. He has a girlfriend and I'm hopefully soon going to have my boyfriend back, that's all I need to remember, as I try and block out whatever romantic fantasies this city is making me have.

Chapter Twenty-Two

Still one week, four days until the abseil, but I've got one other Tower of Terror to conquer first.

All day I've been surprised at how small the Eiffel Tower looks on the skyline of Paris. Wherever we've been in the city, it's being poking out from behind buildings, but not towering over them like I expected. But now that I'm standing underneath it, it seems flipping enormous.

'Well, here we are,' says Ben.

'Here we are indeed.'

Paris has done a pretty good job of distracting me with its fancy boutiques, delicious patisseries and beautiful buildings. But now, as the sun is setting, it's finally time for us to go up the tower.

'Hopefully it should just be dark by the time we get up the top.'

I don't know why but that makes me feel worse. I desperately want to chicken out, but I don't feel like I can because Ben's already reserved and paid for the tickets.

I look up at the lattice of ironwork and I can see all the way up through the gaps. It's doing little to calm my racing heart.

'Are you sure it's safe? I mean, wasn't it built as a temporary structure for a fair?'

'It's one of the world's most iconic, and probably most visited, attractions. I'm pretty sure that they've made sure it's safe.'

I glance back up. I'm still not convinced. My stomach's churning with nerves and I feel sick.

'Come on, Abi. It'll be good training for your Spinnaker challenge.'

My muscles go rigid with fear. I've been trying to banish thoughts of that abseil from my mind, but now, standing next to this tower, it's starting to seem a whole lot more real.

'Is this taller than the Spinnaker?' I ask, not knowing what would make a more comforting answer.

'Yeah. But don't worry, we don't have to go up that high if you don't want to. We can stop at one of the lower floors. The views are better the higher you go, but the point of us going up there is to tick it off your list, so don't feel like you have to go up high. And if you really don't want to go up, you don't have to. I mean we're at the Eiffel Tower, and we've done the rest of Paris pretty much in a day. Joseph was never specific about what had to be done.'

'I know,' I say, thinking that it would be so easy not to bother. I could take a photo right here beneath the arches and be done with it. But there's a part of me that wants to go up. To prove to myself that I can do this. My fear of heights has held me back for so long and if I'm going to stand any sort of chance of going down the Spinnaker Tower in less than two weeks' time, then I've got to at least try and get a head for heights.

I take a deep breath and look Ben in the eye. 'Let's do this,' I say determinedly.

Ben smiles. 'OK then.'

He turns and walks towards the queue for pre-booked tickets, and before I know it we're shuffling along in a throng of tourists waiting impatiently for the lift.

'It's not too late,' whispers Ben as we finally board the lift.

I smile half-heartedly. He's so supportive, I couldn't have picked anyone nicer to have done this with.

The lift creaks into action and whizzes us God knows how many metres above the ground. Too many to think about. There's no turning back now.

We decided to give the first floor a miss, not only would it mean walking up stairs when my legs are already aching from all of today's sightseeing, but it would also mean I'd almost certainly chicken out of going up any higher.

Having looked at the diagram of the different stages at the bottom, I'd decided I'm not brave enough for the top of the tower – the thought of both the height and the glass elevator that takes you up to it reduced my legs to jelly.

When we reach our floor I let the others get off first, before I slowly make my way out of the lift. I get about a foot or two outside before stopping.

I'm hit first by the wind that whistles round my ears. It feels so much colder up here. Maybe it's psychological. Or maybe it's simply that dusk has given way to nightfall while we were queuing to get up here.

The whole of Paris is coated in a blanket of darkness with twinkling lights that look like giant strings of fairy lights. It's breathtaking. For a minute I'm so mesmerised by the view that it takes me a while to get a sense of how high up we are. When I do, I start to stagger backwards, getting as far away from the edge as I can.

'Are you OK?' asks Ben. He instinctively grabs my arm and I cling on to him with both hands and pull him towards me.

'It's beautiful,' I whisper, a slight stammer to my voice, my fear clearly evident.

'Isn't it?' says Ben looking round.

I know my hands are clammy and sweaty and my nails are probably digging into Ben's arms, but I can't move them. He's like my safety blanket. I feel OK as long as I'm clinging onto him for dear life.

'Shall I take your photo?' he asks.

'I can't let go,' I say, suddenly terrified that he's going to move.

He pulls his camera out and slips his other arm round my waist before spinning me round gently. He lifts his arm out and takes another selfie of us.

'It's not like we're going to see anything anyway,' he says, laughing. 'It'll just come out black behind us.'

'So we could have taken a photo anywhere and pretended.'

'I did give you the option.'

'I know. But I'm actually OK.'

'I think my arm would say otherwise.'

I automatically release my grip but stay huddled into him.

'I'll keep you safe,' he says. 'It's a bit easier like this than with you threatening to break my skin with your nails.'

He's smiling and I know he's not serious. For one thing the hoodie he's wearing is way too thick for me to be able to break the skin under it, but having someone holding him in a Chinese burn can't have been the most comfortable thing.

'Do you want to see the rest of the views?' asks Ben.

'I don't think I can go any higher,' I say honestly.

'I meant walking round the outside.'

He drops his arm but before I can panic he takes my hand and gently leads me round the platform.

'Now don't squeeze too hard, I can't ride a bike with one hand.'

I giggle and try to loosen my grip.

'Can't you ride a bike one-handed? I'm sure I can.'

'Abi, the bike-riding expert.'

I mentally try and picture myself riding one-handed and I think back to the cycling proficiency I had to take at school.

'What about when you need to signal?'

Ben laughs and leans down closer to my ear. 'I'll let you into a secret. I can ride no-handed. But still please don't bugger up my hand.'

'Wow, no-handed. You're my hero,' I say, joking and tilting my head playfully.

Ben turns towards me and his hand gravitates to my free one and we suddenly find ourselves facing one another with our hands swinging in the breeze.

If ever there was a perfect moment for a first kiss, then this would be it. It's so cheesily romantic and perfect that I almost want to laugh at the irony that I'm here in this position with Ben. But I don't. I keep my head tilted and look straight into his eyes.

Blimey, the pheromones that this city is pumping must be emanating from here as it feels as if they've been kicked up a notch.

'Do you two want your photo taken?' asks an American woman as she walks past us, smiling. 'Y'all look so cute up here.'

I smile and feel my cheeks blush.

'That would be lovely,' says Ben. 'Might be nice to have a photo of us where I don't have some sort of mutant arm in the picture.'

'Go back against the railings,' says the woman, taking Ben's camera from him.

I'm about to protest about moving from the safety of the inside of the tower, but Ben starts gently leading me back. I dread to think how close to the edge we are. I start to shake, but he pulls me in close and puts both of his arms around me.

'Say cheese,' says the woman.

I barely mumble something, too unsure as to whether I'm nervous about being near the edge or being so close to Ben.

The woman snaps away and finally content she hands the camera back to us.

'Y'all are such a photogenic couple. Have a great rest of your trip,' she says before shuffling off.

I try and mutter that we're not a couple, but I can't quite get the words out.

'Do you think Joseph will be suitably jealous of your trip now?' asks Ben, releasing me from the bear hug and leading me back towards the safety of the wall.

For a minute I realise that I haven't even been thinking about Joseph since we got up here, and it breaks the spell I'm under as it hits me that nothing romantic is going to happen with Ben. He's got Tammy and I'm hopefully going to get Joseph back. Whatever I'm feeling isn't real, it's just the city getting under my skin. It's all those cheesy rom-coms I've watched and books I've read.

'I've had enough,' I say. 'Can we go back down?'

I've got to get away from this romantic setting. We're due back at the station soon for our train home, and right now the dingy railway station with its grime and shifty-looking characters is exactly what I need to purge these thoughts of Ben from my brain.

Ben leads me back down to the lifts and we descend the tower in silence. I look at him as he stares down at the floor and I wonder if he felt the same way I did in that moment where I wanted to kiss him. Or was he thinking about his girlfriend?

'You all right?' he asks as he catches me looking at him.

I blush and cough. 'Yes, fine. Just thinking back over today,' I say, lying.

'It's been a great day,' he says, smiling. 'I can't believe how much we packed in.'

'I know. I'm going to be exhausted at work tomorrow.'

'Yeah. At least I've got an easy day in the shop. My dad's coming down so I can always hide out the back pretending to do inventory while taking a sneaky sleep.'

'Lucky you.'

'I thought you'd taken the morning off?'

'I'd planned to, but after the debacle with that hotel client last week I cancelled it. I'm trying to prove to Rick that I'm all conscientious by working long hours. It's not even like I could work from home.'

I'm still not brave enough to do that after my letter from HR.

We get out of the lift and try to orientate ourselves before walking in the direction of the metro.

'Well, you can have a sleep on the journey home. That'll give you about four hours to drool on my shoulder.'

'Oi,' I say, giving him a shove.

He shoves me back and I feel like we're drunk teenagers.

He grabs my arms and holds them above my head so I can't hit him any more.

'That's not fair,' I say, wriggling and laughing.

He looks at me, smiling back. 'I don't like to play by the rules.'

He holds my gaze and I suddenly feel like he's going to kiss me. He actually leans down towards me.

I turn my head and Ben drops my arms.

'Shouldn't we be getting back to the station, our train will be going soon,' I say, ignoring what was just about to happen.

It seems it's not only me that's getting carried away in the city of love.

'Yes, you're probably right,' he says, clearing his throat. 'We don't want to miss it or else we'll never make the train back down to Pompey.'

I wish we could click our fingers and get home. It's such a long way. By the time we get back on the train to St Pancras and then a couple of tube changes to Waterloo, we still have another hour and a half on the train down to Portsmouth. It all seemed so easy when we were booking it, but I'm absolutely exhausted from our sightseeing extravaganza.

'So, that's another thing ticked off the list, then,' says Ben.

'I know,' I say, realising it's my last challenge with him and therefore the last legitimate reason – according to Tammy – to see him.

'Have you given any more thought to your own list?'

'A little,' I say. In truth, I've done a lot of thinking. Since the other day when we were talking in the pub, I've started to think about what I really want. And not just what would be on mine and Joseph's joint bucket list, but what would make me happy.

'You have? What's on it?'

I feel a bit silly saying my list out loud. It was one thing passing Joseph's off as my own, but that was already honed and crafted.

'Come on, I'm not going to laugh.'

'Promise?'

'Promise,' says Ben as we head down into the metro station and work out which direction we're going in.

'OK. I want to learn to bake. I don't mean get to *Great British Bake Off* standard, but I would like to be able to make a pastry without having to buy it ready-made, and I'd love to make a scone that wasn't rock hard.'

'And what else?'

'I enjoyed being outdoors when I went windsurfing, but thought it was a bit physical, so I'd sort of maybe like to learn to sail.'

I'm wrinkling my face up as I keep expecting Ben to heckle, as by his adrenaline-junkie standards that is pretty tame.

'You couldn't live in a more perfect city to learn. I think they do lessons at the outdoor centre.'

'They do,' I say, nodding.

Our train comes in and we jump on board.

'What else?'

'That's as far as I've got so far.'

It's pathetic, I know that it's so short, but it's not that I don't want to do more, it's that I'm not sure what I want to do. I know that I want to do more travelling, but I don't know where. I need to do some proper research.

'Well, you've not got long before Joseph's list is over and you'll be starting your own.'

'No,' I say, thinking about what that means in terms of both my fate with Joseph and my friendship with Ben.

I don't want to think of that now. I don't want to ruin what's been a perfect day.

'What a wonderful day,' I say, more to myself than Ben.

'It really was,' says Ben. He gives me a look similar to the one he gave me at the bottom of the Eiffel Tower.

I look out the window into the dark train tunnel as if watching the passing scenery. I can't bring myself to look in his eyes.

The sooner we get to the Eurostar and get back home, the sooner this city and all its bloody romance will stop clouding my mind with thoughts of Ben, and I can focus on the man I really want – Joseph.

Chapter Twenty-Three

A week tomorrow until the abseil. No more challenges left, no excuse thought of, no Joseph coming back to me – looks like I've got no choice but to go through with it …

'I can't believe you have a boyfriend,' I say to Sian as I put on my lipstick.

I look at her in the mirror, sitting on my bed. She looks different. She looks … happy. There's a warmth in her eyes that I haven't seen before, and there's definitely more smiling than scowling.

'I don't have a boyfriend. We haven't had that talk yet.'

'*Yet*. So you're going to have it,' I say, turning to her. My cheeks are starting to hurt from smiling. I didn't think it was possible to be so happy about someone else's love life. I've been waiting so long for it.

Since our impromptu pub crawl last weekend, Sian has been on three dates with Pete. For once she's kept her knickers on. Apparently they're getting to know each other before they do the deed.

It's only a matter of time before they're officially an item.

I just can't believe how quickly it's all happened. She's gone from the queen of one-night stands, to a veritable ice maiden, to picking my brains about where's best for romantic picnics.

'Right, are you ready?' asks Sian as she stands up from the bed and grabs her bag.

I recognise that look in her eyes. It's the one that I used to get when I was on my way to Joseph's. That absolutely-can't-wait-to-see-them look.

'Yes,' I say, putting on my jacket and flicking my hair out of the collar. I'm going to have to get it cut again soon. I've grown quite attached to my bob, but my hair's grown so much that it's almost reaching my shoulders.

'Great.'

It's Friday night and we're meeting Pete, Ben and the rest of the Snowdon crew at a nearby pub. On the walk over Sian treats me to a blow-by-blow account of her date. Luckily with no bedroom antics to hear about I can for once relax and listen to her story without cringing my way through.

Much to Sian's disappointment we're the first to arrive at the King Street Tavern. We secure a round table with a good view of the door, despite the fact that the pub is fairly small and it would be hard not to spot to us wherever we sat.

Sian heads off to the bar to get us a drink and I busy myself with my phone. Ben emailed me the photos of Paris this afternoon and I posted them straight to Facebook. I can't resist having another look at them. They're mainly of me, but there are a couple of our joint selfies.

I look at my notifications, and see that people have liked my photos. I check out the list of who and I'm taken aback. It takes me a minute for the words 'Joseph Small has commented on your photo' to sink in.

My hands start to shake as I click on the little icon. Damn my sweaty fingers – the touchscreen won't register my swiping. I wipe my fingers on my jeans and give it another go, and this time it takes me through to the page.

He's commented on the photo that Ben took of me from the side looking out over the Seine. I'm gazing wistfully over at the Parisian buildings on the opposite bank. It's the perfect shot and I had no idea he was taking it. I read Joseph's comment and stare at it in disbelief.

Joseph Small
I always wanted to go to Paris with you.

I can't believe he wrote that. I read it again just to make sure that my eyes aren't playing tricks on me. My mind immediately goes into overdrive. I try and interpret it in every way possible. Does it mean that he still wants to go to Paris with me, or that he did when we were dating?

My heart's racing as I consider that my plan might be working.

I mean, he's seen my photos, and he's interacting with me. He's not just liked a photo, but he's taken the time to comment. And not only that, that comment had a semi-romantic undertone.

Sian deposits a glass of wine on the table in front of me and I practically throw the phone back into my bag.

'What are you up to?' she asks as she sits down on the bench.

'Oh, just checking Facebook,' I say casually. My voice is ever so slightly squeakier than usual, and my cheeks must be flushed because they feel like they're burning. Surely she's going to twig that something's up.

She wouldn't understand my excitement about the comment. With her not knowing about my real motivation for completing the list she wouldn't get what it could mean. In her eyes I'm getting over Joseph. She made her feelings quite clear about him when we broke up, list or no list. I doubt she'd be pleased about him making contact now.

'That's what I should do,' she says pulling out her phone. 'I'll check in on Facebook – then Pete will know we're already here.'

She taps away at the screen before putting it down on the table.

'You really are smitten,' I say, laughing.

She tries to shrug it away, but she knows as much as I do that it's true.

Luckily for Sian her patience isn't tested for too much longer as the door to the pub opens and in walk Pete and Ben. They're closely followed by Laura, Giles and Doug and our group is complete.

As everyone says their hellos and sorts themselves out with drinks, I realise how pleased I am to be reunited with the Snowdon crew. I just hope this time there won't be a crazy Tammy interruption.

'So you liked the photos then?' says Ben as he sits down next to me and sips his pint.

'They're lovely. You've got a real eye for it.'

'It's one of my little hobbies, but it helps when the subject matter is pretty.'

'Yeah,' I say nodding. 'I guess Paris is the ultimate photographer's dream.'

Ben opens his mouth to say something, but he stops short.

'What?' I ask.

He smiles, before taking another sip of his drink. 'Nothing.'

'You'd never guess what just happened,' I say, turning my head to check that Sian isn't listening. She's practically sat on Pete's lap and something tells me that she's not aware that anyone else is even in the room.

'What?'

'Joseph commented on one of the photos,' I whisper, leaning close to Ben. 'You know the photo you took of me looking out across the Seine.'

He nods his head.

'What did he say?' he asks, without looking at me, his eyes firmly glued to the table.

'He said, "I always wanted to go to Paris with you".'

The words are already etched into my memory.

He nods again, but doesn't say anything.

'Well, what do you think? Is it a good sign?'

'It sounds like he's still into you.'

My heart begins to beat a little faster. Having a man interpret it that way too makes it all the more special.

I know that I've been doing my list to get Joseph back but there was always part of me deep down that thought I would never succeed. But with that one line he's given me hope that I haven't been wasting my time.

A smile spreads across my face. For the first time I actually feel like I want to abseil off the tower.

'Anyone want to play a game of bar billiards?' asks Laura from across the table.

'I do,' says Ben, standing up.

'Great. Abi, do you want to play too? Girls against boys?'

'Sure,' I say, standing up and walking to the game in the corner. I've only played a couple of times, but was really rubbish both occasions.

'Looks like you guys had a great time in Paris,' she says as she positions herself next to me and chalks her cue.

'We did,' I say, looking at Ben, who's taking the first shot and nodding.

'The photos look amazing. You were lucky with the weather.'

'It was perfect. Not too hot and not too cold.'

'I went once in the summer and it was stifling, not to mention it stank.'

'I did tell her that everyone says not to go to Paris in August,' says Giles, rolling his eyes. 'She wouldn't listen though.'

'I wanted to do al fresco dining so I needed to go when it was warm. Learnt my lesson though. I loved the photo of you two up the Eiffel Tower. It looks almost romantic.'

There's a twinkle in her eye and I know what she's thinking.

It hits me that I never stopped to consider what Tammy would have thought of the pictures. I'd put them up and tagged Ben and never gave it another thought. I was so hellbent on what it could do to make Joseph jealous that I hadn't thought about what implications it might have on Ben's relationship.

'So, was it romantic?' she says leaning into me and lowering her voice.

I look up at Ben as he takes his shot and think back to our almost kiss. It was romantic, but I can't tell Laura that. I don't even want to admit that to myself.

'Don't forget, Ben has a girlfriend,' I whisper back.

That ought to shut her up – it's pretty hard to argue with.

She looks back at me before looking at Ben and whipping her head round back at me.

'You mean he didn't tell you?' she says. Her eyes wrinkling and her brow furrowing.

'Tell me what?'

'That he broke up with Tammy.'

'What?' I say, my voice barely audible.

'Abi, you're up,' says Giles.

I'm confused for a second before I realise that he's talking about the bar billiards. I go up to the table on autopilot and I take my shot, not really caring that I miss as I want to get back to Laura.

In my absence Giles has wrapped his arms around her and they look like they're having one of their cute moments. I'm desperate for it to be his turn so that I can get her back on her own.

When did Ben break up with Tammy? Was it after Paris? Was it because of Paris? Had he felt what I had? Why hasn't he told me?

As if my mind needed anything else to whirl around it after Joseph's Facebook comment. I nibble my fingernails as I wait impatiently for Laura and Giles to take their turns.

All the while I'm watching Ben out of the corner of my eye. He's not acting any different. He doesn't look like a heartbroken man. He's not like the shell of a person that I was when I broke up with Joseph.

'When did they break up?' I ask, as soon as I'm alone with Laura again.

'Before we went to Snowdon.'

'What?' I say, a little too loudly and Giles looks up at us.

That doesn't make any sense.

'But what about her turning up and them going off to the B&B?'

'Apparently,' says Laura, lowering her voice and arching her eyebrows, 'she wanted to try and convince him that they should get back together. Ben being the nice guy he is didn't want to reject her in front of everyone so they went to talk.'

'And they didn't get back together?' I say, not so much a question but a statement to try and get it straight in my head.

'No, it's over and I think from what Giles says that it's for good this time.'

It doesn't quite sink in. Ben's been single for the past two weeks, during which time I've spent hours and hours alone with him, and yet he didn't think to mention it.

'I honestly thought you knew,' says Laura. 'I mean those photos on Facebook ... I thought you two were getting together.'

This doesn't make sense. What has Ben being playing at? If only I'd known there was nothing but my feelings for Joseph standing in our way in Paris. That moment when I thought I wanted to kiss him, I could have.

'Why didn't he tell me?' I repeat out loud.

Laura and I both stare at Ben and he must sense it. He turns to us and looks taken aback that we're both looking directly at him.

'What? Have I got beer round my face?'

'Nothing,' Laura and I say in unison, making us seem even more shifty.

Ben shrugs his shoulder and takes his turn on the bar billiards table. Unsurprisingly Laura and I are getting well and truly trounced, but we're far too busy trying to work out what's going on in Ben's head.

Giles pots the winning ball, and celebrates with an air punch.

'See, girls suck,' he says, putting his hands on his hips in a superhero pose.

Laura hits him playfully before slipping her arms around him. She subtly leads him towards the bar, leaving Ben and me together.

'Want a rematch?' asks Ben.

I shake my head. I'm in no mood for games.

'Why didn't you tell me about Tammy?'

Ben's mouth drops open and he looks totally caught off balance.

'Whoa,' he says, running his hand through his hair. 'Who told you? Giles?'

'Laura.'

'Ah,' he says. 'Figures.'

'So …'

I can't believe he's leaving me hanging.

'I didn't know how to bring it up.'

'Right, so when we were in the pub talking about your trip to the B&B, or when she phoned when we were in Paris, neither of those were good opportunities to mention it?'

'It's not that I didn't want to tell you. In fact, it's the opposite.'

I'm about to ask him what he means, when I see Joseph walking into the pub with Marcus.

'Joseph,' I say.

'Exactly,' says Ben.

'What?' I look up at Ben, confused. He's got his back to the door and he can't possibly have seen him walk in.

'Nothing,' he says, sighing.

'Joseph's here,' I say, staring in disbelief.

Ben looks round.

'Which one is he?'

'The one with the waves in his hair.'

Ben nods. 'Aren't you going to go over and see him?'

Joseph gets to the bar and turns round and we immediately lock eyes. He smiles, before walking towards me. He taps Marcus on the arm and mutters something to him as he passes.

My knees are starting to buckle and I wish I could grab onto Ben to steady myself, but he's walked away, leaving me alone and unsupported.

'Abi,' says Joseph, bending down and kissing me on both cheeks. I'm motionless and let him, too scared to move. As his lips brush my cheeks I feel my whole body tingle.

'Hi, Joseph. I wouldn't have expected to see you here.'

It's not his kind of pub. It's got real personality, with its shabby-chic interior and homely feel. It's far from the shiny floorboards and bright spotlights that the bars he usually goes to have.

'I'll come clean with you. I came to see you.'

'How did you know I'd be here?'

Unlike him, my movements aren't so habitual.

'Sian tagged you on Facebook as being here and Marcus and I were in Southsea drinking and we thought we'd pop by.'

Ah, Facebook, the twenty-first-century stalker's tool.

I manage to smile at him. I can't believe he's here.

'I hope you don't mind me coming. Your new boyfriend wouldn't mind?'

Joseph is nodding his head towards Ben who's talking to Sian and Pete. I think my ears should be burning because from the not-so-subtle glances in my direction I can tell me talking to Joseph is the topic of conversation.

'He's not my boyfriend,' I say. 'He's just a friend.'

'A friend you went to Paris with.'

'Yep, just a friend,' I repeat.

So he *was* jealous.

'That's a relief to hear.'

I search his hypnotic eyes, trying to work out how he feels. Has my list worked? Is he here to get back together with me?

I feel my mind spinning out of control. I no longer know what I think. I would have thought that seeing him would have made me really happy, but the truth is it's just adding to the confusion. I can't work out why I'm so mad at Ben about keeping the secret about his break-up with Tammy. But seeing Joseph in front of me, my feelings for him come flooding back and the hope that I've clung on to since our break-up is still there.

I look over Joseph's shoulder and see Ben putting on his jacket. He's saying goodbye to the rest of our table and before I can catch his eye he's gone.

'Abi,' says Joseph. 'I think we should talk.'

My eyes flick between him and Ben, and I'm torn.

The last time Joseph said those words to me I knew exactly what was coming, and this time I sense he's about to say the opposite. Up until now I've wanted nothing more than to have that conversation, but something's stopping me.

I desperately want to go after Ben, to see what's happened and why he's leaving so suddenly.

'I feel like there's so much I want to say to you, Abi,' says Joseph, snapping my attention away from the door.

I look back into Joseph's eyes and I'm sucked into them. It's almost like I can see our relationship played back in them. The nights I spent tracing shapes on his chest when we lay in bed, our country-pub Sunday lunches, the times we sipped wine in the intervals at the theatre. So many times I found myself lost in those eyes – they're almost hypnotic.

'I want to explain why I broke up with you, and how I've started to regret my decision. I want to know if there's any hope of us getting back together.'

I feel like I'm out of my trance but realise that it's too late to go after Ben. He'll be on his bike and will probably have pedalled halfway home.

I try to focus on what Joseph's just said. Did he really want to know if there was a chance we could get back together?

'Am I wasting my time? Do you want to hear what I've got to say?'

'I do,' I say, nodding. Isn't this, after all, what I've been working towards with the list?

'Ah, Abi,' he says grabbing my hands. 'That's what I needed to hear.'

Chapter Twenty-Four

Joseph's come back with a week to spare ...

Sian's been giving me evil looks for the past half an hour, and although I don't want to hear what she has to say, I know I can't avoid her for ever.

I know instinctively that she's not going to approve.

'I'm just going to go and speak to Sian,' I say to Joseph and Marcus.

I still can't believe that they're here. It's all too much to take in – my plan seems to have worked and Joseph wants me back. I'm still waiting to talk to him properly, but it's awkward with my friends and Marcus here.

'OK,' says Joseph.

He's looking at me with his puppy-dog eyes like he used to when we first started dating. The same eyes that made me fall in love with him.

As I approach Sian, Pete wisely goes to stand with Giles. I'd go and stand with him too if I thought I could get away with it.

'Well, go on then,' I say, sinking down into the seat next to Sian.

'I don't know what you mean,' she says, her lips pursed. She folds her fingers back to look at her nails.

'About Joseph.'

'So I take it you're getting back together with him?' she says, still not looking at me.

'Well, we haven't really talked about it properly, but he's hinted that he thinks he's made a mistake. So it looks likely.'

'Right, and he just figured that out. After three months?'

'I guess sometimes people need time to realise how they really feel.'

Sian laughs hollowly. 'Are you sure he didn't just see the photos of you and Ben in Paris and get jealous?'

'I don't think so,' I say, thinking back to when I'd seen him at the supermarket. It felt like there was something he'd wanted to say then too.

'So why hasn't he said anything to you before? He could have gone round to your flat at any point in the last three months, but instead he waited until now. He let you go through all that heartache and misery for nothing.'

I shrug, I don't want to think about that.

'Can't you just be happy for me? This is what I want.'

'Is it really? What about Ben?'

'What about him? Where did he go anyway?'

'Where do you think? God, Abi, for someone so smart you can sometimes be so bloody stupid.'

She's folded her arms and is starting to raise her voice.

I look round the pub self-consciously and see that all our friends are looking at us. I suddenly wish I hadn't talked to Sian here. I should have waited until we were somewhere more private.

'So, Ben left because Joseph arrived?'

'Of course he did. Can't you see how much he likes you?'

'No,' I say, shaking my head. 'He broke up with his girlfriend two weeks ago and didn't bother to tell me. If he really liked me surely I'd have been the first person to know.'

She rolls her eyes at me.

'Abi …'

'What?' I wish she'd just spell out whatever it is she wants to say. She clearly thinks it's the most obvious thing in the world, but I don't get it.

'He probably didn't tell you because he was scared you didn't feel the same way.'

'But I'm sure he doesn't have feelings for me,' I say, shaking my head. 'It doesn't make sense because he's been helping me with the list. I mean, why would he do that when he knew I was doing it to get Joseph back.'

I'm trying to unravel what's been going on, before I realise what I've just said.

Sian's eyes widen and if her face looked like thunder before, then now it looks like it's a full-blown tropical storm.

'What do you mean the list was to get Joseph back? How would it get him back?'

Her eyes are glowing in a way that reminds me of the Demon Headmaster in the books that I read as a kid. I'm almost afraid lasers are going to come shooting out of them and frazzle me in my seat.

'Abi, what do you mean?'

I know that I've got no option but to come clean.

'The list was Joseph's,' I mutter.

'Joseph's?' she says, her brow wrinkling in a way that would not be attractive if the wind changed.

'Yes, I found his list in a book in that box of my things he dropped off at my flat, and I thought that if I did everything on it then he might come back to me.'

'All that stuff about you doing the list to get over him, you made that all up?'

I slowly nod my head.

'You lied to me. I'm your best friend and you lied to me.'

The anger has given way to whispering incredulity, which is almost worse.

'I didn't want to, but I knew you wouldn't approve.'

'Of course I wouldn't approve. It was one thing to support you doing this crazy bucket list when I thought it was your idea, but knowing that these weren't things you'd picked and that you were just doing it for him,' she hisses, gesturing in Joseph's direction. 'I was so proud of you. I've been telling Pete how remarkable it was that you were taking charge of your life and rebuilding it after your heartbreak. Taking the bull by the horns and doing all those things you'd never dreamt of doing. I couldn't believe how you'd picked yourself up from the mess you were in and dusted yourself down. And now I find out that it was all for him? It was some stupid plan to get him back.'

'It wasn't *that* stupid,' I say sulkily. 'It worked, didn't it?'

'Congratulations!'

'Can't you just be happy for me? You know how much I love Joseph.'

'Be happy for you? You've lied to me for months. And yes, I know how much you say you love Joseph, but how much does he love you?'

'Sian …' I say, not wanting to go there. If I'm getting back together with him, I don't want her to slag him off to my face.

'No, come on. He loved you so much that he dumped you.'

'People make mistakes.'

'Yes, they do. But, Abi, honestly, it took him three months to realise. And do you still want him? I mean, now that you've met Ben and done all those things?'

'Ben and I were only friends because of the list. What Joseph and I had was different.'

'Oh, yes, it was different. I know exactly how it was different. He's all wrong for you.'

I can feel the tears welling up behind my eyes. This is not what I want to hear.

'You know I tried to support you when he broke up with you and I bit my lip and didn't tell you what I really felt.'

'Oh, come on, you were quite clear that you didn't think he was right for me.'

'But did you ever consider why?'

'You never think any man is good enough. Up until last week I never thought you'd think any man was worthy of a relationship.'

'Ah, yes, Sian the man-hater. So maybe I'm harsh on men, but not on the good ones, Abi. Don't you see?'

'So what's so wrong with Joseph then?'

I look over her shoulder and see him propping up the bar in his freshly pressed chinos with his neatly tucked-in shirt hidden under a monogrammed jumper.

'Don't you remember what he was like with you? Think back.'

'I remember he was kind and generous. He used to spoil me with meals out and presents.'

'Yes, he did, but he never listened to you. He never knew what you liked. He was always buying you clothes that you'd never have picked yourself. And remember when he bought you carnations on your birthday, and you hate carnations. You never said anything, you just took them.'

I remember. It's true – it wasn't the first time that he'd given me carnations and I'd dropped hints about not liking them whenever we saw them. But when he got them for my birthday I just thought it was nice of him to buy me flowers.

'And that time that he took us to that bistro and insisted on ordering you mussels and you had to eat that whole tub.'

I shudder at the thought. Those slimy, chewy things. I'm almost gagging at the memory.

'And what about when he made us go to that bar in Gunwharf even though you didn't want to go there on principle after they chucked us out that time.'

It's true, all those things did happen, but it doesn't mean to say that we're not meant to be.

'I'm not saying he's not a nice guy, he is. But he's never convinced me that he's *your* nice guy. He seemed to think that you should fit in with how he lived his life, without getting to know the real you.'

I'm desperately fighting back the tears. In our twelve-year friendship, Sian has never spoken to me like this.

'You've clearly never had what I had with Joseph. You don't understand how I feel,' I say, almost pleading with her.

'Abi …'

'No, Sian, look I'm sorry that I lied. I truly am. I've never lied to you before and I thought I never would, but despite that, you can't change my mind about Joseph.'

'I just wish you'd see what I can see,' she says, her tone changing to sadness.

'And I wish you could see what I can.'

I hate fighting with her but sometimes she can be so stubborn. She thinks she knows my relationship with Joseph, but how can she? How could anyone except me and him know what went on?

I look over at him again and sigh. Even if she's right and it would be a disaster getting back together, surely I have to try. Wouldn't I always regret it if I didn't?

Sian and I seem to have reached an impasse and neither of us is budging.

'I'm going to go,' says Sian.

'Stay, please.'

I'm not ready for her to go just yet. I feel like I need to get her on side before I talk to Joseph – it's like I need her blessing.

'Abi, I am so mad at you. Have you any idea how it feels to find out your best friend's been lying to you for months?'

She stands up and slips her bag on her shoulder.

'Please, Sian, let me explain.'

'I thought you already had, and FYI it wasn't good enough.' She sighs and gives me a look of disappointment.

'You know what the really silly thing is? I thought you were an inspiration. The way you pulled yourself out of that break-up depression and turned it into something positive. You had this whole new lease of life and it really made me stop and think. It made me realise that I've had my life on hold ever since I broke up with Ted when I arrived at uni.

'It actually spurred me on with Pete when he suggested going on a date. It made me stop and consider it rather than dismissing it. All because of what I thought you'd done. And now I find out it was based on a lie. And to top it all off, you had the nicest guy at your fingertips and you've let him slip through them.'

She walks over to Pete without so much as a backward glance. She whispers to him and he finishes the rest of his pint and pulls on his coat. I watch them say their goodbyes to the others, before they walk out of the pub.

I have never known her to be so angry. It's even worse than the time she had to interview Katie Hopkins for her newspaper.

Tonight started off so well, and here I am an hour later having driven off half of the group. I look up at Giles and Laura and I wonder how long it will take before they abandon me too. Doug is nowhere to be seen. He probably left when Ben did.

'How to clear a pub in minutes.' Giles laughs as I walk up to them.

'As if I didn't already feel like a dick,' I say, trying to smile.

'Dare we ask what happened?' says Laura, her eyes scrutinising me.

'It's a long story, and all my fault,' I reply.

I'm already starting to feel sick as the adrenaline that started to pump round my veins as soon as Joseph made an appearance has started to wane. Add to that the exhaustion of arguing with Sian, and I'm truly beat.

Laura's looking at me as if she wants me to elaborate, but I can't face it.

'So, um, Joseph,' says Giles.

I nod. I feel slightly funny talking about him with Giles, now that I'm confused about Ben leaving the pub, and I don't know where my head's at.

'Are you ...?'

It seems to be the question on everyone's lips.

'Maybe,' I say.

I know that I was quite adamant about my feelings when I was talking to Sian but part of that was because of her reaction.

Joseph's ears must be burning as he walks over to us.

'Do you want another drink, Abi?'

I look down at my empty hands. I have no idea where my drink ended up or whether it was even finished. But a drink is exactly what I need. Something with a kick that will steady my nerves.

'Actually, yes, I'll have a Baileys.'

He looks at me for a minute and then nods. 'OK, then, and can I get you two a drink as well?'

'Actually, I think we might get off too,' says Giles.

'Really?' I say, trying to plead, but after the car crash that tonight has been I can't really blame them.

'Yeah, I think an early night will do us some good,' says Laura. 'Especially as we're tackling the spare room mess tomorrow.'

'On second thoughts, why don't we stay and get completely hammered so we can be hungover all day tomorrow,' says Giles, raising his eyebrows.

'Nice try,' says Laura. She picks up her bag and leans over to give me a quick kiss on the cheek. 'Are you OK getting home?'

As we pull away I nod and tell her that I'll be fine. The least Joseph can do to make up for trampling on my heart is to walk me home.

'See you at work on Monday,' says Giles as they leave.

'Was it something I said?' asks Joseph, as he walks back over and hands me my drink.

I take it and immediately sip the creamy liquid. It hits exactly the right spot. I look round and realise that we're alone.

'Where's Marcus?' I ask, half expecting him to be chatting up a woman in the corner of the pub.

'I sent him home,' he says shrugging. 'I thought he'd get in the way.'

'Oh.'

I'm beginning to wish Laura and Giles had stayed as now we don't have the safety net of other people.

'I figured I'd be staying at yours, so it was probably best for him to get a taxi home before the queues got too big.'

I'm taken aback. I can't believe he so blatantly said he was coming back to mine. It's pretty presumptuous, and totally not going to happen. I'm clearly not that easy, which loosely translates as I haven't shaved my legs in weeks and I haven't had a bikini-line wax since he dumped me. But does he really think that we're going to have some magic conversation and then pick up right where we left off? Was he expecting to stay at mine tonight and then go back to our usual routine of going to the diner for lunch tomorrow?'

'Um, the closest you're going to get to mine is when you walk me back there on your way to the taxi rank.'

Joseph raises his eyebrows at me in a way that used to make my knickers ping off all on their own.

'Oh, really? Where's this willpower come from?'

'From having someone rip out my heart and stamp on it.'

Did I say that out loud? I can't seem to stop blurting out thoughts that were meant only to rattle around my head.

'Ouch,' says Joseph, putting his hands theatrically to his heart. 'I guess I deserved that. So walking you home it is then.'

I smile weakly.

It's so weird, for months I've been dreaming about this moment, and now that it's here it feels so alien. I was never lost for words around him before, whereas now I'm struggling to know what to say.

'I totally understand that I can't come back to yours but, Abi, you've got to know how much I've missed you.'

He places his arm around me and leans in close to my ear. His hot breath warms my neck as he talks and I tingle all over.

It's the one time in my life that I'm actually thankful that I have hairy monkey legs, because the fear of him seeing them is stronger than my willpower.

It's not only that I've missed him, but I also haven't had sex for three months.

'Joseph,' I say, pushing him away. 'If this is going to happen, then we have to talk about everything, and *if* we do get back together, it would have to happen slowly. We're not just going to pick up where we left off. We'll have to go out on dates, and see how it goes.'

'Dates?'

'Yes,' I say, nodding. 'You'll have to put in some ground work and I want you to get to know the real me.'

'The real you?'

He looks confused, but until I started the list I don't think I knew who the real me was. I'd been so caught up in my relationship with Joseph and fitting into his life that I never gave him the opportunity to see who I was.

He's clearly taken aback but I really mean it. I'm not going to be a pushover. If he wants me, he's going to have to work for it.

'OK,' he says. 'If that's what it takes.'

I breathe a sigh of relief.

'So, why don't you tell me what you've been up to over the last few months? From the look of your Facebook you've been quite busy.'

We settle down at the table my friends so hastily vacated and talk. Not about our relationship and his feelings, but about what's happened since we broke up. I tell him about the different challenges, without explicitly telling him about the list.

As we talk I try to banish thoughts of Sian and Ben. I've got what I wanted, surely that's what matters.

The bell rings for last orders and I decline another offer of a drink from him. Any more and I'm likely to cave and invite him back, hairy legs and all.

We manage to make it back to my flat with me batting his groping hands away at various points in our journey.

'So,' he says as we stand on the front steps of my apartment block.

'So ...'

It feels like one of those awkward moments on a first date where you're not sure whether to go in for the kiss or not. But I don't have to wonder for long as Joseph launches himself at me.

He swoops me up in his arms and the next thing I know his lips are on my mine.

It's a familiar and sexy kiss and it's making my resolve weaken.

'I'll call you for a date, and we'll have that talk,' he says, propping me upright and walking down the stairs.

He flashes me a smile with his perfect white teeth and I wave as he leaves. My legs are a little too wobbly to allow me to walk up the steps just yet, so I stand there for a moment, watching him go.

When I finally get the power back to my legs, I head into my flat. Walking into my familiar space, I lock the door and throw myself onto my bed.

It seems like I've got what I wanted. So why the bloody hell am I feeling so confused?

Chapter Twenty-Five

One week exactly to the abseil, and I've pretty much got Joseph back ... My throat's a little sore and I'm starting to feel a bit dizzy. Have you heard that there's flu going round ...?

The door to the bike shop jangles as I push it open.

Ben wasn't joking when he said the shop was busy on a Saturday. There might only be a dozen or so people in the shop, but it's absolutely buzzing. The customers don't seem like your usual casual Saturday browsers. Everyone here means business and there's some serious shopping being done.

I spot Ben over in the corner with one of his expensive bikes, bending down at the foot of a tall, skinny fair-haired man, as if he's trying to judge the optimum seat height.

He stands up as the man rotates his leg, and there's much muttering and nodding going on between the two.

Perhaps I shouldn't have come. Ben's clearly in the middle of something, but my mind's been thinking of nothing else since last night. This morning, instead of waking up ecstatic that my plan to snare Joseph back appears to have worked, all I felt was guilty about Ben leaving the pub.

I'm hoping that by clearing the air with him it will leave me free to be happy about Joseph.

I'm about to turn and leave, thinking that I can come back later this afternoon when the shop is emptier, when I see Ben's spotted me. He says something to his customer before walking in my direction.

'Hi,' I say, for the first time nervous to be around him.

'Hi,' he says, in a very matter-of-fact un-Ben-like way. There's no hint of his usual smile on his face or in his voice.

I really shouldn't have come.

'Was there something you wanted? I'm a bit busy at the moment, well, the shop's packed,' says Ben, turning and pointing as if I'm an idiot who's failed to notice.

'Yes, I see that. I'd been hoping that we could go and have a chat, maybe over your lunch break if you're busy?'

'I don't really get a lunch break on a Saturday.'

'Not even a teeny, tiny coffee break?' I say, wincing and hoping. All I need is twenty minutes away from the hustle and bustle – Ben's distracted eyes keep watching the customers around his shop.

He sighs loudly, clearly sensing that the quickest way to get rid of me is going to be to agree.

'Fine, about three? I'll meet you at the Smile Cafe down the road.'

'Great,' I say, wishing I could have toned down my enthusiasm a notch. 'Three it is. I'll see you then.'

I go to say goodbye, but he's already turned and walked back to his customer.

I hurry out of the shop in case he comes back over to tell me he's changed his mind. I look at my watch. It's only eleven thirty, I've got another three and a half hours to kill.

I walk down the little side street and back to Marmion Road, glancing at the shops that line it for inspiration.

I'm only a fifteen-minute walk away from my flat. I could go back there and do some cleaning, or, more likely, box-set-watching, but my feet don't want to go in that direction. Part of me thinks that if I go back there I'll drive myself mad with my thoughts. Southsea doesn't have a huge number of shops, but I'm sure there are enough for me to browse slowly round them and distract myself.

I start in a furniture shop with the most beautiful wooden pieces. I don't often come in here as my flat isn't big enough to swing a cat in, let alone fit in any more furniture. But as I run my hands along a beautiful oak sideboard I start to imagine it in my dream house. My one-day-when-I'm-a-grown-up house. Whenever that may be.

It's the kind of thing that would go beautifully in Joseph's town house. Not that he'd need it, his house is already spectacularly furnished. My stomach lurches at the thought of him. I still can't get over last night's events. I keep replaying them over and over in my mind. The moment that he walked into the pub; the moment he came up to me; and the one where he asked me if there was hope that we might get back together.

It was all too unbelievable, yet it's overshadowed by thoughts of Ben and Sian.

In my head I'd imagined that when Joseph came back to me, he'd sweep me off my feet and we'd head into the sunset, whilst my friends waved and cheered us on. Only Ben's got under my skin. That's why I need to meet with him, to find out what he was trying to say last night before he left. I need to get that sorted before I can think about Joseph and me.

And Sian. Well, that's going to be a harder one.

I climb the stairs and find myself staring at bookcases that are the ultimate bibliophile's dream – they would hold hundreds of books and look fantastically stylish.

I try and distract myself with thoughts of the dream house again, but Sian's voice is now rattling round my head. Her disappointment. Her anger. It's going to take a lot for us to recover from that.

I know from experience that there's no point in going to see her today. She's far too mad at me. She's best left to stew for a few days and whilst she's not going to get any less angry if I see her later in the week, I'm going to be less in danger of having random objects thrown at my head.

I texted her this morning to say sorry. I knew that I wouldn't get a reply but I wanted her to know I was thinking of her.

I rub my eyes as I feel tears start to collect behind them. I'm not going to go down that route again. I'm not going to cry out of self-pity.

I walk out of the shop and back into the fresh air in a bid to try and stop the tears.

I find myself standing outside a bridal boutique and I look at an exquisite dress in the window and wonder what I'd look like in it. It's a real princess dress, full of silk and lace and oomph, nothing like I'd choose for myself.

For a fleeting second I imagine the type of wedding that Joseph would want. I know it would be big and fancy. This would be the type of dress he'd expect me to wear.

Maybe this shopping malarkey isn't going to help distract me after all.

My phone beeps in my bag and my first thought is that it's from Sian, but when I get it out, it's Joseph.

Fancy coming up to the Ship for lunch? We could have that talk x x

The Ship is a pub outside Portsmouth, and I groan at the thought of leaving the city on a Saturday. The two main roads in and out of the city get congested at the weekend, and the thought of having to go out and come back in when it's a beautiful sunny day and so many people are bound for the beach is enough to put me off.

It isn't lost on me that he hadn't suggested coming in to take me out to lunch near where I live, as I know that he hates Portsmouth weekend traffic even more than I do.

I quickly fire back a text, telling him I already have plans and could we do it another day.

Technically I do have time to go out of the city and meet him for lunch and still be back in time to meet Ben, but I need to get my thoughts straight before seeing him.

As I hit send I wonder what's happened to me. Last week I would have bitten someone's hand off to be in the same room as Joseph, and now I'm turning down the chance to hear him tell me what he's thinking.

I shake my head in disbelief.

I force myself to keep walking down the street and next up on the row of shops is a local chocolatier – today I've got no will-power to resist going in. I usually only restrict myself to window shopping. But it's been one of those days.

I'm ordering myself some salted-caramel-filled chocolate when I spot some chocolate-covered honeycomb with marsh-mallows. I buy Ben a dozen, and hope that they'll go some way to getting him to forgive me.

When I leave the shop I look down at the rest of the street and realise that I'm in no mood to shop. Instead I head towards the seafront. Maybe a walk along there will blow the cobwebs from my mind, and maybe blow some sense into me at the same time.

I make it back to Marmion Road and the cafe where I'm meet-ing Ben with five minutes to spare. My feet are aching from walking so far in my little slip-on canvas shoes. I went all the way to the east side of the city, as far as I could without ending up at the nudist beach – I've made that mistake before and being confronted with an old man's willy swinging in the breeze is not what I need to see ever, let alone in the mood I'm in today.

The door rattles as it opens and I see Ben walking towards me.

I wave and smile as if he's going to have trouble seeing me, but at this time in the afternoon there's only me and one other couple in the corner of the room.

'Hey,' I say as he sits down in front of me.

'Hi,' he says, sighing and picking up the menu.

'Busy day?'

'Always is on a Saturday,' he says, shrugging.

He orders a coffee from the waitress and a panini, and I order the same. My mind's racing trying to think of what to say to make a decision about what to have. I'm just relieved he's ordered food as I'd worried he was going to run in and out and we wouldn't get time to talk properly.

'I bought you these,' I say, pulling out the bag of chocolates and handing them to him. He opens the bag.

'Marshmallow and honeycomb,' he says, a small smile escaping through his stony exterior. 'They're my favourite. How did you know?' he says, squinting.

'You mentioned it when we were on one of our tea breaks when we were out riding.'

'And you remembered,' he says, slipping one into his mouth. 'I know I shouldn't when I'm just about to eat but I'm starving.'

'I can't pass judgement, I bought half a dozen for me and I've eaten them all already.'

Ben smiles and I feel like we're going back to how things used to be.

'I'm touched, though, that you remembered.'

I shrug my shoulders as if it's no big deal really.

'So, last night,' I say, tucking my hair behind my ear.

'We don't need to talk about it.'

The waitress puts our drinks down in front of us. Ben busies himself pouring sugar into his coffee and stirring meticulously.

'I think we do. I want to know what you were going to say before Joseph came in.'

Ben looks up at me and holds my gaze before looking back down at his cup.

'What does it matter? Joseph came back, you got what you wanted. This is what you've been working towards the whole time with your list. Don't worry about me and what I was saying. It wasn't important anyway.'

'It wasn't?'

'No, it wasn't. So tell me about Joseph. Are you getting back together?'

The waitress comes back with our food and for a minute I wish we'd ordered something more adventurous that would have taken longer to prepare. At this rate Ben will be out the door in a matter of minutes given that he practically inhales his food.

I try and use the food as an excuse not to answer the question. I can't go into my thoughts about Joseph, as I'm too confused about what I'm feeling.

'So next week is supposed to be the Spinnaker abseil. It's come round quickly, hasn't it?'

'It has,' he says between mouthfuls. 'I'm not going to be able to come along and watch after all. I spoke to Tammy in the week and she wants me to go and watch her race.'

My mouth falls open. I thought they were supposed to have broken up for good this time. I hope she's not trying to get her claws into him again – he deserves someone so much better than her.

Whenever I've thought about the abseil the only thing that made it bearable was the thought of Ben being there. This gives me an even greater reason to get out of it.

'Doesn't matter, I'm not doing it anyway. I'm going to pull a sickie from work.'

'So you're not going to finish the list?'

I push the panini around my plate.

'No. I mean, I'm really proud of how much I've done, but I think the Spinnaker was too ambitious for me and my fear of heights. It paralyses me even thinking about it.'

'And Joseph's back on the scene so there's really no need,' he says. I can detect a hint of sarcasm in his voice. 'I take it that goes for your own list too? No learning to sail or baking.'

'I hadn't really given it much thought.'

I shift uncomfortably in my chair. That's the last thing on my mind at the moment.

'So are you getting back together with Tammy? If you're going to watch her race,' I say, trying to deflect his anger away from me.

I'm staring at his almost empty plate, I can't bear to look at him whilst I hear what he has to say.

'No. She hasn't taken the news of our break-up well and I think she needs me to be there for her – just as a friend, nothing more.'

He pulls out his wallet from his back pocket and throws some money down on the table. He's somehow managed to finish the rest of his sandwich in record time, even for him. I know I should be pleading with him to stay so that we can talk but all I can wonder is how he's not got indigestion.

'I've got to get back to the shop. I've left Harry on his own. I'm glad everything worked out for you and you got everything you wanted.'

He walks out before I can stop him. I'm left watching him and realising that I didn't.

I look down at my panini and push the plate away. I'm not hungry.

I can't let him walk away from me like this. I run over to the till and thrust the money in the waitress's face, not bothering to wait for the change.

'Ben!' I shout as I run down the street after him. 'Ben!'

He turns round and if I thought he looked unhappy to see me before, now he looks angry.

'I've got to get back to work.'

'But I don't understand what's going on.'

'What's going on?' he says with an almost manic laugh. He runs his fingers through his messy hair, before pushing up the arms of his long-sleeved T-shirt. 'What's going on is that I'm disappointed. Do you even realise how much you've changed over the last few months? You've become a different person to the unconfident and scared girl I met on Hayling Island. Watching you cycling and pushing yourself even though you were terrified. That day in Paris you had this energy about you and it was like watching a butterfly emerge from a chrysalis. So what's going on is that I'm disappointed that Joseph's come back and you're giving up on the list when you were so close to finishing it. And I thought you were going to take charge of a new list by yourself and sort out what you wanted from life.'

I feel like I've been winded and my eyes are hot as the tears are starting to burn.

'Maybe I won't change if we get back together. Maybe I'll carry on with the new me.'

'Do you believe that?' he asks.

I don't believe it. That's part of the reason I'm so conflicted about Joseph. I know he hasn't changed and whilst he's still a man that I want, I'm not so sure he'll want the woman I've become.

Ben takes my silence as an answer and goes to walk away again.

'I can't help that I'm in love with him.'

'Oh, right. You love Joseph. Of course you do,' he says turning round to face me again.

'I do,' I say, suddenly very conscious of how loud my voice has become on a public street. I'm sure there are passers-by that are taking a great interest, but I'm so livid with Ben that I'm not noticing them. 'And what would you know about love anyway?'

'Excuse me?'

He steps closer to me and I can see the anger glowing in his eyes.

'Look at you and Tammy and your on/off relationship and your fear of getting hurt. You're clearly not capable of having a proper relationship and being in love with someone.'

'Clearly,' he practically spits at me. I'm surprised I'm not wounded by the venom that came with it.

He turns and walks away from me, and this time I let him. I've got nothing left to say, and he's made it quite clear how he feels.

Our friendship was going to be over when the list finished anyway and this makes it even easier to sever all ties.

Chapter Twenty-Six

Five days until the tower and five days to find some mental strength to actually go through with it.

I can't remember the last time I was glad to come into the office on a Monday. I practically jumped out of bed this morning, so pleased to have an excuse to get out of my flat and distract myself from my thoughts.

I nearly went crazy over the weekend thinking about Joseph, Ben and Sian. In the end I drove up to see my parents for lunch, hoping it would take my mind off things, only it made matters worse. My mum kept trying to pump me for information about my break-up with Joseph and asking me what I'd done wrong. I came back madder than ever.

I look up as Giles walks into the office and he looks over at me awkwardly. He's obviously spoken to Ben. My nostrils flare at the memory of my argument with him and I start to feel angry again.

'Morning,' he says. 'Coffee?'

'Morning. I've got one,' I say holding up my mug and smiling weakly. So much for coming to work to get away from everything.

He smiles and walks off, and I'm relieved. For an awful moment I thought he was going to say something to me about Ben and I'm not in the mood.

I flip open my diary for the week and groan as I see the words Spinnaker Abseil ringed in red for Saturday. Ben's words echo round my head about not completing the list. I'm beginning to think that I have to do it. As if it isn't bad enough that I am going through emotional hell, I feel like I've got to put myself through actual hell at the end of the week. That's just the cherry on top.

The only thing I can hope is it will be like the full stop to this part of my life. Whatever happens with Joseph will be the future and it will be like a new beginning; a fresh start.

My phone rings and I pick it up, trying to pump as much enthusiasm into my voice as I can, as it's an outside line.

'Good morning, Design Works, Abi speaking.'

'Abi, it's Melissa.'

'Oh, hi, Melissa. How are you?'

Melissa's a curator at one of the local museums and I've been designing the panels for her latest exhibition. Thinking of which, I scan my diary – they were being delivered this morning. Perhaps she's ringing to tell me how awesome they look.

'I've been better.'

'What's wrong? Have the panels not turned up yet?'

I look up at the giant office clock and see that it's still early – only ten o'clock. There's still plenty of time for a morning delivery.

'Oh, no, they're here.'

'And?' I say, forgetting that Melissa can't see my rolling hand move in a bid to get her to elaborate.

'And they're the wrong size. All of them. Nothing fits on our backing panels.'

I rub my forehead and scrunch my eyes shut. Why was I so excited to come to work this morning?

'What do you mean, they're the wrong size?'

'Most of the long panels are far too short, maybe fifty or sixty centimetres too short, and then the small panels that were to be hung on the walls are too big. They don't fit into the spaces we've allowed for them.'

'But I don't understand. We double-checked all the measurements together in the room and I personally checked all the dimensions on the order to the printer.'

'Well, I phoned the printer first and they said the dimensions were the ones sent over. They've emailed me a copy of the order form and they match what has been delivered.'

'But they can't be,' I say, the words getting stuck in my throat.

'We've got three days until the Duchess of Cornwall comes to open this exhibition. Three days! So your company is going to have to get the work redone as it's *your* mistake.'

My heart sinks. Those panels cost the museum thousands of pounds, and now we're going to have to pay for new ones out of our budget. Rick is going to be livid. It will come to a lot more than we've billed them for design time.

'I'll need to speak to Rick,' I say, thinking that I am powerless to agree to anything.

'He's my next phone call,' she spits down the phone. 'I was going to phone him first but as you did the designs I thought you might have been able to shed some light on what happened.'

I'm speechless and again I realise that she won't be able to see the sincere look of confusion on my face.

'I honestly don't know what happened.'

'You've got three days to fix it. *Three days.*'

The phone line goes dead and for a moment I stare at the receiver in disbelief before I put it down again. I know those measurements were correct. I'm sure of it. In all my professional life I've never, ever messed up dimensions before. One mock project as a student when I was working in centimetres rather than millimetres was enough to show me how careful I always had to be.

I dig around in my office drawer for the project folder and pick up the purchase order I'd done. I compare them to the dimensions on my handwritten paper from when we measured the exhibition space and they're the same. How did it go so wrong?

'Abi!' I hear being shouted across the open-plan office.

I shudder at the ferocity of his voice. There's no doubt that Melissa was true to her word about phoning Rick as soon as she hung up from me.

I slowly rise out of my chair and walk over to his office. All my colleagues are looking at me. They're pretending not to, but I can tell they're wondering what I've done to invoke the wrath of Rick. He's one of life's naturally happy people, and he sounds mad as hell.

I walk into his office and see that the scowl on his face matches the tone of his voice.

'What the fuck happened?'

'I don't know,' I say, slinking down into the chair opposite him. 'I double- and triple-checked those dimensions. I don't understand.'

'Well, something must have happened.'

Rick spins from side to side in his chair, his hands folded as if he's waiting for more of an explanation from me.

'The order form for the panels is here and it matches the notes I made from the exhibition. It makes no sense.'

'Well, Melissa's just sent over an email with a photo, and it's pretty obvious. You've designed the files at the wrong size.'

He swivels his screen round so that I can see it.

'But none of the graphics are distorted,' I say in horror.

I'd expected there to have been some cock-up at the printers and for the files to have been printed at the wrong size. But none of the pictures are pixelated; everything is scaled to the right ratio.

'They've got to have been designed at that size in InDesign,' I say, wondering how that's possible.

'I know. You made a mistake.'

I look at the photo of one of the too-small panels and it looks exactly like my design. Could Rick be right? Could I have fucked up?

'There's one way to tell,' says Rick. 'Where are your original design files?'

I sigh and tell Rick the file path and watch in horror as it loads. He clicks on the file information to see the panel size.

'Here you are, the first panel is 600 mm by 600 mm.'

'But that's not right at all,' I say, shaking my head. 'That's a square. Nothing I designed was square.' There's no way that I would have got the dimensions that wrong in InDesign.

'This is crazy,' I say. 'It's like someone has opened the files, changed the sizes and re-ratioed the content to fit.'

'Abi, will you just admit that you made a mistake? You know there's nothing I hate more than dishonesty.'

I can feel myself starting to shake. 'But I didn't get the dimensions wrong, I didn't do this. Someone else has tampered with my work.'

I think back to the missing design files and all of a sudden it seems like someone's out to get me. Linz. It has to be her.

She's extremely competent with InDesign, she was even there at the museum meeting. She would have known how absolutely vital it would have been to have got the sizes exactly right. All signs point to her.

'Who would go to such lengths? Look, it's one thing to make a mistake, it's another to try and cover your arse with crazy accusations. You've been with the company a long time, Abi, and up until this year we've always been really happy with your work. But lately you've been really erratic. What with the disciplinary letter we sent you regarding your extended home-working. Then there's your unpreparedness with the Vista clients, you not taking care of that memory stick, and now this, which is going to cost us thousands. I'm beginning to think that you aren't really invested in the company any more.'

My heart is racing and my mind is whirring. Is he saying what I think he's saying? I get the impression that I'm in for more than a slap on the wrist.

'Hang on,' I say, trying to keep up and process what's gone on. 'What about my purchase order? It's for the same dimensions that are on the paper list, for the files I designed to the same size. Melissa said she'd checked the purchase order with the printers and it matched the panels.'

'What are you saying, that there are two purchase orders?' Rick shakes his head before bringing his hand up and rubbing his eyes. 'Abi, this is sounding nuts.'

'I know, I know. But listen, someone sabotaged my work before when the files were deleted, and now this.'

'You don't honestly believe that, do you?' he says, looking at me with incredulity.

'What else am I supposed to think? I didn't do this. I didn't mess up with these dimensions.'

Rick shakes his head. 'Abi, I can't stand liars and with the money we'll now lose on this account and your recent poor performance, in the old days I'd be firing you right about now. But with all the tribunals and legislation these days, I can't. So instead I'm going to suspend you. For all I know it's you sabotaging the company. Maybe you're making it look like someone else is doing this stuff.'

I scrunch my face up. 'Why on earth would I do that?'

'Who knows? Maybe you're defecting to start your own company or you've got a new job.'

Now who's the crazy paranoid one?

'Look, I'm as confused about all this as you are. All I know is one of my most trusted designers has let me down, but until we get to the bottom of it I've got no choice but to suspend you. I'll get HR involved and there'll be a resolution, one way or another,' he says.

I'm not going to think of the fact that I don't know of anyone that's ever been suspended from work and then reinstated. I know it's code for giving HR time to go through the proper disciplinary procedure before they fire me so the agency doesn't get dragged through a tribunal.

I can't think what it would mean if I did lose my job. What with my rent having increased and me having used my little cushion of savings to do the list, I'd be in big trouble.

'Get your bag and leave as soon as possible,' says Rick.

I walk out of the door and all eyes in the office are on me. Everyone can sense what's happened and whilst everyone's looking, no one is making eye contact with me.

I walk over to my desk, retrieving my bag and shutting down my Mac. I can't face putting up an out-of-office or tidying anything away. I just want to get the hell away from here.

I turn to walk out of the office when Linz comes bounding up to me.

'Abi,' she says in a quiet voice. 'I can't believe you're going.'

Word has obviously travelled quickly round the office.

I shrug my shoulders. 'Well, I'm hoping it won't be permanent.'

'I hope so too. I can't imagine working here without you.'

She gives me a sympathetic puppy-dog look and for a minute I think she's going to burst into tears. She reaches over to me and pulls me into a hug.

'I've learnt so much from you. I was beginning to think of you as my mentor. I can't believe you're not going to be here,' she whispers.

She pulls out of the hug and gives me one of her winning smiles.

'You'll keep in touch though, won't you? We still need to do that advanced windsurfing course.'

I'd rather stick pins in my eyes. I look at her smiling sadly at me and I wonder if this is all for show. Perhaps this is the final part of her plan to convince others that's she's not masterminded this whole thing. Pretending she cares and she's sorry I've left when deep down she's responsible.

God, she's good. She almost has me believing her for a split second.

'Goodbye, Linz,' I say through gritted teeth.

I'd love nothing more than to shout at her and grab her by the ponytail to make her confess. But I've got to rise above it, as that really would be the final nail in my coffin with HR.

I push past her and carry on towards the back stairs. I don't want those from the other companies in the building to see me do my walk of shame.

'Abi, what's going on?' asks Giles, grabbing my arm.

'I've been suspended,' I say, almost in a whisper as the magnitude of what's happened starts to hit me.

'What for?'

'There was a cock-up with the dimensions of the exhibition panels.'

'And Rick's suspending you for that?'

'Not just that,' I say sighing. 'There was the lack of printouts at the Vista meeting too.'

'But that wasn't your fault.'

'And my poor performance when I was away. It's just a suspension, but between you and me, I think Rick wants me gone. The only way I'm going to save my job is to prove that I didn't mess this up,' I say, sighing.

Giles's eyes blink in rapid succession as he tries to keep up with what I'm saying.

'Prove you didn't do it? What, you think someone else did it, like the missing files?'

'Uh-huh.'

Rick was right, it sounds ridiculously far-fetched.

'Do you need any help?'

'I think I might,' I say, smiling, relieved that I've got one person in the office I know I can trust. 'I'll call you tonight to fill you in.'

'OK. Now take care,' he says, rubbing my arm.

'Thanks.'

I don't know whether it's the sympathetic look on Giles's face or the fact that I'm leaving the office via the back stairs in the middle of the day because I've been suspended pending firing, but I just about make it down the fire escape before I'm in floods of tears.

Why is this all happening to me?

Sian and Ben aren't talking to me, and now the only stable thing in my life – my job – is being taken away from me.

I guess I could focus on Joseph walking back into my life, but I can't help but think that my break-up with him and the pursuit to get him back have landed me in this mess in the first place.

As I see it, there are two ways I could go with this. Sorting out my friendships and proving that I didn't sabotage my own career; or going back to my flat, ordering a takeaway Chinese and having the mother of all moping sessions. And right now, I choose moping.

Chapter Twenty-Seven

Tomorrow is the dreaded abseil, but with Joseph back on the horizon and me suspended, I've got absolutely no reason to do it – yet I'm not exactly jumping with joy . . .

I've been semi-unemployed Abi for all of four days. Four days and I'm already bored.

After spending the rest of Monday in stunned silence and denial, watching episode after episode of *Grey's Anatomy*, by Tuesday reality had sunk in.

I decided that maybe I shouldn't be hanging around in suspension limbo, and should look for a new job instead. I started the day in a flurry of activity getting excited that this could be my new start. I reasoned that I'd been in my job for seven years and perhaps it was time to spread my wings and have a fresh challenge. I earnestly looked at the jobs pages online, and then remembered how few design agencies there are in Portsmouth. After applying for a random design job that I'm not suited to, I had the brainwave that I'd go freelance. Seven years of contacts surely would mean that I'd be able to get some work.

I began making list after list of possible leads and things I'd need to do to get it up and running. I set up my own free website on Weebly and searched my Mac for things I could put in my portfolio, but aside from a freebie book cover that I designed for my friend who self-published, I had nothing that didn't belong to the agency.

I'd always intended to grow a little sideline for when I had my 2.4 kids, only with me not getting anywhere close to that stage in my life, I hadn't done anything about it.

Pissed off that I'd spent the evenings in my twenties going out drinking and watching too many box sets rather than setting up a side business, I sulked for the rest of the night and put on more *Grey's Anatomy*.

On Wednesday I had an even better brainwave: I could still go freelance, and start my own company from scratch designing book covers. My self-published author friend said there was a huge demand for good cover art and since I love books, it would be perfect. I spent the morning researching other firms that offered similar services, and decided that there was room in the market.

Then I had probably the best idea ever, which was to write my own book. What better way to get my cover art noticed than to write a bestseller that would storm the charts and have everyone wondering who designed the cover? I'd always wanted to write a Jilly-Cooper-type bonkbuster.

But by midnight I had exactly the same number of words written as I had at midday. Zero. I'd spent most of the afternoon and evening trying to come up with a sexy man's name to rival Rupert Campbell-Black. I went to bed exhausted and depressed.

Yesterday, I got up thinking that I'd move from Portsmouth. With Joseph potentially back on the scene, I widened the search to include the surrounding towns like Chichester and Petersfield. I even started to imagine that I could move in with Joseph to make a new commute easier and to save me from financial ruin. It was a win-win situation. But then I started to think of him and our relationship and my head started to spin. I'd been putting off seeing him all week as I still didn't feel ready to hear what he's got to say.

Really could my life be in any more of a mess?

The only saving grace in this whole thing is that now that I'm suspended I don't have to go through with that terrifying abseil and, with Joseph potentially wanting me back, I have no reason to finish the list, no matter what Ben said.

When I woke up this morning, I didn't know what to do. I've realised I don't want to start my own business. There aren't any jobs locally. I can't write a bestseller. If I'm honest, I don't want a new job. All I want is my old job.

And that's when it hit me: I'm only suspended – I've still got time to fight to get my job back.

I've been at the company for seven years and apart from letting things slide when I was moping post-Joseph, I've done nothing but good work.

I love my job, my colleagues, and, when they don't constantly change their mind, I love my clients. Pat the office manager always keeps the biscuit tin well stocked and I've just got my leather seat perfectly moulded to my bum. I don't want to start somewhere new.

Is that bad? There are still plenty of things that I could achieve there and the company is expanding all the time so it's not like I've got no room to grow.

And even if I didn't want my job back I feel like I need to clear my name. What sort of reference would Rick give me if I got fired? Who would dare employ me?

If I'm going to leave Design Works it's going to be on my terms.

I dial a number on my phone and wait for it to be connected.

'Hiya,' says Giles, the smile evident in his voice.

'Hey, any news?'

I know I probably should start with some niceties to be polite, but I was born three weeks early and I've been impatient ever since. When I told him the whole story of the suspension on Monday, he'd offered to do some digging at work, and I'd finally rung him back this morning to give him the go ahead. It's been the most agonising two hours waiting for an update.

'Hang on.'

I hear a loud clatter that I recognise as him opening the bar on the fire escape.

'Right, then, I've managed to get Sue from finance to pull up the purchase order and she found that there had been two created. Your original one, and another one.'

'There are two?' I say, wondering how he'd got Sue from accounts to do anything nice. She usually barks at me and writes me emails in capital letters telling me that I haven't done my paperwork properly.

'That's right. She said it would have usually been flagged up on the system, but she'd had a note on her desk asking her to cancel the first one, so she had.'

My heart's starting to race. Up until now I'd started to believe that Rick had been right, that I'd been so distracted lately that I'd fucked up. But here is proof that I hadn't. Unless I somehow forgot that I'd created a whole other purchase order and written a note cancelling the first – and even I know that's unlikely.

'So when was it done?'

'Um, the second one was created at seventeen twenty-five on 19 April.'

I usually have a terrible head for dates and times, but I know categorically where I was at that time.

'I wasn't in the office,' I say, relieved that I haven't had some weird spell of memory loss. 'I left work at five on the dot as Ben and I got the train up to London, the night before we went to Paris.'

A jolt of pain hits me as I fleetingly remember Paris and then subsequently my argument with Ben.

'It says your name on the order.'

'But I didn't send it.'

'Is there anyone else that could have used your account?'

I rack my brains and screw up my eyes. 'Well, Linz has been doing some of the orders for me, as she hasn't got her own finance login yet, and I've been showing her how to use it.'

The words tumble out of my mouth. I've been showing her how to use it, and how to get my job.

'Then it must have been her. Rick's already given her the Vista account to work on – it's only going to be a matter of time before he takes her on permanently and gives her your job. She must have planned it all along. We just need to present the evidence to Rick and then you can have your old job back.'

'Hang on there, Columbo, what evidence? It says I did the order, it doesn't prove it was her,' I say with a big sigh.

'Yeah, but you know it couldn't have been you. Have you still got your train ticket?'

I scratch my head. 'Probably. I expect it's still in my backpack.'

'Great, I'll talk to Rick and –'

'Giles, I think you've done enough ... hello?'

I'm talking to my phone but there's no one there. Giles has hung up.

I can feel the perspiration starting to form on my brow. What's he saying to Rick? I slip my shoes on and wonder if I should go to the office. No, I think, sitting down on the couch. I don't want to cause a scene.

I wanted to phone Rick when I'd worked out what I was going to say, and when I had a considered rational explanation. I don't think having half the evidence and accusing Linz, the golden child, of orchestrating some crazy scheme to oust me is going to cut it.

My phone buzzes into life and my office number comes up.

'Hello,' I say, hoping that it's Giles and that he hasn't managed to find Rick.

'Hi, Abi,' booms Rick. 'Giles has just given me the two purchase orders and he's flapping around saying something about Linz interfering with your work.'

I take a deep breath. 'I know this all sounds crazy, but I was on a train to London, and someone cancelled my original purchase order. I've probably got the train ticket to prove that I wasn't in the office, but you've got to believe me.'

'It should be easy to check if you were in the office or not. I'll email IT now and get them to send me everyone's login and logout times. What was the date and time?'

'Seventeen twenty-five on 19 April.'

I hear the tip tap of keys as Rick types and I can't quite believe that he's doing this. I got the impression on Monday that he was looking for any reason to get rid of me, but now he's actually listening and co-operating.

'OK, so I've sent that to them and we'll see what they come back with.'

'Thanks, Rick. Look, I know that my work was shoddy earlier on in the year and I freely admit that. I was going through some stuff and I let it interfere with my work and I shouldn't have done. But I feel I've worked so hard since then. With the Vista account and the work on the Spinnaker pitch. I don't think I gave you much of an impression of how much I love my job and think I'm an asset to the company. I know it sounds crazy to accuse Linz of this, but someone's been sabotaging my work and the only person I can think of is her. I mean, she's ambitious and she wants to be taken on permanently. She's made no secret of that.'

'That's no reason for her to have done these things,' says Rick. '*If* they have been done by someone else.'

'I know it sounds far-fetched, but she's the only person that would have access to my finance login and be able to do the purchase order.'

'Abi, it wasn't Linz that did it.'

'I know that it sounds ridiculous, but it had to be her.'

'It wasn't.'

'You don't know that for sure,' I say, pacing my living room so much that I'm thinking I'm going to wear a track into the floor.

'I do know that for sure. You'll have to trust me.'

I'm about to point out that it's hard for me to trust the person that practically sacked me earlier on in the week, but I bite my tongue. I don't want to piss him off when I'm getting him on side.

'So you believe that someone was trying to sabotage me?'

'I'm considering it.'

I know it's not a total vote of confidence, but it's an improvement from Monday.

'What changed your mind?' On Monday he'd been so dismissive that he'd almost laughed at me.

'Well, Linz did. I was talking to her about your museum meeting and she told me about how thorough you had been with the measurements and it just didn't add up.'

Neither does the fact that Linz has been scheming to get me fired and then is trying to convince Rick that it wasn't me.

'I can't work out what's going on,' I say, so confused.

In my head Linz is both Snow White and her wicked step-mother. I no longer know what to think.

'It has to be someone that could have logged into the finance package as me and changed the files in InDesign.'

'The InDesign angle doesn't really help us as most of the account managers know how to use basic bits of it. Here we go – I've got an email back from IT. The only people in the office at that time were Fran, Greg, Heidi, Linz, Giles, Pat, Isla from accounts and Jo. Whilst Pat would be all over the finance programme I doubt she'd be able to manipulate the files in InDesign, and if she could she's been wasted all these years. As for Isla, she's about as creative as a black spot and Jo's felt the brunt of you going. So that leaves Fran, Greg, Heidi or Giles.'

I think through the list. Giles can be discounted as I know it's not him. Fran and Greg are my fellow designers and they've been with the company almost as long as me – we're like siblings so it couldn't be them. And Heidi, well I don't know her very well – she works on the web team with Giles – but I can't see why she'd be out to get me. Although I did spill a drink on her shoes at the Christmas do …

I still think the finger should be pointing at Linz as no one else has a motive.

'I just don't understand why anyone would do this.'

'I don't understand how anyone could have got your password to login to the finance package,' says Rick. 'You don't have it written down anywhere, do you?'

I shut my eyes and wish I could turn back time.

'Abi ...'

'I sort of have it written in the back of my work diary.'

'Abi, what's the number one rule of computer security? Don't write your passwords down.'

'But there are always so many to remember,' I say in a whiney voice. I have a terrible, terrible memory for these things and we keep having to change them.

'Right, so that's that mystery's solved – now to find out who did it.'

I sigh. We're no Sherlock and Watson.

'I've got an inkling of who it could be, I just need some time to do some fact-checking.'

'It can't be anyone but Linz. She's the only logical candidate.'

'Abi, it's not Linz.'

'Then who do you think it is? Can you at least give me a clue?'

'Not until I'm certain. Look, come and do the Spinnaker abseil tomorrow. I know how much you wanted to do it and whatever happens I believe that it wasn't you that did this. If you want to come back to work then you can.'

'Really?'

'Of course. So ten o'clock tomorrow morning at the tower.'

'Or I could come to work on Monday instead?'

'Come on, Abi, you were the inspiration for the abseil. Plus, I sort of have a plan regarding the saboteur and I need you involved.'

'OK,' I say, wondering if I should cast my net wider on the job front. There must be something else I'm qualified for other than graphic design …

We say our goodbyes and my heart feels a little lighter.

I only hope that Rick gets to the bottom of this, as I don't really want to work there in fear that my work's going to disappear or come out wrong again.

But on the upside, if I'm not going to get fired, then I won't be getting evicted, so that's one thing in my mess of a life that I don't need to worry about. Now I just need to work out the fight with Sian and sort out my love life. But somehow I don't think that's going to be as easy.

As if on cue, the doorbell buzzes and I spring up to let Joseph through the main doors. I know it's him without asking. He's on time, as he always is, on the button of midday. He'd asked to meet for lunch as he had a client meeting round here and I've put off seeing him for long enough this week. I can't hide from him for ever.

'Hello, you,' I say, opening the door of my flat. His right hand is lifted as if he is about to knock, and as he brings it down he reaches over and rests it round my waist, pulling me into him.

I hadn't expected him to kiss me, but I find myself melting and any resolve or resolution in my mind of how things are going to be different this time and how I'm going to be more like myself melt away. Because at this moment in time, I'd do anything he wanted.

He stumbles through the door and I hear it slam behind him as he pushes me up against the wall and kisses me more furiously. The hand that had been resting on my back is now moving under my shirt and he's teasing me with his fingertips as he traces the pattern of my bra.

I'm going to have sex with Joseph.

My mind races through the mental checklist. Yes, I showered this morning, yes, my legs are shaved and whilst my bikini line hasn't been waxed into action lately I don't think it's going to be like some jungle exploration.

He starts nibbling down my neck and I can hear myself groaning involuntarily with pleasure. It's been a long three months.

Then it hits me again. I'm going to have sex with Joseph.

I instantly snap my head up straight and push him back.

He looks at me with hurt puppy-dog eyes.

'What's the matter,' he says.

'I want to take things slowly, remember. And you said you were going to tell me why we really broke up.'

My body is cursing my brain for its rationality as every part of me is crying out to be touched and caressed by him. But I've had a lot of time to think this week and if we're getting back together it's going to be a proper relationship – one where he gets to know the real me. Which means taking things slowly, including bedroom activities.

'Do you want something to drink?'

'No, I want you,' he says, trying to grab my hips and pull me back into him as I walk into the kitchen.

'And I want you,' I say, my body still cross with my mind. 'But we'll get there. We've just got some stuff to work out first.'

Joseph perches himself up against my kitchen unit whilst I make myself comfortable on the sofa. He's always looked so out of place in my flat. My mixture of Cath Kidston prints and kitsch knick-knacks seem to clash with his well-groomed, well-turned-out self.

'What's to work out? I want you back, you want me back. We're back together. End of.'

Does he really think it's that easy?

'We need to talk about why we broke up in the first place. You can't just dump someone after a year without a real explanation and then pick back up a few months later. I've changed, for starters. I haven't been sitting around waiting for you.'

I've been doing a crazy list of tasks instead, whilst waiting for you.

'But surely that's all in the past? Don't you remember how good things used to be?'

'I do,' I say, nodding, and trying not to replay the montage of our best moments in my head. 'But you didn't remember how good things were when you broke up with me. Doesn't that tell you something? You thought there was something wrong in our relationship. You said we weren't compatible.'

Joseph sighs and sits down in my wicker rocking chair. I try not to laugh as his weight sends it flying back and for once he loses his cool composure.

'I don't know what happened, or really what I said. It was just that you were talking about our anniversary and it all got a bit much. I'd seen my mum in the week and she reminded me that I ought to be settling down and I guess I panicked. I think I'm at that age where everyone expects me to be getting married and having kids and I felt trapped by it all.'

I try and listen to what Joseph is saying. For months I agonised over what I'd done and how I'd caused our break-up, but from what he's saying I realise it's all about him. It's not really that I wasn't right for him or there's anything wrong with me as a person, it's that he got freaked out. Which is ironic as he was the one that was always so committed. He assumed we were boyfriend and girlfriend from the get-go. He timetabled our relationship, I just slotted in.

'I thought that I still had too much I wanted to do before I got to that stage, and I felt I wanted to be single to do it.'

The words take a moment to sink in. I think of his list and how naive I've been. It wasn't that he wanted someone to do those tasks with, those were things he wanted to do himself, alone.

'So, what's changed? Why don't you want to be single any more?'

'I realised that I was listening to the wrong people. So what if I'm thirty-six. Forty's the new thirty, right? I've still got bags of time before I have to have a wife and kids. It's not like I've got a ticking biological clock,' he says, laughing.

No, but I bloody well have, I suddenly want to scream.

'Does that mean that you still see us as a bit of fun – that it's nothing serious?' I say, my heart catching in my throat. Ever since he broke up with me I've fixated on how he was the one, but clearly he doesn't feel the same.

'Of course not. Abi, I really do love you. You're different to the other girlfriends I've had in the past. I mean, for starters you didn't fall at my feet when we broke up, you reinvented your look and started throwing yourself into biking and windsurfing and doing all these amazing things, and it made me realise what I'd given up.'

I'm stuck between being dumbfounded that the list actually worked exactly as planned and at the fact that one of the key reasons he wants me back is that I didn't go begging for him when we broke up.

'It's weird as I've never really been single. I've always found myself in a relationship straightaway when I've broken up with someone, only this time I didn't. And that's got to mean something, hasn't it? Like I couldn't easily replace you.'

Or that he hadn't met anyone he liked.

This isn't how I'd fantasised about this conversation going.

'I guess I realised that there's no hurry, is there? You're only thirty – we've still got lots of time to worry about all that grown-up stuff. I just want us to enjoy ourselves a bit. When I saw your Facebook photos, and I saw you with that other guy, I realised I wanted to be him. I wanted to be riding with you downhill and whisking you off to Paris. I mean, why don't we go? This weekend. We can hop on a plane tonight and have a dirty weekend. What do you say?'

The elastic in my knickers almost pings off at the thought of being wrapped up in crisp white sheets with a naked Joseph.

But unfortunately for the horny side of me, my brain is still running the show.

'I can't, I've got plans. I'm abseiling down the Spinnaker tomorrow. For work.'

'Oh,' says Joseph, the smile fading off his face. 'But I thought you got fired?'

'Suspended. I did, but it's a long story.' I don't have the mental energy to cope with filling him in on what's going on work-wise – I need to concentrate on one drama at a time.

'OK, but let's do something special. Let me take you out somewhere after your abseil. What time is it?'

'Ten.'

The butterflies are already building in my belly as there's less than twenty-four hours to go.

'OK, well, why don't I meet you after and I'll take you away somewhere as a surprise? It might not be Paris, but I'm sure I can think of something.'

'Would you come to the tower too, for moral support?'

It feels strange that Ben is not going to be there for the end of my list, because he's been there for practically everything else, and I could really do with having someone there.

'Um, OK, yes.'

'Thanks.'

With Joseph watching I'll not be able to chicken out. And perhaps there's something poetic about having him there for the end of the list. I'll have completed it and he'll whisk me off into the sunset and we'll live happily ever after, just like I wanted.

Joseph starts talking about where we could go, but right now I can't see past the tower. It's not only the fear that I'm going to be dangling off a tiny bit of rope hundreds of feet in the air, it's the fact that the list is coming to an end.

I'm going to get what I want, yet I can't help feeling that I don't want the list to be over.

Chapter Twenty-Eight

Two hours to go until my list is complete (we'll gloss over the fact that means I have to throw myself off the tallest building in Portsmouth . . .).

I can't believe that today's the day that I'm probably going to die. If not from falling from a massive height when the abseil rope breaks, then from a heart attack at 500 feet. There are so many scenarios and ways that this abseil could go horribly wrong, and I seem to have made a montage in my mind that showcases the best of them. But at the same time, I know I have to do it.

Rick's pretty much given me no choice but to go ahead with it. And as much as I hate to admit it – Ben's right. I need to finish the list. I need to prove to myself that I can do anything I set my mind to.

I shudder at the thought of the abseil, but have to put it from my mind. There's something else equally terrifying I've got to do first.

I ring the doorbell and hold my breath as I wonder if anyone will answer it.

Sian's housemate Angela opens the door and I brace myself to be told that Sian's not there.

'Hi, Abi, Sian's in the living room,' she says breezily, holding the door open.

I hesitate for a moment wondering if it's some sort of trick, before I thank Angela and walk into the lounge.

'Abi,' says Sian in shock as she pulls herself away from Pete.

Ah, Pete. I hadn't counted on Sian not being alone. Suddenly I feel that I shouldn't have come. There's something about Pete being Ben's friend that makes me feel awkward.

They're a picture of domestic bliss. He's in baggy tracksuit bottoms and an old band T-shirt and she's in her bright pink dressing gown with fluffy slippers. Her legs are resting on his as they sit with their hands cradling giant mugs of coffee that smell delicious.

Joseph and I would never be found in such a position. He has a rule that if you're out of bed then you shower and dress immediately. Dressing gowns are merely a decorative feature hanging on the back of the bathroom door.

'I'm sorry to interrupt,' I say, suddenly nervous to be around my best friend.

'I'm going to grab a shower,' says Pete diplomatically and he kisses Sian on the head before leaving.

'So, I thought I better come and see you as I'm on my way to do the abseil and I couldn't die without at least attempting to make things better.'

'You're so melodramatic. No one is going to die. You're going to get down that tower just fine. Look at everything else you've done over the last couple of months. It's been incredible.'

The fact that Sian is talking to me gives me the confidence to sit down next to her without fear of being strangled. Her anger appears to have subsided. Clearly Pete has a calming effect on her.

'Yeah, but for all that other death-defying stuff I've done, Ben's been by my side.'

'And he's not coming today?'

'No,' I say, shaking my head and wishing it weren't the case.

'What happened?'

'We had a big fight about stuff. I don't think he was too pleased about Joseph and me getting back together, and then I said some mean stuff ...'

'Jeez, you really are trying to drive everyone away, aren't you? And Pete says that you might've lost your job. I was going to come round, but I was still so cross at you.'

'I know, there's a lot to fill you in on. But first, I'm sorry for lying to you. I wish I'd been honest with you from the start. Do you think you'll ever be able to forgive me?'

'Well, I guess now that I feel sorry for you being an unemployed bum, I'm going to have to.'

'Ah, well, I think I've been reinstated,' I say. 'It's a pretty long story and I haven't got time to tell you now, but I promise I will later.'

Sian raises what I call her journalistic eyebrow. It's the one that goes nuts when she senses a story.

'You promise?'

'I do,' I say, smiling that I've got my friend back, and so easily. I hope that Pete is 'the one' and they never break up as she's much less of a pit bull now she's with him.

'Right, well, I better get going to the tower,' I say in a way that sounds as if I'm being condemned to death at the Tower of London, rather than doing an abseil.

'Do you want to wait and I'll get changed and come with you? I don't like to think of you being on your own.'

'Actually, Joseph is coming with me,' I say, wincing. I've just won her round, I don't want to antagonise her.

'Oh, right. So you are getting back together with him?'

I shrug. 'I am, but I want it to be on my terms. I've changed a lot and I want him to know that.'

Sian nods. 'Well, I can't say I'm happy, but at least that's something. I just hope this time that it's not all rose-tinted glasses. I'm sorry. I shouldn't have said that. I had a big talk with Pete about it and he told me to stay out of it, that I don't know what goes on in private. So, if you think Joseph is so special and he's worth doing this whole list for, then I won't make it any harder for you.'

I lean over to hug her. That's the nicest thing she could have possibly said to me at the moment, and the most surprising.

'I'll let you know how I get on,' I say, standing up.

'Do, but you'll be fine. You know you're stronger than you think you are.'

'Thanks, Sian.'

I get up and realise that I'm delaying the inevitable. The next building I enter will be the Tower of Terror. Imposing da-da-da music echoes round my brain and my stomach lurches.

Looking up at the tower from the bottom is terrifying – it's far more imposing than the Eiffel Tower. It looks like it reaches all the way into the sky with no end in sight. It's making my head spin and I feel dizzy. I don't know if I'm even going to be able to go up to the platform, let alone abseil off it.

'Ah, I was beginning to think you might have changed your mind,' says Rick as I walk into the lobby.

'If only,' I say wistfully, wondering whether it's too late to go back to my freelance business idea. 'So did you manage to get any more evidence?'

'I did. I've pretty much got the proof I need now, thanks to IT tracing who fiddled with the design files.'

My shoulders drop a little with relief. I've not been going crazy after all, and Rick's got proof.

'And you're still not going to tell me who it is?'

'Not until I'm a hundred per cent sure, which means waiting for the final part of my plan to fall into place.'

I still suspect Linz. I look over at her in her tight leggings and her Design Works T-shirt that looks like it's been surgically stretched over her chest. She looks so smug as she laughs with Giles, but she'll be laughing on the other side of her face when it comes out that people know what she's done.

Whilst I'm scanning the room, I try and see if I can spot Joseph, but he doesn't seem to be here yet. I guess I am a bit early. Instead, I spot Fran and walk over to talk to her.

'Abi,' she says wrinkling her face in surprise. 'You're the last person I expected to see here. Can I just say that I was really sorry to hear about your suspension; it's not the same without you.'

'Thanks, Fran.'

'It was just so sudden – one minute you were there, and the next – poof – you were gone!'

'Yeah, but I think I'll be back pretty soon,' I say lowering my voice. I know I shouldn't be saying anything, but Rick did just say he had proof of who set me up, which means I think it can be less of a secret. And besides, I know that Fran isn't Linz's biggest fan.

'What do you mean?'

'Well, between you and me, I didn't mess up on the museum account. Someone sent a fake order and changed all my files.'

'They did what?' she says.

I can see the look of surprise on her face. It's not something I'd have believed if it hadn't happened to me either.

'I know, it's shocking, right? But anyway, Rick has it all under control.'

'He does?'

'Yes. He won't tell me who, but he says he's got evidence of who did it.'

'Really?' she says, her eyes widening.

'Uh-huh. IT got involved and they've been able to identify who modified the design files. Some sort of digital thumbprint. Very CSI if you ask me. I think Rick's waiting until Monday to have it out with this person, which is a bit mean as they're here today and they've got to do this abseil.'

The colour seems to drain from her face, clearly because I've reminded her about her descent down this awful tower. I'm surprised that I'm still standing upright at the mere mention of it, but here I am. My legs might be jelly-like but they haven't bolted for the door yet.

'Don't worry about the abseil,' I say. 'I'm terrified too – we can do it together.'

'I'm not worried about the stupid abseil,' she says, snapping. I'm taken aback as she is usually so calm and mild mannered. 'I'm more concerned about the fact that I'm going to get fired.'

She shakes her head and when I lock eyes with her I see that they're almost glowing red with rage.

'It was meant to be her that took the blame and got fired, not you,' she says, pointing a finger at Linz, who is stroking Rick's arm.

I don't have time to think how inappropriate it is that Linz is touching the boss as the pieces of the puzzle are starting to fall into place.

'You? You're the one that set me up? You're the one that deleted my files and messed up my museum project?'

'Yes,' she says, sighing. 'Only I thought I'd covered my tracks. It was meant to be Linz that took the fall, not you. I thought that everyone would assume it was her before you even got to the suspension stage.'

'But why?'

I can't process this quickly enough. Nice, quiet Fran is actually quite vindictive. I knew she was a little strange after the fake-baby thing, but talk about always being the person you'd least expect.

'Why do you think? Look at her,' she says, pointing again at Linz.

I watch as she tips her head back and laughs, pawing at Rick's stomach as if to show her appreciation of whatever the joke is.

'She's been here five minutes and she's already muscled her way onto two of my accounts. She's got Rick wrapped around her little finger, and I wouldn't be surprised if it was only a matter of time before I got edged out and she got my job.'

'But that's crazy!'

'Is it? Have you ever known Rick invest so much time in another member of staff? He's been having extra meetings with her, taking her to the pub in the evenings, I even heard they went to Goodwood Races together.'

'That's no reason to sabotage your own career.'

'Well, I didn't expect it to backfire. I didn't think Rick would look that closely. I thought that he'd be so disappointed that Linz had lied to him that she wouldn't get past her three months' probation and then everything would go back to normal.'

I stare at her and wonder if the fear of the abseil has made me go mad and that I am, in fact, hallucinating this far-fetched chain of events.

Before I can double-check my facts, Rick has walked over to us. 'Fran.'

'Rick,' she says, no hint of happiness in her voice. 'I know you know, and you can stuff your job. I've had enough of working for someone like you.'

Oh, no, she didn't.

'That's fine, Fran. You can come in on Monday to collect your things.'

She turns on her heels and walks away.

'I don't believe it,' I say, shaking my head. 'I never imagined it would be her. I assumed it was Linz.'

I instantly feel guilty as in my head I'd already acted as judge, jury and executioner condemning her for what she'd done.

'I knew it couldn't be Linz,' says Rick. 'I'm going to have to tell people in the office because it's going to come out anyway, but Linz and I have started dating. We've decided that it's probably best if she doesn't work for us as it would be a conflict of interest, and I think she's going to go to another agency.'

I feel knocked over with the revelations. I open my mouth to say something, but nothing comes.

'Unfortunately for Fran, she happened to go onto your finance login and do the order at the exact same time we were having our first kiss in the meeting room. It was a pretty iron-clad alibi for Linz. I know I could have told you that sooner but I was embarrassed by how it looked.'

I wonder if he means because she's an employee or the fact he's old enough to be her dad.

'This is unreal,' I say, finally.

'I know. It doesn't seem very real to me either, and I know that people are going to be disapproving about the age gap, but you know what? She makes me happy. I mean, doesn't she have the most infectious smile?'

It's certainly infectious in the way chickenpox is, leaving you feeling all uncomfortable and itchy. I simply nod. He's happy and Linz is leaving the company, meaning I won't have to see that perky, ponytail-bobbing whippersnapper look so bloody cheerful all the time, which makes me happy.

I have to admit I feel the teeniest bit guilty that I've been so scathing of her as she's clearly done nothing wrong. Well, except shagging the boss. A mental image flashes through my mind of Rick getting down and dirty and I shudder. That's all sorts of wrong.

I'm just pleased that I can be reinstated and come back to work without the fear of sabotage.

'Ah, would you excuse me, my …' I was about to slip and call Joseph my boyfriend, but that's not right. He can't just go back to that. And he's never really been just a friend. 'My Joseph's here,' I say finally.

I slip away from Rick, still trying to make sense of what's happening.

'Hi,' I say, smiling at Joseph.

'Hi, Abi, sorry I'm a bit late. I had to queue to get in the car park. You'd think that people would have better things to do with their Saturdays than come here.'

Yes, it truly is a mystery why people would want to come to a designer outlet village with restaurants, shops, bowling alley and cinema on a Saturday.

'Thanks for coming, despite the traffic.'

'It's no problem. You know I've always quite fancied doing this myself.'

'Oh, have you?' I say, trying to bite my cheeks in a bid to stop them from going purple with shame.

'Yeah, I'll see how you get on first, though,' he says chuckling.

I try and stifle a laugh but it gets stuck in my throat. Something tells me that when I require medical attention after my fainting/panic attack/heart attack he'll change his tune.

'Right, guys,' says Rick loudly. 'Now that we're all here, Natasha is going to take us for a quick safety briefing, before we go up to the viewing platform to start getting ready.'

My stomach starts to churn and I cross my legs so that I don't wet myself in fear.

I can't do this. There's no way I can possibly do this. What the hell was I thinking? I'm like an ostrich – I wasn't made to leave the ground. Even my big boobs weighing me down like gravity boots are a sign from God that I'm not destined to go up high.

'I'll see you back here before we go to the viewing platform,' I say to Joseph as we're whisked off to the briefing.

On a scale of one to ten of being petrified, I was a ten before we went for the safety briefing, now I'm pretty much at a hundred. It did absolutely nothing to ease my nerves. Instead, it made me realise how much could go wrong that I hadn't considered.

The waivers we had to sign have made me wish I'd got round to writing a will and putting on more sensible underwear. The thought that the medical staff that pick me up off the ground will find me wearing white novelty Snoopy boy shorts that turned pastel pink after a red washing incident is a tad embarrassing. I'd picked them thinking they'd be the pair least likely to give me a wedgie whilst in a safety harness.

'Are you OK, Abi?' asks Joseph as I meet him back in the lobby.

I want to scream that of course I'm not bloody OK, but I nod weakly instead.

'You'll be fine when you get in motion. That initial lean back will be really mentally tough, but as soon as you're dangling and you feel that the safety ropes have got you you'll feel fine. The wind will be whistling around your ears – it will be great.'

I blink in horror.

I hadn't really considered leaning back or feeling the wind in my hair or dangling at 500 feet. Right now I'm psyching myself up simply to get in the lift and get onto the viewing platform.

'Let's go,' he says, taking my arm and shuffling me towards the lift along with my colleagues.

I see Giles out of the corner of my eye trying to give me a thumbs up, but my vision has started to go hazy and I'm not in control of my body enough to respond to him. I can almost feel it shutting down.

'Right,' says Natasha. 'We'll hold you up here for a bit and then when it's your turn we'll hook you up to the safety equipment.'

'I can't do this,' I say, whispering to Joseph, my voice shaky and uneven.

I instinctively reach out and grab his arm, hoping he'll be my anchor.

'Abi, you'll be fine. They do this all the time up here – it's perfectly safe.'

I look at him and I wonder if he realises how scared of heights I am. I don't think we went anywhere in our relationship that put it to the test.

'But I'm scared,' I say in a whisper.

'Of course you are, but you'll be fine. Wow, check out that view,' he says, throwing off my arm, causing me to stumble backwards. He walks towards one of the giant windows and rests his head against the glass.

I hold onto a nearby chair and ground myself, taking a deep breath and trying to remember how well I did at the Eiffel Tower.

At least here it feels safe as we're inside.

'I can see your flat from here,' Joseph says. 'Come see.'

He's beckoning me over and my legs actually start to obey him. I don't make it all the way to him, but I do see my road facing out onto the common. What would have once been a row of impressive Victorian hotels is now a selection of flats in various states of repair.

'Cool, huh,' he says, smiling. 'Oh, by the way, I bought you this. Thought you might need the energy.'

He reaches into his coat pocket and pulls out a paper bag and I'm touched. He's brought me a present.

I reach out and take it without going any closer to him, and I pull out the Danish pastry from inside.

How thoughtful, I think, until I see the raisins poking their ugly head from it.

'Thanks,' I say, planting a fake smile on my face. 'I think I'll save it for when I get to the bottom. I've got a bit too much adrenaline pumping round at the moment to eat it.'

I shove it in my bag and it reminds me of what Sian was saying about his gifts and not listening to what I liked. The image of Ben and the surprise on his face when I pulled out his favourite chocolates springs to mind, and I realise that it's not that difficult to remember what people like, especially when you care about them.

'You know, looking at this view makes me jealous of what you're about to do,' he says, leaning his head on the glass to get a better view.

'Well, why don't you do it with me?' I say, suddenly realising that this is how I can get down the tower.

'What? I'm sure it's too late and they won't have space,' he says, shrugging his shoulders.

'But there is space. Fran has dropped out, so you can take her spot. You can come down with me and hold my hand.'

With Joseph by my side I might actually make it down.

'Um, but I'm not dressed. I can hardly abseil in chinos.'

I'm about to point out that we are next to a shopping centre where I'm sure he could buy something more appropriate, but I stop as I realise something.

'You're not going to do it, are you?' I say as the penny starts to drop.

'Not today. Maybe one day,' he says looking back out at the view.

And then it hits me. It's like the rest of the things on his bucket list – they're all just ideas, but he's never actually going to go through with them.

He's got no intention of abseiling down this tower – it's just a dream, a mere fantasy. He doesn't have the inclination to go through with it.

And I realise in that moment that I don't want a boyfriend like that.

I want someone who will experience life with me. Whether it's through a list or on the spur of the moment. But Joseph isn't that person – he's too stuck in his ways. And whilst that might have been fine for me once, it's not fine for the new Abi. I want to really live life, and as comforting as it always was to do the same things every weekend, I don't want to go back to that.

'Is that for you?' he says, turning to me and snapping me out of my thoughts.

'Is what for me?'

'That, there. It says, "Go, Abi! Go!"'

I forget that I'm up so high in the sky and I go up to the window railing and follow Joseph's finger. There, on a roof top, in giant letters, is an enormous sign. I spot the unmistakable minaret of the mosque behind it, and realise that the rooftop has to be Ben's bike shop.

A smile lights up my face and my fear drains away. It's the same feeling that crept over me when I went up the Eiffel Tower. It's as if Ben is there squeezing my hand. He is with me after all.

I turn to face Joseph and he has confusion written all over his face.

'You were right, when you broke up with me,' I say, my voice losing its shake. 'When you said we wanted different things from life – you were so right. When we broke up I started doing this bucket list to get over you, with all these crazy things that I'd never wanted to do or even thought it was possible for me to do. But you know what? I did them. And it proved to me that I could do anything I set my mind to. But more than that, it's opened my mind up to who I want to be. And who I want to be with.

'I want to be with a doer, Joseph, not simply a dreamer. I've lived more in these last few months than I have in years and I can't give that up and get back together with you.'

'Is this because I won't abseil? I can change my mind if it is.'

'No,' I say, shaking my head. 'It's not. It's about me and who I've become,' I say honestly. Ben and Sian were right about how much of a different person I am now from the one that Joseph let go.

'But I don't understand, I thought you wanted me back?'

'I did, but I realise now how wrong that was. I'm sorry, Joseph, for messing you around, but I've got to follow my heart.'

'And that's leading you to the person who made you that sign. That guy from Paris?' he says with a sneer to his voice.

'I guess so,' I say as my head catches up with my heart. 'I'm sorry.'

I walk away from Joseph and realise how foolish I've been. All this time I've been doing these tasks to get him back and little did I know they were driving me further away from him.

Natasha asks for volunteers to go first and I immediately put my hand up. I've got to go and see Ben, now. And my fear of heights is not going to get in the way of me getting the man that I want.

As Natasha helps me into the safety gear, all I can think of is Ben. I'm oblivious to which of my work colleagues is coming down with me, because in my head I'm imagining Ben's by my side.

I barely notice anything as I'm strapped into my harness and led onto an outside platform. A man explains briefly what's going to happen, yet I'm on autopilot. I ignore the wind rattling around the helmet that's been fixed on my head.

I lean back as instructed and my brain stops whirling long enough for my heart to start racing and my breathing to speed up.

I can't believe I'm actually going to do this. I daren't look anywhere but straight in front of me because if I get any sense of the height I think I'll grab hold of the instructor in front of me and never let go.

'Deep breaths, Abi,' says Giles.

I look over in surprise to see him next to me.

'You're going to do great.'

I smile back at him. I *am* going to do great. I made it out here onto the platform, that's a lot further up than I ever thought I'd get. And if I'm already feeling proud of that accomplishment it's only going to feel better at the end.

The man at the top instructs us to move and I know this is my last opportunity to wimp out. If I chicken out halfway down I'm going to be stuck there for what will feel like an eternity before I'm rescued.

'You ready?' asks Giles.

I nod. I know the adrenaline won't last for ever and if I don't go now I'm not going to be able to move at all.

'On three then. One, two, three.'

Much to my amazement my knees bend and I push myself away from the wall. It feels like I'm floating rather than falling. As my legs hit the building again and I release more rope, I start to relax. From this angle I can only see the white tiles of the building. The rope holding me is super strong and thanks to the harness wedgie (damn you, Snoopy pants), I feel surprisingly secure.

I'm sure the views around are wonderful, but all I can focus on is the white building in front of me. For all I know, I could be doing this anywhere. But I don't care. The point is I'm doing it. *I'm actually doing it.*

My heart's beating ever quicker as it tries to keep up with my mind. What with Fran revealing it was her that set me up and me realising my true feelings for Ben, it's too much to take in.

I can't believe that I'm finishing this list. It's been one of the most incredible experiences of my life. I know now that Ben was right – I have to carry on with my own.

'Nearly there,' says Giles.

For a moment I'm distracted and I almost look down, but I know if I do I'll freeze.

'Focus on the list,' I mutter to myself as I try and work out what I'd put on it.

I want to go on a safari. Not one you do on a package holiday, but one where you go for a week or so and stay in tents and actually rough it.

A sudden gust of wind blows me slightly to the left and I instantly tense up and scrunch my eyes closed for a moment.

I want to climb the rest of the Four Peaks.

I take a deep breath and kick off again.

I want to learn to bake so that I can be confident in the kitchen.

I want to learn to knit properly so I can make jumpers that are wearable in public.

I want to travel more, and go somewhere on a whim.

But first of all, I want to kiss Ben and I want to tell him how I really feel.

Hands grab my shoulders and for a second I wonder what the hell is going on before I realise I'm at the ground.

How the bloody hell did that happen?

'You did it, Abi!' says Giles, slapping me on the back.

'Oh, my God, I did!' I say as I put my feet on the ground.

I almost fall straight backwards onto my bum as my legs are buckling as if they're made of Slinky springs.

I let the man unharness me and I slip off my helmet.

I know Ben said he was going to watch Tammy race but I've got to at least try and see if he's at his flat. My hair must be sticking up at all angles from my ponytail and I'm all sweaty and gross. I probably should go home and change first, but I can't. I have to go now.

I'm about to turn and bolt when I spot a face in the crowd. I think I'm hallucinating as I see Ben standing right there in front of me.

Maybe all that adrenaline has done funny things to my brain. But it looks like he's standing next to Laura, smiling at me.

I walk up to him, slowly at first, then as I get closer I break into a jog. I haven't had time to think about what I'm going to say, but as I reach him I suddenly know what I want to do. I want to throw my arms round him and kiss him, but I can't do that, can I?

All I can say is that Ben must be telepathic because no sooner have I reached him than he puts his hand on the small of my back and pulls me towards him. His lips graze mine and he looks at me before closing his eyes and tilting his head. And – bam! – we're kissing.

I feel his other hand tracing the side of my face and settling on my neck. I reach my hands forward and place them happily on his chest, before I use them to push him off me.

He stops immediately.

'I'm sorry,' he says. 'I couldn't help it. I was so proud to see you come down the tower, and I was so pleased to see you and I –'

I lean over and kiss him again.

Pulling out of it, he's suddenly quiet, a small smile forming on his lips.

'You were wrong, Abi Martin. I am capable of being in love, and I know that because I've fallen head over heels for you.'

My legs were just starting to strengthen after the abseil, but I now go weak at the knees as that's the most romantic thing anyone's ever said to me.

'Well,' I say, taking his hands in mine. 'It's a good job, because I've started my own list, and number one on it is to have a relationship with you.'

'Is that right?'

'Uh-huh. What do you reckon? Are you up for ticking that off with me?'

'Absolutely,' he says, pulling me back into him and wrapping his arms around me. He leans down and gives me the most incredible kiss.

I'd say that this new list has got off to a pretty good start.

Epilogue

'Slow down,' I say, laughing. 'You're going way too fast – it's going to spin off out of control.'

'I can't go any slower – it seems to be either stop or go with this motor,' he says, looking at his foot. But in looking down, he's lost control and the clay throws itself all over the wheel.

'Stupid bloody thing,' says Ben. He picks up the strewn-about clay and slams it back down again onto the now still wheel. He rubs his head in frustration, depositing a bit of clay in his hair and making it stand up in a Tintin quiff.

My heart does a somersault and I bite my lip. He couldn't possibly look any sexier.

'You've just got to take it easy,' I say, sitting down behind him and balancing myself. I carefully scrape up his clay and mould it back into a ball, before putting his hands around it. I wrap mine over the top à la *Ghost*, and as I depress the pedal and ease the wheel slowly round, I help Ben shape it.

'Now this is a bit more like it,' he says, the lightness coming back into his voice.

I have to say I've enjoyed the pottery. For the first time since embarking on our new joint bucket list, I've found something that Ben can't do that I can. It's nice to be the one coaxing and encouraging for a change.

We've rented a little cottage in the Lake District, and whilst for most of the week Ben's had me hurtling head first down questionable paths on my bike and hiking up what seem like sheer cliff faces, today was my choice of adventure, and I chose the shed at the bottom of the garden that has a little potter's wheel and kiln. The whole reason I'd chosen this particular cottage – well, that and the hot tub ...

'Got something on your mind, have you?' says Ben, laughing.

I look round at the pot we're making – it looks undeniably phallic. I haven't been paying attention, too lost in thinking about last night's steamy hot-tub session.

'Must be a Freudian slip.'

'Oh, really,' says Ben removing his hands and running them along my thighs.

'Oi, watch my trousers, clay hands,' I say, jumping up.

It only seems to spur him on as he gets up, his hands outstretched.

'These clay hands want to show you how good they are off the potter's wheel.'

He reaches over to me and slips them under the waist band of my trousers and pulls me in close.

'Do they now?'

'Uh-huh.'

I scan the window of the shed to make sure we're not visible to onlookers; it's pretty secluded so I think we're safe.

His hands slide under my T-shirt and up my back as he slowly leans over and kisses me.

I close my eyes and think how lucky I am that I'm now working my way through the list that I call *the bucket list for living happily ever after.*

Abi's Guide to Bucket Lists

Now, a bucket list really should be full of stuff that you've always wanted to do, not torturous things that have you quaking in your boots like the list of Joseph's that I did.

So instead of putting yourself into your ex's shoes and living out their dreams, write your very own bucket list – one that will inspire you to live a little, and here's how I recommend you do it.

1. *Choose two or three Travel Destinations:*

Before I met Ben I booked holidays based on last-minute deals, using the checklist of cheap booze, sizzling temperatures and proximity to the beach. I'd never really got the travelling bug, and therefore my 'where to' bucket list was pretty empty. But after some head scratching I thought of three.

First up: a European city break. Not only are they easy to do on a weekend and therefore involve taking minimal time off work, but with cheap flights they won't cost you the earth. Meaning there won't be many excuses not to tick them off your list quickly.

I chose Florence and Siena for my list. Not only is there the lure of all that yummy pasta and fantastic coffee, but they also have amazing art collections. And they're not the most unromantic of places, perfect to go with my lovely new boyfriend...

Next up is somewhere a bit further afield. That place tucked away in the back of your mind that you've always wanted to go to, somewhere dreamy. For me, that place is the Maldives. I'm picturing a little wooden bungalow on stilts over crystal-clear waters and bright white beaches. The perfect place for something like a honeymoon (nudge, nudge, Ben).

Then there's that once in a lifetime trip – or at least I hope mine will be ... I'm definitely not doing it twice. Something like a safari, a diving holiday or a camper-van trip round New Zealand. On my list is – a trip to Tanzania to trek up Kilimanjaro followed by a safari. Um, can you guess who came up with this? Ben thinks I'll get up Kilimanjaro no problem, since I've managed to conquer Snowdon. I'm not brilliant at geography but I'm thinking that Kili is a bit bigger, and the risks of altitude sickness a bit higher. But Ben keeps telling me to focus on the cute fluffy lions and lofty giraffes that I'm going to see after.

2. Pick up a new hobby

So I've binned the Spanish lessons. I can now successfully go to tapas restaurants and order meatballs – mission accomplished. Yet there are other hobbies I've always wanted to acquire but never given the time to start.

I recommend picking a couple of things that you've always wanted to learn to do, but never had the time. Then make the time!

I decided I wanted to learn to knit and to bake. I've started both and I'm pleased to report they're going better than the español. I started off knitting Ben a jumper (I'm still convinced that the Colin Firth Christmas jumper is a good one) but I've scaled down my ambitions and am now knitting a scarf. As for the baking, I'm getting pretty good and my waistline is testament to that – let's just say those post-Joseph break-up pounds are not going anywhere.

3. Day trips

Places where you have to get glammed up or get togged up in overalls. I'm thinking tea at the Ritz or walking over the millennium dome. Things you can do in a day that are as far from your average day as you can get.

On my list is having dinner at Heston's The Fat Duck. It's a four-hour feast that I think will blow me away, and with the prices charged a real one-off experience for me!

4. Add some life goals

Ideally you should think about where you want your life headed and how you can get there. They should be slightly obtainable;

marrying Ryan Gosling as amazing as it might be is probably a bit far out of reach. But writing a novel or getting a few rungs up the career level might not be. In my life-goals section are to own a house (my bank balance is laughing at that one) and to start up my own business (well, Ben wants lots of kids and a little bit of flexible working would help).

And that's my new bucket list in a nutshell.
I probably should have made a list like this
in the first place, but then I never would
have met Ben …

Acknowledgements

I once mountain-biked down the most dangerous road in the world in Bolivia. Or at least I would have done if I hadn't cried my eyes out after the first two metres and spent the rest of the day in the support van following the riders that did complete it. You see that's what happens when you try and do something on your ex's bucket list just so you can impress them. Despite that being one of the worst things I've ever done it did inspire this novel, so thank you to that ex for breaking up with me back then and setting me on the path to writing this novel.

My agent Hannah Ferguson also deserves a huge thank you for helping to come up with the idea for this novel. It was a bit of an uphill struggle and as always she put up with my neurotic emails and I'm incredibly thankful she keeps me as a client.

This is my first book with the imprint Zaffre, and it's been lovely getting to know everyone. To Joel and Claire especially, thank you for your editorial notes and your enthusiasm for the novel.

A huge thank you needs to go to the readers, bloggers, fellow authors and Team Novelicious for their support –

especially keeping me sane on Twitter. Also to the amazing bloggers who have reviewed my books or featured me on their blog, thank you so much. To my lovely real-life friends and family, your endless support and interest in my books often astounds me – thank you!

My two lively children Evan and Jessica deserve special thanks as they have to put up with a forgetful mum and a messy house (as any time not feeding the baby or playing Duplo are spent tapping away instead of cleaning). Lastly, my husband deserves the biggest thank you. Thanks for putting up with all the self-doubt, all the ham, egg and chip dinners we have to have when I haven't had time to cook, and for buying me lots of Maltesers when I'm editing. You know I met him whilst ticking 'trek to Everest base camp' off my bucket list. You see actual proof that bucket lists can lead you to love…